W9-BQS-696

# THE BEST
# MAINE
# STORIES

**Edited by Sanford Phippen,**
**Charles Waugh, and Martin Greenberg**

*Down East Books*

"The Viking's Daughter" by Arthur Train. ©1927. Reprinted by permission of the Estate of Arthur Train.

"Maine" by Margaret Osborn. ©1944 by The Atlantic Monthly Company. Reprinted by permission of David D. Osborn.

"The Lesson" by Sam Brown, Jr. ©1970. Reprinted with permission from the February 1970 issue of *Yankee* Magazine, Yankee Publishing Inc., Dublin, NH 03444.

"Prayer for the Dying" by Willis Johnson. ©1982 by Willis Johnson. Reprinted from his volume *The Girl Who Would be Russian and Other Stories* by permission of Tilbury House Publishers.

"Berrying" by Rebecca Cummings, from *Kaisa Kilponen,* Coyote Love Press. ©1985 by Rebecca Cummings. Reprinted by permission of the author.

"Greg's Peg" by Louis Auchincloss. ©1950 by Louis Auchincloss. Reprinted by permission of the author.

"The Search" by Virginia Chase. ©1983 by Puckerbrush Press. Reprinted by permission of the author.

"Step-Over Toe-Hold" by Sanford Phippen. ©1982 by Sanford Phippin. Reprinted by permission of the author.

"The Ledge" by Lawrence Sargent Hall. ©1960 by Lawrence Sargent Hall. First published in *The Hudson Review,* Vol XI, No. 4, Winter 1958-59. Reprinted by permission of the author.

"Ollie, Oh. . ." by Carolyn Chute. ©1982 Carolyn Chute. Reprinted by permission of John Farquharson Ltd., agents for Carolyn Chute.

"They Grind Exceeding Small" by Ben Ames Williams. ©1919. Copyright owned jointly by heirs of Florence T. Williams (widow); Ann Williams Wardwell; Roger Chilton Williams; and Ben Ames Williams, Jr.; reprinted with their permission.

"Small Point Bridge" by Stephen Minot. ©1969 by Stephen Minot. Reprinted by permission of the University of Illinois Press.

"Head of the Line" by Gladys Hasty Carroll. ©1942 by Gladys Hasty Carroll. Reprinted by permission of the author.

"The Soldier Shows His Medal" by Ruth Moore. ©1945, 1973. Reprinted by permission of The *New Yorker* Magazine, Inc., where a shorter version of the story appeared under the title "It Don't Change Much."

Text design by Janet Mecca. Cover design by Edith Allard.
Color separation: Four Colour Imports, Louisville Ky.
Printed at Capital City Press, Montpelier, Vt.

9   8   7   6   5   4   3   2   1

Library of Congress Cataloging in Publication Data

The best Maine stories / edited by Sanford Phippen, Charles Waugh & Martin Greenberg.
  p.  cm.
  ISBN 0-89272-351-3 :
  1. Short stories, American—Maine. 2. Maine—Fiction
I. Phippen, Sanford, 1942– . II. Waugh, charles. III. Greenberg, Martin Harry. IV. Title: Maine stories.
PS548.M2B47  1994
813'. 010832741—dc20

94-5391
CIP

# THE BEST MAINE STORIES

# CONTENTS

## Summer

## Fall

# CONTENTS

## Winter

## Spring

# SUMMER

*As he watched Dizzy standing so unselfconsciously in the lamplight in her brown overalls, her cheeks flushed from running uphill and damp with the mist that clung in hundreds of tiny drops to her hair and eyelashes, he wished that he had a daughter like her. Did they breed girls of such sort in cities?*

The Viking's Daughter

# THE VIKING'S DAUGHTER

## I

BAR HARBOR, Mt. Desert, Maine

Desire to retain your services in important matter. Please come at once. All expenses paid. Money no object.

ALLISON DINGLE

The telegram had arrived at a moment when Mr. Tutt — the rest of the office force, with the exception of Miss Sondheim and Bonnie Doon, having departed for a vacation — was feeling particularly old and lonely.

"Dingle? Dingle? Ever hear of him, Bonnie?" He tossed the yellow sheet toward the ambulance chaser. "Look him up in *Who's Who.*"

Mr. Doon reached for the unwieldy red volume that always stood on the end of the table alongside the Bible, the *World Almanac, Burke's Peerage, Bartlett's Familiar Quotations,* the *Shakespearean Concordance, Bibby's Pocket Dictionary* and *Ploetz's Manual of Universal History.*

"Dingal — Dingball — Dingbat — Dingel — here he is: 'Dingle, Allison; b. Yonkers, N.Y., Sept. 30, 1870; s. Thomas and Sarah Jane D.; m. Mary Haskell, of Brooklyn, N.Y., April 15, 1904.' Gee! This guy certainly hates himself! They write their own obituaries, you know! Claims he's a manufacturer, financier, author, genealogist, agrostologist —"

"What's that?" asked Mr. Tutt.

"Got me!" answered Bonnie. "But whatever it is, he says he's it!"

"What clubs or societies does he belong to?"

"Union League, Yale, Sons of the Revolution, Society of American Wars, United Order of Americans, President of the Breakfast Food Manufacturers' Association, Vice-President of the Nordic Society — there's nearly a page of it!"

"He's everything but a Blue Goose and a Sacred Camel!" declared Mr. Tutt.

"Anyhow, I guess he's good for a ticket to Bar Harbor." Bonnie replaced the book. "If you don't feel like taking such a long trip this hot weather, I —"

Now, although Mr. Tutt had always insisted that New York was par excellence the finest summer resort upon the American continent, he was at this particular juncture yearning to get out of it. In the first place, there was absolutely nothing doing in the office of Tutt & Tutt; in the second, the weather had been unspeakably hot; thirdly and lastly, he hated to be left there all by himself when everybody else was off having a good time, and even the Saturday-night meetings of the "Bible Class" at the Colophon Club, where they played deuces wild and everybody raised on a red and black nine, had been temporarily suspended.

Besides, strange as it may seem, in spite of the fact that Mr. Tutt was by birth a New Englander and had fished most of the inland waters of the state of Maine, he had never visited the sea-coast, although he probably knew more of its early history than most of the native inhabitants. He had passed many a winter evening beside his sea-coal fire in his musty old library on Twenty-third Street, smoking innumerable stogies and reading of the earlier expeditions from France and England to the North Atlantic coast nearly two decades before the Pilgrims landed at Plymouth in 1620.

Champlain was one of his favorite heroes, and he was familiar with the fact of his picturesque but ill-starred expedition, which, under the charter of Henry of Navarre, King of France, and the leadership of Pierre de Guast, Sieur de Monts, had visited the coast of Maine in 1603, discovered the island of Mt. Desert, and attempted unsuccessfully to establish a colony at the mouth of the St. Croix River, where most of his followers had fallen victims to starvation, scurvy and Indian arrows. Hence Mr. Tutt's interest in

Mt. Desert was not social, nor even professional, but historic.

He had always wanted to go to Mt. Desert; and now the chance was being offered him — all expenses paid — by the distinguished Mr. Allison Dingle. Send Bonnie Doon in his place? Perish the thought! It made no difference who or what Mr. Dingle might be, or the nature of the matter in which the latter desired to retain him. "Service" was the motto of Tutt & Tutt.

So Mr. Tutt gave Bonnie Doon a paternal smile.

"It is very kind of you to suggest going in my place," he said. "But as I read his telegram, Mr. Dingbat demands my personal attention."

"Dingle is the name," corrected Mr. Doon with hauteur.

His employer rose.

"I shall honor the call of this patriotic manufacturer of dry cereals," he announced. "You and Miss Sondheim can hold down the office furniture while I am gone."

Thus it was that Mr. Tutt, at five o'clock the next morning, had found himself in the wilds of Maine. He had gone via Boston and debouched at Bangor, tired and rather cross, after a sleepless night in the Pullman; but having snatched a cup of coffee at the station restaurant and transferred himself to the back platform of the train, he had begun to revive. As he rattled down the single track to Ellsworth and the Mt. Desert ferry, Mr. Tutt, breathing into his tobacco-tanned lungs the cold air in which the balsam of pine forests was mingled with the breath of the ever-nearing sea, revived more and more.

Later he stood clinging to his hat in the bow of the "Norumbega" as it churned across the bay toward the mountains that ranged themselves like a row of gigantic elephants over the island of Mt. Desert, passed through a narrow channel between some small spruce-covered islands, called The Porcupines, and threading its way among the yachts lying in the harbor, bumped at length against the Bar Harbor pier. Mr. Tutt had enjoyed every minute of that beautiful sail, and it was by reason of his desire not to miss anything, and his consequent commanding position in the bow of the steamer, that he was the only passenger to observe the tableau at that moment being enacted upon a neighboring float at which lay a small stubby white launch.

A girl in khaki overalls and blue jersey, her yellow hair cupped by a round blue worsted cap, was standing in the stern, evidently engaged in saying good-bye to a white-flanneled young man upon the float, who seemed disinclined to let go her hand. They evidently had a great deal of importance to say to each other, and they were much too engrossed to notice either the approach of the "Norumbega," or the inquiring presence of Mr. Tutt.

"All ashore that's going ashore!" yelled the mate as the hawser looped one of the piles; and Mr. Tutt, grasping his carpetbag, descended the plank.

Reaching the pier, he turned to see what further might have happened. The launch was by this time a couple of hundred yards from the float, scudding for the open bay, the girl looking back, one hand upon the wheel, and waving good-by with the other.

A trimly gaitered chauffeur relieved Mr. Tutt of his carpetbag, conducted him to a shining limousine, whirled him through the town and up a half-mile of curving bluestone drive to a chateau surrounded by pines upon the summit of a neighboring hill.

It was a sparkling day, one of Stevenson's "green days in forests, blue days at sea." The odor of roses drifted from the garden near by; across the tree tops he caught the glint of the ocean.

Mr. Tutt would have liked to throw himself down on the lawn, stick his face into the hot grass, and maybe roll about and kick his old heels in the air; but a portly, pink-faced manservant was standing upon the marble step beneath the porte-cochère.

"Mr. Dingle wished me to say that he will be down in a few minutes," he said. "Breakfast is at nine o'clock. Shall I show you to your room, sir?"

So Mr. Tutt turned his back on the sunlight outside and followed the butler through a shadowed entrance hall, hung with armor and mounted trophies, and up the heavily carpeted stairs, to a vast white bedchamber, adjoining an equally vast bathroom, resplendent in tile and gleaming nickel.

At the door of this natatorium, Mr. Griffin, the gentleman in waiting, paused.

"How do you like your bath, sir?"

"Er — medium, I guess," temporized the old lawyer.

The eyes of the stately one enfiladed Mr. Tutt's congress shoes, string tie and rusty old frock coat. Elevating the carpetbag upon a supercilious finger, he inquired unhopefully, "Shall I lay out some other clothes for you, sir?''

Mr. Tutt, who had thrown himself at full length upon a lounge and was feeling in his pockets for a match, waved him aside.

''No,'' he replied. ''In point of fact, I haven't got any. And you needn't bother to open that bag, either. There's nothing in it but a toothbrush, a pair of socks, a bundle of stogies and my last copy of the *Influence of Wealth in Imperial Rome.*''

''Very good, sir. Thank you, sir,'' said Mr. Griffin.

''Not at all!'' said Mr. Tutt.

## II

''I'm a Nordic,'' said Mr. Allison Dingle, half an hour later, with one eye on the butler. ''And,'' he added with a significant nod at Mr. Tutt across the breakfast table, ''we Nordics must hang together.'' He drained his cup of coffee nervously and poured half a pitcher of cream over the cereal on the plate before him. ''Oh, I'm not a pessimist! All I mean is that we Nordics, who furnish most of the back-bone, muscle and moral character to the American nation, ought to present a solid front to any attempted relaxation of the immigration laws. America ought to be for the American — the real ones! We ought to breed true,'' he waved a stubby arm, ''particularly since we live in a country where the really good elements in the stock have a chance to rise to the top. There's where we put it all over the English and the Germans, who weaken the strain by inter-marriage within an artificial nobility already run to seed!''

An egg-shaped spoon jingled. Mr. Dingle was addressing an imaginary audience of thousands.

''Yes, sir! 'Out of a democracy of opportunity we have created an aristocracy of achievement!' There is no wealth, no honor, no public position which is not within the grasp of any man who has it in him. Look at the Vanderbilts, the Astors; at Rockefeller, at Carnegie, at Ford — and, in a more modest degree, myself! These men had nothing except their natural inheritance of brains and moral fibre, and the other dominant characteristics of our race.''

He leaned back in his wicker chair, which creaked ominously, a short, snugly-tailored fat man with restless gray eyes.

''When did you come over?''

Mr. Tutt regarded him abstractedly.

"Me? The ferry landed me at the Bar Harbor pier about twenty minutes ago."

"I know that — I meant your people. When did they come to America?"

"I haven't the remotest idea."

Mr. Dingle refused to be placed in the position of entertaining a mongrel.

"'Tutt' sounds like a Scotch name," he mused, ignoring his guest's admission of ignorance. "We Dingles are Scotch. 'Dingwell' the name was originally, until it was unfortunately corrupted over here to 'Dingle.' There is a barony in the family. The first Lord Dingwell dates from 1609. My personal forbears were naturally not in the direct line, but were merely of good, honest yeoman stock, who came over somewhere toward the beginning of the last century. I find genealogy rather interesting to play with. Everybody should have a hobby, don't you think?"

"I certainly do," agreed Mr. Tutt.

Mr. Dingle cast his other eye at the tall Englishman who was fussing at the side-table.

"That will be all, Griffin," he said impatiently. "You needn't wait." Griffin reluctantly retired, and his master arose and closed both doors leading off the breakfast porch.

"We may as well get down to business," continued Mr. Dingle as he sat down again. "Your time is valuable and so is mine — and I have a golf engagement at ten o'clock. Try one of these." He extended a gold case containing a row of oversized cigarettes, each bearing the intials "A. D." surmounted by a discreet crest.

Mr. Tutt produced a withered stogy.

"I'll smoke my own brand, if you don't mind."

Mr. Dingle helped himself and returned the case to his pocket.

"Well, the fact is I'm up against a delicate situation. Every rich man has to face the possibility of blackmail, I suppose, but this is different from the ordinary run. . . . The trouble is Robert insists on marrying the girl. He's only twenty-two, and still in college. All my hopes are centered on him. I want him to take my place in the business world — to start where I leave off — and so far, he has come right up to scratch. But last Sunday he broke the news to me that he wanted to get married. At first, naturally, I supposed that it was some girl friend of his whom I knew, whose parents come up here in the summer — from New York, Philadelphia or Boston. Then I discovered that this woman had been a waitress at the village tearoom, and that she is the daughter of a — of a lobsterman.''

Mr. Dingle paused to allow the full horror of the disclosure to sink in.

''Yes, sir! The daughter of a common fisherman — a man who gets his living by catching lobsters. Imagine my son tied up for life to a woman like that! It would ruin him socially — and in a business way too. Ridicule is the one thing that kills a man. Lobsters! It would spoil all my daughter's chances of making a proper match. There is a young Englishman of title over here just now, who is quite attentive to her. If he knew about this lobster business he'd run like a rabbit!''

Mr. Tutt nodded.

''No doubt he would. . . . Have you seen the young lady?''

''No! And I don't want to. Whatever she looks like — and I assume that she must be good-looking or Robert wouldn't have fallen for her — such a marriage would be preposterous — a calamity.''

''Do you know anything against her except that she is a lobsterman's daughter?''

''That's all I want to know. I don't want to be allied with that sort of people.''

''What's her name?''

''Her name?'' Mr. Dingle's gray eyes held the glint of ice. ''Her name,'' he announced, ''is Dizzy Zucker — and she comes from Mud Island!''

Mr. Tutt experienced a certain sympathy for his dogmatic host. Dizzy Zucker of Mud Island! It certainly sounded like bad news!

''What do you want me to do?'' he asked.

''Go there and buy her off.''

''But suppose she won't be bought off?''

''Every woman has her price. I'll pay her anything she asks, so long as it doesn't get into the papers; buy the whole island rather than have my only son married to a lobsterman's daughter! Can't you see the headlines? Mud Island! There'd be photographers and reporters swarming all over it! I've no idea what kind of a name Zucker is — Italian probably, or maybe it's Portuguese — there are a lot of them scattered along the coast. But that's the least of my troubles. I could even swallow Mud Island! What I can't stomach is the lobsters — and the girl's front name! Dizzy might mean anything. I can't find out from Robert whether it's her surname, her Christian name — if she is a Christian — or a nickname. If it's the last, she probably drinks. I don't know how a girl would get a name like that in any other ways — unless she was an acrobat or suffered from vertigo. Some of these islanders are a tough lot." He leaned back and patted his forehead with his napkin. "Dizzy! Lobsters!" he muttered.

"Where is this Mud Island?"

"Thirty miles offshore from Bass Harbor Light. I'll send you over, when you're ready, in my motorboat. You'll get there in a couple of hours. If money won't turn the trick, maybe your powers of persuasion will. I appreciate that what I'm asking you to do for me is a bit unusual, and I'll not forget it. Do whatever is necessary, and if you're successful, you can fill out your own check and I'll sign it without looking to see how much it's for. I've a lot of other business — and my present attorney isn't altogether satisfactory."

He was the kind of client all lawyers dream about.

"I've only one suggestion," said Mr. Tutt, "and that is that you go with me. It would be much safer if you were on hand to sign your check and close the transaction yourself. If I went alone, the girl might change her mind while I was making my report to you, or perhaps tell your son."

"There's something in that," agreed Mr. Dingle. "We'll go together, and start after luncheon. Now I must hustle off to the golf club. Meantime try to amuse yourself."

"I'd like a chance to talk to your son before we go," said the old lawyer. "It might be wise to get a slant on the young lady through him."

"All right. But you'll find him very obstinate. He simply won't talk to me! In fact we're barely on speaking terms. However — see you at one o'clock. Ta-ta!"

### III

From where Mr. Tutt stood on the veranda, awaiting the arrival of the Younger Dingle, he could see the whole grand sweep of Frenchman's Bay. Eastward stretched the hundred-harbored coast, promontory after promontory lying in echelon. Behind him, on the hill, crows summoned one another to council in the pines, squirrels scampered over carpets of pine needles. The air was tonic to the old lawyer's soul.

"What a place to live!" he exclaimed as, with his eyes wandering over the horizon festooned with the smoke of distant steamers bound for Halifax or New York, his thoughts flew back three hundred years to the day when Champlain in his *patache,* a tiny open boat with lateen sails and oars, had come coasting by the reefs and rocks, the bays and harbors of the then unknown coast, until he had sighted the bare summits of *Les monts désert* from which the island took its name. Hardy explorers those, who, braving shipwreck, starvation and savage enemies, had come in their tiny shallops to found a new empire for the King of France!

The seascape shifted its lights and shadows to suit the play of the old man's fancy. The low-lying islands became the shelter of Spanish buccaneers, their rakish schooners hiding behind clumps of trees to swoop down upon the unconscious fishermen, — that far-off sloop, carrying its load of lumber from Eastport to Boston, changed to a Portuguese caravel, a Norse trireme, a shallop of the Cabots, or the quaint bark of the brave De Guast with his motley company of nobles and vagabonds, — a crew of whom François Villon would have loved to sing — of gamblers, cutthroats, gay young blades of Paris, bloods of the court of Henry IV, and thieves fleeing the torture of the galleys. Mr. Tutt knew the stories of all of them. Under the still, blue, burning sky he saw the mists enveloping De Guast's fragile vessel amid the crags of the long-sought islands; heard the surf roaring along the barren granite shores; watched the creaming of the sunken reefs, the flapping sails of the pinnace; heard the boom of cannon above the songs of Lescarbot and the patter of Latin prayers. Did Dingle suspect the debt he owed De Guast?

"How do you do, sir?" The words, in a clear, boyish voice, brought Mr. Tutt to himself. Robert Dingle, tall, brown, was extending his hand. Mr. Tutt recalled the scene on the float. It was thus that he had first seen him. His heart warmed to the young man. Was Dingle, Sr., on the right track, after all? In his self-assumed capacity of adjuster-general of the universe, Mr. Tutt resolved to get at the bottom of the matter.

"How about a walk in the woods?" he suggested, with his gentlest smile. "I don't often get such a chance as this — That is, unless you have an engagement."

The boy shook his head.

"No," he replied; "as it happens, I've nothing whatever to do this morning. I'll be delighted to show you a little of Mt. Desert."

They wandered up the hill back of the house, through the pines, to an open sunny spot on the very crest covered with gray rein-deer-moss.

Mr. Tutt made no effort to force the conversation, but there was something so sympathetic about the old man's kindly face and courteous manner, that they had not rested there twenty minutes before Robert had told him the whole story of his love-affair with Dizzy Zucker.

"It all seems so foolish and unnecessary!" declared the boy, as he lay on the bed of moss with his hands locked behind his head, looking up at Mr. Tutt. "If Father would only just see Dizzy once, and talk to her — but he won't even let me bring her to the house! It isn't as if she were an uneducated girl, — Dizzy goes to college. You see, I'm on our college glee club and we gave a concert at Colby, winter before last. Dizzy was on their reception committee. I thought she was the grandest girl I'd ever met, so honest and capable and lovely to look at. I guess she liked me pretty well, too, although she didn't say so.

"I went back to college, but I used to think of her a lot, and once I sent her a book of poetry — Yeats, you know — and got a letter from her, saying she hoped we'd meet again sometime — nothing much, but very friendly and nice. Well, the following summer Dad rented this place here in Bar Harbor in order to give my sister a chance to meet what he calls the 'right sort' of people, and when I got here I found that Dizzy had taken a job in the village tea-room. Of course, after that, I saw her all the time."

"That was a year ago?"

"Yes. I didn't see her but once last winter. You see, Dizzy's father died a long time ago, and she has always lived with her mother and grandfather on the island, except when she has been away at school and college, or working. Last March her grandfather was taken sick with pneumonia and they sent for her to go back. He died, and she stayed on there to look after her mother, who is quite an old lady and can't be left alone. I saw Dizzy for a couple of days during the Christmas vacation while she was visiting her brother in Boston. I want her to go back to college again this autumn, but she says she ought not to leave her mother; and that, anyhow, they couldn't afford it unless she makes a lot of money this summer lobstering. It makes me feel like a perfect rotter to be hanging around here doing nothing, while she's hard at work over on the island.

"I suppose Dad would like me to marry the daughter of somebody just like himself, who'd made a few millions in mining, or insurance, or electric lighting, or canned goods, and is satisfied to spend three or four months here in the summer going out to a lot of fat luncheons and dinner parties. He talks a lot about wanting to have me begin where he leaves off. Well, where is he leaving off? As far as I can make out, it's at the Kebo golf course and the Pot and Kettle Club. I don't mind coming up here in my college vacations and swinging a golf club for a week or so, in order to be near him, but I'd a darn sight rather be off camping in the woods, or taking a walking trip in Switzerland, or putting in a couple of months with Grenfell in Labrador.

"Perhaps Dad shouldn't have sent me to college if he wanted me to be the perfect type of American business go-getter. It isn't that I don't like business. I do. I really enjoy it a lot. I'm pretty good at figures and I've taken a lot of courses in economics and banking. But I've taken others, too — in philosophy and fine arts — and I think there's something in life besides money." He considered a moment. "I want to be perfectly fair to Dad. I'm not sure he really values money any more than I do, but he confuses the kick he gets out of making it — it's his form of sport, you see! — with the thing itself. That's his fallacy. He says he judges people by what they've done, whereas he really judges them by what they've got. I agree that manufacturing breakfast-food is a high and honorable calling, only I don't see why the man who makes it is any better than the woman who passes it around the table.

"And then, of course — speaking confidentially — Dad is bugs on this Nordic business. To hear him you'd think the present generation of Dingles were of undiluted English blood. You got all this talk of his about our being merely 'good honest yeoman stock'? Well, I looked that good old yeoman stock up, and the first Dingle to come over was a ticket-of-leave man whose family had to pay his debts to get him out of jail. And Dad's paternal grandmother was a French Creole born in Martinique. I don't suppose he counts her in at all!

"He's just as muddled in his theories about racial inheritance as he is over that democracy-of-opportunity-and-aristocracy-of-achievement bunk of his, in which he measures achievement simply by how much money a man has got. It seems to me that it's not how much a man has got, but how he gets it that counts. I'm ready to become an aristocrat by achievement in the breakfast-food business and carry on the prestige of the Dingle family, but I'm going to marry whom I choose!

"I don't regard it as any particular favor to me for Dad to load me up with all his money. I'd enjoy life exactly as much as a retailer as if I were a wholesaler, — selling athletic goods, writing ads or raising chickens, so long as I do it with the right girl. From what Dizzy tells me, there's a lot of excitement in the lobster business. Dad is too pig-headed even to look at her! Once I told him her name and where she came from, he shut up like a clam. He won't even let me use the launch to go to see her. . . . Can you keep a secret?" Mr. Tutt nodded solemnly. "So she has to come over here to Bar Harbor to see me!"

"How does she get here?"

"In her own motorboat. She can make it in four hours and a half. . . . I haven't any money of my own, but I can work. If Dad won't give his consent to our marriage I can marry without it. I'm fond of Dad, but he doesn't need a lawyer half so much as a little broadmindedness. He at least ought to be willing to listen to me."

"I'll do my best to see that he listens to me," said Mr. Tutt.

## IV

It is a scant mile from the top of Malvern Hill, where the million-aires live, to the boat wharf, where the real life of Bar Harbor cen-tres, — the steam-laundry, the bakery, Hodgkin's fish-market, Nickerson & Spratt's feed-store, Mr. Angelo's peanut-stand, Charlie Parker's canoe-float and supply-store, and the Dirigo landing, where once in a blue moon you can find an old-time Portugee seaman with rings in his ears. Thither it was that Mr. Tutt, who always gravitated toward the genuine rather than the artificial, leaving behind him the gray-stone château of good old yeoman Dingle, took his way. From the bluestone drive he emerged upon a broad concrete highway lined with flower-bedecked stone walls and, smoking a contemplative stogy, strolled down West Street toward the harbor.

Here descending a hill, he passed a small grocery store where prominent in the window stood a pyramid of parti-colored packages labeled Dingle's Korn Pops. America was surely the land of opportunity! Contemplatively, he continued, pausing to buy a package of peanuts from Mr. Angelo, and arriving eventually at the steamboat wharf, where he sat down on one of the piles.

Engrossed in the view and otherwise fully occupied in eating his peanuts, he was rudely accosted from below: "Avast there! What ye doin' with them shells?"

Directly beneath him lay an exquisite mahogany launch nearly a hundred feet in length. Flags fluttered at her bow and stern, her brass blazed in the sunlight and the waves reflected themselves in dancing ripples on the green of her shining water-line.

Her red-faced captain, no less immaculate, glared up at the old lawyer.

"Don't y' s'pose I've got suthin' better to do than pick up your peanut shells?" he demanded.

"Sorry. Very careless of me. . . . Have a peanut?"

"No, I won't!"

"Sorry. My mistake. . . . Nice launch you've got there. . . . Have a cigar?"

The captain's austerity melted, as did that of most people when Mr. Tutt was around.

"Thanks, don't mind if I do." He made a fair catch. "Yes, she's a pretty good boat."

"Who does it belong to?"

"Feller named Dingle."

"Don't say! I've heard of him."

"Like to come aboard?"

"I sure would!"

Thus it was Mr. Tutt made another friend.

V

The bell of the launch jangled, the dial registered "Full Speed —
Reverse," and the "Arrow" churned back into a whirlpool of seeth-
ing foam.

The launch, bearing the two elderly men on their cynical adventure, had raced seaward for an hour, slicing through the rollers,
while the silhouette of Mt. Desert sank lower and lower over the
stern. Then on the uttermost purple rim had lifted a gray shadow,
growing in definition each instant as they leaped toward it, until it
had become an island with ruddy granite cliffs and fir-capped prom-
ontories; lonely, yet beautiful, and seemingly uninhabited save
by the snowy gulls that spotted its rocky shores or flickered
against the background of its black pines.

"That's Mud," announced the captain. "Nothin' much else between us an' Lisbon."

At that moment he observed a jagged, barnacle-covered rock,
not quite awash, apparently rushing directly at the "Arrow," and
gave a frenzied jingle.

"That was a close one!" he ejaculated, gazing anxiously at the
island across the maelstrom created by the "Arrow's" abrupt ret-
rocession. "It's been some time since I was over here."

He slipped the lever to "Ahead" and the launch hummed in a
sweeping half-circle around the nearest promontory.

"That's the harbor — such as it is."

They were at the mouth of a narrow cove the shores of which,
littered with buoys, nets and lobster-pots, rose everywhere in
steep gravel banks to where it joined the meadow. At the farther
end, a few weatherbeaten gray shanties clustered about a sagging
wharf. Unless one wanted to shin up the slimy piles, it was difficult to see how one could get up there.

"Tide's goin' out. I'll have to set you ashore in the tender," the
captain allowed. "I'll run in ez fur ez I darst."

With her engines at "Slow" the "Arrow" nosed a hundred yards
or so in toward the wharf, the anchor was dropped, the dinghy
lowered.

"Wait for us, captain," ordered Mr. Dingle, as he climbed in,
followed by Mr. Tutt. "We'll be back inside an hour."

"All right, sir. I can't stay in here 'count of the tide, but I'll hang around close as I kin. I'll be watchin' out fer ye.''

Mr. Tutt looked about him, sniffing the reek of tar and seaweed. So this was Mud Island! Again the grim suspicion came creeping over him that, after all, Mr. Dingle might be right. How could any girl who lived in such a place, even if she had gone to college, make a suitable wife for a young man of Robert Dingle's tradition and environment? Well, they would see. But first, how were they ever going to climb up that almost perpendicular bank? Slipping and sliding, his congress shoes filled with loose gravel, Mr. Tutt, followed by his fat client, scrambled up the slope and collapsed panting on a bed of juniper at the top. There was no suggestion of a road; no sign of life except the footpath that straggled around the cove to the group of houses on the opposite side. There was not even a cow in sight.

"This is a hell of a place!" grunted the perspiring Mr. Dingle. "That girl must live over in one of those hovels."

They walked along the path, which presently ducked over the dune and quartered the stony beach left bare by the receding tide. A grizzled gaffer with incredible ringlets was searching among the stones, watched from a distance by a small freckle-faced boy. The ancient one looked up at their approach.

"Ain't seen a knife-blade, have ye?" he cackled at Mr. Dingle. "I lost one here some'res ever so long ago. I dunno where it is." The cracked voice was plaintive.

"I have not!" snapped Mr. Dingle, stepping aside into a mudhole.

"He's all right!" called out the small guardian, approaching. "That's only old Pop Mullins. He's cracked, but he won't hurt nobody. Been lookin' for that knife-blade for the last thirty years. He's eighty-seven. Folks never dies here . . . . Dizzy Zucker? Sure, I know where she lives. You keep on this path round the cove, an' up over that hill thar, an' through the grove, an' you'll see it. Big yaller house.''

It was a glittering afternoon. About them the meadow was sprinkled with daisies and wild roses. Beyond the reddish rocks of the headland they could see myriads of white horses racing shoreward across a bay of indigo. The air was full of grassy smells, pungent with the odor of thyme, juniper and sun-dried moss, the breeze fragrant of fir and balsam. From overhead the sun burned hot upon their backs. Through the drone of bees and the rasping of locusts came the faint syncopated tinkle of unseen cowbells, the occasional bleat of sheep.

"It's a fine afternoon," admitted Mr. Dingle. "These folks have a pretty nice place to live in — if they are able to appreciate it."

The path led up the hill, traversed a grove, and unexpectedly emerged upon the other side of the promontory. A horizon of unbroken ocean encircled them. From the beach below came the roar and rattle of breakers. A solidly built two-story house with a cupola, surrounded by tall pines, faced the sea a hundred yards back from the edge of the cliff. Beside the open door of a shed, piled high with birch logs, a hatchet lay upon a wood-block, the ground littered with white chips. Smoke was rising from the kitchen chimney.

"Go ahead. You must do the talking," directed Mr. Dingle.

Mr. Tutt knocked on the kitchen door, which was opened by a pleasant-faced woman, spotless in white calico.

"Does Miss Dizzy Zucker live here?" he asked.

"Yes," answered the woman, "here's where she lives. She's out at present. But if you want to bargain for lobsters, it isn't any use, for she's all contracted up with Gains & Foster down to Boston."

"We're not looking for lobsters," answered Mr. Dingle stiffly. "We want to see her about something else."

"Well, if you want to try to find her, she's gone over to read to old Captain Freeman. He's stone-blind. She reads to him 'most every afternoon. You can follow the path right along the cliff."

They strolled on and entered the fragrant woods again, pausing frequently to enjoy the ocean-glimpses through the trees.

"Say!" unexpectedly exclaimed Mr. Dingle, as they gazed through a framework of spruce and hemlock at the blue white-flecked bay. "This would be some site for a summer cottage, wouldn't it? Just look at that view! A fellow could buy one of these islands and have it all to himself. Don't suppose it would cost hardly anything to speak of. He could have a regular place over at Bar Harbor, with all the society he wanted, and come over here every day or so to — to —"

"— to live?" suggested Mr. Tutt.

The path circled back through the pines and they found themselves once more on the edge of the meadow overlooking the cove.

Here, in a patch of sun, a tall old man with snow-white hair and beard was sitting with closed eyes, his head resting against a pine trunk. Beside him, flat on her stomach, lay a girl reading aloud — the girl Mr. Tutt had seen that morning on the float. She lifted her eyes at their approach.

"I beg your pardon," said he. "Are you Miss Zucker?"

"Yes," she said, without moving, "that is my name."

"Would it be convenient for you to have a few moments' talk with us — on a matter of business?"

"That's all right, Dizzy," boomed from the old man's lips. "Don't you bother about me. You must 'a' read more'n an hour already. Go ahead and talk to these folks."

Miss Zucker scrambled to her feet. She was still dressed in her khaki overalls. She had presented a pretty enough picture in the early morning as she stood in the stern of the launch with her hand upon the wheel; now, close at hand, Mr. Tutt perceived that she had real beauty.

"What do you want to speak to me about?"

Mr. Tutt, ignorant as he was of all feminine artifices, could not but wonder whether the blue cap and jersey had not been selected with an eye to contrast, for against them her bobbed yellow locks and clear sunburned skin looked almost golden. They made her eyes sky blue, her white teeth whiter. She stood easily erect, with her head thrown slightly back as if she were looking out to sea. Although her shoulders in the tight jersey looked absurdly small, she was only half a head shorter than Mr. Tutt — and Mr. Tutt was a tall man. Her expression was frank and direct.

"I haven't any lobsters — if that's what you want," she added.

Mr. Dingle rubbed his chin and looked at his companion.

"Allow me to introduce myself." The old lawyer bowed. "My name is Tutt — Ephraim Tutt — and this is Mr. Allison Dingle."

Miss Zucker flushed under her tan — flushed to the top of her temples, the tips of her ears.

"Tutt — Dingle? I never knew anybody by those names," interjected Captain Freeman. "You're not island men, are you?"

Mr. Tutt, repressing a natural desire to explain that they were Nordics of good old yeoman stock, admitted that unfortunately they were not island men.

A moment of mutual embarrassment followed, relieved by a

totally unexpected diversion.

Miss Zucker pointed suddenly to the cove.

"If that's your launch, she's in trouble!" she exclaimed. "Looks to me as if she were aground."

A single glance was enough to satisfy them that the "Arrow" was, indeed, in trouble, for she lay canted on her side high out of water in mid-channel, surrounded by a flotilla of skiffs and lobster boats, while Captain Hull waved his arms and shouted ineffectually at the cosmos.

"Never ought to have come in on ebb tide," interjected the blind man, towering to his feet. "It's plumb crazy. You don't know much about this coast, I reckon."

"Better come along and see if we can't get her off!" cried the girl, running swiftly down the hill, followed by Mr. Tutt and his client.

"She's hard and fast on the bar!" she shouted to them over her shoulder, as she climbed into a dory and pushed off.

"Say," panted Mr. Dingle, "this is awkward!"

A crowd of perhaps twenty islanders was gathered on the beach, yelling encouragement and jocularities at the unfortunate Hull, who, waist-high in the water and assisted by the mate, was attempting to lift the bow clear of the mud.

"I got trapped just like a lobster, b'gosh!" he shouted. "We come into the dog-goned cove all right, but when I went to turn around to git out, I got stuck on this here dog-goned mudbank. Tide must 'a' dropped jist enough to ketch us."

He grasped the bow in his arms and heaved. The thin mahogany cracked.

"Look out!" You'll rip the engines out of her!" warned the girl. "You can't move until the tide comes in."

"And when will that be?" inquired Mr. Dingle.

"About six to-morrow morning."

"Dear me, this *is* awkward!" repeated Mr. Dingle.

The girl, who had been surveying the situation from a dory, came rowing toward them.

"Your launch is all right," she said. "Lucky the bottom where she went aground is soft and level, and will distribute the weight of the engines so that they won't tear through. She'll lie there safe enough until morning."

"Isn't there any way for me to get back to Mt. Desert?" inquired Mr. Dingle, addressing Dizzy for the first time directly.

"Cap'n Higgins might take you over in his dory. He puts on an outboard motor — she makes nearly six knots."

"How long would it take?"

"About six hours."

"But I wouldn't get home until one o'clock to-morrow morning!"

"Besides which, you haven't as yet accomplished your purpose in coming here," warned Mr. Tutt.

"Looks as if we'd have to spend the night. Do you know of anybody who would put us up?" asked Mr. Dingle.

"The Duncans might take you in. They sometimes accommodate people," she replied. "Shall we go there and see?"

They followed the duck board that constituted the main street toward a frame house planted in the middle of a field. Four adults, three men and one woman, rocking on the porch and regarding the horizon with studied unconcern, stolidly awaited their approach. The men were all in their shirtsleeves and collarless, apparently taking turns spitting over the crazy balustrade.

"Good-evening, Mrs. Duncan," said Dizzy. "These gentlemen want to spend the night. Can you accommodate them?"

Mrs. Duncan seemed to be suffering from acute indigestion.

"No, I can't!" she snapped, after a lengthy silence.

"She can't!" echoed the last spitter. "School-teacher's stayin' here."

"I'm sorry. We'll try Mrs. Godkin."

The man at the other end of the row spat joyously.

"She's full too. The coastwise missionary's got her only room."

Mrs. Duncan's turtle eye was fixed upon a tin can containing one dingy geranium.

"Why don't you take him in yourself?" she inquired, adding enigmatically, "I guess what's good enough for one is good enough for another."

Dizzy turned to her companions.

"Do stay with us. Mother will be delighted to have you," she said cordially.

Already, the sun's red ball was rolling on the purple horizon and the shadows of the pines were shooting across the field. A wind chill from the mists of the Bay of Fundy drew down the hill.

"Really, this is most embarrassing," said Mr. Dingle in an aside to Mr. Tutt. "What the dickens are we going to do?"

"Unless you want to sleep out here in the meadow, I guess you are going to spend the night at Mrs. Zucker's," succinctly replied Mr. Tutt to Mr. Dingle.

The shipwrecked Son of the Revolution turned humbly to the daughter of the islands.

"Er — really, I hardly know what to say," he stammered. "I — er — hate to impose upon your mother; but if there's nowhere else —"

"There isn't!" she laughed. "You will be entirely welcome. If you can amuse yourselves looking around the town for a few minutes, I'll dash ahead and get things ready."

"Well — it's awfully good of you," began Mr. Dingle, but already the girl had turned and was running light-footedly up the hill.

He stared helplessly at Mr. Tutt.

"Say!" he ejaculated. "I wouldn't have had this happen for a million dollars!"

## VI

Mr. Tutt and Mr. Dingle watched Dizzy Zucker disappear among the pine trees.

"No, sir! I wouldn't have had this happen for a million dollars," repeated the manufacturer miserably. "Imagine coming over here to try to buy off a — er — blackmailer, and then finding yourself forced to accept her hospitality and spend the night in her house! It's — it's grotesque!"

"Oh, it isn't so bad as all that," Mr. Tutt encouraged him. "In fact, it seems to me to be almost providential. It puts us on a solid and amicable footing at the very start, and gives us plenty of time to feel our way along instead of hurrying roughshod through negotiations that will probably require very delicate handling. In fairness to the girl herself, you ought to find out something about her, first hand; anyhow, that will be necessary in order to make up our minds what to offer her."

"Well, as I told you before we started," replied Mr. Dingle doggedly, "I'll buy the whole damned island before I'll let my son marry into a lobsterman's family. It doesn't look as if it would cost much either. I don't believe the land is worth over fifty dollars an acre cleared, if that; and uncleared, it's practically worthless. What bothers me is how you are going to broach the subject. She might take it into her head to get mad and throw us out of the house, and then where would we be?"

"Right here in this meadow," admitted Mr. Tutt.

"You'll have to wait until morning before you try to talk business with her," warned Mr. Dingle. "Anyhow, as you say, the more we know about her, the better we'll be able to calculate what to offer. How about giving the village the once-over, as she suggested? What a wretched-looking place! I don't believe they've even got a church! How do you suppose they manage to make a living?"

"From the sea, I suppose," answered Mr. Tutt. "Don't you think we'd better go back and try to arrange to have Captain Hull and your crew taken care of for the night? They can't sleep on the "Arrow.""

Captain Hull and the engineer were just coming ashore in the dinghy as Mr. Tutt and Mr. Dingle reached the beach, where a reception committee composed of the entire population of Mud Island, including old Pop Mullins, was awaiting their arrival. The sand-bar on which the "Arrow" had gone aground was now clear out of water, and she lay high and dry across the mouth of the cove.

"Darned if I had any notion there was any such tide here as that!" declared Captain Hull in extenuation of his error, as he climbed shamefacedly out of the dinghy. "Must be over two fathoms if it's an inch!"

"Tide averages eleven foot," replied Captain Freeman, who had seated himself on a tar barrel and was interrogating the witnesses to the disaster. "There won't be a part'cle o' water in this cove two hours from now. You kin walk acrost it anywheres."

"I was diggin' clams this mornin' right where your propeller lies," announced another ancient mariner.

"Say, Joe, you didn't see nuthin' o' that knife-blade of mine out thar, did ye?" inquired Pop Mullins. "I lost it ever so many years ago, an' I've been lookin' fer it ever since."

"Sorry, Pop, but I didn't," answered the other old man in a

kindly tone. "I heard you lost one and I'll keep an eye out fer it."

"What sort of a knife was it?" asked Mr. Tutt.

"It were an oyster knife — a new one," replied Pop. "That is, it were a new one when I lost it. I guess it would be kind o' rusty by this time."

"Come up to the store and I'll buy you another," volunteered the lawyer.

Pop appeared overwhelmed by such munificence.

"Wa-ll, na-ow, that's kind of ye, I'm sure," he said with an embarrassed smile. "I don't know ez I ought ter let ye do so much for me."

"It won't do no good," declared Captain Freeman. "Dizzy buys him a new knife every six weeks or so, and he just puts 'em away somewheres and goes on lookin' for the old one."

"No matter," said Mr. Tutt. "I'd like to buy him a knife."

"Go along, Pop," urged the crowd. "Let him git ye a new one."

Headed by Pop Mullins, Mr. Tutt and Mr. Dingle, the crowd moved in single file along the duck board toward the group of shanties constituting the village. A flight of steps, so high as to seem almost like a ladder, led up to the door of a weatherbeaten combination post-office and grocery store which stood on the side of the hill. Two little girls and a wizened old man with a nutcracker face stood staring down at the approaching throng.

"Hi, Henery!" yelled someone. "This man's goin' to buy Pop a new knife. Got one?"

"Reckon I hev," mumbled Henery. "Come on up an' I'll see what there is."

"Henery's postmaster," explained Pop as they laboriously climbed the steps. "He's been postmaster pretty nigh ez long's I kin remember. He come from Lowell, Massachusetts, time of the war — didn't ye, Henery?"

"I sure did, Pop," answered the wizened one. "I come here the year President Lincoln signed the Emancipation Proclamation. Lowell was my home. I used to know Gen. Benjamin F. Butler well. But I had a hankerin' fer the sea, an' this seemed a likely place . . . . How'll one o' them do ye?"

"How much is it?" asked Mr. Tutt.

"A quarter. It's the kind Dizzy allus gits fer him."

"Thank you very much," said Pop, pocketing the knife. "You'll find Henery a very interesting man."

"You say you came here during the Civil War?" challenged Mr. Dingle suspiciously. "How old are you, may I ask?"

"I'll be eighty-nine next month," said Henery. He lifted off his ragged wig, disclosing an entirely bald skull. "This ain't my own haar, ye see. But there's plenty o' folks livin' on this island older'n I be. Take old Captain Higgins — he's nearly a hundred."

"Where does he live? I'd like to meet him," said Mr. Tutt.

"First house to the right at the end of the street," replied the postmaster. "Pop will be glad to show ye."

The sun had sunk below the horizon, leaving behind it a fan of gold. Overhead the sky was dappled with pink clouds. The reflected light bathed the weather-beaten sheds and dwellings, and the no less weather-beaten faces of the old folks about them, in a magic sheen. The pines upon the promontory stood like bronze pillars against the deep blue. Mr. Dingle felt as if he were in a strange mysterious world, unlike anything which he had ever known before and in which nothing was real. They bade the postmaster good-night and walked on. Standing apart a hundred yards up the hill was a shanty no bigger than a large doll's house.

"That's whar Cap'n Higgins lives," said Pop. "He most allus goes to bed at sundown, but I'll rout him out. He'll be glad to see ye."

The doll's house was perhaps eight feet high by seven feet square, with tiny windows, surrounded by a fence inclosing a miniature garden of phlox, sunflowers and hollyhocks.

Pop pounded on the closed door with his fist.

"Ahoy, Cap'n Higgins!" he cackled. "Got visitors fer ye! Let down your companionway!"

A muffled bellow came from somewhere under the roof, there was a heavy creaking, the door opened a crack, and a huge white beard protruded from it.

"Who's thar?"

"It's me — an' some men from the mainland," explained Pop.

The door opened wider, a shaggy head appeared in the aperture, and its owner came forth, stooping, and stood up. Erect, he was nearly as tall as the rooftree of his house.

"Glad to see ye," he said in a deep husky voice, extending a gnarled, blue-veined hand, first to the manufacturer and then to

Mr. Tutt. "I can't ask ye to come in, 'cause there ain't room. There's hardly space fer the cats after I get in."

"What a delightful house you have!" remarked Mr. Tutt. "It's the smallest one I ever saw."

"Yes, it's a pretty good house. I built it myself," agreed Captain Higgins, obviously pleased at the compliment. "When I gave up the sea about twenty years ago I had to have some place to live, an' havin' no family and not wantin' to go to any o' them seamen's homes or such places, I set to and built myself this house. I've lived here ever since."

"May I peek in?" begged Mr. Tutt.

"Sure! Look all ye want."

Captain Higgins picked up the white kitten that was purring between his ankles, and stepped to one side. Mr. Tutt bent his head and thrust it through the door. A rag carpet covered the floor, white dimity curtains hung across the windows, the unpainted walls were gay with lithographs. One side was completely filled with a modern, highly polished stove. There was a rocking-chair, but no bed. A ladder led upward to a manhole in the ceiling.

"Where do you sleep?" inquired the lawyer.

"I bunks 'tween decks," explained Captain Higgins. "There's just room for my mattress under the keel — I mean the ridgepole. I tried to make it ez much like my old quarters aboard the 'Sarah N. Higgins' — my old barkentine — ez I could. Below decks, I've got my little galley and cabin, and I've got my berth above. It's mighty snug and shipshape. It wasn't allus ez pretty ez it is now, though. Miss Zucker, a young lady who lives here — she's quite a near neighbor o' mine — gave me the picters and put up the curtains for me."

"We are spending the night at her mother's," explained Mr. Tutt.

"Wa-al, ye couldn't have a nicer place to stay!" declared Captain Higgins warmly. "The Zuckers are jest about the finest people on this island, or anywheres else, I reckon. They was among the first to come here way back in the time when nobody knew whether these islands belonged to France or England. I sailed with her father an' her gran'ther an' her great-gran'ther. They was all deep-sea men who could take a ship around the Horn or through the Strait of Malacca when there weren't no lighthouses or markin's on the reefs — just crammed full sail on her and sent her boomin' through."

"Do they still breed good sailors hereabouts?" asked Mr. Tutt provocatively.

"They do that — men an' women! I don't want to see any man handle a boat prettier than this here Dizzy Zucker, the young lady I spoke of. You know how Deer Island men rate, I reckon. They won't have none but them to sail the big international cup races. Well, Deer Isle is only eleven miles south of here, and the men on all these islands rate as Deer Island men. It's in the blood — they're loyal. They'll see ye through and they'll stick by ye. Now take Dizzy. She's one of the smartest girls ever I see — college-eddicated an' able. She could go anywheres an' be welcome — be an ornament to any society. But would she go away an' leave her mother? Not she! Lor' bless ye, she looks after every sick woman and child on this island! And that's sayin' suthin' when there ain't a nurse or a doctor or a midwife nearer than Swan's Plantation — fourteen mile by water. Dizzy's one of our selectmen now. She was elected unanimous last November."

"Indeed!" exclaimed Mr. Tutt. "Is there much party feeling here?"

"Pretty strong. We've got thirty-seven voters, with a reg-lar Republican majority of five. It hasn't changed, so fur ez I know, in ten years. Dizzy was on both tickets."

"What an extraordinary old man!" declared Mr. Dingle as they said good-night and walked on. "And a very garrulous one. He seems to have a rather high opinion of the Zucker family."

"Well, can you blame him?" mused Mr. Tutt.

## VII

It was dark by the time they reached the top of the hill, and they found their way through the grove to the house by the light shining through its windows. Perhaps, thought Mr. Tutt, it was by the light from those same windows that Captain Freeman and Captain Higgins had shaped their homeward courses on their return from far-distant ports across the seas. Inside, they could see Mrs. Zucker moving about her shining kitchen, and from the crack of the window came a pleasant smell of cooking.

"I don't know how you feel about it," growled Mr. Dingle, "but

I've never been more embarrassed in my life. I don't see how I can partake of that woman's bread and salt, and then turn right around and offer her money to keep her hands off my son. I'd rather not take a bite to eat. But to be honest, I'm as hungry as a bear.''

"I'm glad the situation has not deprived you of your appetite," replied Mr. Tutt. "I think we are exceedingly fortunate in having such a comfortable place in which to spend the night. I'm quite hungry myself."

"Well, knock and get it over with," said Mr. Dingle, and Mr. Tutt knocked.

"No trouble at all," declared their hostess, leading them into the kitchen. "No trouble at all. I'm always glad to have any friends of Dizzy's stay with us — that is, if there ain't too many of 'em. Only I'll have to ask you to wait a few minutes more while I get supper. You just make yourselves comfortable there around the stove. . . . Sure, smoke all you want to. A sea-captain's wife is used to tobacco.''

Dizzy was not in evidence, but from the darkness outside came the sound of chopping, and presently she came in bearing an armful of wood.

"I'll just run down to the car and get a few lobsters," she said, depositing the wood and picking up the lantern which she had left beside the door. "I won't be five minutes."

"It's certainly most hospitable of you," murmured Mr. Dingle, as he took off his overcoat and settled himself as near the fire as seemed reasonably safe. "You really needn't cook any lobsters on my account."

"Oh, that's all right! Lobsters take the place of chickens with us," explained Mrs. Zucker."I hope you both like 'em. Chicken feed is so high these days — an egg is quite a luxury. But lobsters take care of themselves. Thank God for the lobster, I say! When my great-grandfather, Isaac Weyman, moved over here from Swan's Plantation in 1823, these islands were all covered with fine farms. Salt was hard to get in those days and the islanders used to trade with any French or English vessels that came along — two pounds of fresh beef or mutton for one of salt. Think of that! They didn't do nearly so much fishing as you'd think. That came later. They were real homesteaders. I've heard Gran'ther say that folks along the coast — including Boston and New York and Philadelphia — all lived just about the same — not much difference between city and country."

"I take it that your husband was a deep-sea sailor," commented Mr. Tutt.

"Yes; he and his father and gran'ther before him," she answered. "They all followed the sea. My husband was drowned when Dizzy was five years old, so Gran'ther Zucker came to live with us. He was a pretty old man by that time, so he took up lobsterin'. He died of the pneumony last winter."

She paused and sighed. From the stove arose the sound of sizzling, accompanied by a delicious aroma.

"Gran'ther Zucker was a wonderful old gentleman," she continued. "He'd been most everywhere in the world. Him and Cap'n Freeman, his chum, sailed round the Horn together in 1871. They most always shipped in the same vessel when they could. . . . Gran' ther was terrible fond of Dizzy. Summers he taught her how to sail an' trawl an' make lobster pots, and winters he taught her out of books. 'Twas him prepared her for college. She's a senior now at Colby."

"Do many of the young people from the island go to college?" asked the lawyer.

"Most all the boys and girls that's fit to go. I don't hold with educating the whole kit and caboodle. But the general run goes either to Colby or Bates or the University of Maine. They work summers and go to college in winters."

"And then what?" suddenly inquired Mr. Dingle, who was gradually shedding his embarrassment.

"The majority of 'em become doctors or lawyers or business men, and the girls get married and settle down in the cities. It's a great shame!"

"How do you mean — a shame?" Mr. Dingle leaned forward.

"I hold they ain't near so happy, nor don't begin to live near so well as they would if they stayed right here on the island. My husband, Captain Zucker, said he'd sailed all over the globe, up and down, crisscross and sideways, and there weren't any prettier place than the Maine coast — and no climate anywheres that could touch it."

"That was your idea, too, in settling on Mt. Desert, wasn't it,

Mr. Dingle?'' said Mr. Tutt innocently.

"Why, yes — certainly,'' agreed Mr. Dingle.

"And look how much it costs to live in those places!'' she rattled on with the volubility of one who rarely had a chance to talk herself out. "My son, Lester, who's a doctor in Boston, he can't lay by anything. He's smart too. But what with a wife and four children, he's never been able to contribute toward sending Dizzy to college. She's earned her way — every cent of it — waiting on table, an' clerkin' an' teachin'. She's a real smart girl, if I am her mother.''

"Did you say she was in the lobster business?'' inquired Mr. Dingle timidly.

"I don't know as I said it, but she is,'' answered his hostess. "Gran'ther Zucker had a fine string of traps, and when he died last winter it took all Dizzy's savings to pay for his illness and the funeral. D'y' know, there weren't a decent coffin this side of Bass Harbor? Anyhow, I was left all alone here, so she came back and carried on the business. She's doing well too — makes all her own traps an' everything. Next winter she aims to take me along to live with her, while she finishes her course and gets her degree.''

"Don't you look forward to seeing her married?'' hazarded Mr. Tutt.

"I haven't seen anybody near good enough for her yet,'' declared Mrs. Zucker, turning to the stove.

At that moment the young lady herself entered the kitchen, carrying a basket.

"Aren't they beauties?'' she demanded, throwing back the cover.

Mr. Dingle looked in. He seemed fascinated.

"Are those lobsters?'' he exclaimed. "I always supposed they were red.''

"You're learning,'' Mr. Tutt informed him.

As he watched Dizzy standing so unselfconsciously in the lamplight in her brown overalls, her cheeks flushed from running uphill and damp with the mist that clung in hundreds of tiny drops to her hair and eyelashes, he wished that he had a daughter like her. Did they breed girls of such sort in cities? He wondered what his client thought about it. He continued to wonder when, ten minutes later, she came downstairs dressed in a trim, one-piece frock of dark-blue worsted edged with white, and began deftly to set the table.

The old lawyer had never eaten a more savory meal — broiled live lobsters with drawn butter, hot muffins, new potatoes in their jackets, fresh corn on the cob, griddlecakes and maple sirup, blueberries and cream, coffee.

"I'm supposed to be dieting," announced the manufacturer ruefully. "But I'm going to cut loose for once. I wish my chef could cook like this."

Replete, they sat and smoked in the spotless kitchen, while the two women cleaned up and washed the dishes. Just as they finished, Captain Freeman entered.

"Heard you men were here," he said. "Wa-al, you kin rest easy. Your boat seems all right and your crew are over to Putnam's. Thought you might like to know where they was. Anyhow, a 'gam' with a strange vessel is always agreeable."

"Glad to see you, Captain Freeman," cried Dizzy, leading the blind man to a chair. "Did you have any trouble finding your way across the lot?"

"Nary a bit! I see as well by night as by day. I been walkin' that path now nigh on seventy years."

"May I offer you a stogy?" asked Mr. Tutt.

"No, thanks. I never got used to seegars," replied the old man. "Yes, sirs! I kin remember when old Captain Lester Zucker built this house — Dizzy's great-gran'ther. That was in 1849, when everybody was all het up over the gold in Californy. He must 'a' been around ninety at that time. He run the blockade during Revolutionary days, fit the Barbary pirates, an' was with Commodore Perry in 1812. Yes, born right here on this island. His great-gran'ther settled here in 1698. He's buried up thar in the grove — spelled his name L-e-i-c-e-s-t-e-r. Unless the marble cutter made a mistake, he spelled Zucker different too — Z-o-o-k-e."

"That's right," nodded Mrs. Zucker. "They used to spell it that way, but they changed it, 'cause folks always mispronounced it."

Captain Freeman exhaled a cloud of smoke rivaling in size that of Mr. Tutt.

"There used to be an *h* in it, somehow. Wa-al, it don't make no difference. But Captain Lester, he was quite interested in things like that. Told me he went somewheres in London once and paid to have it all looked up. But his son, Cap'n Isaac, never bothered about it none.''

''We don't pay much attention to names around here,'' commented Mrs. Zucker. ''Maybe we do spell it wrong, but what of it? A name don't mean anything, when you come to study it. There's Miss Duncan — she's always so ashamed because her great-great-great-great-grandmother was a full-blooded Kennebec Indian. I figured out she's only a one-sixty-fourth part.''

''Zactly!'' agreed Captain Freeman. ''And if the Indian had been a buck instead of a squaw, Miss Duncan might have inherited his name, spite o' the fact that she had sixty-three other ancestors, just as closely related to her, named entirely different.''

Dizzy had been scribbling on the back of a paper bag.

''On that basis,'' she remarked, ''and allowing four generations to a century, a person who traced his ancestry back three hundred years would have 4,096 ancestors, from any one of whom he might have got his name.''

Mr. Dingle showed signs of interest.

''I really never thought of that before,'' he ruminated. ''But, of course, it's quite true.''

''Three hundred years ain't such a long time,'' mused Captain Freeman, ''albeit a good many changes kin take place. I remember when all these islands was populated thick. Every inch of shore line was took up with farms, although no one did much farming. What they did was to build boats. You could hear the calkin' irons ringin' all the way from Calais to Biddeford Pool. I've seen sixty-two vessels built right in this very cove where you ran aground — brigs, barkentines, schooners an' full-rigged ships. Every man was a sailor, an' his ambition was to sail his own ship. There was a heavy coastwise trade in salt cod an' lumber, an' to the Bahamas and West Indies. Occasionally a feller would take a sportin' chance and try Madeira, Lisbon, Algiers and Constantinople. The islanders was rich then. If a man died, his widow would invest what he left, in a ship — one thirty-second or one sixty-fourth.''

''The lumber trade was a very active one,'' contributed Mr. Tutt.

'''Twas so!'' agreed Captain Freeman. ''An' a good deal of lumber that started for Boston an' New York never got farther than the captain's farm. There's lots of houses on this island built from lumber that was dumped ashore on the way by, an' paid for the consignor as lost at sea.''

''There must have been a lot more goin' on here in those days than there is now,'' said Mrs. Zucker.

''Oh, them was lively times!'' declared the captain. ''We had a lot of social life — corn-huskin's, clambakes an' quiltin's. Folks was always visitin' around. I remember rowin' a girl fourteen miles to a huskin' over on Dog Island once.''

''Dizzy's father and I sailed and rowed twenty-five to find a preacher to marry us,'' said Mrs. Zucker. ''Took us all day to get there — and then he was out! He'd rowed eleven miles to Duck Island to bury a man.''

''Conditions haven't improved much in that respect,'' said Dizzy. ''There isn't a doctor or an undertaker nearer than fourteen miles by water. Of course, now that there are motorboats, it isn't so bad.''

''Not unless there's a storm on,'' qualified her mother. ''There's been many a soul passed out, and many a child born, on this island without assistance from doctors. But, of course, gasoline has made a big difference.''

Mr. Dingle had been listening attentively.

''What you say, Captain Freeman, interests me extremely,'' he remarked. ''What has been the reason for the decline of prosperity on these islands?''

''Steam,'' answered the old sailor. ''It killed the coastwise trade, just as it did the overseas. There weren't no use building brigs an' schooners when one tug could tow a string o' barges half a mile long. So we quit ship-buildin'. Ever since then the folks on these islands have been livin' on their hump, more or less, although the hump don't amount to nothin' to speak of.''

''That's when we began lobsterin',''  said Mrs. Zucker. ''If steam took away our carryin' trade, it enabled us to market our fresh fish and lobsters.''

''What does it cost per pound to ship from here to Boston?'' asked Mr. Dingle.

''Six cents,'' answered Dizzy. ''Three cents to Rockland and three more to Boston. A power-smack calls here a couple of times a week. I can sell direct for thirty-five cents a pound, or pay freight and try to profit by the fluctuations in price.''

"We couldn't do no sech thing before steam," said Captain Freeman. "Some folks is inclined to lament modern inventions, but I hold there's a good deal to be said for 'em . . . . Don't y'want to turn on the radio, Diz, before I go?"

"Dizzy vanished into the adjoining room and presently through the open door came the strains of "Valencia."

"That's Russell's orchestra over at the Swimming Club in Bar Harbor," she said. "I tried New York and Boston, but there was nothing interesting."

"Wa-al, I must be gettin' along an' give you folks a chance to git to bed," said Captain Freeman, after the music had stopped. "Glad to have met you."

"I tell you it's a great comfort on a winter's night when there's a storm ragin', to sit here snug an' warm an' listen to a concert or an opry or a good speech, just like the folks on the mainland," remarked Mrs. Zucker appreciatively. "Makes you ferget you're miles out to sea. We heard the President's speech just as clear as if he was upstairs . . . . Wouldn't you like to turn in?"

Mr. Tutt and Mr. Dingle agreed it would not be a bad idea at all.

Lamp in hand, high above her head, the girl guided the two men up the narrow stairs.

"This was Gran'ther's room," she said, throwing open a door. "I hope you won't mind sleeping in the same bed." She put down the lamp, lingering for a moment to make sure that they had everything they might need.

It was a square, high-ceiled corner room, curtained with old-fashioned English chintz and furnished in heavy San Domingo mahogany. Upon the mantel stood an elaborate model of a Chinese junk, done entirely in ivory. A seaman's brass-bound chest stood in one corner, a tall secretary in the other, and upon the walls hung several prints of vessels under full sail. Mr. Dingle commented upon the beauty of the furniture, admiring the grain and polish of the mahogany. Her grandfather had brought it all himself from San Domingo more than sixty years ago, Dizzy said, and there were a lot of curious old things downstairs in the parlor collected by the great-grandfather who had been interested in family history. So far, Robert had not been mentioned, neither had there been any reference to the business which had brought them there. As she closed the door softly behind her, Mr. Dingle said, "I wonder what that girl thinks of us.''

''I don't know what she thinks of us,'' answered Mr. Tutt. ''But I know what I think of her,'' he added as if to himself.

## VIII

It soon became obvious that the night in Gran'ther Zucker's bed was not going to be a success. Neither of them was used to sleeping with anybody else, a ghostly light pervaded the room, the patchwork quilt was too hot, and something was evidently preying upon the Dingle mind. The manufacturer tossed restlessly from side to side, sighing and groaning, and occasionally giving vent to distraught outcries. The lobsters had evidently been too much for him.

Mr. Tutt stood it as long as he could. At last he arose. A gibbous moon hung low over the pines. From the beach below the house came a muffled roar. From Gran'ther Zucker's bed came a roar equally muffled, hollow and unearthly. Mr. Tutt stood shivering by the window, for the air that came through it was chill.

''It is a nipping and an eager air,''' quoted the lawyer, as he slipped on his frock coat. '''The glowworm shows the matin to be near, And 'gins to pale his ineffectual fire.''' He tiptoed to the door. '''Rest, rest, perturbed spirit'!'' he remarked to the huddled form.

Downstairs it was warm and cozy, and the range shone red. Mr. Tutt, lighting first a lamp, then a stogy, started on a voyage of exploration. His first survey of Great-gran'ther Leicester's collection of curios proved disappointing — nothing more than a glass case containing a few Indian relics, a stuffed and rather mangy seaotter, a small brass cannon. Mr. Tutt placed the lamp on the center table holding the radio, and sat down. A little reading perhaps might soothe his weary nerves enough to induce sleep. But he could see nothing to read. There was not even a magazine lying about. Usually people left something on the center table, if only a photograph album. He glanced beneath it. Stacked against the legs was a row of books evidently removed to make room for the radio — a copy of *Chambers' Miscellany of Useful and Entertaining Facts*, which Mr. Tutt knew by heart; *Ben Hur*, the *Christmas Carol*, *Webster's Dictionary*, and a heavy volume bound in black leather and held by an iron clasp. He picked it up, blew off the dust and lifted the cover.

"To the most high and mighty Prince James, by the grace of God, King of Great Britain, France and Ireland, defender of the faith, etc., the translators of the Bible wish grace, mercy and peace through Jesus Christ our Lord." One of the original copies of the King James version.

Mr. Tutt, with the volume upon his lap, turned to its faded record of births and marriages. The first entry was barely decipherable:

> Our Lady's Day, 1639, Leicester Bayard Villiers Zouche married to Mary Cavendish Montagu Drummond, of Eastlake, Hants.

Followed page upon page of births, deaths and marriages, during which the name Zouche became in turn Zouke, Zooke, Zooker, and finally Zucker. Two Christian names appeared over and over again — among the men, that of Leicester; among the women, that of Desire. The final entry was:

> Sept. 6, 1903, born to Abner and Mary Zucker, a daughter — Desire.

The creaking of the staircase awakened the old man from the reveries conjured by the record, and he looked up to see Desire herself standing in the doorway with a lantern in her hand, dressed in oilskins, a sou'wester and rubber boots.

"Good-morning, Desire," he accosted her. "Where are you going at such an early hour?"

"It's not early," she replied. "It's after one. I have to go and pull my traps. . . . I'm sorry you couldn't sleep."

"What do you know about this?" he asked, pointing to the first entry in the family Bible.

"Yes, that is the way the name used to be spelled. Great-gran'ther went into it all very carefully. There's a family tree over in the corner which carries it back ever so much farther."

She reached behind the bookcase and pulled forth a great scroll which he helped her to unwind.

At the top of the trunk, opposite the date 1308, appeared the name Zouche of Haryngworth; at the bottom, among a hundred or more tiny leaves, that of Leicester Bayard Villiers Zouche.

"The oldest barony in England," mused the old man.

"Is it?" she inquired. "Well, that's where the Zuckers came from, and" — she laughed — "the way we figured it out to-night, I must be nearly one ten-millionth part of a Haryngworth!"

"Whatever the percentage, you're all wool and a yard wide, my dear," he answered.

"Well, none of those things count much around here," she commented.

At the moment there was a noise from above. Mr. Tutt hurriedly rolled up the scroll and replaced the book as Mr. Dingle sleepily made his appearance.

"What are you two making such a noise about?" yawned the manufacturer.

"I was just going to ask Mr. Tutt if he wouldn't like to come out and help me pull my lobster traps," answered the girl.

"Sure, I'll come! Why don't you join the party, Dingle?"

"Do!" cried Desire. "There's going to be a lovely sunrise."

Mr. Dingle hesitated.

"Well, I'll go — as far as the beach," said he.

"Oh, come on!" urged Mr. Tutt. "Be a Nordic!"

## IX

The moon had set, and in place of it a pale luminosity yielded the sleeping islands as, swinging her lantern, Desire led the way across the meadow to the wharf, where a fifteen-foot motorboat was made fast. Here she unlocked a small shanty and brought out two sets of oilskins, which in the case of Mr. Tutt just reached to his knees and in that of Mr. Dingle trailed upon the ground — the long and the short of it. The latter climbed in dubiously.

"If we upset I'd have a swell chance to float in these things!" he muttered, wedging himself in the stern between two half barrels, dimly visible by the light of the lantern which the girl had placed near the winch-head amidships. Down there underneath the piles, it was pitch black, clammy as a charnel-house, — the boat, a ferry for lost souls. He meditated flight, but, during the instant that pride withheld him, the engine started with a sputter and they chugged swiftly out into the darkness.

Too late! His heart sank. On its way down it encountered his stomach.

"Ugh!" he groaned. "What on earth is in those barrels?"

"Bait," answered the girl laconically.

Mr. Dingle pinched his nose between his fingers. "Wad sord of baid?"

"Refuse from the sardine factory."

So far the water had been smooth; now, as they neared the mouth of the cove, the launch began to rock gently but ominously.

"Ugh!" groaned Mr. Dingle again. He could see nothing — it was as if his sight had gone entirely into his nose. He felt that all would soon be lost. Once around the promontory, the full force of the ocean-swell struck the launch, tossing it about like a chip, while an icy breeze smote him in the face and whisked away his outcries. In the darkness he clung to the barrels like a frenzied cat, as amid lashings of spray and spin-drift the frail cockleshell that stood between him and death reared, hung in mid-air and plunged with an angry roaring of the propeller downward again into bottomless black craters. He entirely forgot the terrible odor from the barrels. They were headed straight for Spain! The end could not be delayed for long!

"H-how far out are y-you g-going?" he shouted in agony to the girl, who stood calmly holding the tiller.

"A couple of miles. If you set your traps on a rocky lee shore like this, you lose most of 'em in the winter. The big storms toss 'em around and smash 'em to bits. So I go out where I can get good clear bottom."

Two miles? They would not outride such a sea for a hundred yards! And then a whiff from the sardines upset his universe. He leaned weakly against the nearer barrel, clasping it with convulsive tenderness.

Unexpectedly and without preliminary, the sea turned lead color instead of black-green. Between plunges, he could see Mr. Tutt clutching at his sou'wester in the bow. The sight gave him comfort. They were literally both in the same boat, anyhow! But with the coming daylight the waves seemed even more mountainous. It was incredible that the launch could climb — climb — climb to their awful summits or survive the never-ending coast down into eternity. And then, with an abandonment of all hope, he realized that they were beyond sight of land. They were in a wilderness of waters. On every side, within arm's length, death yawned for him with gigantic, hissing, foam-flecked jaws.

"Isn't this — far — enough?" he gasped.

Suppose this was really to be the end! What a useless and utterly absurd way to die! Just to put out to sea for no purpose whatsoever — on a sort of bet — and be drowned! A ridiculous performance! Not even in his own boat! His life simply thrown away before he'd had half a chance to enjoy his money and the position that he'd made for himself! What good his fine house over at Bar Harbor, his apartment in New York, his fine car, his chef — Griffin? He could not die and lose everything like that! And yet he felt sure that drown he would. He realized that he was miserably afraid.

In that black moment in which he clung face to face with death, he was forced to acknowledge that, so far as he was concerned, he was no more a Nordic than he was a Latin or a Celt. The ghost of his Creole grandmother arose from the waves and shook an admonitory finger at the little man paralyzed with terror. Why had he always tried to gloss her over? His own grandmother! What was the use of pretending that one was anything in particular, when, as that girl had proved last evening, one had had four thousand ancestors only three hundred years back? — and millions before that? As he prepared to meet his God, Mr. Dingle confessed that he was a fraud. And there was Robert! He could not leave Robert yet — so young, so inexperienced — to face life alone. If, before he died, he could only see him safely married to the right girl!

At that instant the sun broke through the gray bank of cloud upon the eastern horizon and the leaden world became one of purple and bronze. It shone through Desire's wind-tossed hair, turning it and her oilskins to bright gold. All that had been vague, vast and mysterious became definite, close at hand and natural. They were not out of sight of land, after all! Somewhere off there to the right he could see the island cliffs. Desire looked at him and smiled. Suddenly Mr. Dingle felt an immense and reposeful confidence in the stalwart, erect, fearless, young figure beside him. She was strong and brave and resourceful. She would not let him drown! And she was gentle and kind. She wished him no evil. How easily she could have disposed of him had she been so minded! Instead

she had protected him — saved his life! He experienced an un-
bounded admiration for her capacity — as he already had for her
lithe beauty.

"Hold on tight now!" she cried as she ran the launch up into the
wind and shut off the engine. "There's one of my pots!"

They were drifting rapidly astern toward a white object that
bobbed and ducked. Desire threw over the wheel, seized a gaff,
and pulling in the buoy, tossed the warp over the davit-block, took
a turn around the winchhead and started the engine again. Then,
as the line ran up over the side, she coiled it deftly in the bottom of
the launch.

"Here it comes!"

Leaning down below the davit, she heaved aboard the main
trap. The winch rumbled again and she drew in another, — the
bridle trap. With the two traps dripping on the stern sheets, she
once more shut off the engine. The main trap was empty, the second contained three greenish monsters. Desire swiftly unfastened
the bottom that closed the door below the guy line, removed the
bait bag, tossed the contents overboard and refilled it with a handful of the sardine refuse from the barrel in front of Mr. Dingle.
Then, thrusting the trap overboard, she opened the other, reached
in and took out the lobsters, threw one into the water and the two
others into an empty keg, rebaited the trap and shoved it after its
fellow, all before the six fathoms of warp that held the two traps
together had run out.

"Wish I could do anything as well as that," thought Mr. Dingle
admiringly. "She's as sure as Helen Wills!"

Her nonchalance communicated itself to him. He no longer
believed death to be so imminent.

"Why did you throw one of 'em overboard?" he asked.

"That was a seed lobster," she announced — "a female. Of
course we mustn't keep those. And one of the others was a
shedder."

"A what?" bellowed Mr. Tutt from the bow.

"A shedder — a lobster that has shed its shell. Every year they
crawl down into the mud and rocks and do that, beginning from
the middle of July to the first of August, depending on what sort of
a winter we've had. When it has been mild — like this year — they
begin to shed earlier. A shedder is soft, but if he's full length we

keep him and hold him in the car until his shell grows again."

Once more they raced head on into the waves, stopped, drifted down upon another buoy, kept off to gaff it, and ran before the wind while Desire pulled in and unloaded the pots.

Many were empty and some were badly damaged, with broken bows, or cracked sills and rungs, several having the funnel eyes, through which lobsters entered the trap, half-torn from the heads.

"The sea treats 'em rough," she commented. "I have to spend half my time mending my traps. I lose quite a few too, — guy-line frays off or the warps break and sometimes a trap will catch in the rocks and refuse to come up for keeps. But it's a fairly good business. If the lobsters go back on us we take to trawling or fall back on ground and hand lines. I can carry six tubs of trawls right in this boat. We get seventy-five cents a quintal — that's a hundred and twelve pounds — for hake, and seventy-two cents a quintal for cod. We pack 'em in hogsheads — drums, we call them — holding eight quintals apiece and ship to Boston and New York. It's all right in summer; great fun in fact — as you can see."

"Great!" echoed Mr. Dingle, beginning to feel like a hardy mariner. He was really enjoying himself a little, although now and again a particularly big surge would make him catch his breath. The sun by this time was well up, the wind had gone down, and the sea, deep blue and sparkling, was covered with boats. He felt reasonably confident that if any accident happened someone would come to their rescue. He started to hum:

> *"All's well on the land;*
> *All's well on the sea!"*

Was it? Surely it was — on the sea! Even if this girl were not a suitable mate for a boy of Robert's wealth and social opportunities, she would be a splendid wife for anybody who had to make his way in the world. If Robert were beginning now at the bottom instead of the top! There really wasn't such a terrible difference between the lobster business and any other, except that it took a lot more skill and courage. For an instant his Napoleonic mind dallied with the idea of a gigantic lobster trust.

"What are you thinking about?" he yelled to the lank figure in the bow.

"I was just wondering whether or not a lobster was a fish," answered Mr. Tutt.

The bait kegs were empty, the bottom of the launch full of writhing crustaceans, when Desire, having pulled her one hundred and twenty-sixth trap, headed the launch shoreward. Running with the wind, it was hot, and they took off their oilskins.

"Certainly a fine-looking girl," admitted Mr. Dingle. "Put her in a ball gown and she — No, by thunder, I'd rather keep her in a sweater!"

Confronted with her frank and disarming smile, he felt decidedly ashamed of himself. Really, he'd never seen a prettier girl — of that type.

"I was thinking over what you said yesterday about Nordics," mumbled Mr. Tutt as he bent over in the cockpit to light a stogy.

At the entrance of the cove, Desire steered the launch alongside a huge floating car into which she tossed her catch of forty-three.

"The smack will be by here Friday," she said; then, shading her eyes, she added, looking toward the beach, "I see the 'Arrow' is afloat again."

A young man who had been awaiting them on the wharf arose at their approach. His face wore an expression of amusement.

"Hello, Diz! Hello, Dad! Hello, Mr. Tutt! Where have you been?"

"Oh, just for a little sail after lobsters," replied the elder Dingle airily. "What are you doing here, Robert?"

"I got nervous when you didn't turn up last evening, so this morning I hired a launch myself and came to look for you."

The constraint between father and son had disappeared. In fact there was no constraint apparent upon the part of anyone as they all walked back together to the house.

Mrs. Zucker was standing on the porch.

"Breakfast ready!" she called. "Come right in and sit down!"

Mr. Dingle, who up to that time had not thought of food, ate ravenously of cereal, hot rolls, bacon, griddle-cakes and coffee. He was not only content; he was positively happy, the final factor in his absolute satisfaction being the gayly colored package of Dingle's Korn Pops that stood in the middle of the table.

"Well," said Mr. Tutt, as he joined his client for a postprandial smoke upon the piazza, "how shall we go about this business? Will you speak to the girl or shall I?''

Desire and Robert had wandered off toward the grove.

"How do you mean?" demanded Mr. Dingle, vaguely.

"You haven't forgotten the purpose of your visit, have you?"

Mr. Dingle fidgeted. "Naturally — not!" he said. "But I don't want to be too hasty. When it comes to matters of this sort I don't believe in too much interference with other people's lives."

They looked at each other and grinned. "Absolutely, Mr. Dingle?"

"Positively, Mr. Tutt!"

"In that case I might as well beat it back to New York," said the lawyer. "How soon before you start for Bar Harbor?"

"I think I'll spend the day here with Robert," replied his client. "The 'Arrow' can run you up to Bangor in time to catch the afternoon express. Incidentally, how much do I owe you?"

Mr. Tutt pondered for a moment.

"One hundred dollars," he said finally.

"A hundred dollars! Nonsense! That's not enough! Besides, you had your expenses."

"My fee is one hundred dollars — or nothing," replied the old lawyer. "I've always wanted to see Mt. Desert, and anyhow, I've had a swell time."

Mr. Dingle peeled a bill from the roll in his pocket.

"Well, there you are!" he protested. "But you make me feel pretty cheap."

"That's what I set out to do," muttered Mr. Tutt to himself as he went into the house. Presently he returned carrying Great-gran'ther Leicester's family Bible.

"You might stick your nose in that," he suggested — "after I'm gone!"

Desire and Robert waved at him from the promontory as he shot out of the harbor, and Mr. Tutt blew them a kiss. Two hours and a half later he shook hands with Captain Hull on the steamboat landing at Bangor.

"Here's the hundred dollars I promised you," he said. "You certainly did your part of it. But how on earth did you know just where to run the 'Arrow' aground?"

"Oh, that was easy," replied that worthy sea-dog. "I was born on Mud Island, although I ain't been thar since I was a boy."

Mr. Tutt stopped halfway up the gang-plank.

"And I forgot to pay you for that package of Korn Pops," he remarked. "How much did it cost?"

"Oh, that's all right," said Captain Hull.

*Born in Boston, Arthur Train (1875-1945) graduated from Harvard, became a lawyer, and served for many years as an Assistant Attorney General of New York. He wrote mainly at his summer residence on Frenchman's Bay in Bar Harbor, specializing in works of mystery and crime. Mr. Tutt, a shrewd but kindly lawyer, was his most popular character. This story appeared in THE SATURDAY EVENING POST in 1927 and was reprinted in MR. TUTT AT HIS BEST (1961).*

*Margaret Osborn* ————————————— *1944*

# MAINE

Silent at the tiller, Arnold threaded the boat through the rock pillars, going with the tide. High overhead we could hear the long moan of the foghorn, and the pure ring of Machias Light bell came over the water, sounding as if from nowhere, far off, and near us was the slapping of water against the rock and the screaming of the gulls.

The island loomed high in the fog that lay against it in heavy bands, the dark of the cliffs towering up, and off the shore huge broken columns that rose straight out of the black water, ancient portions of the face of the cliffs, half lost, fearful, and ruined. The water pulled around them, and where the fog lifted we could see it rolling in and breaking in a wide smoking line against the foot of the cliffs. We could see the deep holes of the caves and against them the gulls turning and dipping. Above them the fog was so thick we could not see where the cliffs ended.

We rounded the point into dead calm, the short sound of the engine echoing secretly back. We went straight along the lee shore; the cliffs seemed gradually to slope down to a steep, long slant of dark stones, and suddenly we came onto the harbor, a little crescent, narrow and deep and full as it could be packed of fishing boats. We came in on high tide, thirty feet. It was flush, beautiful, and very dark. Black Harbor.

We tied up to the dock. Arnold fussed with the gear of the boat, putting her to rights. Lundberg and I hauled up the heavy stuff, our shirts and dungarees wet with fog.

Arnold had sent word to Turner to meet us at the store. We went up there and found a message to let him know when we got in. We telephoned and sat down to wait.

The place was poor. The fishermen sat on the steps of the store or hung around two men pitching horseshoes. One of them spoke to Arnold. They looked at Lundberg and me and looked away, vague and polite. They were curious and hostile. There were no women about, only one girl, very handsome in a coarse way, with a sullen, captive look like something wild. She stood on the steps of the store; the men bantered her, and every now and then she'd shout back, in a speech so singsong we could not understand. She also looked at Lundberg and me, sly and savage, taking us in as strangers and as men.

We bought a few provisions and then moved our stuff up onto the road behind the store, and soon we saw Turner coming with his horse and wagon. He drew up and Arnold went to meet him. Turner got down from his wagon. He was a little, hard, spare man from the mainland. He was thin and dried out with small burning eyes. Arnold introduced us. His speech was laconic and clipped but he was friendly and welcomed us. I watched the intensity of those eyes set in his dry, beaten face. They looked as if only a little would be needed to start a fire that would consume him.

It was getting late, so we loaded our stuff into the wagon and started off. The dirt road ran along through thick woods of pine and spruce. The thin, furry-looking horse went fast, in a rickety trot with a break in it, and Turner kept slapping the reins on his back so he had no chance to slow down. We had about six miles to go, Turner told us. He talked along to Arnold, looking sideways at Lundberg and me, reminding Arnold where to get water, what had happened during the winter — so many sheep lost, a death in the village, a birth, a quarrel. "Mrs. Turner'll be glad to see you up to supper," he said. "We make our dinner at noon." It was the first time he had mentioned her, and I wondered what she'd be like. A little woman, I thought, dried up like him, and burning away too.

The pine woods thinned; we came out of them and crossed a bridge over a stream and were in open pasture on top of the cliff. The smell of salt came rich and heavy from the sea. The fog was thick and we couldn't see to the edge of the cliffs; there was only the rigid outline of bare, wind-shaped trees that grew along them. We skirted a rough, scrubby piece of land and he drew the horse up. It was dusk. We dragged the stuff out and he leaned over the wheel.

"You'll be coming along up to supper," he said, "when you're fixed." We thanked him and he drove rattling off into the fog.

We lit a lantern and worked for an hour against the dark, getting the tent up and things in order. All the time we could hear the fog-horn sounding very close. When we were through it was clean dark, and suddenly the flash from the lighthouse fell on us, once — a pause — away — a long pause — then return. The light fell like that across the mist, soft, bathing everything, then away.

We went along the path to the lighthouse, taking a lantern. The worn path ran very close along the cliff. There were droppings of sheep on it and rough little stones. The caves were at the foot of these cliffs, Arnold said; Southern Head, he called them. Here the sea pounded day and night, and the sheep that sometimes fell down from above were washed into the caves and turned over and over. Every now and then, in a flash from the lighthouse, we saw the white, naked, wind-bent trees. We heard the sea far down below and the foghorn close and heavy.

The path curved along and came to a flat rocky place and in front of us, right on the edge of the cliff, was the lighthouse, low and white, with a round tower. To one side was a small building, some sort of shed and outhouse combined. The flash of the light revolved high over our heads and the horn was shattering and harsh; it made a humming reverberation all around us against the stone. Inside, against the small windows of the main building, we could see the shadow of someone moving.

We went up the path to the door. Turner opened to us. He looked small and dry, standing aside and bidding us enter. We felt awkward going into the warmth, light, and odor of a strange place. We stood a second in the doorway and then we saw Mrs. Turner. She was standing by the table, which was laid for supper. There was a lamp on it and light was thrown up behind her.

She was a huge woman, not fat, but beautifully built and huge. It was surprising that she was young and so big, and she didn't seem possibly Turner's wife. She was silent and a little sullen-looking and beautiful. She had heavy black brows and a great knot of hair, and strong breasts and thighs, and there she stood and

Turner was introducing us. There was nothing juicy about her.
She was Northern. But she wasn't burning up like Turner; she was
smoldering.

From the beginning Lundberg didn't take his eyes off her. He
has a way with women. He gets them with his cold and passionate
desire without an ounce of feeling for them. I've never seen one
that didn't try to please him.

Mrs. Turner didn't speak much; she passed us the food and
waited on us. She didn't even smile at first. When the food was all
set out she came and sat down at the table across from Arnold and
Turner, next to Lundberg and me.

Arnold said, "It's a pleasure to be here and taste your cooking
again, Mrs. Turner." Turner looked across at her with a quick
look of pride.

"You're real welcome, Mr. Arnold," she answered.

Her voice was high and loud. It had a rasping quality. I thought,
When she's old that voice will be strong medicine. Now she's the
kind of woman to rouse desire in a man. I saw Lundberg's nostrils
open when he looked at her. Turner watched her, too, all the time
with that queer burnt look in his eyes. He was a little man and
harsh, but not without a sort of power.

We ate in the kitchen. There was a parlor on the other side of the
entrance. The whole place was whitewashed; it was very clean,
but untidy and littered. There was a musty smell, and the air was a
bit close. Plants grew in tins and boxes in the windows. There
were a rocker and a sewing machine with the top down and
covered with magazines and papers — no books. There was something restless in the place; it would be hard to read there — doing
would be better. The roar of the foghorn outside made a trembling
in the room, and the light revolving was reflected in the mist
against the windows on first one side and then the other. In
storms, they said, the sea came up high against the cliffs and made
a tremendous sound.

"Seems like it would come in, times, and get us," Lottie Turner
said.

She cleared supper away. She moved carelessly, noisily, with
large gestures. She piled the dishes at the sink, beside a pump
painted blue. We sat at the table with Turner, who told us about
the lobster traps. We could set at the foot of the cliffs, he said. "Go

straight down, if you've a mind to." He went around from the harbor in a boat. "You'll burn the shells," he said, looking sidewise at us, and we could have a sheep from him and fishing and shooting, he offered us. He was the game warden.

All this time she moved back and forth, and Lundberg followed her with his eyes. Sometimes she looked at him; she didn't look at Arnold or me. In the little low, white room, with the light of the oil lamp, she seemed incandescent, moving strongly with her great breasts and thighs.

When supper was cleared away she lit another lamp and came over to the table. Turner got out a game they played — "sixty-seven," it was called. It was played with cards, chips, and scores in which one could abet the other. We all drew our chairs up around the table. Again she sat opposite Turner and next to Lundberg and me. The light fell full on her, on her arms and her cheeks. The throat of her plain dress was open. She had a clean, musty odor like the room, with a faint sweetness in it, a bodily sweetness such as an animal would have. She gave it out when she moved.

We played the game for an hour. Outside the foghorn roared and the mist against the windows was illumined. The whole thing seemed rounded and strange like a dream.

Lottie Turner had grown less shy. She laughed from time to time with a queer, explosive, schoolgirl's laughter, harsh like her voice. Those bursts of slightly uncouth laughter did not break her dignity. In her roughness she was more desirable. She leaned a bit away from me and toward Lundberg, who never left her with his eyes. He could not stare directly at her; he glanced down continually at her breast and arm close to him, almost against him.

When the game was over we thanked them, said good night, and went home along the path. We were silent, all of us tired. Lundberg whistled softly a little tune over and over, off the key and with no ending.

We slept hard that first night, on our two cots, with some blankets, for the third put down on the ground. The last thing I saw was the light turned on the side of the tent: a flash — a pause, away — a long pause, then return.

That next morning the sun shone. By afternoon the fog closed in again. Fog or strong weather was part of the hugeness up there. When the fog broke and there was a calm, free summer day there

seemed suspense in it, like a person holding his breath; it was brilliant, with that hardness of light that neither ripples nor expands,
and has beneath it a foundation of darkness.

I don't know when he became her lover. The beginning was that
first night, though, and all the nights after were the same, with a
growing intensity between them that shut the rest of us out. There
were little things, too, after a while. They would touch knee
against knee under the table, or their hands would meet passing a
dish, and in the game she favored him and helped him to win. I
don't know how much Turner knew; he never made a sign and he
never appeared to see anything. He was gone every afternoon on
his exacting rounds of the lobster traps, which took him each time
clear around the island; and every afternoon, after the first few
days, Lundberg was gone, too, up to the lighthouse.

That was how it went. From the first she was his. With him she
was a creature for his wants and no telling when they might veer
somewhere else or when she would tire him with her passion.
Perhaps he was her first lover. There was a feeling of life unspent
in her, virginal and strong.

The days went along. We did turnabout at cooking and keeping
the tent. We hung our sheep and trapped the lobster that Turner
had allowed us. Lundberg and I cut steps in the cliff to go straight
down instead of around by the cove. Arnold and I spent the day
working at our pictures; every morning Lundberg pounded his
typewriter and was gone every afternoon; every evening we all
three went up to the lighthouse to supper, to the game of "sixty-
seven," to Lundberg and Lottie Turner, and Turner looking on.
The whole day and all we did came back to that, the five of us sitting in that low, whitewashed room with its musty odor, filled
with the dry, laconic burning of Turner, the casual ruthlessness of
Lundberg's desire, and the passion of Lottie, which filled the room
with an intense vibration. All this while she served the supper and
cleared away, and we laughed and talked with Turner of fishing
and trapping, of the tides, the village news, and afterwards drew
our chairs against the table to play.

Once I saw them. It was afternoon. I'd knocked off from my
work and gone up to the lighthouse for water. With the bucket in
my hand I was crossing toward the well when they came out of
the house. There was fog, they hadn't seen me, and I stopped, not

knowing whether to call out or be quiet. She stood above him on
the step and he turned around to her and with a rough gesture she
caught his head against her breast. Then she released him and he
went down the steps and along the path to the cliff. She called
after him in that strange, harsh voice of hers, holding her hand
against her mouth. She looked fine standing on the step. The collar
of her dress was wide open. Her hair was disordered; the great
knot of it was barely held up in the back, and there was something
triumphant about the stand of her whole body. He turned and
waved his hand and disappeared into the fog. I waited until she
went indoors and filled my bucket at the well.

It was when we'd been there a month that, one afternoon, Lundberg didn't go to the lighthouse. He came with me to the village to
see, he said, the girl I was doing, the strange, coarse girl we'd seen
that first afternoon. I'd told him about her. She lived with her
mother and five brothers in a long, gray-weathered house, very
dirty inside; she helped with the nets and was as strong as a man,
and though only sixteen she was no longer a virgin. The mother
was thin and sandy-haired, with enormous ears and startled,
stupid eyes.

Lundberg watched them all afternoon in the rambling, sagging
house. They had a last flare of power, he said, in the midst of the
degradation of their ways. He was going to write about it and
about the girl. Her name was Pearl Crandall and he stayed talking
to her after I'd started home, sitting on the steps of the house, rolling a cigarette the way he did, turning it quickly in his hands,
while she stood running her foot back and forth in the dust and
eyeing him and laughing. She'd been mending a net of her
brother's and she had it trailed over her arm and down behind
her. Her hair fell into her eyes. She had on a fisherman's jacket
and a short dress. Her feet were bare and very dirty, and her legs
were firm and strong with coarse skin on them. I thought, She has
the violence of a Goya. It was some time before Lundberg caught
up with me on the way home.

That night we were late for supper. Turner was standing in the
open doorway, the light streaming out past him.

"We were minded to think you weren't coming," he said. "Lottie was fearful her supper would be spoiled." Lottie was silent and
sullen, her brows drawn together. Sitting in the rocker, she pushed

it back and forth.

"I was painting," I said, "down at the village; it's a good walk back."

Lundberg went over to the sewing machine, next to Lottie, and picked up a magazine from the pile lying on the top.

"And I went with him, Mrs. Turner," he said, "and got an idea for a story, and fooling around with it made us late. Forgive us," he said. "We're a bad lot."

His back was turned to us. There was laughter in his voice and a stroking softness. She got up and we went to the table. She looked bewildered, and the tenseness in the air remained.

The next day I was off to the other end of the island. Lundberg didn't come with me. In the evening Lottie Turner was glowing. She hardly bothered to hide her feelings. In the last flare of Lundberg's desire, without an overt motion, they seemed to own each other, to be alone in the room. Turner was very dry. He talked little and made mistakes in his game. Finally he got up and left the room, saying he was going to attend to the light. She offered to help him. He waved his hand and went out without answering and was gone some time.

When Turner came back he carried our lantern. He set it absently down on the table. The game was over, and, standing above it and looking down, it threw an added light directly up against his face, and it seemed to me that I saw him for the first time: his beaten thinness, his defeat, his burning, and his lasting, sterile power. He said, "It's coming on to rain. I figure it will blow up and rain hard. We're in for a storm." There was water on his coat and his hair. We said good night, turned up our collars, took our lantern, and went out. The heavy drops were beginning to fall.

It rained all night, drumming down above us on the roof of the tent, drumming its sound and texture into our dreams, and all day it rained, and the next day and the next. We stayed inside. Every evening the odor, warmth, and glow of the lighthouse room with the storm outside was like a narcotic. I remember those evenings passed in a blur. There was a lull in the tenseness and a sense of remote and shut-in quietness.

Then the storm cleared. The third day the wind dropped, by evening the rain ceased, there was a struggle of light in the west, and the next morning the sun was strong and hot. When, after lunch, I started for the village Lundberg said he was coming along.

When we got to the Crandall place Pearl wasn't around. Mrs. Crandall was there; Pearl was off up the shore, she said, by the small cove, with the boat. Luke was gone with her. She'd be back come evening, maybe.

The small cove was the only opening there was in the cliffs. It was there with the tide down, a little piece of beach, rock, and sandy soil, a hollow hardly bigger than your hand, a resting place in the long line of cliff. We'd come on it going down our steps and half wading, half climbing along the shore. The fishermen used it when the tide was low. When the tide rose there wasn't an inch of it left.

I stayed waiting for a chance to draw Mrs. Crandall. Lundberg, after sitting around with us, went off along the road. I worked late and then I went down to the village for the post. Turner's horse was unhitched, tied up to the block. His wagon was there full of stuff. He didn't seem to be around. He was out with his boat, someone told me. One of the Crandall boys came in as I was leaving. It was Luke. I asked him where his sister was.

"Left her up to the small cove, Mr. Haven," he said. He grinned. I went out of the store and along the road toward home.

The late slanting sun glinted on everything. The pine woods smelled strong and clean after the rain. There was no dust.

A little way along I heard the wheels and Turner came up to me in his wagon. He stopped and offered me a lift. I said I'd walk. "It's good tonight after the storm."

"Yes," he said. "Yes." He lifted the reins. "I give your friend a row in from the small cove. He and Pearl Crandall. They nigh got caught with the tide. He got kinda wet. He'll be coming along right smart, I reckon." He looked at me sidewise, the reins suspended. "It don't pay folks that don't know the tide fooling along the cliffs — or folks that don't belong making it with the wimmen either." His voice rasped. He spat over the wheel, pulled the reins, and went on.

I stood in the road and waited for Lundberg. That was where he'd gone and that was what Luke Crandall meant when he grinned. It was true what Turner said. I'd heard it before, but it wasn't Pearl Crandall I was bothered about, or her mother or her brother Luke.

I went and sat down by the side of the road. The orange light of the sun slanted level through the woods behind me onto the stones and dirt. I was thinking of how Lottie Turner had seemed to me that first night.

When Lundberg came along he was walking fast, his head back. He was wet to the waist. I called out to him. He stopped short.

"Were you waiting for me, Pete?" he asked.

"Yes," I said. "I saw Turner. He told me you'd be coming along."

"Turner?" said Lundberg. He made a face. "He caught me out — damn him," he said. "Suppose he told you. I had to take a lift from him too. We were all stuck with the tide. God, I'm wet," he added. "Let's walk."

He lit a cigarette and we started off. We walked for a while in silence except for the swishing of Lundberg's wet clothes.

"Listen," he said suddenly. "The tide was way out when I got there. They were through, nearly, with the traps and I hung around and the brother went off with the boat. She stayed with me. I thought we'd get up by the steps, climbing along the shore. She said she'd often gone the other way, over the cliffs. It seemed all right, but we stayed too long. We stayed a long time, and Turner caught us."

I turned my head and looked at Lundberg. He met my eyes. "Sure," he said, "together . . ." His face contracted. "The tide was turned and coming in fast. We'd have both known it — only then. But Turner rowed by and, coming back, he shouted to us to go with him. It was too late. There wasn't a chance of getting out. That row back to the harbor," Lundberg said, "God, that cooled me off."

"Turner is full of knowledge," I said.

Lundberg laughed shortly. "Pearl Crandall," he said. "It's not the first time nor the last with her."

It's not Pearl Crandall, I thought, but I didn't say it. We walked fast and were silent the rest of the way back.

We were right on time for supper. The sun had set and it was dusk when we got to the door. No one opened to us; there didn't seem to be anyone there.

"Funny," Arnold said. "Don't they expect us?"

Generally the door was ajar, the lamps lit, and we walked in and they were there ahead of us and supper was laid. We knocked again. Then we heard a noise overhead and then someone coming down the stairs. A pause at the bottom and Turner opened the door. In the half-light he seemed as narrow as a ghost.

"Come in," he said. There was something gone from his voice and something else in the place of it, a guarded harshness.

We went in. "There's nothing wrong, is there?" Arnold asked. "You were expecting us, weren't you?"

"We were expecting you," Turner answered. "Lottie'll be down. Come in."

He lit the lamps, and while he was trimming the wick of the second one Lottie Turner came into the room. She didn't glance at Lundberg but came straight to me and said very loud, "Well, supper'll be ready in a minute. Set down, won't you?"

At supper she waited on us in silence without her usual rough, shy sallies. She set the dishes heavily on the table. She didn't eat much, and afterwards sat with her elbows on the oilcloth and gave occasional uncouth outbursts of laughter at things we said. They were loud, without coquetry, and they were unsteady. Her brows were drawn together, she didn't speak to Lundberg, but once when he crossed the room I saw her follow him with her eyes; her mouth trembled and a minute later she burst out laughing again.

She had on a different dress from the one she usually wore, a more elaborate dress, made of cloth instead of print. It was maroon color and smelled of camphor. She must have dragged it out and put it on at the last moment. It didn't fit her; it marred the nobility of her body and made her look fat. The sleeves were too short and it was fastened somehow close across the neck. The color was unbecoming to her; for the first time she looked plain.

Arnold noticed her dress when she came and sat down next to him after supper was cleared away, and the lamplight fell strong on it. "You look very fine, Mrs. Turner," he said. His voice filled the awkward silence.

"Oh," she said dully, "I ain't fixed out much, Mr. Arnold." Turner was coming back to the table, the game of "sixty-seven" in his hand. He stopped, shaking the box of chips up and down.

"Mrs. Turner," he said, rather loud, "was minded to style herself a little because the company's going. We always aim to send them off right. Ain't that true, Lottie?"

The blood ebbed away from her face, leaving the color marked in blotches on the surface of the skin. She gave a laugh which choked off. Turner came to the table and set the game down.

"Going?" said Arnold. "Who? I don't understand."

I was sitting next to him. Under the table I put my hand on his knee. Lundberg leaned over and lit a cigarette at the chimney of the lamp.

"We didn't tell you, Dick," he said. "Pete and I got a wire from Sweeney this afternoon. We've got to be moving tomorrow." He looked at Turner. "It's too bad," he said. "It breaks up everything. I guess, Dick, you'll have to hold the fort alone."

"Well, by God," said Arnold, "you fellows —"

Lottie was silent. I didn't look at her. I looked at Turner. He had met Lundberg's look with his burning little eyes and now he was bending down, setting the piles of chips neatly out on the table.

"Seems that's about it," he said. "We hate to see folks go when they could have stayed, but it looks like this time it was a settled thing." He sat down and drew his chair up to the table and started dealing the cards.

We were silent. Arnold choked on his surprise. Lottie had turned very white. We played stupidly and Turner called the points in his dry voice with a sort of drag in it. Before the game was ended she got up, saying she must go see to the light.

"Set still," Turner said. "I'll go." But she was already in the corner lighting the lantern, and he didn't rise.

She came to the table with the lantern in her hand. "I'll say good night," she said in a loud voice and held out her hand to each of us. When she touched Lundberg's she looked straight over his head; her mouth was drawn in a line and her brows met. She towered there, big and uncouth in her clumsy dress, which seemed hardly able to hold her body. She hesitated and then turned and went out. Turner had not moved. His eyes were fixed on the cards in his hand. He set them down on the table and rose.

"There'll be fog in again come morning," he said. "I reckon you'll want to turn in early, making your start tomorrow." He spoke to me, ignoring Lundberg.

"Yes," I said, "we'll be going along now."

"Well I'm damned," Arnold said. Lundberg had him by the arm and they went out together through the door. I followed. At the door I looked back. Turner was still standing by the table.

"Turner," I said, "we owe you for the sheep, the boat, and all your trouble, and for the board too."

He waved his hand. "I ain't takin' narthin' for it," he said.

"But . . ." I said.

"It'd been arranged before this," he said. "I ain't takin' narthin'."

It was finished. "Good night," I said, and went along to join the others.

They hadn't waited and were well ahead of me. I could see their lantern swinging back and forth. The stars were out overhead but they were dim. I remembered Turner had said there would be fog tomorrow. He knew the weather like his hand.

In the tent we said nothing. Lundberg seemed to have fixed it with Arnold. "I'll take you over in the morning," he said, his voice angry and restrained.

It was my stint at cooking. I should have to be up early, so I packed my bag and got my paints together after the others had turned in. My blankets were ready on the ground. Long after I was through and wrapped in them I watched the light turn on the tent: a flash — a pause — away — a long pause — then return. It moved in my sleep in a deep unease.

It was gray light when I woke. The fog was in. My blankets were wet with it and I could hear the hoarse, long-drawn sound of the foghorn coming across from the tower. I got up slowly and dressed and went outside the tent to wash and start the fire. The water in the barrel was almost gone when I'd done washing, so I took a bucket and went up to the lighthouse. I walked along the path, looking down at the little stones and sheep droppings I'd seen the first night, and heard the sea way below and felt the jar of the horn as I got nearer.

There was no one about; everything was quiet. I went to the well and filled my bucket. The base of the lighthouse tower looked huge and very white and round. The air was pure and heavy with the smell of salt. There were a few sheep grazing a patch of grass near the shed. The horse was gone, his worn and dirty blanket hanging on the rail. Turner was off early on his rounds.

I started back slowly, my bucket as full as it would hold. The fog had lifted and thinned in the way it sometimes did, with what seemed a strange and whimsical passion of its own. The light was pale and very beautiful, and it seemed to me that I should never get enough of that strange thrill of loneliness and awe that came from passing so near, so very near, the edge of that high cliff, hearing below the savage, weary movement of the sea. I set the bucket down. This was the last time I should be here or know this place.

Now I had a great desire to lie flat on the ground and feast on the impelling violence and beauty. The light struck down singly on the cliffs and I could see the dark shine of the water. Lying there, I could see its great swell and lift, the line of foam, and the black, wet hollows of the rocks. The hoarse vibrating sound of the lighthouse came, and far off, as on that first day, the sound — pure, remote and haunting — of Machias Light bell that was never still.

I drew in a great breath of the sea and the grass, bitter and lovely, and then I saw her washing, turning over, heavy and terrible at the foot of the cliffs below me: Lottie Turner, washing there, caught — turning and turning on the rocks below — her hand stretched out, her head and the weight of her body very plain in the pale light. I could not get my breath and I lay staring and unbelieving and terribly afraid. She was the shape of death itself; her body looked not tiny but huge still, down there, turning with a fearful casualness and abandon — her body powerful and alone in the dark red dress against the bitter dark rocks and gleaming water.

I felt my heart pounding and my breath was dry in my throat. We would reach Turner. Something must be done. I got to my feet, stumbling against the water bucket, spilling it over onto the ground. The roar from the lighthouse tower struck me like a voice calling out. Around me the fog was shifting already and was closing in again. I looked down once: the gleam of the water was receding. Through my mind, as I turned, went what Arnold had said — how the creatures falling in fog or storm turned over and over in the sea below, washed into the dark caves by the powerful and restless water. Had she fallen as they, blinded with fog, or was it a storm greater than any they could know?

"Seems like it will come and get us, times," she said, and now she was down there. "Seems, times, like it will come right in and get us," laughing in her harsh and ugly voice. I kept hearing that as I went down blindly toward the tent, the brush and brambles tearing at my ankles. I saw the crash and impact of the spray against the lighthouse, but the current that had caught Lottie Turner was more powerful, terrible, and casual than the sea. I could see Turner standing by the table, the lamplight on his face, and his little burning eyes. The shattering roar of the lighthouse horn, like a desperate voice, struck me again and again. "Seems like it will come right in and get us."

I reached the tent and found myself standing, holding the empty bucket in my hand. I'd picked it up and carried it without knowing. It felt insanely light; I set it down. As I did so Lundberg came out of the tent, rumpled and half awake, the lines of sleep still in his handsome, smiling face.

"Well, Pete, old boy, that was a long, sweet night," he said, and then: "What's the matter? You look as if you'd seen a ghost."

I stared at him. I could not speak. "It's not getting you down, this island, is it, Pete?" He laughed, and then he yawned and stretched with the wide stretch of waking. "God," he said, "am I telling you, I'll be glad as sin to get off it and stand again on hallowed ground."

And once more he laughed, that strong easy laugh of his, narrowing his eyes and throwing back the beauty of his head. I stood there, and his words seemed to fall down cold between us, and for that instant I could find nothing to shape what I had to say.

---

*Margaret Osborn, about whom the anthologists could discover little information, was born in Saunderstown, Rhode Island, and was the sister of the noted author Oliver La Farge. Much of her life was devoted to social causes in the South. The above story apparently was her first sale. It appeared in THE ATLANTIC MONTHLY in 1944 and was reprinted in O. HENRY MEMORIAL AWARD PRIZE STORIES OF 1944.*

*Sam Brown, Jr.* ————————————————— *1970*

# THE LESSON

It seemed at the time as though it was all Harry's fault — that's my cousin, Harry — but in retrospect I have to admit that I was almost, if perhaps not quite, as much to blame as he was. I tended to blame him partly because he was older than I — nearly nineteen, while I was sixteen and a half — but also partly, I realize now, because I needed a scapegoat so as to keep my good intentions from seeming to pave the wrong road. But hell-bent they were, and I with them; and just because it was Harry's idea does not eradicate the keen pleasure I took in first following Harry and then acting as his accomplice.

Poaching lobsters was what we were up to — I say "poaching" now, as I did then, not merely because it was technically that, but because it sounds more innocuous than "stealing" or "robbing." But robbery it was, in fact — larceny of the highest order — for we were depriving a man not merely of the fruits of his labor, but of the source of his entire income. A good analogy would be the theft or destruction of row after row of a wheat farmer's crop, irreplaceable until the next year's harvest. The enormity of our crime didn't occur to me, of course, at the time. I was a summer visitor who was exposed at home mostly to professional men, people like my lawyer father, whose sources of income were pretty much all in their heads. You can rob a lawyer of every bit of material worth he owns, and he can still practice law in a borrowed suit; but a lobsterman with consistently empty traps cannot earn his living.

But as I say, none of this was evident to Harry and me that summer; we were just caught up in the excitement of the theft, on open water (why, right in plain sight!), of those little creatures whose meat we found so succulent when boiled the next afternoon in our rocky grotto on the shore. Our fathers, who were brothers, had regularly brought their children to the Maine coast for a vacation which always included several lobster feeds. Ever since our folks had introduced us to the dish when we were ex-toddlers, we had both loved fresh lobster, boiled in salt water under seaweed, dunked in melted butter, and eaten on a barnacled rock above the swirling tide.

This summer, Harry's family had sent us up to their shore cottage a week before they came up for their August vacation, and we were to "open the place" and keep constructively busy in a "safe" environment. The week before, Harry had been picked up by the police along with several friends on charges, later dropped, of disturbing the peace, and he and his parents were ready for a temporary separation. My parents were receptive to their suggestion that I accompany Harry, principally, I think, because they did not much approve of the girl I was dating at the time, a moist-eyed, giggly gazelle I had taken quite a shine to. There was nothing at all wrong with her, but to parents I guess a teenager's girlfriend is generally either idiotic or slatternly, or both. And so we were sent to Maine as a way of keeping us off the streets. Ironically, we would probably have been into less real trouble in suburban Boston.

Our first day there together had been easy enough to kill, opening padlocked doors and shuttered windows, sweeping out minimal living space, de-mousing our sleeping quarters, and getting in a supply of food. But our adolescent interest in constructive projects was typically limited, though our energy was typically not; and after two nights of filling the silence with jokes about our school chums and arrogantly smoking cigarettes openly in the house (even Harry had not yet dared do so in front of his parents), we were bored.

"Hey, Mark." Harry that morning was sprawled indolently over a chair leaned up against the sunlit kitchen window. "Let's do something."

"Sure." I fumbled for a cigarette. "Feel like a swim or something?"

"Naw. 'S too cold." Harry fingered a shade pull and looked out the window toward our rude boathouse. "We might get the dory out."

"Okay." I peered out the door toward the bay in the direction Harry was looking. Blinding bits of sunlight were bursting like continuous shrapnel from the surface of the water. It hurt to look. A bit to the left of this fiery display was a reef, an island really, partially exposed even at high tide, surrounded by a great many lobster buoys, tiny bobbing specks that trailed in kite-tail fashion off toward the eastern point of the mainland. Something larger bobbed evenly near the reef. "Hey, Harry," I said, "there's a lobster boat."

"Lobster!" Harry sat up. "Hey, that's for us." He got out of the chair expectantly. "Whaddya say, lobster feed tonight?"

"Good idea." I dragged on my cigarette, still looking out at the lobster boat with its tiny single helmsman, chugging now to a new buoy off the reef. The boat slowed, its stern heaving sluggishly, and the lobsterman hooked a buoy and began to haul in the line. "We'll have to drive over to Evans' Wharf to the lobster pound. Got any money?"

"Yeah. Some." Harry, too, watched as the distant lobsterman gracefully pulleyed the heavy trap to the gunwale, flipped open its lid, and began to toss back into the sea the many undersized lobsters which customarily were caught in it. Harry was silent for a moment. "You still want to work on the dory?" he asked.

"Sure. Nothin' else to do. But let's go get some lobsters first. And butter. And hey!" I squashed out my cigarette with slight nervous agitation. "Maybe we could get some beer!"

"Yeah." Harry obviously wasn't listening very closely. We both loved beer, but had never been able to get any except when our parents, mellowed by a vacation cocktail, had allowed us each a can. I was thinking now that we might drive around until we found an out-of-the-way grocery store where Harry's deep voice and mature height might pass for those of a twenty-one-year-old. Surely Harry would be interested. "Some beer, eh, Harry?"

"Wait a minute." He screwed up his eyes, peering at the distant boat. "Why don't we save our dough? *We* could do that."

"We could do what? Save dough on beer? How?"

"No, *we* could do *that* —" he gestured — "in the dory." He turned to me. "Pull some traps. He does it alone. There's two of us. *We* could do *that.*"

"Pull traps?" I paused, reflective. "But we don't have *any,*
Harry — ?"

"Yeah, but *he* does."

"You mean, steal his lobsters?" I felt let down. "Aw, we can buy
'em."

"Look at him. He throws out most of all of 'em anyway. We
wouldn't take the big ones. No problem. Hey, Mark?" Harry's
eyes flickered. "Let's get at that dory."

I was not convinced. Theft did not particularly appeal to my
moral sense, and I wasn't sure I'd know how to haul a trap. But
those reasons could not be expressed publicly, of course; so I said,
"I don't know, Harry. Suppose we get caught?"

"Caught? With what evidence? Anyone comes by, we just toss
'em back in the bay. And what lobsterman that you know of ever
takes his boat out at night?"

"You mean we'll go out and pull traps in the dark?" I asked.

"Sure," Harry said. "Aw, we'll be able to see okay out on the
open water. And there won't be any chance of being caught by a
nosy lobster boat at *night.*"

That pretty well did it. I was still uneasy about the idea of theft,
but Harry had obliterated any argument I could, at that age and
under those circumstances, effectively present. I almost (but not
quite) wished that Mom and Dad were around so that I could protest that it would be impossible to pull it off without their knowledge. But what the hell, I thought; it sounded pretty darn exciting.

That afternoon, we lugged out the family dory, strenuously
shoved it down the ramp into the water, marked the obvious
leaks, hauled the boat out and caulked it, and lowered it in again
to let it swell. It wouldn't really be tight for a couple of days and
until we'd caulked it again, but it was not an old boat and would
certainly serve us that night. Then, sweaty and happily absorbed
in our project, we drove off to seek beer.

After we'd driven for about five miles, we saw a little grocery
store on the left. MORRILL'S STORE, a sign said, and another sign
proclaimed COLD BEER TO GO. We pulled in, got out of the car,
and went into the store. I was jittery, so I let Harry lead the way.

A middle-aged man with wire-rimmed glasses jutted up behind
the counter. "H'lo, fellas," he said. "What can I get you?"

Harry tried to look casual as he surveyed the glass-doored refrigerator compartment behind the counter with its army of assorted beers, ales, and soft drinks. "Hmm," he said. "Guess I'll take two six-packs of, uh, Miller's."

The man turned and procured the beer without a blink. He put it on the counter. "Anything else, fellas?" he asked brightly.

"No, thanks," Harry said, and paid for the beer. We walked out quickly, waiting until we were in the car again to cackle delightedly at each other. "You hot ticket!" I said. "Tut-tut," said Harry, "all in a day's work." We chuckled for several minutes. I felt exuberant; my last trace of uneasiness had disappeared. We were men! And we were going on a lobstering adventure!

We ate a regular supper that evening, figuring that we'd have our lobster feed the next afternoon after our midnight excursion. The time passed slowly until after dark; we had a can of beer each and played some cards, but were really too nervous to do anything well. We each lost a hand of gin rummy through pure carelessness, discarding the wrong cards, and ultimately we lost interest.

Finally, after looking out the windows for hours (forty-five minutes, perhaps), Harry decreed that it was dark enough to set out. We put on our jackets, climbed into the boat, and began to row stealthily out through the slightly choppy water. There was no moon; not a vessel was in sight on the bay. The perfect crime!

"Here's one." Harry was at the oars. "I'll back up to it. You grab it." The black water swirled around the stern as Harry maneuvered the boat toward the small bobbing buoy. The breeze gusted a bit, whipping cold droplets of water from the wet oars across my face. I shivered. Off to my left, a few lights glimmered on the point beyond our house; straight ahead was the faintly visible reef, and far beyond was the dark horizon. The buoy was far colder and heavier than I had imagined it would be, but I got it into the boat all right. I wondered if it was the beer that was making me a little shaky.

Harry shipped the oars. "Lemme give you a hand." Together we pulled the slimy potwarp up over the transom. The darned thing was bigger around than it looked lying in coils on the shore near Frank's Lobster Pound, and the slime made it hard to grip. But, with a few grunts and an occasional loss of balance, we got the line all the way up — and there came the trap: it emerged darkly, with a rush of water, and banged against the boat.

"Hey! Not so loud!" Harry said. I fumbled, and the trap slipped back a foot or so and submerged with a swish. "Sorry!" I whispered hoarsely. "Couldn't help it." "Well don't let it *slip*, for God's sake!" Harry's breath was hissing through his teeth now. It was hard work. We pulled together and got it lodged precariously over the gunwale, where it teetered and drained noisily.

Suddenly we heard a noise like a wet towel being snapped loudly several times — FWADASAPAPAP — and we practically lost the trap again. "What the hell was *that*?" I gasped. Then it dawned on us that it was a lobster, flapping his tail as he always does out of water in a vain attempt to propel himself back into the sea. We both broke into hoarsely voiceless laughter. "Damn lobster!" Harry said. From then on it was easier. We emptied the lobsters into the boat (they all seemed undersized to us) and let the trap gently — "Watch it now!" — back into the water, smiling even as we panted, and occasionally imitating both the lobster's flapping noise and our own earlier fright, *"Fwadasapapap!"* and wheezed laughter. We were having a ball!

We worked for perhaps twenty-five minutes, pulling three traps, before we had what we thought would be an ample feed for the two of us: about eight rather small lobsters. To ease our consciences, we did leave two or three large lobsters in the last two traps. "It's kinda funny," Harry remarked as he swished the lobsters around in the bilge, "there's so few of 'em in any one trap." I pulled on the oars. "Well, Har," I offered, "you don't get rich lobstering." We didn't say much else till we got to shore.

The next afternoon we built a fire in the shadow of a large overhanging rock near the high-water mark not far from the house. The horizon was misty, but the sun was out and our beer was cold and plentiful, and we felt pretty good. "Darn fine catch, captain!" Harry said as he cracked open his third claw. Butter dribbled randomly down my chin and the breeze ruffled my hair and T-shirt. Behind us, the fire cracked and smoked. I smiled broadly and took a quick pull at my beer. "You bet," I said.

"Hey, Harry, there he is again." Across the dancing sunlit ripples, we could see the lobsterman hauling his traps near the reef-island. Harry sloshed a chunk of lobster up and down in the can of melted butter and wiped his chin. "Seems to me I recognize that white buoy with the blue band," he said, and threw me a grin. "How 'bout you?"

"Can't recall. Does it go *fwadasapapap?*" We both roared. The lobsterman, we noticed, wasn't throwing out any undersized lobsters from these traps. "Guess we saved him some trouble." "Anything to help a fellow lobsterman," Harry said. We roared again, our laughter becoming the tear-producing giggles that leave one weak in the stomach and euphoric. Only in adolescence can this kind of gentle sadism be so amusing; I wonder, in retrospect, what had gotten into us.

The success and pleasure produced by our initial poaching experiment buoyed us for an inevitable second night of crime, and the confidence inspired by that success led to a third. Before we knew it, we had poached four nights running, becoming bolder each time, ultimately taking only the biggest lobsters and actually throwing the undersized ones back into the bay. This move was perhaps the unwisest of all, at least as far as escaping detection was concerned, for it left each trap completely empty at eleven p.m. and hence likely to be nearly empty when the owner pulled them next morning. Like all amateur criminals, especially those whose intent is far less malicious than the damage done, we did not give sufficient attention to the details which can lead to detection. We also failed to give enough credit to our unidentified victim, the lobsterman. He turned out to be far more wise, and we far more stupid, than we had imagined.

On the fifth night of poaching, Harry and I set out at about ten thirty, a little later than usual, after having a couple of beers each in the house. We were positively heady, not so much from the liquor as from an inflated sense of our own powers. We had hauled heavy traps, eaten free lobster, and drunk illegal brew for nearly five days straight without a hitch, and we were, I fear, more than a little wild-eyed and arrogant. The world, so to speak, was our lobster. And so we donned our light jackets and pushed off into the unusually still water of this particular night without even lowering our voices. Harry made an obscene noise from the stern seat, and I laughed so hard that I nearly dropped one oar into the water. Harry grabbed it with a great clatter, and we whooped a bit as the dory lurched awkwardly.

We were in the midst of hauling our third trap — giggling and joking about the heavy slime on the potwarp — when Harry suddenly became still and said, "Shsh!"

I stopped giggling and put one hand on the dripping gunwale. "What?" I whispered.

"Motor." I looked up and listened. From not too far off at all came a putt-putt-putt. The lobster boat!

"Where is it?" I whispered.

"Can't see," Harry replied, tensing. "No lights?"

"Quick! Drop the trap!"

"No, don't drop it! Too loud! Lower it!"

We eased the trap into the water and hurriedly cast the line and buoy after it. "Let's get out of here," Harry said, and quickly put the oars in the water and began to row.

The putt-putt of the approaching vessel grew louder and clearer. No doubt about it, it was a lobster boat. But why no lights? I froze in the stern seat, my eyes darting around trying to see through the heavy moonless night. Suddenly the reef exploded in light. To the right of it, a powerful searchlight threw its beam onto the reef, then began knifing in other directions. *My God,* I thought. *The lobsters!*

In our haste we had completely forgotten that several lobsters lay partly submerged in the bilge of the dory. Absolute evidence! We'd be killed!

"Throw 'em out!" he whispered frantically, pulling at the oars as fast as he could without making a racket.

"Too many," I said. "Cover 'em!" I yanked off my jacket and bid Harry do likewise. He shook his head vigorously and kept rowing. I managed to get all the lobsters under my jacket (which became immediately soaked in bilgewater) just before the searchlight struck us. Straightening up from a crouch, I saw Harry's nervous face and awkwardly positioned body piercingly illuminated against an invisible background. Harry froze.

The searchlight bobbed a bit and pushed ahead until it was nearly upon us. The putt-putting died to a low rumble, and some smaller lights went on, revealing the dim outlines of a high prow, a long hull, and a stiff little cabin. The searchlight clicked off, and over its dying lens came a voice.

"Evenin', boys." Pause.

"H-hi," Harry stammered.

A flashlight clicked on and played on the two of us and the dory. The waves lapped at the hulls of both boats and seemed, impossibly, to drown the sound of the engine's muffled burbling. Harry moved the oars a bit in the water and tried to look relaxed.

"Out f'r a row, boys?" Pause.

"Yeah," Harry said. He gestured toward the shore. "We — we're in there. Our house." The flashlight beam caught his face and he turned his eyes toward me. "We kind of like to row. Good dory."

"Yes 'tis, boys," the faceless voice replied evenly, almost softly. The flashlight beam moved to me, then to the floor of the dory.

"You always leave your jacket in the bilge, son?"

I shivered. A small breeze rippled my T-shirt. "Warm night," I said weakly. It was warm, but not so warm as to make one discard a jacket carelessly in the bilge. He would catch us. I knew he would!

The pale beam of light slid around the edges of my jacket as it partly floated, partly lay over the lobsters. I held my breath; Harry and I stared in terror at it. What if one of the lobsters should crawl out? What if —

FWADASAPAPAP.

The jacket flapped; the flashlight clicked off. An enormous silence followed. I could hear nothing but the pounding in my ears.

FWADASAPAPAPapap.

"Boys." Pause.

"Boys, you row right over here." The voice had a new note of quiet but powerful urgency. Harry swallowed hard and backed the dory clumsily up to the side of the lobster boat.

I looked up from the stern and saw the gradually visible face of the lobsterman. He wore a small dark yachting cap pulled low over a large, sharp nose and hollow cheeks. His neck seemed too thick for the thin face; but his eyes quickly distracted me from the rest of him. He had the quietest, most unfathomable eyes I had ever seen. They could have been intensely angry or thoroughly benign; I could not tell. But they scared me to death.

"Boys," he said. "Someone's been pullin' my traps." He leaned over the gunwale and I noticed a slight tremor in his hands and face. "I make a livin' on them traps. If they're empty, I got nothin'.''

He paused for a moment, staring deeply at Harry, who was transfixed, frozen to the oars. The lobsterman straightened up slightly and reached into his boat. When he leaned over again, one hand held a plank of wood, and the other a shotgun.

I was about to yell out, but the lobsterman began to talk in his quietly urgent way before I had a chance. I checked myself. ''Boys,'' he said, ''I want you to see what'll happen if I ketch them poachuhs.'' With a sudden thrust he chucked the plank over the dory. My eyes followed it to where it splashed heavily into the water just beyond our gunwale. Before I could turn my gaze again toward the lobster boat, the silence was shattered with a deafening blast that caused me literally to jump off my seat and Harry to drop the oars into the dory with a clatter. There in the foaming water which rocked our boat bobbed the two halves of the former plank.

When I looked back, breathless and with heart pounding furiously, the lobsterman was putting his shotgun back into the boat. He settled himself down with hands on the gunwale again and looked at us, his jaws working.

''I don't shoot folks,'' he said. ''But I don't mind shootin' a boat if I have to.'' He paused for emphasis and lowered his voice. ''Mighty hard swimmin' ashore at night.''

In another moment, he had straightened up, taken the helm, and revved up the engine. The lobster boat putt-putted to a deafening staccato, spun heavily away from us, and left the dory on a rising swell which made us lunge to keep our balance. Harry grabbed the oars.

''Holy God,'' I said. ''Holy, holy God.''

''Throw 'em out!'' Harry fairly shouted. I grabbed my jacket and threw out the lobsters as fast as I could. Harry pulled at the oars and we headed for shore, both of us shaking rather badly.

As I reflected much later on our narrow escape, I realized that the lobsterman would have been perfectly justified in sinking our dory that night instead of merely shattering a plank. This fact has given me an enduring respect for the principle that no man is automatically entitled to the fruits of another's labor. But more important, I think, is the fact that he chose *not* to sink the dory; for he impressed our minds indelibly with a lesson about the efficacy of charity in matters of justice. He was a remarkably wise man.

*A mystery man to the editors, Sam Brown, Jr., lived in Saratoga Springs, New York, when he submitted this story to YANKEE magazine, which published it in 1970. It was reprinted in A TREASURY OF NEW ENGLAND SHORT STORIES (1975).*

# PRAYER
# FOR THE DYING

The day Yakov Kaputin died, he managed to make the nurse understand that he wanted to see Father Alexey. Yakov had lived in America for thirty years, but he did not speak English. He scribbled a faint wiggly number on the paper napkin on his lunch tray and pointed a long knobby finger back and forth between the napkin and his bony chest. "You want me to call, do you, dear?" the nurse asked in a loud voice that made Yakov's ears ring. Yakov could not understand what she said but he nodded, *"Da."*

When the telephone rang, Father Alexey was just dozing off. It was July. Crickets were chirring in the long dry grass outside his window. The priest was lying in his underwear listening to a record of Broadway show tunes on the new stereo set his mother had bought him. His long beard was spread out on his chest like a little blanket. The window shade was down and a fan was softly whirring.

He thought it was the alarm clock that rang and tried to turn it off.

"Mr. Kaputin wants you to come to the hospital," the nurse said.

He did not know how long he had slept. He felt shaky and unfocused.

"I can't," he said.

"Is this the Russian priest?"

"This is Father Alexey." His voice seemed to come from somewhere far away. "I'm busy just now."

"Well, we're all busy, dear." The nurse paused as if waiting for him to see the truth in that and do the right thing.

"What is it this time?" Father Alexey asked with a sigh.

The nurse began to converse chattily. "I just came from him. He's a real sweetheart. He wrote your number down. He didn't touch his lunch, or his breakfast. I don't think he feels well. Of course, we can't understand a word he says, and he can't understand us. . . ."

"He *never* feels well," Father Alexey said irritably. "You usually do not feel well when you have cancer."

"Well," the nurse said indignantly. "I've called. I've done *my* duty. If you don't want to come. . . ."

Father Alexey sighed another large sigh into the receiver. He hated the hospital. He hated the way it smelled, the way grown men looked in johnny coats, the way Yakov's bones were all pointed. Besides, it was very hot out. During the entire morning service not a hint of a breeze had entered the church. In the middle of a prayer he thought he might faint. He had to go into the Holy of Holies and sit down.

"It's not a matter of 'not wanting,'" he said pointedly. "I'll have to adjust my schedule. That's not always easy to do. I don't know when I can be there. I have to try to find a ride."

He lay for a while longer with the fan blowing on him, his hands clasped on his soft white stomach. The sheet under him was clean and cool. He looked tragically at the window shade. It was lit up like a paper lantern.

Father Alexey lived next to the church in an old house with a cupola, fancy molding, and derelict little balconies. A rusty iron fence tottered around the unmowed yard. Once every seven or eight years one or two sides of the house got a coat of paint. The different shades of paint and the balusters missing from the little balconies gave the house a patched, toothless look. On rainy days water dripped down the wall next to Father Alexey's bed. He complained to Mr. Palchinsky, the president of the Union of True Russians, which owned the house. Mr. Palchinsky got the Union to provide each room with a plastic bucket. Father Alexey would have tried to fix the roof himself but he did not know how to do it. Yakov said he knew how to do it, but he was too old to climb a ladder and besides they did not have a ladder.

Yakov's room was next to Father Alexey's. Each night after the old man said his prayers he would say good night to the priest through the wall.

Father Alexey did not always answer. Yakov was a nice man, but he could be a bother. He was always telling stories about himself. Yakov in Galicia. Yakov in the Civil War. Yakov in the labor camp. Yakov tending flower beds for some big shot in White Plains. Father Alexey knew them all. And whenever he made an observation with which Yakov did not agree, Yakov would say, "You're young yet. Wait a while. When you're older, you'll see things more clearly."

The priest knew it was one of the things people in town said about him: He was young. He tried to look older by wearing wire-rimmed glasses. He was balding, and that helped. Not that it was a bad thing to say, that he was young. If people really wanted to be disparaging — as when the Anikanov family got mad at him because he forgot to offer them the cross to kiss at their mother's memorial service — they went around reminding their neighbors that he was not Russian at all but an American from Teaneck, New Jersey; if they knew about his mother being Polish they called him a Pole; they brought up the fact that he once had been a Catholic. If they wanted truly to drag his name through the mud, they called him a liberal, even though he almost always voted Republican.

Yakov had been in the hospital before, once when he had his hernia and once for hemorrhoids. This time, even before they knew it was cancer, he sensed he wouldn't be coming home. He was, after all, almost ninety years old. He carefully packed his worn suit, the photographs of his wife, his Army medal, some old books that looked as if they had been rained on, into cardboard boxes, which he labeled and stacked in a corner of his room. He left an envelope with some money with Father Alexey and also his watering pail for his geraniums. When the car came to get him, he didn't want to go. Suddenly he was afraid. Father Alexey had to sit with him in his room, assuring him that it was all right, he was going to get well. He carried Yakov's suitcase out to the car. Yakov was shaking. When Father Alexey waved good-bye the old man started to cry.

The hospital was in the city, fifteen miles away. Once a week, on Thursday, the senior citizens' bus took people from the town to the shopping center, which was only a mile or so from the hospital, and you could get a ride if there was room. But if you did not have a car and it was not Thursday, you had to call Mikhail Krenko, the dissident. He had a little business on the side driving people to the city for their errands.

Krenko worked nights on the trucks that collected the flocks from the chicken barns. He had arrived in town one day after jumping off a Soviet trawler. It was said that he offered a traffic policeman two fresh codfish in exchange for political asylum. People suspected he was a spy. They were almost certain he had Jewish blood. Why else, they asked themselves, would the Soviets have given him up so easily? Why had he come to live in a godforsaken town that did not even have a shopping center?

Krenko was a small man with limp yellow hair and a round face like a girl's. He chewed gum to cover the smell of his liquor, sauntered with his hands in his pockets and did not remove his hat upon entering a house, even with an ikon staring him in the face. In. the churchyard one Sunday, people overheard him call Mr. Palchinsky — *"Papashka"* — "Pops." Anna Kirillovna Nikulina told of the time she rode to the city with him and he addressed her as Nikulina — not even *Mrs.* "Here you are, Nikulina," he said. "The drugstore."

Some female — an American; young, by the sound of her — answered when Father Alexey dialed his number.

"He's in the can," she said.

"Well, would you call him, please?" he said impatiently.

"Okay, okay. Don't have a kitten."

She yelled to Krenko. Father Alexey heard her say, "I don't know — some guy having a kitten."

When Krenko came on the telephone, the priest said as sarcastically as he could, "This is Father Alexey — the 'guy' from your church."

"Hey, you catch me hell of time, with pants down."

"I called you," Father Alexey replied stiffly, "because one of my parishioners happens to be very ill."

He hung his communion kit around his neck and went to wait for Krenko in the sparse shade of the elm tree in front of the house. Only a few branches of the old tree still had leaves. In some places big pieces of bark had come off. The wood underneath was dry and white as bone.

Across the street from where the priest stood was the funeral home. Sprays of water from a sprinkler and a couple of hoses fell over the trim green grass and on the flowers along the walk. Father Alexey held his valise with his holy vestments in one hand and in the other his prayer book, a black ribbon marking the place with the prayers for the sick. He could feel the sweat running down his sides.

He thought what it would be like to strip off his long hot clothes and run under the spray, back and forth. He saw himself jumping over the flowers. He could feel the wet grass between his toes. Setting down his valise, he took off his hat and wiped his face and balding head with his handkerchief. He fluttered the handkerchief in the air. In a minute it was dry.

From behind him a window opened. He heard Mrs. Florenskaya call. He pretended not to hear her. He did not turn around until she had called him for the third time.

"Oh, hello, Lidiya Andreyevna," he said, holding the bright sun behind his hand.

"Somewhere going, *batyushka?*" the old woman asked in her crackly voice.

"Yes," the priest said reluctantly.

"Good," Mrs. Florenskaya said. *"Ich komme."*

The Union of True Russians had bought the house along with the church building next door. It had been a fine, sturdy house, the home of a shipbuilder; the church had been the stable for his carriage horses. The Union divided the house into rooms and flats and rented them. At one time, they had all been occupied. Everyone was gone now, dead or moved away — mostly dead. The whole parish had grown older all at once, it seemed. Now with Yakov in the hospital, Father Alexey was alone in the old house with Mrs. Florenskaya. Every day she shuffled up and down the empty, echoing hallway in her slippers and Father Alexey would hear her crying. In nice weather she cried out on the porch. The first time he heard her — it was shortly after he had arrived to take over the parish, his predecessor, Father Dmitri, having been transferred back to New York after a prolonged bout with the bottle — Father Alexey had run upstairs to see what was wrong. Mrs. Florenskaya listened to his beginner's Russian with a happy expression on her face, as if he were trying to entertain her. Then she replied in a mixture of English and German, although he did not know any German, that a bandit was stealing spoons from her drawer.

He no longer asked.

After a minute the front door opened and the little woman came spryly down the stairs carrying a cane she did not seem to need. A paper shopping bag and an old brown purse hung from one arm. She was wearing a kerchief and a winter coat.

"Where going *Sie,* little father?"

When he told her about Yakov, she sighed heavily, "Old people just closing eyes," she said. Her chin started to wobble.

"Aren't you hot in that coat, Lidiya Andreyevna?"

She pulled a wadded tissue out of her pocket. "*Sie* young man, *Sie* can *arbeiten.* I am old." She wiped her nose, then lifted her chin in the air. "I *arbeiten* in Chicago," she said proudly. "In fine hotel."

Father Alexey looked down the empty street.

"He's late," he said.

"*Ja,*" the old woman said emphatically, as if he had confirmed all she had said. "Many *zimmer* taken care of; wash, clean, making beds."

A short distance from where they stood the road dropped steeply to the river. Father Alexey could see the far bank and the dark pines of the forest beyond. The sky was blue and still. The leaves were motionless on the trees, as if they were resting in the heat. Above the brow of the hill, Father Alexey saw two heads appear then slowly rise like two plants pushing up into the sun. The heads were followed by two bodies, one long, one square. They came up over the hill and slowly in the heat toward the priest and Mrs. Florenskaya. They were dressed for the city, the woman in a dress with flowers, the man in a dark suit and tie. The woman was the long one. The man was hewn sheer and square like a block of stone. As they drew near, the man took the woman's arm in his thick hand and stopped her short of the shade. They looked back down the road. The man checked his watch.

Bending around the priest, Mrs. Florenskaya peered at them with curiosity.

"Good heavens," she said in Russian. "Why are you standing in the sun? Come here, dearies, with us."

The man gave them half a smile. "It's all right," he said as if embarrassed. But the woman came right over.

"Thank you," she said, as if the shade belonged to them. "That hill! We had to stop four times. Stepanka, come join these nice people." She pulled him by the arm. "Now that's much better — no?"

Father Alexey introduced himself and said in Russian that the weather was very hot.

"Fedorenko," the man said but he did not offer his hand. He added in English: "My wife."

*"Ach, Sie sprechen Englisch!"* Mrs. Florenskaya said delightedly. "I, too!"

From time to time Father Alexey had run into them in the market or on the street. The man was Ukrainian , the woman Byelorussian. The woman would always smile. Occasionally the man nodded stiffly. On Sundays Father Alexey would see them pass by on their way to the Ukrainian church.

"Are you waiting for someone?" the man's wife asked, continuing the English. "We're supposed to meet Mr. Krenko here."

"He was supposed to be here ten minutes ago," the priest said.

"We're going to do a little shopping," the woman informed them. "Stepan's not allowed to drive. It's his eyes. They wouldn't renew his license. We're going to get some glasses for him. He doesn't want them. He thinks they'll make him look old."

"Not old," her husband said sharply. "Don't need it. What for spend money when don't need it?"

"You see?" she said hopelessly.

As they waited the sun grew hotter. They inched closer together under the tree. They could see the heat coming up from the road and from the shingles of the roofs that showed above the hill. Mrs. Fedorenko fanned her face. Mrs. Florenskaya unbuttoned her coat. They stared longingly at the shimmering spray of water across the way. There was a rainbow in the spray and the water glistened on the green grass and flowers and lawn sign on which the undertaker had painted in gold an Orthodox cross beside the regular Christian one.

Finally they heard an engine straining. Up over the hill through the waves of heat came Krenko's car. It was a big car, several years old, all fenders and chrome. Upon reaching level ground it seemed to sigh. It came up to them panting.

Krenko pushed open the front door.

"You're late," Father Alexey told him. With a look of distaste, he set his valise with his holy vestments on the zebra-skin seat cover. Mr. and Mrs. Fedorenko climbed into the back, followed by Mrs. Florenskaya, who nudged Mr. Fedorenko into the middle with her bony hip.

"Where is she going?" Krenko said.

"Ask her," the priest shrugged.

"Where you going, lady?"

"Never mind," Mrs. Florenskaya said.

"Not free, you know. Cost you money."

"*Ja.* Everything all time is money."

"Ten dollars," Krenko said.

"*Ja, ja.*"

"You have?"

Mrs. Florenskaya took a rag of a bill out of her pocketbook and waved it angrily under Krenko's nose. She put it back and snapped her purse. "Everything is money," she said. Tears suddenly rolled out from under her eyeglasses.

"Crazy old woman," Krenko muttered.

"May we go?" Father Alexey said.

They drove around the block onto the main street of the town. On the street was the market, the bank, the hardware store, the laundromat, the Hotel Nicholas the Second, and the variety store. Part way down the hill Krenko stopped and blew the horn.

"Another passenger, I presume?" Father Alexey said.

"Make it when sun is shining," Krenko said.

From a door marked PRIVATE stepped Marietta Valentinova, the famous ballerina who lived over the hardware store. A white cap with a green plastic visor kept the sun from her small severe face. Krenko got out and opened the front door, giving her a mock bow, which she ignored.

"Good afternoon, Marietta Valentinova," Father Alexey said. *"Ya yedu v gospital."*

The ballerina glanced at his valise. One corner of her small red mouth lifted. "The hospital? Well, I thought you have been looking thin," she teased him in English. "That's the trouble with being monk: no wife to feed you."

"It's Yakov Osipovich," he said, reddening.

"So," she said. "Shall you move over or must I stand in sun all day?"

"Maybe you get in first, lady," Krenko said. "With such little legs you fit better in middle."

"I will thank you to pay attention to your own legs. And also to your manner. Who do you think you are, blowing that horn?"

"Like joking with her," Krenko winked when the priest got out to let the ballerina in.

"How about the air conditioning?" Father Alexey said when Krenko got back behind the wheel.

"Okay. First got to put up all windows," Krenko said. He turned a switch. Air blew out from under the dashboard.

"I think that's the heat," said Father Alexey.

"Is okay," Krenko said. "Got to cool up."

They drove to the bottom of the hill and turned up along the river. The water lay flat and colorless between banks of colorless clay. Soon they were in the woods. The road ran over the tops of the hills and down to stream beds filled with rocks. The undergrowth was dense and tangled and they could no longer see the river. They passed a farmhouse with a barn propped up by poles. In a clearing slashed in the woods a mobile home squatted like a gypsy, its children and its trash strewn around the yard.

The air was blowing out of the vent, but the car was stifling. They were squeezed together, Father Alexey with his valise on his lap. Marietta Valentinova smelled Krenko's sweat. She moved a fraction closer to the priest, who had pulled out his handkerchief and was wiping his face.

"If I don't get some air, I am going to faint," Marietta Valentinova said.

Krenko clicked the switch another notch. The hot air blew out harder.

"Sometimes takes couple minutes," he said.

"In a couple of minutes we will be cooked," the ballerina said. "Can't you see I'm dying?"

"Hold it!" Krenko said. He felt under the dashboard. "Now is coming."

Father Alexey wiggled his fingers in the air blowing on his knees. It was still hot.

"Now is coming," Krenko said confidently.

"Open a window," the ballerina commanded.

"You going to let all the air condition out...."

"Did you hear me?" she said in a voice so severe that everyone at once rolled down the windows.

"Thank God," said the priest as the wind blew in on them. They put their hands out into it, groping for a current of coolness.

After a while, Mrs. Fedorenko said, "It was very hot in New Jersey, too. That's where we lived."

"Hot like hell," Krenko agreed, although he had never been to New Jersey. "Here is not hot."

"I am very glad to hear that this is not hot," the ballerina said. She held a hanky over her mouth as they passed a chicken barn.

"More hot in California," Mr. Fedorenko said. "I been all over United States. Many Ukrainian people live in California. Many Russian, too," he added for the benefit of the ballerina, who had cocked her ear toward him, showing him her profile, the raised eyebrow. "And many Ukrainian. Not same thing."

"Do tell us about it," the ballerina said haughtily. To Marietta Valentinova there was no such thing as a Ukrainian. That was modern nationalistic nonsense. What was the Ukraine? — *Malorossiya,* "Little Russia." They were all Russians.

"You are from New Jersey, *batyushka?*" Mrs. Fedorenko asked to change the subject.

"Yes. It is very hot in New Jersey. I haven't been to California."

"*I* in Chicago *arbeiten,*" Mrs. Florenskaya said.

"You were saying something about the *malorossy,* I believe?" the ballerina said.

"Not Little Russians, lady. Ukrainian."

"All right, Stepanka. Did you hear? *Batyushka* also lived in New Jersey."

Mr. Fedorenko folded his heavy arms. "Don't call us *malorossy.*"

"I don't call you anything," the ballerina smiled coldly.

"No?" Mr. Fedorenko pushed forward his big chin. "What are you calling ten million Ukrainians? The ones Russia starved?"

"If you are speaking of the Soviet Union, I'll thank you not to call it Russia," the ballerina said. "I hate that word — *soviet.*"

"Okay," Krenko said. "Long time ago — okay?"

"I have a question," Father Alexey said.

"You, too," said Mr. Fedorenko accusingly. His face was very red.

"Me, too? What?" said the priest.

"Stepanka," Mrs. Fedorenko implored.

"I see you Four July parade. See you turn away when Ukrainian club marching by. You don't remember, huh?"

"I didn't turn away."

"I wouldn't blame you if you did," the ballerina said. "I certainly would."

"I didn't."

"That's enough, Stepanka."

"Maybe I just looked somewhere else," the priest said. "There is a big difference between looking somewhere else at a given moment and turning away."

"Of course there is," Mrs. Fedorenko assured him.

"I know how is seeing," her husband said.

"All right, Stepanka. What were you going to ask before, *batyushka?*" You said you had a question."

"I don't know," the priest said dejectedly. After a moment he said, "I guess I was going to ask why everyone is speaking English."

"You're absolutely right," Mrs. Fedorenko said. "You need to practice." And then she said something in Russian, or Ukrainian, or Byelorussian, which Father Alexey did not quite catch. In the conversation that followed, he heard many words he knew but there were many words in between — they spoke so quickly — which he could not understand.

Then there was silence.

He looked around and saw the others looking at him.

*"Nu?"* the ballerina said.

*"Shto?"* he asked. "What?"

*"Shto ty dumayesh?"*

*"Shto?"*

Heavens, my dear Father Alexey," the ballerina changed to English. "We are talking about poor Mr. Kaputin. Haven't you been listening?"

"Of course I've been listening."

"Well, then?"

"Well, what?"

"Does he have much pain? Is he getting any weaker? You did say you were going to see him? He's not going to last, is he?"

"Yes, of course, Marietta Valentinova. I know. I understand." He had picked out Yakov's name in the wash of words that flowed back and forth between them, but he had heard the word, he thought, for "flowers," and he assumed they were talking about the old man's geraniums. Yakov grew them in his window box. They were big, healthy flowers, all from pinchings from other people's flower pots, and it was the thing you saw when you walked past the house. Instead, they had been discussing his funeral. Father Alexey shifted the valise on his lap. His clothes were stuck to him.

"The nurse said he wasn't feeling well," he said. "Who knows what that means? The last time they said the same thing and I went all the way to the hospital and there was nothing wrong with him. He was fine. He just wanted someone to talk to. I walk in and he says, 'I'm glad you came, *batyushka.* Have you paid my electric bill? I think I paid it before I came here, but I can't remember.' I told him everything was taken care of. 'That's good,' he says. 'I was worried. So how are you, *batyushka?* It's hot out, isn't it?' That cost the church ten dollars."

"Don't blame me," Krenko said. "They don't give the gas away."

There were more farms, more rocky fields, and unpainted houses that tilted one way or the other. Then more woods broken by raw-cut clearings full of stumps and weeds and plastic toys and house trailers on cement blocks.

Of the farms and houses, Father Alexey could almost pick which were Russian, which American. None of the people in them had money, you could see that easily enough, but the American ones almost seemed to be the way they were out of stubbornness. There was something willful, in a savage, defiant way, about the broken porches, the rusty machinery outside the barns. The Russian yards were unkempt only with weeds and overgrown grass and the woods coming closer and closer. They had little gardens, just tiny patches, with flowers and a few vegetables. Father Alexey started to get depressed.

"Did you ever think," he said, looking out the window, "that you would be here?"

No one said anything.

"Are you speaking to me?" Marietta Valentinova said.

"Yes. To anyone."

"Who would ever think they would be here?"

"Then why did you come?"

"Personally, I came for my health."

Mr. Fedorenko gave a guffaw. His wife pulled at his sleeve.

"It's true. Why else would I leave New Jersey? I had a nice place to live in. When I danced I got good write-ups. You should see the people who came to my ballets. You could barely find a seat. The only thing was, the air was no good to breathe. All that pollution. If you dance, you must have air. So where does a Russian go? You've got to have a church. So you go where there are Russians. At least in New Jersey there were people with intelligence," she added over her shoulder toward Mr. Fedorenko.

"So many people lived in New Jersey!" Mrs. Fedorenko said before her husband could say anything. "We like it here, though," she added, patting Mr. Fedorenko's thick square hand. "We've had enough big things — the war, DP camps. After the last camp we went to South America. On Monday morning you turned on the radio and if there was a revolution you did not have to go to work. Too many things. Here it is small and quiet. Stepan always wanted to live next to a river. He says that with a river you will never starve."

"I live in this place eighteen year," declared Mrs. Florenskaya. *"Achtzehn jahr,"* she added for Father Alexey's benefit. "All in this old house."

"Eighteen years," said the ballerina sadly. "I couldn't stand this place so long." But she already had been in the town more than half that.

Father Alexey calculated. Eighteen years ago he was nine years old. It was a whole year in his life, but all he could remember of it was being in the fourth grade and Sister Rita St. Agnes being his teacher, a stern woman with thick black eyebrows who had seemed to take to him after his father died. "The boy with the laughing eyes," she called him affectionately. Sometimes he'd looked into the mirror to see why she'd called him that. The eyes belonged now to a not very old person who was expected to be full of

answers for people far older than he, people who were afraid of
getting sick and of nursing homes and hospitals and of what was
going to happen to them. He dispensed answers like the holy
water he flung on heads and shoulders at feast-day processions.
Answers for death and fear and sadness and stolen spoons. And in
all his life he had only lived in New Jersey with his mother and in
the monastery in New York and now in a little town no one had
ever heard of. How could he know?

In another eighteen years he would be forty-five. How much
would he know then? Would he see things more clearly, as Yakov
said? Krenko and the ballerina might still be around. Krenko probably would be in jail or involved in some scheme, making money
one way or another. The ballerina would be an old woman if she
were still alive. The others would surely be dead. Most of the people in the parish would be dead.

He was becoming more and more alone in the world.

The shopping center was on a broad avenue that ran between
the interstate highway and the city. Once the road had had fine
old houses with wide porches and broad lawns and beds of mari-
golds and tulips. A few of these houses remained, but now dentists
and lawyers had their offices in them. The rest had been torn
down for the fast-food restaurants, gas stations, and bargain stores
that lined the road with their bright, colorful signs like a crowd at
a parade. Krenko drove into the shopping center parking lot and
discharged his passengers in front of the K-Mart store. He would
be back for them in about two hours, he said.

Father Alexey let the ballerina out and got back in the front seat.
His cassock was wet and wrinkled where the valise had been.

"Look like you piss yourself," Krenko laughed.

In the hospital Father Alexey carried his valise in front of him to
hide the wet place. Two teenaged girls snickered behind him on
the elevator. A small boy who got on with his mother gawked up
at him all the way to the seventh floor. "Hey, mister — you look
like something," the boy said.

Father Alexey marched to the nurses' station and set his valise
down impatiently. Then he remembered the wet place and
covered it with his prayer book.

"You're here for Mr. Kaputin?" asked the nurse who was there.

"Yes," Father Alexey said curtly. "Are you the one who

called?''

''No, that was Mrs. Dinsmore. She's gone off shift now.'' The nurse came out into the corridor. She was a tall woman with narrow shoulders and graying hair. Even before she said anything, Father Alexey knew from the look on her tired face that Yakov was going to die.

''The doctor has been in,'' she said.

He followed her to the room. Yakov was asleep, long and gaunt under the sheet. There was a sweet thick smell in the room. Yakov's bones looked as if they might pop through his face. With each breath his mouth puffed out like a frog's throat. On the stand beside his bed was the ikon from his bureau at home and a small vase of daisies whose petals were dropping off.

Father Alexey touched the old man's arm.

Yakov's eyes blinked open. For a while he stared up at the priest.

''It's you,'' he said.

''How are you feeling, Yakov Osipovich?'' Father Alexey asked in Russian.

''I saw my mother.'' Yakov's voice was hoarse and very old. He took a long time between his words.

''Where did you see her?''

''She went away. There are fewer Russians, *batyushka*. . . .''

He began to talk incoherently, something about apples in his father's orchard. The words came out in pieces that did not fit together, as if something inside of him had broken.

The nurse brought a glass of tea. Father Alexey cooled it with his breath.

''Here, Yakov Osipovich,'' he said, raising the old man's head. The tea rose halfway up the glass straw, then sank back into the glass.

''Try again, Yakov Osipovich. Pull harder.''

''Shall I try?'' the nurse asked.

Father Alexey took his communion kit from around his neck. ''I don't think it matters,'' he said.

The nurse went out quietly, leaving the door ajar.

Father Alexey arranged articles from his kit and others from his valise on the stand beside Yakov's bed. He put on his holy vestments. He took the ribbon from the place he had marked in his book, and turned through the pages to the prayers for the dying.

He read quietly, occasionally making the sign of a cross over the old man's head. Yakov gazed up at him in silence and a kind of wonder, his mouth agape.

The priest softened a piece of bread in a little wine.

"Yakov Osipovich," he said. "Are you sorry for your sins?"

The old man looked from the priest's face to the hand with the bread. Then his eyes closed. Father Alexey shook him. "Yakov Osipovich," he said. "Say, yes."

He tried to put the bread into Yakov's mouth but the old man's teeth were clenched. He slipped the bread between Yakov's lips, tucking it back into his cheek. Eventually Yakov's mouth began to move. He chewed fast, as if he were hungry.

Yakov opened his eyes just once more. Father Alexey was putting his things away. He heard Yakov's voice behind him. The old man was looking at him calmly.

"How did you come?" he said.

The priest sat down beside him. "I found a ride. Are you feeling better?"

"Then you have to pay."

"Don't worry about it, Yakov Osipovich."

"Well, I'll straighten it out with you later, *batyushka.*"

Krenko was parked outside the emergency door in a place marked DOCTORS ONLY.

"You make me wait long time," Krenko said. Father Alexey could smell liquor on him.

"I'm sorry."

"Not me, I don't care. But little dancing lady going to be mad like hell."

Marietta Valentinova sputtered at them half the way home. Tiny drops of saliva flew from her mouth and landed on the dashboard. Father Alexey watched them evaporate, leaving little dots. At last she stopped. They became aware of his silence.

"*Batyushka?*" Mrs. Fedorenko said.

After a while Krenko said, "Well, you got to go everybody sometimes."

"Where going?" Mrs. Florenskaya said.

"Mr. Kaputin," Mrs. Fedorenko told her gently.

"*Ja, alles,*" the old woman said. "*Alles kaput. Mein mann, meine*

*Kinder. Alles* but me.''

The sun was gone from the window shade when Father Alexey got back to his room and lay down on his bed. It was still light, it would be light for a while yet. He turned on his fan to move the air and looked at the wall through which Yakov had said good night. He heard Mrs. Florenskaya in the hallway upstairs. She was starting in again.

The priest switched on the stereo set with the record from the afternoon. But still he could hear her.

''Christ,'' he said, and turned up the volume very loud.

*A former reporter who moved to Maine in 1966, Willis Johnson (1938-    ) was born in Norwalk, Connecticut, and has been writing full-time since 1975. He has won a Pushcart Prize and had this story, which first appeared in TRI-QUARTERLY in 1982, selected for PRIZE STORIES: O. HENRY AWARDS 1984. His first collection is THE GIRL WHO WOULD BE RUSSIAN (1986).*

# BERRYING

F ootsteps, followed by a hacking cough, sounded in the spare room above. Matti Kilponen and his wife Kaisa both looked up to the smoke-darkened plaster of the ceiling. Kaisa jabbed the sewing needle into the worn brown trousers she was mending. "Why did you bring her here?" she hissed.

Matti looked up from *The County Observer,* spread out on the round kitchen table. "You know she didn't have anyplace to go. And she almost died from the influenza. You can see that she is weak. And she said she wanted to be around womenfolk."

Matti returned to the newspaper, his finger underscoring the line of print, his lips mouthing the English words. Only when he had finished the column did he look up at his wife and say, "It's just for a few weeks. Until Nestori gets back from the quarries at the coast. There's work there now. It says so. Right here."

Kaisa sat stiffly, her arms crossed, the sewing untouched on her lap. She stared across the kitchen at the rain streaking the windows in the gray dusk.

"You don't think she could stay in the woods alone, do you? Not the way she is now. Remember . . . the Bible says, 'Do unto . . . .'"

"They're not married!"

"They're as good as married. All these years."

At Kaisa's feet a coffee-colored dog named Karhu stretched and then nestled his huge muzzle onto his wide front paws. Kaisa looked down at the dog and broke the thread with her teeth. She folded the trousers neatly into thirds and dropped her thimble into the cigar box she used for sewing notions. "And what if he doesn't come back?'' she asked, her mouth tight. ''Do we just keep Lena the way we kept Karhu?'' She didn't trust that the bent, red-whiskered man with the odd twitch to his eye would return. When Matti had brought them home through the rain that afternoon, *Komia* Nestori, or Pretty Nestori, had dropped Lena's meager bundle, wrapped in a wet brown shawl, and had spun to go. With the dog barking beside her, Kaisa had reluctantly called out to him to come in for coffee, but Nestori hadn't even turned to look. ''He probably has no intention of coming for her. He's going to take his money and go away. To Canada. Or Minnesota.''

''He'll come.'' Matti yawned and reached for the heavy silver watch in his pocket to check against the clock that ticked between the two front windows. ''Put the dog out, and let's go to bed,'' he said, picking up the lantern.

Again there was the hacking cough from above.

Over the years, Matti had spoken of Lena Hakola in such admiring terms that Kaisa sometimes wondered whether or not he carried a spark for her. It didn't seem to matter to Matti that she was skinny, or that her gapped teeth were stained from years of chewing tobacco, or that her frowzy hair was never pulled back into the neat bun that all modest Finnish women wore. The two never stopped talking. It seemed that they had already resurrected every Yankee, every Canadian, every Finn who had ever worked in the lumber camp. Every meal Lena had cooked. Every storm that had raged. Every tree that had been felled. Every dollar lost to gambling and whiskey. Every accident. Every hard time. Every good time.

Lena's eyes snapped and laughter rattled from her when she recalled some incident. With Lena, Matti quipped in a way he never did with Kaisa. Only when Lena, with a dingy handkerchief to her mouth and her eyes swollen with tears, broke down in a spell of coughing, did they stop.

No one could say that Lena didn't try to please Kaisa. With the first light of dawn, Lena was up, poking kindling at Kaisa when she started the morning fire. When the coffee was ready, Lena sat between Matti and Kaisa slurping steaming coffee from her saucer just as Matti did from his. Kaisa could barely taste her own coffee for listening to Lena's noisy inhalations. Although to tell the truth,

Matti had been drinking his coffee as noisily for years, and Kaisa had barely noticed.

Whenever Kaisa went into the barn to do her morning chores, Lena was there. Always talking. The cows balked at her strange touch and were skittish when she coughed. The usually docile animals jumped and kicked, and milk spilled.

Despite the many years of praise Kaisa had received for her crusty bread and tasty stews, Lena offered up advice from her years of experience as a cook in the lumber camp. "When I make it in the camp...." she'd begin, so that the blood would boil in Kaisa's head.

As soon as a meal was over, Lena would dash to the slate sink, insisting that she would be the one to wash dishes. "Why don't you go rest?" Kaisa would say as she hovered close by, watching Lena haphazardly dip greasy plates, forks and knives into water that was barely warm. And afterwards, Lena would grab the broom to flick at the crumbs around the table. When Lena, finally exhausted, did go upstairs to lie down, Kaisa would stealthily pick the dishes out of the pantry cupboard to wash them again in water that steamed and turned her hands red. And then she'd wield the broom with a sore vengeance, attacking the four corners of the roomy kitchen, moving the woodbox aside to get every woodchip and splinter, and rolling the long rag floor runners to carry outside and beat so that not a speck of dust dared linger.

The more Lena tried, the worse it got with Kaisa so that she became quieter and quieter. And the quieter Kaisa grew, the more Matti tried to make up the difference with Lena.

Lena no longer chewed tobacco, but she did now smoke a pipe. Several times a day, she lit the pipe, dribbling shreds of tobacco and leaving behind the heady scent of Prince Albert.

"I don't like the way it smells," Kaisa complained to her husband as she scooped up bits of tobacco from the table. "And look at the mess!"

Matti took Lena aside and suggested that she not smoke inside the house. After that, Lena smoked on the front stoop with the dog Karhu beside her, thumping his stub of a tail as she rubbed his back.

Kaisa, seeing how the dog seemed to be taking to Lena, sometimes poked in the pantry for a bit of gristly meat or a scrap of bread. And then, with a good deal of noise, she rattled the dog's tin dish, watching in satisfaction as he greedily dashed to her. At such times, though, Lena seemed to take no notice.

When the dog, with the look of a scruffy brown bear, had appeared at their door one morning, Kaisa, not heeding Matti's caution, had given it the remainder of her porridge mixed with a raw egg and milk. "If the dog wants to stay," she had said, "we'll keep it for a cow dog. All the farms have cow dogs. And since he resembles a bear, let's call him Karhu."

Karhu, however, proved to be worthless with cows. His barking drove them in the opposite direction of the barn, and at midday when they should have been comfortably chewing their cuds in the shade of a tree, the dog would excite them. Matti threatened to get rid of the dog, but Kaisa wouldn't hear of it.

But one evening as they ate supper, Kaisa suddenly said, "Maybe we should do away with that good-for-nothing dog. He's not earning *his* keep around here!"

Lena looked up in surprise.

Matti ignored his wife.

It was a fine August morning when Matti told the two women about the blueberries. Knowing how much Kaisa enjoyed picking berries, he felt sure that Lena would be of the same persuasion. And perhaps, he thought, with a few berries to pick, Kaisa might slip into a more cheerful frame of mind.

"You know where I mean. On the ridge above Pottle's," he said. And then to tempt his wife further, he added, "As thick as — As grapes! They've *never* grown so plentifully."

"Lena, you stay here and rest," Kaisa said, her eyes flashing with excitement. "It's a long walk. Too far for you. And steep. You'll get tired if you go."

But Lena wouldn't hear of it. She wouldn't mind the walk. She wanted to help. Going out into the sunshine would be healthful. And she wouldn't get tired. And if she did get tired, she would just sit down and rest. Look how much better she was already after just a few weeks. Yes. She would go. To keep Kaisa company.

"But going so far will make you cough," Kaisa said.

"I don't cough so much now," Lena insisted. "I'll go with you."

There was no convincing her otherwise.

"Oh, I almost forgot to tell you," Matti added, increasingly hopeful that berrying would make Kaisa more agreeable. "George Pottle has pastured his bull in that big field. You'll have to go around. There's no trusting a bull."

As soon as the few morning duties were out of the way — the cows milked, the dishes washed, the kitchen neat and tidy, a pot of beans baking for supper in the oven — Kaisa collected two lard pails, a cooking pot and a shiny milk bucket. Handing the two lard pails to Lena, she set the larger containers on the table for herself.

She filled a glass jug with hot milky coffee and slid it into a worn woolen stocking to keep it hot. From the crock on the pantry shelf, she reached for a handful of rusks and grabbed for two white mugs. Putting all of these into a birch bark pack which she shrugged over her shoulders, she pulled a faded purple kerchief from the hook by the door and tied it under her chin.

Matti was sharpening his scythe at the grindstone and watched as the two women left the dooryard. Kaisa, with the pack over her shoulders, carrying the cooking pot and milk bucket, scurried two steps ahead of Lena. And behind Lena, Karhu followed.

"I've never told you," Lena puffed, trying to keep pace with Kaisa's stride, "that back in Finland, my aunt — that would be my mother's sister — met her Maker because of a bull. What a tragic story! It happened that she was taking her nice little cow to her neighbor's for a little loving. You know what I'm saying, eh? That bull had no idea when he saw my aunt leading that cow that he should be grateful. There was nothing left of Lempi *Täti* they said. I never saw her myself. But they told me." And after a moment's reflection, she added, "We won't go through that pasture, eh? We'll go around. Just the way Matti said, eh?"

"If you're so worried, maybe you should go back."

"No! No! I'll help you pick berries. And we'll make a blueberry soup. Nice and sweet, eh? But I won't go near that bull."

Kaisa's step quickened. Behind her, Lena walked faster. The dog Karhu, with his black nose to the ground, wandered off into the bushes.

"I see that you made beans this morning," Lena huffed. "Sometime I'll make beans for you. Matti likes my beans. In the lumber camp, those men, they said, 'Lena!' they said. 'Lena, you make good beans!'"

Kaisa's lips tightened. She eyed a small white cloud. "Matti *likes* my beans," she said, her feet wanting to fly.

But the faster Kaisa walked, the faster Lena walked, her breathing becoming labored, the two lard pails clinking unevenly.

"When I go back to Finland," Lena started, her voice breathy, "I'll tell your people how you let me stay here. And I'll go back in style, too. Maybe a new black coat. A new shawl. And new hat with flowers. And everyone will say, 'Lena! Lena, you went to America, and now you're a rich woman!' I'll tell everyone how you and Matti took care of me when I was sick and Nestori went to work in the quarry. I'll go and take greetings to your mother and your sisters. Now what did you say their names are? Liisa and — ? and — ?" Lena stopped to cough, her dirty handkerchief to her mouth.

"Liisa and Anni!" Kaisa snapped, turning to wait for Lena. "And how do you think you'll get back to Finland? You don't have that kind of money." Kaisa fumed. Even she had long ago given up the idea of going back to her homeland.

They passed the stone wall that marked the line to George Pottle's farm and soon came to the white house encircled with a wide veranda and a big steep-roofed barn with its pointed cupola. Every time she passed George Pottle's house, Kaisa wanted to peek in one of the curved front windows. Just to see what was inside. She imagined it must be very fine. Finer than she had ever seen. But the two women walked past with perhaps even a little more haste.

"It's shorter if we go through," Kaisa said as they paused to rest at the edge of the big field. Rich and green with lush clover, it was a field large enough for a whole herd of cattle. All for one bull, Kaisa thought. What a good life he leads. But where was he? She squinted, peering across the pasture. Glancing at Lena from the corner of her eye, she blurted, "Let's go," and jerked the heavy thick strands of barbed wire apart.

"You heard what Matti said!" Lena cried, shrinking back from the fence. "He said to go around. I told you about my aunt. I won't go."

"*Voi! Voi!* How much time will we lose if we have to go around?" Although earlier Kaisa had had no intention of crossing through the field, she now felt that she wanted to insist.

"Are we in so much of a hurry that we'll risk our lives? Don't you see? Behind those bushes?"

Even from where she stood, Kaisa could see that the black bull was enormous. As a rule, she was sensible enough to have a mighty respect for the power of such a creature. But today, her annoyance with Lena made her tongue careless. "As though we couldn't go faster." However, with a shrug, she headed for the steep tangled path that ran alongside the green pasture.

The dog Karhu, though, scooted under the barbed wire into the thick clover.

"Come back!" Kaisa demanded. "Karhu!"

The dog turned to look.

"Come, Karhu —" Lena crooned.

But the coffee-colored dog sat, wagging his stubby tail.

"Leave him," Kaisa said, trudging up the steep path. "If he thinks he's going to chase that bull, he'll learn fast enough."

"Come, Karhu — Come —" Lena called again, slapping her hands together invitingly. But then, she, too, hurried along.

The trail was far from smooth. Brushy growth, fallen logs and jutting rocks provided obstacles for each step. Flying branches slapped Lena's cheek, and thorny brambles snarled her hands.

At last, though, Kaisa and then Lena emerged from the tangle of dark woods onto the bright sunny ledge. At their feet were patches of blue amongst gray rock, for blueberries grew everywhere, as abundantly as Matti had said.

Kaisa sighed.

Beyond were the roll and peak of mountains to the west. Neat patchwork fields and farms dotted the distant hills. A lake, seemingly no larger than Kaisa's shoe, nestled in the green valley below. And there was the tiny village of Edom with two rising church steeples. Kaisa felt so close to God at the moment that her heart was suddenly sweet with goodness for Lena.

"Well!" Lena exclaimed, her face red from the climb. "Look at that! I've never seen so far. It's not as flat as in Finland. Maybe we can see where Nestori went, eh? And so many berries." And then she started to cough. But despite her hacking, she continued to speak, "Remember in Finland? The berries were so small? One here. One there," she coughed. "What work to fill the dish. But we did it. We had to. Times were so bad. My mother one time made porridge from wood shavings. And then from straw. What bad times they were! But we picked berries when we could. Remember?'' she said, coughing.

"Remember? Of course, I remember!''

Kaisa had always loved berrying. Loved to feel the sun on her hunched shoulders. Loved to slide her kerchief off and feel the breeze in her hair. Loved to view the world from such a height. But not today. Today she had Lena Hakola.

"And the *lakka* berry,'' Lena continued. "Remember the *lakka*?'' There's nothing like the *lakka* in this country. I've never seen it here. Have you? I don't suppose they grow here at all. Maybe in Minnesota. There are many Finns in Minnesota. And plenty of work on the iron range. Maybe the *lakka* grows there, too. What do you think? Do you think the *lakka* grows there?''

"No! It doesn't grow there at all!''

"Oh — But you remember the taste?''

Kaisa did remember the taste. She remembered it each June when the days were long and the summer heat was still a promise. Like a raspberry in shape but orange in color. Low to the ground. A single berry to the stem. What Finn didn't remember the *lakka* and long for its taste.

"Do you think I am so simple that I have lost my memory? Of course I remember the *lakka*. You pick here,'' Kaisa said, "and I'll go over there. That way we won't trouble each other.''

Kaisa slid the pack that had grown heavy with the climb from her shoulders and stood it against a rocky shelf that glistened with strands of shining quartz. And then she started to pick.

As the berries fell into her pail, Kaisa's troubles with Lena were forgotten. Her fingers worked quickly. The round dusky-colored berries bounced, rolling in the empty space, plopping softly as the bottom covered. Not a leaf. Not a stem. Not a green berry marred the blue of the growing mound. Her fingers flew. She breathed deeply and smiled, pausing for an instant to look out over the world — the mountains, the woods, the farms, the village. God was with her.

She picked faster than ever. And the faster she picked, the more she thought of Lena. And the more she thought of Lena, the more she realized how shamefully she had acted. But from this moment, she resolved, her heart full of song, she'd be kinder. More understanding. Kaisa clasped her hands together and bowed her head, her eyes smarting, "Help me, Heavenly Father," she prayed. "Give me patience and understanding."

Already the milk pail was full. She carried it to the little rock shelf where she had left the coffee. Reaching for the still-warm jug, she filled one of the cracked mugs for herself, and then, her heart glowing, she poured coffee into the other mug as well and called, "Lena! Come for coffee!"

"Coffee? Coffee? Just what I was waiting for," Lena panted, even before Kaisa could screw the lid back onto the coffee jug. "And, yes, I'll take a *korpu,* too." She crunched one of the cinnamon and sugar sprinkled rusks, dribbling crumbs down her narrow chin. "I've never made good *korpu* myself," Lena said as she chewed the crusty bit. "But I don't make good *nisu* either. And you need to make good *nisu* to make good *korpu,* eh? Maybe you can show me, eh? Then when Nestori gets back, I'll make good *korpu* so that he can take it in the woods. Ohhh — !" she exclaimed, spying the milk pail mounded with firm plump berries. "You're full already? Look at my pail," she laughed, tilting the half-full lard pail for Kaisa to see. "Not as many. And not as clean, eh?"

"Maybe if you'd save the eating for later, you'd have more!" Kaisa snapped. Lena's mouth was stained dark with blue. And who'll clean those? Kaisa wondered. Lena's pail was messy with twigs and leaves. Her berries mushy. Not like Kaisa's, so clean and dry they wouldn't need to be picked over at all. But Lena's berries! Like Lena herself. Kaisa gulped her coffee and hurried off to fill the cooking pot.

As she picked, she heard a barking from below. Karhu? Was he chasing that bull? She should have known better than to leave him. They had had enough trouble with George Pottle, what with that cow they used to have getting into his corn. She stood, running her hand over the small of her back. Stiff. But the pot *was* filling. Just a while longer. Then home. But what about Lena? Probably still didn't have that first lard pail full. And messy! Never had Kaisa seen such messy berries.

Again she heard the faint barking from below.

At last she called out to Lena, "I'm going home. No. No. You stay," she said when Lena's unkempt head popped over the crest of the ridge. "My kettle is full. Matti will want to eat. You come home for dinner when you're through."

"But...." Lena started.

"No. You stay here and have a good time," Kaisa chirped. "So many nice berries. And I'll leave the rest of the coffee for you. By this rock. Do you see?" she asked, holding up the woolen stocking, swollen with the jug inside.

Balancing the brimming cooking pot in the crook of one arm and the overflowing milk bucket in the other hand, Kaisa hurried off into the shadowy woods. With each step down the steep trail, she skirted tangled branches that reached out for her and loose rocks that threatened to send her flying. With each step, berries bounded from her too-full containers. She tried holding the cooking pot by the handle but felt so unbalanced that the walking was even more difficult. At last, though, her feet found a rhythm.

*Well, Kaisa,* she found herself thinking. *You didn't keep your resolve, did you? You're not acting very Christian towards Lena.*

She snorted.

*You bully her.*

"I do not!" Kaisa's arms ached with the awkwardness of carrying the berries.

*But she wanted to leave. She hates to pick berries. Anyone can see that.*

At that moment, Kaisa stumbled, her foot catching on a root that snaked from the ground. As she twisted to regain her balance, berries bounced in the air. She straightened. Although her heart was pounding, she felt smug that she hadn't lost her grip on either the cooking pot or the milk bucket. She blew at a wisp of hair that slid out from under the purple kerchief and brushed against her nose. Her arms creaked with stiffness.

Pausing to rest at the upper edge of the pasture, she stooped to place first the milk bucket and then the cooking pot at her feet. There was no sign of the dog. Nor could she see the bull. To cross through the field would take but half the steps of the rough trail. She looked to the sun. It was high. And the bull was nowhere to be seen. Maybe sleeping under a tree in the far corner. Or maybe Pottle had taken him in. She remembered Lena back on the hilltop picking her messy berries. She'd be coming along anytime. Talking. Talking. Although it wasn't in her nature to be so, Kaisa's anger towards Lena had made her reckless. Surely, she thought, she was spry enough to cross that field in no time.

Kaisa reached over the stone wall and through the thick strands of barbed wire to set the cooking pot and then the shiny milk bucket on the other side. She found a spot where she could crawl under the taut wire. As she inched through, her kerchief caught and then the back of her skirt. *"Voi hyvänen aika,"* she muttered, yanking at the kerchief until she heard a faint tear. "Oh, for goodness sake."

Picking up her berries, she stood to survey the pasture. It was still enough. She wet her lips. Her mouth felt dry. She took one step. And then another.

The berries bounced as she walked, rolling to the ground. Nearly there, she thought, when the distance behind her equalled that yet to go. Her heart thumped against the metal of the cooking pot. She was walking quickly, one foot seemingly chasing the other.

She was almost running. The berries jounced into her path. She held her hand along the rim of the pot, trying to stop the flying berries. She saw where she would squeeze through the fence. Next to some young poplars.

She didn't hear but felt, through the soles of her hard black shoes, the thunder of the bull's approach. Her legs, entangled in the coarse dark material of her long skirt, groped mechanically. She clutched the cooking pot so that it dug into her arm. Still the round berries flew into the air. She knew she should drop them. She knew that the cooking pot and pail impeded her flight but was unable to let them go. She saw in a blinding instant the huge black bull bearing down on her.

She saw its head lower. The wide horns twist. Heat eased into the fleshy part of her, just below the ribs. Her neck spun and snapped. She knew not to move, to become as limp as the ragbag hanging in the woodshed, to not try again for the fence. Blueberries rained down on her, soft and cool. As gentle as spring mist.

Seconds or minutes or hours later, she lay with her face buried in sweet grass. She heard the far-off raspy call of a crow. From the great stillness, she knew that the bull was no longer there. Her head beat thickly. The berries? Where were the berries?

And then pain.

For a long while she lay still, her eyes too weighted to open. She knew that Matti would want his dinner, and she wondered

whether he had thought to stir the beans. She groped for the knot
in her kerchief, fumbling with it over the open wound. She whimpered because her clothes were torn.

She inched towards the fence. Lena. Lena would be coming.
Lena would see her. The prickly barbs of wire reached out, grabbed
her.

She thought of the clock on the shelf between the two front windows. The steady tick. Never stopping. She looked to the glaring
sun to judge the time. But she couldn't remember which way was
east.

Matti would go for the doctor. She had never seen the doctor
before. Had taken care of their ills herself. He would look at her,
see such a private part. She wanted to get home to wash herself.
The *sauna* would be cold. But there would be water. And soap.

Struggling to her feet, she glimpsed the faded purple kerchief,
now darkly stained as she clutched it to herself. She fought back a
rush of nausea. Again she remembered the *sauna,* needing to get
there.

It was in the *sauna* that Lena found her.

For the better part of a week, Kaisa didn't know one day from
another. She would wake and ask for water, seeing sometime Lena
and sometime Matti. She fretted about the lost berries, begging
Matti to go back and find them. Because he felt so helpless, Matti
climbed to the ridge and filled the cooking pot and milk pail he
had earlier retrieved. The berries were as clean as though Kaisa
herself had picked them. He carried them up to the loft bedroom
to show his wife. She smiled and drifted off to sleep.

Perhaps it was the rooster's first tentative morning call, or perhaps it was the faint glow of dawn just painting the horizon that
woke Kaisa. Or perhaps it was that she was hungry, hungrier it
seemed than she could ever remember being. It was strange to her
that she was alone in the room that she had shared with Matti all
these years. She slid her feet onto the cool floor and tried to stand,
but because of the nagging pull below her ribs and the weakness
in her legs, she fell back onto the pillow.

She took assurance in the familiar shapes in the dusky shadows.
The gentle curve of the footpiece of the iron bedstead. The cold
bedroom stove with its long pipe to the chimney. The smooth pitch-

er and bowl on the low commode. The gauzy curtain, barely stirring at the open window. From down below she heard Lena's voice, full of chatter so early in the morning. The dog Karhu barked from outside. The scent of coffee wafted upstairs, reminding her of her hunger.

She called to Matti, but her voice had no strength and wouldn't carry.

The sky turned from pink to violet, and although she had been watching, she wasn't able to say just when it happened.

She was, instead, remembering the fright. The heat. The pain. She remembered crawling through the fence, clutching the kerchief to the oozing hurt. She remembered the water spilling in the *sauna*. Lena carrying her. Lena holding a cup for her to drink. Lena crooning as she changed the dressing.

Kaisa insisted that Matti help her down the stairs to the kitchen for breakfast. As Lena fluttered about, Kaisa sat at her place at the round table, a shawl over her shoulders, and her long brown hair hanging loose.

"Soon you'll be as good as new," Lena clucked. "Oh, my!" And she flittered to Kaisa's side, taking up her limp hand to kiss it. "Ohhh — ! You haven't eaten for five days. And now you're hungry, eh? I'll make you a good breakfast. Then you'll be strong. Five days!"

Although Kaisa lacked bodily strength, her sight was as good as ever. Already she had spotted yesterday's crumbs on the table. The bright runner that ran along the middle of the floor was stained, the other two gritty and askew. Dishes were piled at the slate sink.

She caught her husband's eye as she picked up a biscuit, the bottom as black as the stovetop. But she turned it to butter it, so the black wouldn't show. Lena hovered close by, tense as a bird ready for flight, while Kaisa took a spoonful of beans. Kaisa glanced at Matti who waited with a dribbling knifeful ready to shovel into his open mouth. Never had she tasted such salty beans! They were *hot* with salt!

"What beans," she said, swallowing. "What beans. I now understand why Matti has talked about Lena's beans all these years." And then she added, "Lena, when I'm stronger, you should show me how to make these beans."

Pleasure flushed over Lena's face. "You like my beans, eh?" she asked, puffing with importance, hustling to the stove to scoop out more from the frying pan. "Now you go ahead and eat. Lena's beans will make you strong."

Kaisa nodded. She glanced at Matti and saw a smile twinkling in his eyes. "And while you're up, Lena, would you get me a little water? The fever, you know. It's made me so thirsty."

*Rebecca Cummings (1944-      ) was born in South Paris, Maine. She has a baccalaureate and M.A. from the University of Maine at Orono. A teacher, she has specialized in stories about Maine's Finnish community. In 1984 the Maine Arts Commission awarded her first prize in a fiction chapbook competition. This story first appeared in her collection KAISA KILPONEN (1985).*

# FALL

*I suppose that I was lonelier than I cared to admit, for I found myself dropping into the empty swimming club before lunch and drinking a cocktail on the terrace that looked over the unfilled pool and the bay.*

Greg's Peg

# GREG'S PEG

It was in the autumn of 1936 that I first met Gregory Bakewell, and the only reason that I met him then was that he and his mother were, besides myself and a handful of others, the only members of the summer colony at Anchor Harbor who had stayed past the middle of September. To the Bakewells it was a period of hard necessity; they had to sit out the bleak, lonely Maine September and October before they could return, with any sort of comfort, to the Florida home where they wintered. To me, on the other hand, these two months were the only endurable part of Anchor Harbor's season, and I had lingered all the summer in Massachusetts, at the small boarding school of which I was headmaster, until I knew that I would find the peninsula as deserted as I required. I had no worries that year about the opening of school, for I was on a sabbatical leave, long postponed, and free to do as I chose. Not, indeed, that I was in a mood to do much. I had lost my wife the year before, and for many months it had seemed to me that life was over, in early middle age. I had retreated rigidly and faithfully to an isolated routine. I had taught my courses and kept to myself, as much as a headmaster can, editing and re-editing what was to be the final, memorial volume of her poetry. But during that summer I had begun to look up from the blue notepaper on which she had written the small stanzas of her garden verse to find myself gazing out the window towards the campus with a blank steadiness that could only have been symptomatic, I feared, of the heresy of boredom. And thus it was with something of a sense of guilt and a little, perhaps, in that mood of

nostalgic self-pity that makes one try to recapture the melancholy
of remembered sorrow, that I traveled up to Anchor Harbor in
the fall.

My wife and I had spent our summers there in the past, not, as
one of her obituary notices had floridly put it, "away from the
summer resort in a forest camp, nestled in that corner of the
peninsula frequented by the literary," but in the large rambling
pile of shingle, full of pointless rooms and wicker furniture, that
belonged to my mother-in-law and that stood on the top of a
forest-covered hill in the very heart of the summer community.
In Anchor Harbor, however, the poets' corner and the watering
place were akin. Each was clouded in the haze of unreality that
hung so charmingly over the entire peninsula. It was indeed a
world unto itself. Blue, gray and green, the pattern repeated itself up and down, from the sky to the rocky mountaintops, from
the sloping pine woods to the long cliffs and gleaming cold of the
sea. It was an Eden in which it was hard to visualize a serpent.
People were never born there, nor did they die there. The elemental was left to the winter and other climes. The sun that
sparkled in the cocktails under the yellow and red umbrella
tables by the club pool was the same sun that dropped behind the
hills in the evening, lighting up the peninsula with pink amid the
pine trees. It was a land of big ugly houses, pleasant to live in, of
very old and very active ladies, of hills that were called mountains, of small, quaint shops and of large, shining town cars. When
in the morning I picked up the newspaper with its angry black
headlines it was not so much with a sense of their tidings being
false, as of their being childishly irrelevant.

By mid-September, however, the big summer houses were
closed and the last trunks of their owners were rattling in vans
down the main street past the swimming club to the station. The
sky was more frequently overcast; there was rain and fog, and
from the sea came the sharp cold breezes that told the advent of
an early winter. I was staying alone in my mother-in-law's house,
taking long walks on the mountains and going at night to the
movies. I suppose that I was lonelier than I cared to admit for I
found myself dropping into the empty swimming club before
lunch and drinking a cocktail on the terrace that looked over the
unfilled pool and the bay. There were not apt to be more than one

or two people there, usually the sort who had to maintain a residence in Maine for tax purposes, and I was not averse to condol-
ing with them for a few minutes each day. It was on a day when I
had not found even one of these that a youngish-looking man,
perhaps in his early thirties, approached the table where I was sitting. He was an oddly shaped and odd-looking person, wide in the
hips and narrow in the shoulders, and his face, very white and
round and smooth, had, somewhat inconsistently, the uncertain
dignity of a thin aquiline nose and large owl-like eyes. His long
hair was parted in the middle and plastered to his head with a
heavy tonic, and he was wearing, alas, a bow tie, a red blazer, and
white flannels, a combination which was even then out of date
except for sixth-form graduations at schools such as mine. All this
was certainly unprepossessing, and I shrank a bit as he approached
me, but there was in his large gray eyes as they gazed timidly
down at me a look of guilelessness, of cautious friendliness, of
anticipated rebuff that made me suddenly smile.

"My name is Gregory Bakewell. People call me Greg," he said
in a mild, pleasant voice less affected than I would have anticipated. "I hope you'll excuse my intrusion, but could you tell me if
they're going to continue the buffet lunch next week?"

I looked at him with a feeling of disappointment.

"I don't know," I said. "I never lunch here."

He stared with blinking eyes.

"But you ought. It's quite delicious."

I shrugged my shoulders, but he remained, obviously concerned
at what I was passing up.

"Perhaps you will join me for lunch today," he urged. "It's *su-
prême de volaille argentée.*"

I couldn't repress a laugh at his fantastic accent, and then to
cover it up and to excuse myself for not lunching with him I
asked him to have a drink. He sat down, and I introduced myself.
I confess that I expected that he might have heard of me, and I
looked into his owl eyes for some hint that he was impressed.
There was none.

"You weren't up here during the season?" he asked. "You've
just come?"

"That's right."

He shook his head.

"It's a pity you missed it. They say it was very gay."

I murmured something derogatory in general about the summer life at Anchor Harbor.

"You don't like it?" he asked.

"I can't abide it. Can you?"

"Me?" He appeared surprised that anyone should be interested in his reaction. "I don't really know. Mother and I go out so little. Except, of course, to the Bishop's. And dear old Mrs. Stone's."

I pictured him at a tea party, brushed and combed and wearing a bib. And eating an enormous cookie.

"I used to go out," I said.

"And now you don't?"

Even if he had never heard of me I was surprised, at Anchor Harbor, that he should not have heard of my wife. Ordinarily, I hope, I would not have said what I did say, but my need for communication was strong. I was suddenly and oddly determined to imprint my ego on the empty face of all that he took for granted.

"My wife died here," I said. "Last summer."

He looked even blanker than before, but gradually an expression of embarrassment came over his face.

"Oh, dear," he said. "I'm so sorry. Of course, if I'd known—"

I felt ashamed of myself.

"Of course," I said hurriedly. "Forgive me for mentioning it."

"But no," he protested. "I should have known. I remember now. They were speaking of her at Mrs. Stone's the other day. She was very beautiful, wasn't she?"

She hadn't been, but I nodded. I wanted even the sympathy that he could give me and swallowed greedily the small drops that fell from his meager supply.

"And which reminds me," he said, after we had talked in this vein for several minutes, "they spoke of you, too. You write things, don't you? Stories?"

I swallowed.

"I hope not," I said. "I'm an historian."

"Oh, that must be lovely."

I wondered if there was another man in the world who could have said it as he said it. He conveyed a sense of abysmal ignorance, but of humility, too, and of boundless admiration. These things were fine, were wonderful, he seemed to say, but he, too, had his little niche and a nice one, and he as well as these things existed, and we could be friends together, couldn't we?

I decided we were getting nowhere.

"What do you do?" I asked.

"Do?" Again he looked blank. "Why, good heavens, man, I don't do a thing."

I looked severe.

"Shouldn't you?"

"Should I?"

"You haven't got a family or anything like that?"

He smiled happily.

"Oh, I've got 'something like that,' " he answered. "I've got Mother."

I nodded. I knew everything now.

"Do you exercise?"

"I walk from Mother's cottage to the club. It's several hundred yards."

I rose to my feet.

"Tomorrow morning," I said firmly, "I'll pick you up here at nine-thirty. We're going to climb a mountain."

He gaped at me in horror and amazement as I got up to leave him, but he was there when I came by the next morning, waiting for me, dressed exactly as he had been the day before except for a pair of spotless white sneakers and a towel, pointlessly but athletically draped around his neck. He was very grateful to me for inviting him and told me with spirit how he had always wanted to climb a mountain at Anchor Harbor. These "mountains" were none higher than a thousand feet and the trails were easy; nonetheless I decided to start him on the smallest.

He did well enough, however. He perspired profusely and kept taking off garments as we went along, piling them on his arm, and he presented a sorry figure indeed as his long hair fell over his face and as the sweat poured down his white puffy back, but he kept up and bubbled over with talk. I asked him about his life, and he told me the dismal tale of a childhood spent under the cloud of a sickly constitution. He had been, of course, an only child, and his parents, though loving, had themselves enjoyed excellent health. He had never been to school or college; he had learned whatever it was that he did know from tutors. He had never left home, which for the Bakewells had been St. Louis until the death of Mr. Bakewell and was now St. Petersburg in Florida. Greg was thirty-five and presented to me in all his clumsy innocence a perfect *tabula rasa*. His mind was a piece of blank paper, of white, dead paper, on which, I supposed, one could write whatever message one chose. He appeared to have no prejudices or snobbishnesses; he was a guileless child who had long since ceased to fret, if indeed he ever had, at the confinements of his nursery. I could only look and gape, and yet at the same time feel the responsibility of writing the first line, for he seemed to enjoy an odd, easy content in his own placid life.

We had passed beyond the tree line and were walking along the smoother rock of the summit, a sharp cool breeze blowing in our faces. It was a breathtaking view, and I turned to see what Greg's reaction would be.

"Look," he said pointing to an ungainly shingle clock tower that protruded from the woods miles below us, "you can see the roof of Mrs. Stone's house."

I exploded.

"God!" I said.

"Don't be angry with me," he said mildly. "I was just pointing something out."

I could see that decisions had to be made and steps taken.

"Look, Greg," I said. "Don't go to St. Petersburg this winter."

He stared.

"But what would Mother do?"

I dismissed his mother with a gesture.

"Stay here. By yourself. Get to know the people who live here all the year round. Read. I'll send you books."

He looked dumbfounded.

"Then you won't be here?"

I laughed.

"I've got a job, man. I'm writing a book. But you're not. Give one winter to being away from your mother and Mrs. Stone and the Bishop, and learn to think. You won't know yourself in a year."

He appeared to regard this as not entirely a happy prognostication.

"But Mrs. Stone and the Bishop don't go to St. Petersburg," he pointed out.

"Even so," I said.

"I really don't think I could leave Mother."

I said nothing.

"You honestly think I ought to do something?" he persisted.

"I do."

"That's what Mother keeps telling me," he said dubiously.

"Well, she's right."

He looked at me in dismay.

"But what'll I do?"

"I've made one suggestion. Now it's your turn."

He sighed.

"Well, it's very hard," he said, "to know. You pick me up, and then you throw me down."

I felt some compunction at this.

"I'll write you," I said. "To St. Petersburg. You can keep me informed of your progress."

He beamed.

"Oh, that would be very kind," he said.

During the remaining two weeks of my visit to Anchor Harbor I walked with Greg almost every day, and we became friends. It was agreeable to be with someone whose admiration was unqualified. He listened to me with the utmost respect and attention and forgot everything I said a moment afterwards. But I didn't mind. It gave me a sense of ease about repeating myself; I talked of history and literature and love; I set myself up as counsel for the forces of life and argued my case at the bar of Greg's justice, pleading that the door might be opened just a crack. Yet whoever it was who represented the forces of his inertia was supplying very cogent arguments against me. I decided that it must be his mother, and I stopped at the Bakewells' one day after our walk to meet her.

Mrs. Bakewell I had made a picture of before I met her. She would be a small grim woman, always in black, mourning the husband whose existence one could never quite believe in; she would be wearing a black ribbon choker and a shiny black hat, and she would never change the weight or the quantity of her clothing, equally inappropriate for St. Petersburg or Anchor Harbor, for any such considerations as season or weather. I saw her thus as small, as compact, as uncompromising, because in my imagination she had had to wither to a little black stump, the hard remnants of the heaping blaze of what I visualized as her maternal possessiveness. How else could I possibly explain Gregory except in terms of such a mother? And when I did meet her each detail of her person seemed to spring up at me to justify my presupposition. She *was* a small, black figure, and she *did* wear a broad, tight choker. She was old, and she was unruffled; her large hook nose and her small eyes had about them the stillness of a hawk on a limb. When she spoke, it was with the cold calm of a convinced fanatic, and beyond the interminable details of her small talk that dealt almost exclusively with Episcopal dogma and Episcopal teas I seemed to catch the flickering light of a sixteenth-century *auto-da-fé*. But a vital element of my preconceived portrait was missing. She showed no weakness for her only child. Indeed, her attitude towards him, for all one could see, demonstrated the most commendable indifference. He had hatched from her egg and could play around the barnyard at his will. I discovered, furthermore, that unlike her son, she had read my books.

"It's very kind of you to take time off from your work to walk with Gregory," she said to me. "I don't suppose that he can be a very stimulating companion for an historian. He never reads anything."

Gregory simply nodded as she said this. She brought it forth without severity, as a mere matter of fact.

"Reading isn't everything," I said. "It's being aware of life that counts."

She looked at me penetratingly.

"Do you think so?" she asked. "Of course, I suppose you would. It's in line with your theories. The Bishop and I were interested in what you had to say about the free will of nations in your last book."

"Did you agree with it?"

"We did not."

Gregory looked at her in dismay.

"Now, Mother," he said protestingly, "you're not going to quarrel with my new friend?"

"I'm going to say what I wish, Gregory," she said firmly, "in my own house."

No, she certainly did not spoil him. Nor could it really be said that she was possessive. It was Greg who kept reaching for apron strings in which to enmesh himself. He seemed to yearn to be dominated. He tried vainly to have her make his decisions for him, and even after she had told him, as she invariably did, that he was old enough to think things through for himself, he would, not only behind her back but to her very face, insist to those around him that she ruled him with an iron hand. If I asked him to do something, to take a walk, to go to a movie, to dine, he would nod and smile and say "I'd love to," but he would surely add, and if she was there, perhaps in a lower tone, behind his hand: "But I'll have to get back early, you know. Mother will want to hear all about it before she goes to bed." And Mrs. Bakewell, overhearing him, with her small, fixed grim smile, did not even deign to contradict.

2

During that winter, when I was working on my book in Cambridge, I forgot poor Greg almost completely, as I usually did Anchor Harbor people. They were summer figures, and I stored them away in camphor balls with my flannels. I was surprised, therefore, each time that I received a letter from him, on the stationery of a large St. Petersburg hotel, protesting in a few lines of wretched scrawl that he had really met a number of very nice people, and could I possibly come down for a visit and meet them? One of them, I remember, he thought I would like because she wrote children's plays. I wrote him one letter and sent him a Christmas card, and that, I decided, was that.

I was in a better frame of mind when I went up to Anchor Harbor towards the end of the following July to stay with my mother-in-law. I was still keeping largely to myself, but the volume of my wife's poems was finished and in the hands of the publishers, and I no longer went out of my way to spurn people. I asked my mother-in-law one afternoon while we were sitting on the porch if the Bakewells were back in Anchor Harbor.

"Yes, I saw Edith Bakewell yesterday at Mrs. Stone's," she said. "Such an odd, stiff woman. I didn't know you knew them."

"Was her son there?"

"Greg? Oh, yes, he's always with her. Don't tell me *he's* a friend of yours?''

"After a fashion."

"Well, there's no accounting for tastes. I can't see a thing in him, but the old girls seem to like him. I drew him as a partner the other night at the bridge table."

"Oh, does he play bridge now?"

"If you can call it that," my mother-in-law said with a sniff. "But he certainly gets around. In my set, anyway. I never go out that I don't run into him."

"Really? Last fall he knew nobody."

"And Anchor Harbor was a better place."

Little by little I became aware that my friend's increased appearances in the summer-colony world was part of some preconceived and possibly elaborate plan of social self-advancement. He was not, I realized with a mild surprise, simply floating in the brisk wake of his mother's determined spurts; he was splashing gayly down a little back water on a course that must have had the benefit of his own navigation. At the swimming club he had abandoned the lonely couch near the table of fashion magazines, where he used to wait for his mother, for the gay groups of old ladies in flowered hats who gathered daily at high noon around the umbrella tables and waited for the sun to go over the yardarm and the waiters to come hurrying with the first glad cocktail of the day. I was vaguely disgusted at all of this, though I had no reason, as I well knew, to have expected better things, but my disgust became pointed after I had twice telephoned him to ask him for a walk and twice had to listen to his protests of a previous engagement. I wondered if he fancied that his social position was now too lofty to allow of further intimacy between us, and I laughed to myself, but rather nastily, at the idea. I would have crossed him off my books irrevocably had I not met him one day when I was taking my mother-in-law to call on old Mrs. Stone. We had found her alone, sitting on the porch with her back to the view, and were making rather slow going of a conversation about one of my books when her daughter, Theodora, came in with a group of people, including Greg, who had just returned from what seemed to have been a fairly alcoholic picnic. I found myself caught, abandoned by my fleeing mother-in-law, in the throes of a sudden cocktail party.

"My God!" cried Theodora as she spotted me. "If it isn't Arnold of Rugby!"

I had always been rather a favorite of Theodora's, for she had regarded, in the light of the subsequent tragedy, her very casual friendship with my wife, of the kind that are based on childhood animosity and little more, as the deepest relationship that she had ever known. And in all seriousness it may have been. Theodora had had little time, in her four marriages, for friendships with women. At the moment she was in one of her brief husbandless periods, and her energy, unrestrained, swept across the peninsula like a forest fire. She drew me aside, out on the far end of the huge porch, hugging my arm as she did when she had had one drink too many and hissed in my ear, with the catlike affectation that purported to be a caricature of itself and which, presumably, a minimum of four men had found attractive:

"Isn't he precious?"

"Who?"

"Little Gregory, of course." And she burst into a laugh. "He tells me that you were kind to him. Great big you!"

"Where on earth did you pick him up?"

"Right here." She indicated the porch. "Right here at Mummie's. I found him in the teapot. The old bitches were stuffing him into it, as if he were the dormouse, poor precious, so I hustled right over and caught him by the fanny and pulled and pulled till he came out with a pop. And now he's mine. All mine. You can't have him."

I glanced over to where Gregory was talking to two women in slacks. His white flannels looked a tiny bit dirtier, and he was holding a cocktail rather self-consciously in his round white hand.

"I'm not sure I want him," I said gravely. "You seem to have spoiled him already."

"Oh, precious," she said, cuddling up to me. "Do you think Theodora would do that?"

"Is he to be Number Five?"

She looked up at me with her wide serious eyes.

"But could he be, darling? I mean, after all, what sex is he? Or *is* he?"

I shrugged my shoulders.

"How much does that matter at our age, Theodora?"

She was, as always, a good sport. She threw back her head and howled with laughter.

"Oh, it matters!" she exclaimed. "I tell you what, darling. Greg will be Number Seven. Or maybe even Number Six. But not the next one. No, dear. Not the next one."

I found it in me to speculate if I had not perhaps been selected on the spot for that dubious honor. Anyway, I decided to go. Conversation with Theodora who believed so patently, so brazenly, in nothing and nobody, always made me nervous. As I re-entered the house and was crossing the front hall I heard my name called. It was Greg. He ran after me and caught me by the arm at the front door.

"You're leaving!" he protested. "And you haven't even spoken to me!"

"I'm speaking to you now," I said shortly.

To my dismay he sat down on the stone bench under the porte-cochère and started to cry. He did not cry loudly or embarrassingly; his chest rose and fell with quiet, orderly sobs.

"My God, man!" I exclaimed.

"I knew you were mad at me," he whimpered, "by the way you spoke on the telephone when I couldn't go on a walk with you. But I didn't know you wouldn't even speak to me when you saw me!"

"I'm sorry," I said fretfully.

"You don't know what you've meant to me," he went on dolefully, rubbing his eyes. "You have no idea. You're the first person who ever asked me to do anything in my whole life. When you asked me to go for a walk with you. Last summer."

"Well, I did this summer too."

"Yes," he said, shaking his head, "I know. And I couldn't go. But the reason I couldn't go was that I was busy. And the reason I was busy was what you told me."

I stared down at him.

"What the hell did I tell you?"

"To do things. See people. Be somebody." He looked up at me now with dried eyes. There was suddenly and quite unexpectedly almost a note of confidence in his tone.

"And how do you do that?"

"The only way I can. I go out."

I ran my hand through my hair in a confusion of reluctant amusement and despair.

"I didn't mean it that way, Greg," I protested. "I wanted you to see the world. Life. Before it was too late."

He nodded placidly.

"That's what I'm doing," he said.

"But I wanted you to read big books and think big thoughts," I said desperately. "How can you twist that into my telling you to become a tea caddy?"

His wide thoughtless eyes were filled with reproach.

"You knew I couldn't read books," he said gravely. "Or think big thoughts. You were playing with me."

I stared.

"Then why did you think you had to do anything?"

"Because you made me want to." He looked away, across the gravel, into the deep green of the forest. "I could feel your contempt. I had never felt that before. No one had ever cared enough to feel contempt. Except you."

As I looked at him I wondered if there were any traces of his having felt such a sting. I was baffled, almost angry at his very expressionlessness. That he could sit and indict me so appallingly for my interference, could face me with so direct a responsibility, was surely a dreadful thing if he cared, but if he didn't, if he was simply making a fool of me . . .

"I hope you don't think," I said brutally, "that you can lessen any contempt that you think I may feel for you by becoming a social lion in Anchor Harbor."

He shook his head.

"No," he said firmly. "Your contempt is something I shall have to put up with. No matter what I do. I can't read or think or talk the way you do. I can't work. I can't even cut any sort of figure with the girls. There aren't many things open to me. You're like my mother. You know that, really, but you think of me as if I was somebody else."

I took a cigarette out of my case, lit it and sat down beside him. From around the corner of the big house came a burst of laughter from Theodora's friends.

"Where are you headed, then, Greg?" I asked him as sympathetically as I could.

He turned and faced me.

"To the top of the peninsula," he said. "I'm going to be a social leader."

I burst into a rude laugh.

"The *arbiter elegantiarum* of Anchor Harbor?" I cried.

"I don't know what that means," he said gravely.

Again I laughed. The sheer inanity of it had collapsed my mounting sympathy.

"You're mad," I said sharply. "You haven't got money or looks or even wit. Your bridge is lousy. You play no sports. Let's face it, man. You'll never make it. Even in this crazy place."

Greg seemed in no way perturbed by my roughness. His humility was complete. The only thing, I quickly divined, that could arouse the flow of his tears was to turn from him. As long as one spoke to him, one could say anything.

"Everything you say is true," he conceded blandly. "I'd be the last to deny it. But you watch. I'll get there."

"With the old ladies, perhaps," I said scornfully. "If that's what you want."

"I have to start with the old ladies," he said. "I don't know anyone else."

"And after the old ladies?"

But he had thought this out.

"They all have daughters or granddaughters," he explained. "Like Theodora. They'll get used to me."

"And you're 'cute,' " I said meanly. "You're a 'dear.' Yes, I see it. If it's what you want." I got up and started across the gravel to my car. He came after me.

"I'm not going to hurt anyone, you know," he said. "I only want to be a respected citizen."

In the car I leaned out to speak to him.

"Suppose I tell them?"

"About my plans?"

"What else?"

"Do. It won't make any difference. You'll see."

I started the motor and drove off without so much as nodding to him.

3

Gregory was good to his word. Every ounce of energy in his small store was directed to the attainment of his clearly conceived goal. I had resolved in disgust to have no further dealings with him, and I adhered to my resolution, but curiosity and a sense of the tiny drama latent in his plans kept me during the rest of that summer and the following two with an ear always alert at the mention of his name for further details of his social clamber.

Little by little Anchor Harbor began to take note of the emergence of this new personality. Greg had been right to start with the old ladies, though he had had, it was true, no alternative. The appearance of this bland young man with such innocent eyes and wide hips and such ridiculous blazers would have been followed by brusque repulse in any young or even middle-aged group of the summer colony, intent as they were on bridge, liquor, sport and sex. In the elderly circles, however, Greg had only to polish his bridge to the point of respectability, and he became a welcome addition at their dinner parties. His conversation, though certainly tepid, was soothing and enthusiastic, and he could listen, without interrupting, to the longest and most frequently repeated anecdote. He liked everybody and every dinner; he radiated an unobtrusive but gratifying satisfaction with life. Once he became known as a person who could be counted upon to accept, his evenings were gradually filled. The old in Anchor Harbor had an energy that put their descendants to shame. Dinner parties even in the septagenarian group were apt to last till two in the morning, and in the bridge circles rubber would succeed rubber until the sun peeked in through the blinds to cast a weird light on the butt-filled ash trays and the empty, sticky highball glasses. The old were still up when the young came in from their more hectic but less prolonged evenings of enjoyment, and Gregory came gradually, in the relaxed hours of the early morning, to meet the children and grandchildren of his hostesses. Friction, however, often ran high between the generations, even at such times, and he found his opportunity as peacemaker. He came to be noted for his skill in transmitting messages, with conciliatory amendments of his own, from mother to daughter, from aunt to niece. Everyone found him useful. He became in short a "character," accepted by all ages, and in that valuable capacity immune from criticism. He was "dear old Greg," "our lovable, ridiculous Greg." One heard more and more such remarks as, "Where but in Anchor Harbor would you find a type like Greg?" and "You know, I *like* Greg." And, I suppose, even had none of the foregoing been true, he would have succeeded as Theodora's pet, her "discovery," her lap dog, if you will, a comfortable, consoling eunuch in a world that had produced altogether too many men.

That Mrs. Bakewell would have little enough enthusiasm for her son's being taken to the hearts of Theodora and her set I was moderately sure, but the extent of her animosity I was not to learn until I came across her one hot August afternoon at the book counter of the stationery store which was a meeting place second only in importance to the club. She was standing very stiffly but obviously intent upon the pages of a large volume of Dr. Fosdick. She looked up in some bewilderment when I greeted her.

"I was just looking," she said. "I don't want anything, thank you."

I explained that I was not the clerk.

"I'm sorry," she said without embarrassment. "I didn't recognize you."

"Well, it's been a long time," I admitted. "I only come here for short visits."

"It's a very trivial life, I'm afraid."

"Mine? I'm afraid so."

"No," she said severely and without apology. "The life up here."

"Greg seems to like it."

She looked at me for a moment. She did not smile.

"They're killing him," she said.

I stared.

"They?"

"That wicked woman. And her associates." She looked back at her book. "But I forgot. You're of the new generation. My adjective was anachronistic."

"I liked it."

She looked back at me.

"Then save him."

"But, Mrs. Bakewell," I protested. "People don't *save* people at Anchor Harbor."

"More's the pity," she said dryly.

I tried to minimize it.

"Greg's all right," I murmured. "He's having a good time."

She closed the book.

"Drinking the way he does?"

"Does he drink?"

"Shockingly."

I shrugged my shoulders. When people like Mrs. Bakewell used the word it was hard to know if they meant an occasional cocktail or a life of confirmed dipsomania.

"And that woman?" she persevered. "Do you approve of her?"

"Oh, Mrs. Bakewell," I protested earnestly. "I'm sure there's nothing wrong between him and Theodora."

She looked at me, I thought, with contempt.

"I was thinking of their souls," she said. "Good day, sir."

I discovered shortly after this awkward interchange that there was a justification in her remarks about Greg's drinking. I went one day to a large garden party given by Mrs. Stone. All Anchor Harbor was there, old and young, and Theodora's set, somewhat contemptuous of the throng and present, no doubt, only because of Theodora, who had an odd conventionality about attending family parties, were clustered in a group near the punch bowl and exploding periodically in loud laughs. They were not laughing, I should explain, at the rest of us, but at something white-flanneled and adipose in their midst, something with a blank face and strangely bleary eyes. It was Greg, of course, and he was telling them a story, stammering and repeating himself as he did so to the great enjoyment of the little group. It came over me gradually as I watched him that Mrs. Bakewell was right. They *were* killing him. Their laughter was as cold and their acclaim as temporary as that of any audience in the arena of Rome or Constantinople. They could clap hands and cheer, they could spoil their favorites, but they could turn their thumbs down, too, and could one doubt for a moment that at the first slight hint of deteriorating performance, they would? I felt a chill in my veins as their laughter came to me again across the lawn and as I caught sight of the small, spare, dignified figure of Greg's mother standing on the porch with the Bishop and surveying the party with eyes that said nothing. If there were Romans to build fires, *there* was a martyr

worthy of their sport. But Gregory. Our eyes suddenly met, and I
thought I could see the appeal in them; I thought I could feel his
plea for rescue flutter towards me in my isolation through the
golden air of the peninsula. Was that why his mother had come?
As I turned to her I thought that she, too, was looking at me.

He had left his group. He was coming over to me.

"Well?" I said.

"Come over and meet these people," he said to me, taking me
by the arm. "Come on. They're charming." He swayed slightly
as he spoke.

I shook my arm loose.

"I don't want to."

He looked at me with his mild, steady look.

"Please," he urged.

"I said no," I snapped. "Why should I want to clutter my summer with trash like that? Go on back to them. Eat garbage. You
like it."

He balanced for a moment on the balls of his feet. Evidently he
regarded my violence as something indigenous to my nature and
to be ignored.

"Theodora's never been in better form," he held out to me as
bait.

"Good for Theodora," I said curtly. "And in case you don't
know it, you're drunk."

He shook his head sadly at me and wandered slowly back to
his group.

4

Gregory went from glory to glory. He became one of the respected
citizens of the summer colony. His spotless white panama was to
be seen bobbing on the bench of judges at the children's swimming
meet. He received the prize two years running for the best costume at the fancy dress ball. On each occasion he went as a baby.
He was a sponsor of the summer theater, the outdoor concerts,
and the putting tournament. He was frequently seated on the right
of his hostess at the very grandest dinners. He arrived early in
the season and stayed into October. What he did during the winter
months was something of a mystery, but it was certain that he

did not enjoy elsewhere a success corresponding to his triumph at Anchor Harbor. Presumably, like so many Anchor Harbor people whose existence away from the peninsula it was so difficult to conceive, he went into winter hibernation to rest up for his exhausting summers.

That he continued to drink too much when he went out, which was, of course, all the time, did not, apparently, impair his social position. He was firmly entrenched, as I have said, in his chosen category of "character," and to these much is allowed. Why he drank I could only surmise. It might have been to steady himself in the face of a success that was as unnerving as it was unfamiliar; it might have been to make him forget the absurdity of his ambitions and the hollowness of their fulfillment, or it might even have been to shelter himself from the bleak wind of his mother's reproach. Theodora and all her crowd drank a great deal. It was possible that he had simply picked up the habit from them. It would have gone unnoticed, at least in that set, had it not been for a new and distressing habit that he had developed, of doing, after a certain number of drinks, a little dance by himself, a sort of jig, that was known as "Greg's peg." At first he did it only for a chosen few, late at night, amid friendly laughter, but word spread, and the little jig became an established feature of social life on Saturday night dances at the club. There would be a roll of drums, and everybody would stop dancing and gather in a big circle while the sympathetic orchestra beat time to the crazy marionette in the center. Needless to say I had avoided being a witness of "Greg's peg," but my immunity was not to last.

It so happened that the first time that I was to see this sordid performance was the last time that it ever took place. It was on a Saturday night at the swimming-club dance, the festivity that crowned the seven-day madness known as "tennis week," the very height, mind you, of Anchor Harbor's dizzy summer of gaiety. Even my mother-in-law and I had pulled ourselves sufficiently together to ask a few friends for dinner and take them on to the club. We found the place milling with people and a very large band playing very loudly. I noticed several young men who were not in evening dress and others whose evening clothes had obviously been borrowed, strong, ruddy, husky young men. It was the cruise season, and the comfortable, easy atmosphere of overdressed but companionable Anchor Harbor was stiffened by an infiltration of moneyed athleticism and arrogance from the distant smartness of Long Island and Newport. All throbbed, however, to the same music, and all seemed to be enjoying themselves. Theodora, in a sweater and pleated skirt and large pearls, dressed to look as though she were off a sailboat and not, as she was, fresh from her own establishment, spotted me and with characteristic aplomb deserted her partner and came over to our table. She took in my guests with an inclusive, final and undiscriminating smile that might have been a greeting or a shower of alms, took a seat at the table and monopolized me.

"Think of it," she drawled. "You at a dance. What's happened? Well, anyway," she continued without waiting for my answer, "I approve. See life. Come for lunch tomorrow. Will you? Two o'clock. I'll have some people who might amuse you."

Since her mother's death Theodora had begun to take on the attributes of queen of the peninsula. She dealt out her approval and disapproval as if it was possible that somebody cared. Struggling behind the wall of her make-up, her mannerisms and her marriages one could sense the real Theodora, strangled at birth, a dowager, with set lips and outcasting frown, a figure in pearls for an opera box. I declined her invitation and asked if Gregory was going to do his dance.

"Oh, the darling," she said huskily. "Of course, he will. I'll get hold of him in a minute and shoo these people off the floor."

"Don't do it for me," I protested. "I don't want to see it. I hear it's a disgusting sight."

She snorted.

"Whoever told you that?" she retorted. "It's the darling's precious little stunt. Wait till you see it. Oh, I know you don't like him," she continued wagging her finger at me. "He's told me that enough times, the poor dear. You've hurt him dreadfully. You pretend you can't stand society when the only thing you can't stand is anything the least bit unconventional."

I wondered if this were not possibly true. She continued to stare at me from very close range. It was always impossible to tell if she was drunk or sober.

"Like his old bitch of a mother," she continued.

"That's a cruel thing to say, Theodora," I protested sharply.

"Do you even know her?"

"Certainly I know her. She's sat on poor Greg all his life. Lord knows what dreadful things she did to him when he was a child."

"Greg told you this?"

"He never complains, poor dear. But I'm no fool. I can read between the lines."

"If she's a bitch you know what that makes him," I said stiffly.

"I was going to ask you tonight to give him back to his mother. She's the one person who knows what you're doing to him. But now I don't want to. It's too late. Keep him. Finish the dirty job."

"You must be drunk," she said and left me.

It was not long after this that the orchestra suddenly struck up a monotonous little piece with a singsong refrain and as at a concerted signal the couples on the floor gathered in a half-circle around the music, leaving a space in which something evidently was going on. The non-Anchor Harborites on the floor did not know what it was all about, but they joined with the others to make an audience for the diversion. I could see nothing but backs from where I was sitting, and suddenly hearing the laughter and applause and an odd tapping sound, I was overcome with curiosity and, taking my mother-in-law, we hurried across the dance floor and peered between the heads that barred our view.

What I saw there I shall never be able to get out of my mind. In the center of the half-circle formed by the crowd Gregory was dancing his dance. His eyes were closed and his long hair, disarrayed, was streaked down over his sweating face. His mouth, half open, emitted little snorts as his feet capered about in a preposterous jig that could only be described as an abortive effort at tap dancing. His arms moved back and forth as if he were striding along; his head was thrown back; his body shimmied from side to side. It was not really a dance at all; it was a contortion, a writhing. It looked more as if he were moving in a doped sleep or twitching at the end of a gallows. The lump of pallid softness that was his body seemed to be responding for the first time to his consciousness; it was only thus, after all, that the creature could use it. I turned in horror from the drunken jigger to his audience and noted the laughing faces, heard with disgust the "Go it, Greg!" It was worse now than the hysterical arena; it had all the obscenity of a strip-tease.

As I turned back to the sight of Gregory, his eyes opened, and I think he saw me. I thought for a second that once again I could make out the agonized appeal, but again I may have been wrong. It seemed to me that his soul, over which Mrs. Bakewell had expressed such concern, must have been as his body, white and doughy, possessed of no positive good and no positive evil, but a great passive husk on which the viri of the latter, once settled, could tear away. I turned to my mother-in-law who shared my disgust; we were about to go back to our table when I heard, behind us, snatches of a conversation from a group that appeared to feel even more strongly than we did. Looking back, I saw several young men in flannels and tweed coats, obviously from a cruise.

"Who the hell is that pansy?"

"Did you ever see the like of it?"

"Oh, it's Anchor Harbor. They're all that way."

"Let's throw him in the pool."

"Yes!"

I recognized one of them as a graduate of my school. I took him aside.

"Watch out for your friends, Sammy," I warned him. "Don't let them touch him. Remember. This is his club and not yours. And every old lady on the peninsula will be after you to tear your eyes out."

He nodded.

"Yes, sir. Thank you."

This may have kept Sammy under control, but his friends were another matter. When Greg had finished his jig and just as general dancing was about to be resumed, four young men stepped up to him and quietly lifted him in the air, perching him on the shoulders of two of their number. They then proceeded to carry him around the room. This was interpreted as a sort of triumphal parade, as though students were unhorsing and dragging a prima donna's carriage through enthusiastic streets, and everybody applauded vociferously while Greg, looking rather dazed, smiled and fluttered his handkerchief at the crowd. Even I, forewarned, was concluding that it was all in good fun when suddenly the four young men broke into a little trot and scampered with their burden out onto the porch, down the flagstone steps and across the patch of lawn with the umbrella tables to where the long pool shimmered under the searchlight on the clubhouse roof. People surged out on the terrace to watch them; I rushed out myself and got there just in time to see the four young men, two holding the victim's arms and two his legs, swinging him slowly back and forth at the edge of the pool. There was a moment of awful silence; then I heard Theodora's shriek, and several ladies rushed across the lawn to stop them. It was too late. There was a roar from the crowd as Greg was suddenly precipitated into the air. He hung there for a split second in the glare of the searchlights, his hair flying out; then came the loud splash as he disappeared. A moment later he reappeared and burbled for help. There were shouts of "He can't swim" and at least three people must have jumped in after him. He was rescued and restored to a crowd of solicitous ladies in evening dress who gathered at the edge of the pool to receive him in their arms, regardless of his wetness. At this point I turned to go. I had no wish to see the four young men lynched. I heard later that they managed to escape with their skins and to their boats. They did not come back.

5

Gregory appeared to have developed nothing but a bad cold from the mishap. He spent the next two days in bed, and the driveway before his mother's little cottage was jammed with tall and ancient Lincoln and Pierce-Arrow town cars bringing flowers from his devoted friends. When he recovered Theodora gave a large lunch for him at the club. Everybody was very kind. But it became apparent after a little that, however trivial the physical damage may have been, something in the events of that momentous evening had impaired the native cheerfulness of Greg's sunny disposition. On Saturday nights he could no longer be prevailed upon to do his little dance, and at high noon his presence was frequently missed under the umbrella tables when the waiters in scarlet coats came hurrying with the first Martini of the day. Theodora even spread the extraordinary news that he was thinking of going with his mother to Cape Cod the following summer. He had told her that the pace at Anchor Harbor was bad for his heart.

"That old witch of a mother has got her claws back into him," she told me firmly. "Mark my words. You'll see."

But I suspected that even Greg could see what I could see, that despite the sympathy and the flowers, despite the public outcry against the rude young men, despite the appeal in every face that things would again and always be as they had been before, despite all this, he had become "poor Greg." What had happened to him was not the sort of thing that happened to other people. When all was said and done, he may have known, as I knew, that in the last analysis even Theodora was on the side of the four young men. And perhaps he did realize it, for he was never heard to complain. Silently he accepted the verdict, if verdict it was, and disappeared early that September with his mother to St. Petersburg. I never heard of him again until several years later I chanced to read of his death of a heart attack in Cape Cod. I asked some friends of mine who spent the summer there if they had ever heard of him. Only one had. He said that he remembered Greg as a strange pallid individual who was to be seen in the village carrying a basket during his mother's marketing. She had survived him, and her mourning, if possible, was now a shade darker than before.

*Louis Auchincloss (1917-      ), born in New York City, was a Phi Beta Kappa at Yale and received a law degree from the University of Virginia. Perhaps most noted for THE RECTOR OF JUSTIN (1964), he has produced approximately twenty-five books of fiction and another ten of criticism. This story first appeared in THE INJUSTICE COLLECTORS (1950).*

# A BUNDLE
# OF LETTERS

FROM MISS MIRANDA HOPE IN PARIS TO MRS. ABRAHAM C. HOPE
AT BANGOR, MAINE

*September 5, 1879.*

M y Dear Mother.

I've kept you posted as far as Tuesday week last, and though my letter won't have reached you yet I'll begin another before my news accumulates too much. I'm glad you show my letters round in the family, for I like them all to know what I'm doing, and I can't write to everyone, even if I do try to answer all reasonable expectations. There are a great many unreasonable ones, as I suppose you know — not yours, dear mother, for I'm bound to say that you never required of me more than was natural. You see you're reaping your reward: I write to you before I write to any one else.

There's one thing I hope — that you don't show any of my letters to William Platt. If he wants to see any of my letters he knows the right way to go to work. I wouldn't have him see one of these letters, written for circulation in the family, for anything in the world. If he wants one for himself he has got to write to me first. Let him write to me first and then I'll see about answering him. You can show him this if you like; but if you show him anything more, I'll never write to you again.

I told you in my last about my farewell to England, my crossing the Channel and my first impressions of Paris. I've thought a great deal about that lovely England since I left it, and all the famous historic scenes I visited; but I've come to the conclusion that it's not a country in which I should care to reside. The position of woman doesn't seem to me at all satisfactory, and that's a point, you know, on which I feel very strongly. It seems to me that in England they play a very faded-out part, and those with whom I conversed had a kind of downtrodden tone, a spiritless and even benighted air, as if they were used to being snubbed and bullied *and as if they liked it,* which made me want to give them a good shaking. There are a great many people — and a great many things too — over here that I should like to get at for that purpose. I should like to shake the starch out of some of them and the dust out of the others. I know fifty girls in Bangor that come much more up to my notion of the stand a truly noble woman should take than those young ladies in England. But they had the sweetest way of speaking, as if it were a second nature, and the men are *remarkably handsome.* (You can show *that* to William Platt if you like.)

I gave you my first impressions of Paris, which quite came up to my expectations, much as I had heard and read about it. The objects of interest are extremely numerous, and the climate remarkably cheerful and sunny. I should say the position of woman here was considerably higher, though by no means up to the American standard. The manners of the people are in some respects extremely peculiar, and I feel at last that I'm indeed in *foreign parts.* It is, however, a truly elegant city (much more majestic than New York) and I've spent a great deal of time in visiting the various monuments and palaces. I won't give you an account of all my wanderings, though I've been most indefatigable; for I'm keeping, as I told you before, a most *exhaustive* journal, which I'll allow you the *privilege* of reading on my return to Bangor. I'm getting on remarkably well, and I must say I'm sometimes surprised at my universal good fortune. It only shows what a little Bangor energy and gumption will accomplish wherever applied. I've discovered none of those objections to a young lady travelling in Europe by herself of which we heard so much before I left, and I don't expect I ever shall, for I certainly don't mean to look for them. I know what I want and I always go straight for it.

I've received a great deal of politeness — some of it really most pressing, and have experienced no drawbacks whatever. I've made a great many pleasant acquaintances in travelling round — both ladies and gentlemen — and had a great many interesting and open-hearted, if quite informal, talks. I've collected a great many remarkable facts — I guess we don't know quite *everything* at Bangor — for which I refer you to my journal. I assure you my journal's going to be a splendid picture of an earnest young life. I do just exactly as I do in Bangor, and I find I do perfectly right. At any rate I don't care if I don't. I didn't come to Europe to lead a merely conventional society life: I could do that at Bangor. You know I never *would* do it at Bangor, so it isn't likely I'm going to worship false gods over here. So long as I accomplish what I desire and make my money hold out I shall regard the thing as a success. Sometimes I feel rather lonely, especially evenings; but I generally manage to interest myself in something or in some one. I mostly read up, evenings, on the objects of interest I've visited during the day, or put in time on my journal. Sometimes I go to the theatre or else play the piano in the public parlour. The public parlour at the hotel isn't much; but the piano's better than that fearful old thing at the Sebago House. Sometimes I go downstairs and talk to the lady who keeps the books — a real French lady, who's remarkably polite. She's very handsome, though in the peculiar French way, and always wears a black dress of the most beautiful fit. She speaks a little English; she tells me she had to learn it in order to converse with the Americans who come in such numbers to this hotel. She has given me lots of points on the position of woman in France, and seems to think that on the whole there's hope. But she has told me at the same time some things I shouldn't like to write to you — I'm hesitating even about putting them into my journal — especially if my letters are to be handed round in the family. I assure you they appear to talk about things here that we never think of mentioning at Bangor, even to ourselves or to our very closest; and it has struck me that people are closer — to each other — down in Maine than seems mostly to be expected here. This bright-minded lady appears at any rate to think she can tell me everything because I've told her I'm travelling for general culture. Well, I *do* want to know so much that it seems sometimes as if I wanted to know most everything; and yet I guess there are some things that don't count for improvement. But as a general thing everything's intensely interesting; I don't mean only everything this charming woman tells me, but everything I see and hear for myself. I guess I'll come out where I want.

I meet a great many Americans who, as a general thing, I must say, are not so polite to me as the people over here. The people over here — especially the gentlemen — are much more what I should call almost oppressively attentive. I don't know whether Americans are more truly sincere; I haven't yet made up my mind about that. The only drawback I experience is when Americans sometimes express surprise that I should be travelling round alone; so you see it doesn't come from Europeans. I always have my answer ready: "For general culture, to acquire the languages and to see Europe for myself;" and that generally seems to calm them. Dear mother, my money holds out very well, and it *is* real interesting.

II

FROM THE SAME TO THE SAME

*September 16.*

Since I last wrote to you I've left that nice hotel and come to live in a French family — which however is nice too. This place is a kind of boarding-house that's at the same time a kind of school; only it's not like an American boarding-house, nor like an American school either. There are four or five people here that have come to learn the language — not to take lessons, but to have an opportunity for conversation. I was very glad to come to such a place, for I had begun to realise that I wasn't pressing onward quite as I had dreamed with the French. Wasn't I going to feel ashamed to have spent two months in Paris and not to have acquired more insight into the language? I had always heard so much of French conversation, and I found I wasn't having much more opportunity to practise it than if I had remained at Bangor. In fact I used to hear a great deal more at Bangor from those French-Canadians who came down to cut the ice than I saw I should ever hear at that nice hotel where there was no struggle — *some* fond struggle being my real atmosphere. The lady who kept the books seemed to want so much to talk to me in English (for the sake of practice, too, I suppose — she kind of yearned to struggle too: we don't yearn *only* down in Maine—) that I couldn't bear to show her I didn't like it. The chambermaid was Irish and all the waiters German, so I never heard a word of French spoken. I suppose you might hear a great deal in the shops; but as I don't buy anything — I prefer to spend my money for purposes of culture — I don't have that advantage.

I've been thinking some of taking a teacher, but am well acquainted with the grammar already, and over here in Europe teachers don't seem to think it's *really* in their interest to let you press forward. The more you strike out and realise your power the less they've got to teach you. I was a good deal troubled anyhow, for I felt as if I didn't want to go away without having at least got a general idea of French conversation. The theatre gives you a good deal of insight, and as I told you in my last I go a good deal to the brightest places of amusement. I find no difficulty whatever in going to such places alone, and am always treated with the politeness which, as I've mentioned — for I want you to feel happy about that — I encounter everywhere from the best people. I see plenty of other ladies alone (mostly French) and they generally seem to be enjoying themselves as much as I. Only on the stage every one talks so fast that I can scarcely make out what they say; and, besides, there are a great many vulgar expressions which it's unnecessary to learn. But it was this experience nevertheless that put me on the track. The very next day after I wrote to you last I went to the Palais Royal, which is one of the principal theatres in Paris. It's very small but very celebrated, and in my guide-book it's marked with *two stars,* which is a sign of importance attached only to *first-class* objects of interest. But after I had been there half an hour I found I couldn't understand a single word of the play, they gabbled it off so fast and made use of such peculiar expressions. I felt a good deal disappointed and checked — I saw I wasn't going to come out where I had dreamed. But while I was thinking it over — thinking what I *would* do — I heard two gentlemen talking behind me. It was between the acts, and I couldn't help listening to what they said. They were talking English, but I guess they were Americans.

"Well," said one of them, "it all depends on what you're after. I'm after French; that's what I'm after."

"Well," said the other, "I'm after Art."

"Well," said the first, "I'm after Art too; but I'm after French most."

Then, dear mother, I'm sorry to say the second one swore a little. He said "Oh damn French!"

"No, I won't damn French," said his friend. "I'll acquire it — that's what I'll do with it. I'll go right into a family."

"What family'll you go into?"

"Into some nice French family. That's the only way to do — to go to some place where you can talk. If you're after Art you want to stick to the galleries; you want to go right through the Louvre, room by room; you want to take a room a day, or something of that sort. But if you want to acquire French the thing is to look out for some family that has got — and they mostly have — more of it than they've use for themselves. How *can* they have use for so much as they seem to *have* to have? They've got to work it off. Well, they work it off on *you.* There are lots of them that take you to board and teach you. My second cousin — that young lady I told you about — she got in with a crowd like that, and they posted her right up in three months. They just took her right in and let her have it — the full force. That's what they do to you; they set you right down and they talk *at* you. You've got to understand them or perish — so you strike out in self-defence; you can't help yourself. That family my cousin was with has moved away somewhere, or I should try and get in with them. They were real live people, that family; after she left my cousin corresponded with them in French. You've got to do *that* too, to make much real head. But I mean to find some other crowd, if it takes a lot of trouble!"

I listened to all this with great interest, and when he spoke about his cousin I was on the point of turning around to ask him the address of the family she was with; but the next moment he said they had moved away, so I sat still. The other gentleman, however, didn't seem to be affected in the same way as I was.

"Well," he said, "you may follow up that if you like; I mean to follow up the pictures. I don't believe there's ever going to be any considerable demand in the United States for French; but I can promise you that in about ten years there'll be a big demand for Art! And it won't be temporary, either."

That remark may be very true, but I don't care anything about the demand; I want to know French for French. I don't want to think I've been all this while without having gained an insight. . . . The very next day, I asked the lady who kept the books at the hotel whether she knew of any family that could take me to board and give me the benefit of their conversation. She instantly threw up her hands with little shrill cries — in their wonderful French way, you know — and told me that her dearest friend kept a regular place of that kind. If she had known I was looking out for such a place she would have told me before; she hadn't spoken of it herself because she didn't wish to injure the hotel by working me off on another house. She told me this was a charming family who had often received American ladies — and others, including three Tahitians — who wished to follow up the language, and she was sure I'd fall in love with them. So she gave me their address and offered to go with me to introduce me. But I was in such a hurry that I went off by myself and soon found them all right. They were sitting there as if they kind of expected me, and wouldn't scarcely let me come round again for my baggage. They seemed to have right there on hand, as those gentlemen of the theatre said, plenty of what I was after, and I now feel there'll be no trouble about *that.*

I came here to stay about three days ago, and by this time I've quite worked in. The price of board struck me as rather high, but I must remember what a chance to press onward it includes. I've a very pretty little room — without any carpet, but with seven mirrors, two clocks and five curtains. I was rather disappointed, however, after I arrived, to find that there are several other Americans here — all also bent on pressing onward. At least there are three American and two English pensioners, as they call them, as well as a German gentleman — and there seems nothing backward about *him.* I shouldn't wonder if we'd make a regular class, with "moving up" and "moving down;" anyhow I guess I won't be at the foot, but I've not yet time to judge. I try to talk with Madame de Maisonrouge all I can — she's the lady of the house, and the *real* family consists only of herself and her two daughters. They're bright enough to give points to our own brightest, and I guess we'll become quite intimate. I'll write you more about everything in my next. Tell William Platt I don't care a speck *what* he does.

## III

FROM MISS VIOLET RAY IN PARIS
TO MISS AGNES RICH IN NEW YORK

*September 21.*

We had hardly got here when father received a telegram saying he would have to come right back to New York. It was for something about his business — I don't know exactly what; you know I never understand those things and never want to. We had just got settled at the hotel, in some charming rooms, and mother and I, as you may imagine, were greatly annoyed. Father's extremely fussy, as you know, and his first idea, as soon as he found he should have to go back, was that we should go back with him. He declared he'd never leave us in Paris alone and that we must return and come out again. I don't know what he thought would happen to us; I suppose he thought we should be too extravagant. It's father's theory that we're always running up bills, whereas a little observation would show him that we wear the same old *rags* FOR MONTHS. But father has no observation; he has nothing but blind theories. Mother and I, however, have fortunately a great deal of *practice,* and we succeeded in making him understand that we wouldn't budge from Paris and that we'd rather be chopped into small pieces than cross that squalid sea again. So at last he decided to go back alone and to leave us here for three months. Only, to show you how fussy he is, he refused to let us stay at the hotel and insisted that we should go into a *family.* I don't know what put such an idea into his head unless it was some advertisement that he saw in one of the American papers that are published here. Don't think you can escape from them anywhere.

There are families here who receive American and English people to live with them under the pretence of teaching them French. You may imagine what people they are — I mean the families themselves. But the Americans who choose this peculiar manner of seeing Paris must be actually just as bad. Mother and I were horrified — we declared that *main force* shouldn't remove us from the hotel. But father has a way of arriving at his ends which is more effective than violence. He worries and goes on; he "nags," as we used to say at school; and when mother and I are quite worn to the bone his triumph is assured. Mother's more quickly ground down than I, and she ends by siding with father; so that at last when they combine their forces against poor little me I've naturally to succumb. You should have heard the way father went on about this "family" plan; he talked to every one he saw about it; he used to go round to the banker's and talk to the people there — the people in the post-office; he used to try and exchange ideas about it with the waiters at the hotel. He said it would be more safe, more respectable, more economical; that I should pick up more French; that mother would learn how a French household's conducted; that he should feel more easy, and that we ourselves should enjoy it when we came to see. All this meant nothing, but that made no difference. It's positively cruel his harping on our pinching and saving when every one knows that business in America has completely recovered, that the prostration's all over and that *immense fortunes* are being made. We've been depriving ourselves of the commonest necessities for the last five years, and I supposed we came abroad to reap the benefits of it.

As for my French it's already much better than that of most of our helpless compatriots, who are all unblushingly destitute of the very rudiments. (I assure you I'm often surprised at my own fluency, and when I get a little more practice in the circumflex accents and the genders and the idioms I shall quite hold my own.) To make a long story short, however, father carried his point as usual; mother basely deserted me at the last moment, and after holding out alone for three days I told them to do with me what they would. Father lost three steamers in succession by remaining in Paris to argue with me. You know he's like the schoolmaster in Goldsmith's "Deserted Village" — "e'en though vanquished" he always argues still. He and mother went to look at some seventeen families — they had got the addresses somewhere — while I retired to my sofa and would have nothing to do with it. At last they made arrangements and I was transported, as in chains, to the establishment from which I now write you. I address you from the bosom of a Parisian ménage — from the depths of a second-rate boarding-house.

Father only left Paris after he had seen us what he calls comfortably settled here and had informed Madame de Maisonrouge — the mistress of the establishment, the head of the "family" — that he wished my French pronunciation especially attended to. The pronunciation, as it happens, is just what I'm most at home in; if he had said my genders or my subjunctives or my idioms there would have been some sense. But poor father has no native tact, and this deficiency has become flagrant since we've been in Europe. He'll be absent, however, for three months, and mother and I shall breathe more freely; the situation will be less tense. I must confess that we breathe more freely than I expected in this place, where we've been about a week. I was sure before we came that it would prove to be an establishment of the *lowest description;* but I must say that in this respect I'm agreeably disappointed. The French spirit is able to throw a sort of grace even over a swindle of this general order. Of course it's very disagreeable to live with strangers, but as, after all, if I weren't staying with Madame de Maisonrouge I shouldn't be *vautrée* in the Faubourg Saint-Germain, I don't know that from the point of view of exclusiveness I'm much the loser.

Our rooms are very prettily arranged and the table's remarkably good. Mamma thinks the whole thing — the place and the people, the manners and customs — very amusing; but mamma can be put off with any imposture. As for me, you know, all that I ask is to be let alone and not to have people's society *forced upon me.* I've never wanted for society of my own choosing, and, so long as I retain possession of my faculties, I don't suppose I ever shall. As I said, however, the place seems to scramble along, and I succeed in doing as I please, which, you know, is my most cherished pursuit. Madame de Maisonrouge has a great deal of tact — much more than poor floundering father. She's what they call here a *grande belle femme,* which means that she's high-shouldered and short-necked and literally hideous, but with a certain quantity of false type. She has a good many clothes, some rather bad; but a very good manner — only one, and worked to death, but intended to be of the best. Though she's a very good imitation of a *femme du monde* I never see her behind the dinner-table in the evening, never see her smile and bow and duck as the people come in, really glaring all the while at the dishes and the servants, without thinking of a *dame de comptoir* blooming in a corner of a shop or a restaurant. I'm sure that in spite of her *beau nom* she was once a paid book-keeper. I'm also sure that in spite of her smiles and the pretty things she says to every one, she hates us all and would like to murder us. She is a hard clever French-woman who would like to amuse herself and enjoy her Paris, and she must be furious at having to pass her time grinning at speci-mens of the stupid races who mumble broken French at her. Some day she'll poison the soup or the *vin rouge*, but I hope that won't be until after mother and I shall have left her. She has two daugh-ters who, except that one's decidedly pretty, are meagre imita-tions of herself.

The "family," for the rest, consists altogether of our beloved compatriots and of still more beloved Englanders. There's an Englander with his sister, and they seem rather decent. He's re-markably handsome, but excessively affected and patronising, especially to us Americans; and I hope to have a chance of biting his head off before long. The sister's very pretty and apparently very nice, but in costume Britannia incarnate. There's a very pleasant little Frenchman — when they're nice they're charming — and a German doctor, a big blond man who looks like a great white bull; and two Americans besides mother and me. One of them's a young man from Boston — an aesthetic young man who talks about its being "a real Corot day," and a young woman — a girl, a female, I don't know what to call her — from Vermont or Minnesota or some such place. This young woman's the most extraordinary specimen of self-complacent provinciality that I've ever encountered; she's really too horrible and too humiliating. I've been three times to Clémentine about your underskirt, etc.

IV

FROM LOUIS LEVERETT IN PARIS<br>TO HARVARD TREMONT IN BOSTON

*September 25.*

My dear Harvard.

I've carried out my plan, of which I gave you a hint in my last, and I only regret I shouldn't have done it before. It's human na-ture, after all, that's the most interesting thing in the world, and it only reveals itself to the truly earnest seeker. There's a want of earnestness in that life of hotels and railroad-trains which so many of our countrymen are content to lead in this strange rich elder world, and I was distressed to find how far I myself had been led along the dusty beaten track. I had, however, constantly wanted to turn aside into more unfrequented ways — to plunge beneath the surface and see what I should discover. But the opportunity had always been missing; somehow I seem never to meet those opportunities that we hear about and read about — the things that happen to people in novels and biographies. And yet I'm always on the watch to take advantage of any opening that may present itself; I'm always looking out for experiences, for sensations — I might almost say for adventures.

The great thing is to *live,* you know — to feel; to be conscious of one's possibilities; not to pass through life mechanically and insensibly, even as a letter through the post-office. There are times, my dear Harvard, when I feel as if I were really capable of everything — *capable de tout,* as they say here — of the greatest excesses as well as the greatest heroism. Oh to be able to say that one has lived — *qu'on a vécu,* as they say here — that idea exercises an indefinable attraction for me. You'll perhaps reply that nothing's easier than to say it! Only the thing's to make people believe you — to make above all one's self. And then I don't want any second-hand spurious sensations; I want the knowledge that leaves a trace — that leaves strange scars and stains, ineffable reveries and aftertastes, behind it! But I'm afraid I shock you, perhaps even frighten you.

If you repeat my remarks to any of the West Cedar Street circle be sure you tone them down as your discretion will suggest. For yourself you'll know that I have always had an intense desire to see something of *real French life.* You're acquainted with my great sympathy with the French; with my natural tendency to enter into their so supremely fine exploitation of the whole personal consciousness. I sympathise with the artistic temperament; I remember you used sometimes to hint to me that you thought my own temperament *too* artistic. I don't consider that in Boston there's any real sympathy with the artistic temperament; we tend to make everything a matter of right and wrong. And in Boston one can't *live* — *on ne peut pas vivre,* as they say here. I don't mean one can't reside — for a great many people manage that; but one can't live aesthetically — I almost venture to say one can't live sensuously. This is why I've always been so much drawn to the French, who are so aesthetic, so sensuous, so *entirely* living. I'm so sorry dear Theophile Gautier has passed away; I should have liked so much to go and see him and tell him all I owe him. He was living when I was here before; but, you know, at that time I was travelling with the Johnsons, who are not aesthetic and who used to make me feel rather ashamed of my love and my need of beauty. If I had gone to see the great apostle of that religion I should have had to go clandestinely — *en cachette,* as they say here; and that's not my nature; I like to do everything frankly, freely, *naïvement, au grand jour.* That's the great thing — to be free, to be frank, to be *naïf.* Doesn't Matthew Arnold say that somewhere — or is it Swinburne or Pater?

When I was with the Johnsons everything was superficial, and, as regards life, everything was brought down to the question of right and wrong. They were eternally didactic; art should never be didactic; and what's life but the finest of arts? Pater has said that so well somewhere. With the Johnsons I'm afraid I lost many opportunities; the whole outlook or at least the whole medium — of feeling, of appreciation — was grey and cottony, I might almost say woolly. Now, however, as I tell you, I've determined to take right hold for myself; to look right into European life and judge it without Johnsonian prejudices. I've taken up my residence in a French family, in a real Parisian house. You see I've the courage of my opinions; I don't shrink from carrying out my theory that the great thing is to *live.*

You know I've always been intensely interested in Balzac, who never shrank from the reality and whose almost *lurid* pictures of Parisian life have often haunted me in my wanderings through the old wicked-looking streets on the other side of the river. I'm only sorry that my new friends — my French family — don't live in the old city, *au coeur du vieux Paris,* as they say here. They live only on the Boulevard Haussmann, which is a compromise, but in spite of this they have a great deal of the Balzac tone. Madame de Maisonrouge belongs to one of the oldest and proudest families in France, but has had reverses which have compelled her to open an establishment in which a limited number of travellers,

who are weary of the beaten track, who shun the great caravan-
series, who cherish the tradition of the old French sociability —
she explains it herself, she expresses it so well — in short to open
a "select" boarding-house. I don't see why I shouldn't after all
use that expression, for it's the correlative of the term pension
bourgeoise, employed by Balzac in "Le Père Goriot." Do you remember the pension bourgeoise of Madame Vauquer née de
Conflans? But this establishment isn't at all like that, and indeed
isn't bourgeois at all; I don't quite know how the machinery of
selection operates, but we unmistakably feel we're select. The
Pension Vauquer was dark, brown, sordid, *graisseuse;* but this is
quite a different tone, with high, clear lightly-draped windows
and several rather good Louis Seize pieces — family heirlooms,
Madame de Maisonrouge explains. She recalls to me Madame
Hulot — do you remember "la belle Madame Hulot"? — in "Les
Parents Pauvres." She has a great charm — though a little artificial,
a little jaded and faded, with a suggestion of hidden things in her
life. But I've always been sensitive to the seduction of an ambigu-
ous fatigue.

I'm rather disappointed, I confess, in the society I find here; it
isn't so richly native, of so indigenous a note, as I could have desired. Indeed, to tell the truth, it's not native at all; though on the
other hand it *is* furiously cosmopolite, and that speaks to me too
at my hours. We're French *and* we're English; we're American
*and* we're German; I believe too there are some Spaniards and
some Hungarians expected. I'm much interested in the study of
racial types; in comparing, contrasting, seizing the strong points,
the weak points, in identifying, however muffled by social hypoc-
risy, the sharp keynote of each. It's interesting to shift one's point
of view, to despoil one's self of one's idiotic prejudices, to enter
into strange exotic ways of looking at life.

The American types don't, I much regret to say, make a strong,
or rich affirmation, and, excepting my own (and what *is* my own,
dear Harvard, I ask you?) are wholly negative and feminine.
We're *thin* — that I should have to say it! we're pale, we're poor,
we're flat. There's something meagre about us; our line is wanting
in roundness, our composition in richness. We lack temperament;
we don't know how to live; *nous ne savons pas vivre,* as they say
here. The American temperament is represented — putting my-

self aside, and I often think that my temperament isn't at all American — by a young girl and her mother and by another young girl without her mother, without either parent or any attendant or appendage whatever. These inevitable creatures are more or less in the picture; they have a certain interest, they have a certain stamp, but they're disappointing too: they don't go far; they don't keep all they promise; they don't satisfy the imagination. They are cold, slim, sexless; the physique's not generous, not abundant; it's only the drapery, the skirts and furbelows — that is I mean in the young lady who has her mother — that are abundant. They're rather different — we *have* our little differences, thank God: one of them all elegance, all "paid bills" and extra-fresh *gants de Suède,* from New York; the other a plain pure clear-eyed narrow-chested straight-stepping maiden from the heart of New England. And yet they're very much alike too — more alike than they would care to think themselves; for they face each other with scarcely disguised opposition and disavowal. They're both specimens of the practical positive passionless young thing as we let her loose on the world — and yet with a certain fineness and knowing, as you please, either too much or too little. With all of which, as I say, they have their spontaneity and even their oddity; though no more misery, either of them, than the printed circular thrust into your hand on the street-corner.

The little New Yorker's sometimes very amusing; she asks me if every one in Boston talks like me — if every one's as "intellectual" as your poor correspondent. She's for ever throwing Boston up at me; I can't get rid of poor dear little Boston. The other one rubs it into me too; but in a different way; she seems to feel about it as a good Mohammedan feels toward Mecca, and regards it as a focus of light for the whole human race. Yes, poor little Boston, what nonsense is talked in thy name! But this New England maiden is in her way a rare white flower: she's travelling all over Europe alone — "to see it," she says, "for herself." For herself! What can that strangely serene self of hers do with such sights, such depths! She looks at everything, goes everywhere, passes her way with her clear quiet eyes wide open; skirting the edge of obscene abysses without suspecting them; pushing through brambles without tearing her robe; exciting, without knowing it, the most injurious suspicions; and always holding her course — without a stain, without a sense, without a fear, without a charm!

Then by way of contrast there's a lovely English girl with eyes as shy as violets and a voice as sweet! — the difference between the printed, the distributed, the gratuitous hand-bill and the shy scrap of a *billet-doux* dropped where you may pick it up. She has a sweet Gainsborough head and a great Gainsborough hat with a mighty plume in front of it that makes a shadow over her quiet English eyes. Then she has a sage-green robe, "mystic wonderful," all embroidered with subtle devices and flowers, with birds and beasts of tender tint; very straight and tight in front and adorned behind, along the spine, with large strange iridescent buttons. The revival of taste, of the sense of beauty, in England, interests me deeply; what is there in a simple row of spinal buttons to make one dream — to *donner à rêver,* as they say here? I believe a grand aesthetic renascence to be at hand and that a great light will be kindled in England for all the world to see. There are spirits there I should like to commune with; I think they'd understand me.

This gracious English maiden, with her clinging robes, her amulets and girdles, with something quaint and angular in her step, her carriage, something mediaeval and Gothic in the details of her person and dress, this lovely Evelyn Vane (isn't it a beautiful name?) exhales association and implication. She's so much a woman — *elle est bien femme,* as they say here; simpler softer rounder richer than the easy products I spoke of just now. Not much talk — a great sweet silence. Then the violet eye — the very eye itself seems to blush; the great shadowy hat making the brow so quiet; the strange clinging clutched pictured raiment! As I say, it's a very gracious tender type. She has her brother with her, who's a beautiful fair-haired grey-eyed young Englishman. He's purely objective, but he too is very plastic.

V

FROM MIRANDA HOPE TO HER MOTHER

*September 26*

You mustn't be frightened at not hearing from me oftener; it isn't because I'm in any trouble, but because I'm getting on so well. If

I were in any trouble I don't think I'd write to you; I'd just keep quiet and see it through myself. But that's not the case at present; and if I don't write to you it's because I'm so deeply interested over here that I don't seem to find time. It was a real providence that brought me to this house, where, in spite of all obstacles, I *am* able to press onward. I wonder how I find time for all I do, but when I realise I've only got about a year left, all told, I feel as if I wouldn't sacrifice a single hour.

The obstacles I refer to are the disadvantages I have in acquiring the language, there being so many persons round me speaking English, and that, as you may say, in the very bosom of a regular French family. It seems as if you heard English everywhere; but I certainly didn't expect to find it in a place like this. I'm not discouraged, however, and I exercise all I can, even with the other English boarders. Then I've a lesson every day from Mademoiselle — the elder daughter of the lady of the house and the intellectual one; she has a wonderful fearless mind, almost like my friend at the hotel — and French give-and-take every evening in the salon, from eight to eleven, with Madame herself and some friends of hers who often come in. Her cousin, Mr. Verdier, a young French gentleman, is fortunately staying with her, and I make a point of talking with him as much as possible. I have *extra-private lessons* from him, and I often ramble round with him. Some night soon he's to accompany me to the comic opera. We've also a most interesting plan of visiting the galleries successively together and taking the schools in their order — for they mean by "the schools" here something quite different from what we do. Like most of the French Mr. Verdier converses with great fluency, and I feel I may really gain from him. He's remarkably handsome, in the French style, and extremely polite — making a great many speeches which I'm afraid it wouldn't always do to pin one's faith on. When I get down in Maine again I guess I'll tell you some of the things he has said to me. I think you'll consider them extremely curious — very beautiful *in their French way*.

The conversation in the parlour (from eight to eleven) ranges over many subjects — I sometimes feel as if it really avoided *none;* and I often wish you or some of the Bangor folks could be there to enjoy it. Even though you couldn't understand it I think you'd like to hear the way they go on; they seem to express so much. I sometimes think that at Bangor they don't express enough — except that it seems as if over there they've less *to* express. It seems as if at Bangor there were things that folks never *tried* to say; but I seem to have learned here from studying French that you've no idea what you *can* say before you try. At Bangor they kind of give it up beforehand; they don't make any effort. (I don't say this in the least for William Platt *in particular*.)

I'm sure I don't know what they'll think of me when I get back anyway. It seems as if over here I had learned to come out with everything. I suppose they'll think I'm not sincere; but isn't it more sincere to come right out with things than just to keep feeling of them in your mind — without giving any one the benefit? I've become very good friends with every one in the house — that is (you see I *am* sincere) with *almost* every one. It's the most interesting circle I ever was in. There's a girl here, an American, that I don't like so much as the rest; but that's only because she won't let me. I should like to like her, ever so much, because she's most lovely and most attractive; but she doesn't seem to want to know me or to take to me. She comes from New York and she's remarkably pretty, with beautiful eyes and the most delicate features; she's also splendidly stylish — in this respect would bear comparison with any one I've seen over here. But it seems as if she didn't want to recognise me or associate with me, as if she wanted to make a difference between us. It is like people they call "haughty" in books. I've never seen any one like that before — any one that wanted to make a difference; and at first I was right down interested, she seemed to me so like a proud young lady in a novel. I kept saying to myself all day "haughty, haughty," and I wished she'd keep on so. But she did keep on — she kept on too long; and then I began to feel it in a different way, to feel as if it kind of wronged me. I couldn't think what I've done, and I can't think yet. It's as if she had got some idea about me or had heard some one say something. If some girls should behave like that I wouldn't make any account of it; but this one's so refined, and looks as if she might be so fascinating if I once got to know her, that I think about it a good deal. I'm bound to find out what her reason is — for of course she has got some reason; I'm right down curious to know.

I went up to her to ask her the day before yesterday; I thought that the best way. I told her I wanted to know her better and would like to come and see her in her room — they tell me she has got a lovely one — and that if she had heard anything against me perhaps she'd tell me when I came. But she was more distant than ever and just turned it off; said she had never heard me mentioned and that her room was too small to receive visitors. I suppose she spoke the truth, but I'm sure she has some peculiar ground, all the same. She has got some idea; which I'll die if I don't find out soon — if I have to ask every one in the house. I never *could* be happy under an appearance of wrong. I wonder if she doesn't think me refined — or if she had ever heard anything against Bangor? I can't think it's that. Don't you remember when Clara Barnard went to visit in New York, three years ago, how much attention she received? And you know Clara *is* Bangor, to the soles of her shoes. Ask William Platt — so long as he isn't native — if he doesn't consider Clara Barnard refined.

Apropos, as they say here, of refinement, there's another American in the house — a gentleman from Boston — who's just crammed with it. His name's Mr. Louis Leverett (such a beautiful name I think) and he's about thirty years old. He's rather small and he looks pretty sick; he suffers from some affection of the liver. But his conversation leads you right on — they *do* go so far over here: even our people seem to strain ahead in Europe, and perhaps when I get back it may strike you I've learned to keep up with them. I delight to listen to him anyhow — he has such beautiful ideas. I feel as if these moments were hardly right, not being in French; but fortunately he uses a great many French expressions. It's in a different style from the dazzle of Mr. Verdier — not so personal, but much more earnest: he says the only earnestness left in the world now is French. He's intensely fond of pictures and has given me a great many ideas about them that I'd never have gained without him; I shouldn't have known how to go to work to strike them. He thinks everything of pictures; he thinks we don't make near enough of them. They seem to make a good deal of them here, but I couldn't help telling him the other day that in Bangor I really don't think we do.

If I had any money to spend I'd buy some and take them back to hang right up. Mr. Leverett says it would do them good — not the pictures, but the Bangor folks (though sometimes he seems to want to hang *them* up too). He thinks everything of the French, anyhow, and says we don't make nearly enough of them. I couldn't help telling him the other day that they certainly make enough of *themselves*. But it's very interesting to hear him go on about the French, and it's so much gain to me, since it's about the same as what I came for. I talk to him as much as I dare about Boston, but I do feel as if this were right down wrong — a stolen pleasure.

I can get all the Boston culture I want when I go back, if I carry out my plan, my heart's secret, of going there to reside. I ought to direct all my efforts to European culture now, so as to keep Boston to finish off. But it seems as if I couldn't help taking a peep now and then in advance — with a real Bostonian. I don't know when I may meet one again; but if there are many others like Mr. Leverett there I shall be certain not to lack when I carry out my dream. He's just as full of culture as he can live. But it seems strange how many different sorts there are.

There are two of the English who I suppose are very cultivated too; but it doesn't seem as if I could enter into theirs so easily, though I try all I can. I do love their way of speaking, and sometimes I feel almost as if it would be right to give up going for French and just try to get the hang of English as these people have got it. It doesn't come out in the things they say so much, though these are often rather curious, but in the sweet way they say them and in their kind of making so much, such an easy lovely effect, of saying almost anything. It seems as if they must *try* a good deal to sound like that; but these English who are here don't seem to try at all, either to speak or do anything else. They're a young lady and her brother, who belong, I believe, to some noble family. I've had a good deal of intercourse with them, because I've felt more free to talk to them than to the Americans — on account of the language. They often don't understand mine, and then it's as if I had to learn theirs to explain.

I never supposed when I left Bangor that I was coming to Europe to improve in *our* old language — and yet I feel I can. If I do get where I *may* in it I guess you'll scarcely understand me when I get back, and I don't think you'll particularly see the point. I'd be a good deal criticised if I spoke like that at Bangor. However, I verily believe Bangor's the most critical place on earth; I've seen nothing like it over here. Well, tell them I'll give them about all they can do. But I was speaking about this English young lady and her brother; I wish I could put them before you. She's lovely just to see; she seems so modest and retiring. In spite of this, however, she dresses in a way that attracts great attention, as I couldn't help noticing when one day I went out to walk with her. She was ever so much more looked at than what I'd have thought she'd like; but she didn't seem to care, till at last I couldn't help calling attention to it. Mr. Leverett thinks everything of it; he calls it the "costume of the future." I'd call it rather the costume of the past — you know the English have such an attachment to the past. I said this the other day to Madame de Maisonrouge — that Miss Vane dressed in the costume of the past. *De l'an passé, vous voulez dire?* she asked in her gay French way. (You can get William Platt to translate this; he used to tell me he knows so much French.)

You know I told you, in writing some time ago, that I had tried to get some insight into the position of woman in England, and, being here with Miss Vane, it has seemed to me to be a good opportunity to get a little more. I've asked her a great deal about it, but she doesn't seem able to tell me much. The first time I asked her she said the position of a lady depended on the rank of her father, her eldest brother, her husband — all on somebody else; and they, as to their position, on something quite else (than themselves) as well. She told me her own position was very good because her father was some relation — I forget what — to a lord. She thinks everything of this; and that proves to me their standing can't be *really* good, because if it were it wouldn't be involved in that of your relations, even your nearest. I don't know much about lords, and it does try my patience — though she's just as sweet as she can live — to hear her talk as if it were a matter of course I should.

I feel as if it were right to ask her as often as I can if she doesn't consider every one equal; but she always says she doesn't, and she confesses that she doesn't think *she's* equal to lady Something-or-Other, who's the wife of that relation of her father. I try and persuade her all I can that she *is;* but it seems as if she didn't want to be persuaded, and when I ask her if that superior being is of the same opinion — that Miss Vane isn't her equal — she looks so soft and pretty with her eyes and says "How can she not be?" When I tell her that this is right down bad for the other person it seems as if she wouldn't believe me, and the only answer she'll make is that the other person's "awfully nice." I don't believe she's nice at all; if she were nice she wouldn't have such ideas as that. I tell Miss Vane that at Bangor we think such ideas vulgar, but then she looks as though she had never heard of Bangor. I often want to shake her, though she *is* so sweet. If she isn't angry with the people who make her feel that way, at least I'm angry *for* her. I'm angry with her brother too, for she's evidently very much afraid of him, and this gives me some further insight into the subject. She thinks everything of her brother; she thinks it natural she should be afraid of him not only physically — for that *is* natural, as he's enormously tall and strong and has very big fists — but morally and intellectually. She seems unable, however, to take in any argument, and she makes me realise what I've often heard — that if you're timid nothing will reason you out of it.

Mr. Vane also, the brother, seems to have the same prejudices, and when I tell him, as I often think it right to do, that his sister's not his subordinate, even if she does think so, but his equal, and perhaps in some respects his superior, and that if my brother in Bangor were to treat me as he treats this charming but abject creature, who has not spirit enough to see the question in its true light, there would be an indignation-meeting of the citizens to protest against such an outrage to the sanctity of womanhood — when I tell him all this, at breakfast or dinner, he only bursts out laughing so loud that all the plates clatter on the table.

But at such a time as this there's always one person who seems interested in what I say — a German gentleman, a professor, who sits next to me at dinner and whom I must tell you more about another time. He's very learned, but wants to push further and further all the time; he appreciates a great many of my remarks, and after dinner, in the salon, he often comes to me to ask me questions about them. I have to think a little sometimes to know what I did say or what I do think. He takes you right up where you left off, and he's most as fond of discussing things as William Platt ever was. He's splendidly educated, in the German style, and he told me the other day that he was an "intellectual broom." Well, if he is he sweeps clean; I told him that. After he has been talking to me I feel as if I hadn't got a speck of dust left in my mind anywhere. It's a most delightful feeling. He says he's a remorseless observer, and though I don't know about remorse — for a bright mind isn't a crime, is it? — I'm sure there's plenty over here to observe. But I've told you enough for today. I don't know how much longer I shall stay; I'm getting on now so fast that it has come to seem sometimes as if I shouldn't need all the time I've laid out. I suppose your cold weather has promptly begun, as usual; it sometimes makes me envy you. The fall weather here is very dull and damp, and I often suffer from the want of bracing.

## VI

FROM MISS EVELYN VANE IN PARIS TO THE
LADY AUGUSTA FLEMING AT BRIGHTON

*Paris September 30.*

Dear Lady Augusta.

I'm afraid I shall not be able to come to you on January 7th, as you kindly proposed at Homburg. I'm so very very sorry; it's an immense disappointment. But I've just heard that it has been settled that mamma and the children come abroad for a part of the winter, and mamma wishes me to go with them to Hyères, where Georgina has been ordered for her lungs. She has not been at all well these three months, and now that the damp weather has begun she's very poorly indeed; so that last week papa decided to have a consultation, and he and mamma went with her up to town and saw some three or four doctors. They all of them ordered the south of France, but they didn't agree about the place; so that mamma herself decided for Hyères, because it's the most economical. I believe it's very dull, but I hope it will do Georgina good. I'm afraid, however, that nothing will do her good until she consents to take more care of herself; I'm afraid she's very wild and wilful, and mamma tells me that all this month it has taken papa's positive orders to make her stop indoors. She's very cross (mamma writes me) about coming abroad, and doesn't seem at all to mind the expense papa has been put to — talks very ill-naturedly about her loss of the hunting and even perhaps of the early spring meetings. She expected to begin to hunt in December and wants to know whether anybody keeps hounds at Hyères. Fancy that rot when she's too ill to sit a horse or to go anywhere. But I dare say that when she gets there she'll be glad enough to keep quiet, as they say the heat's intense. It may cure Georgina, but I'm sure it will make the rest of us very ill.

Mamma, however, is only going to bring Mary and Gus and Fred and Adelaide abroad with her: the others will remain at Kingscote till February (about the 3d) when they'll go to East-bourne for a month with Miss Turnover, the new governess, who has proved such a very nice person. She's going to take Miss Travers, who has been with us so long, but is only qualified for the younger children, to Hyères, and I believe some of the Kings-cote servants. She has perfect confidence in Miss T.; it's only a pity the poor woman has such an odd name. Mamma thought of asking her if she would mind taking another when she came; but papa thought she might object. Lady Battledown makes all her governesses take the same name; she gives 5 pounds more a year for the purpose. I forget what it is she calls them; I think it's John-son (which to me always suggests a lady's maid). Governesses shouldn't have too pretty a name — they shouldn't have a nicer name than the family.

I suppose you heard from the Desmonds that I didn't go back to England with them. When it began to be talked about that Georgina should be taken abroad mamma wrote to me that I had better stop in Paris for a month with Harold, so that she could pick me up on their way to Hyères. It saves the expense of my journey to Kingscote and back, and gives me the opportunity to "finish" a little in French.

You know Harold came here six weeks ago to get up his French for those dreadful exams that he has to pass so soon. He came to live with some French people that take in young men (and others) for this purpose; it's a kind of coaching-place, only kept by women. Mamma had heard it was very nice, so she wrote to me that I was to come and stop here with Harold. The Desmonds brought me and made the arrangement or the bargain or whatever you call it. Poor Harold was naturally not at all pleased, but he has been very kind and has treated me like an angel. He's getting on beauti-fully with his French, for though I don't think the place is so good as papa supposed, yet Harold is so immensely clever that he can scarcely help learning. I'm afraid I learn much less, but fortun-ately I haven't to go up for anything — unless perhaps to mamma if she takes it into her head to examine me. But she'll have so much to think of with Georgina that I hope this won't occur to her. If it does I shall be, as Harold says, in a dreadful funk.

This isn't such a nice place for a girl as for a gentleman, and the Desmonds thought it *exceedingly odd* that mamma should wish me to come here. As Mrs. Desmond said, it's because she's so very unconventional. But you know Paris is so very amusing, and if only Harold remains good-natured about it I shall be content to wait for the caravan — which is what he calls mamma and the children. The person who keeps the establishment, or whatever they call it, is rather odd and *exceedingly foreign;* but she's wonderfully civil and is perpetually sending to my door to see if I want anything. She's tremendously pretentious and of course isn't a lady. The servants are not at all like English ones and come bursting in, the footman — they've only one — and the maids alike, at all sorts of hours, in the *most sudden way.* Then when one rings it takes ages. Some of the food too is rather nasty. All of which is very uncomfortable, and I dare say will be worse at Hyères. There, however, fortunately, we shall have our own people.

There are some very odd Americans here who keep throwing Harold into fits of laughter. One's a dreadful little man whom indeed he also wants to kick and who's always sitting over the fire and talking about the colour of the sky. I don't believe he ever saw the sky except through the window-pane. The other day he took off my frock — that green one you thought so nice at Homburg — and told me that it reminded him of the texture of the Devonshire turf. And then he talked for half an hour about the Devonshire turf, which I thought such a very extraordinary subject. Harold firmly believes him mad. It's rather horrid to be living in this way with people one doesn't know — I mean doesn't know as one knows them in England.

The other Americans, besides the madman, are two girls about my own age, one of whom is rather nice. She has a mother; but the mother always sits in her bedroom, which seems so very odd. I should like mamma to ask them to Kingscote, but I'm afraid mamma wouldn't like the mother, who's awfully vulgar. The other girl is awfully vulgar herself — she's travelling about quite alone. I think she's a middle-class school-mistress — sacked perhaps for some irregularity; but the other girl (I mean the nicer one, with the objectionable mother) tells me she's more respectable than she seems. She has, however, the most extraordinary opinions — wishes to do away with the aristocracy, thinks it wrong that Arthur should have Kingscote when papa dies, etc. I don't see what it signifies to her that poor Arthur should come into the property, which will be so delightful — except for papa dying. But Harold says she's mad too. He chaffs her tremendously about her radicalism, and he's so immensely clever that she can't answer him, though she has a supply of the most extraordinary big words.

There's also a Frenchman, a nephew or cousin or something of the person of the house, who's a horrid low cad; and a German professor or doctor who eats with his knife and is a great bore. I'm so very sorry about giving up my visit. I'm afraid you'll never ask me again.

## VII

FROM LEON VERDIER IN PARIS TO PROSPER GOBAIN IN LILLE

*September 28.*

Mon Gros Vieux.

It's a long time since I've given you of my news, and I don't know what puts it into my head tonight to recall myself to your affectionate memory. I suppose it is that when we're happy the mind reverts instinctively to those with whom formerly we shared our vicissitudes, and *je t'en ai trop dit dans le bon temps, cher vieux,* and you always listened to me too imperturbably, with your pipe in your mouth and your waistcoat unbuttoned, for me not to feel that I can count on your sympathy today. *Nous en sommes-nous flanquées, des confidences?* — in those happy days when my first thought in seeing an adventure *poindre à l'horizon* was of the pleasure I should have in relating it to the great Prosper. As I tell thee, I'm happy; decidedly *j'ai de la chance,* and from that avowal I trust thee to construct the rest. Shall I help thee a little? Take three adorable girls — three, my good Prosper, the mystic number, neither more, nor less. Take them and place in the midst of them thy insatiable little Leon. Is the situation sufficiently indicated, or does the scene take more doing?

You expected perhaps I was going to tell thee I had made my fortune, or that the Uncle Blondeau had at last decided to re-commit himself to the breast of nature after having constituted me his universal legatee. But I needn't remind you for how much women have always been in any happiness of him who thus overflows to you — for how much in any happiness and for how much more in any misery. But don't let me talk of misery now; time enough when it comes, when *ces demoiselles* shall have joined the serried ranks of their amiable predecessors. Ah I comprehend your impatience. I must tell you of whom *ces demoiselles* consist.

You've heard me speak of my *cousine* de Maisonrouge, that *grande belle femme* who, after having married, *en secondes noces* — there had been, to tell the truth, some irregularity about her first union — a venerable relic of the old noblesse of Poitou, was left, by the death of her husband, complicated by the crash of expen-sive tastes against an income of 17,000 francs, on the pavement of Paris with two little demons of daughters to bring up in the path of virtue. She managed to bring them up; my little cousins are ferociously *sages*. If you ask me how she managed it I can't tell you; it's no business of mine, and *a fortiori* none of yours. She's now fifty years old — she confesses to thirty-eight — and her daughters, whom she has never been able to place, are respec-tively twenty-seven and twenty-three (they confess to twenty and to seventeen). Three years ago she had the thrice-blest idea of opening a well-upholstered and otherwise attractive *asile* for the blundering barbarians who come to Paris in the hope of picking up a few stray pearls from the *écrin* of Voltaire — or of Zola. The idea has brought her luck; the house does an excellent business. Until within a few months ago it was carried on by my cousins alone; but lately the need of a few extensions and improvements has caused itself to be felt. My cousin has undertaken them, re-gardless of expense; in other words she has asked me to come and stay with her — board and lodging gratis — and correct the conversational exercises of her *pensionnaire*-pupils. I'm the exten-sion, my good Prosper; I'm the improvement. She has enlarged the *personnel* — I'm the enlargement. I form the exemplary sounds that the prettiest English lips are invited to imitate. The English lips are not all pretty, heaven knows, but enough of them are so to make it a good bargain for me.

Just now, as I told you, I'm in daily relation with three separate pairs. The owner of one of them has private lessons; she pays extra. My cousin doesn't give me a sou of the money, but I consider nevertheless that I'm not a loser by the arrangement. Also I'm well, very very well, with the proprietors of the two other pairs. One of these is a little Anglaise of twenty — a *figure de keepsake;* the most adorable miss you ever, or at least I ever, beheld. She's hung all over with beads and bracelets and amulets, she's embroidered all over like a sampler or a vestment; but her principal decoration consists of the softest and almost the hugest grey eyes in the world, which rest upon you with a profundity of confidence — a confidence I really feel some compunction in betraying. She has a tint as white as this sheet of paper, except just in the middle of each cheek, where it passes into the purest and most transparent, most liquid, carmine. Occasionally this rosy fluid overflows into the rest of her face — by which I mean that she blushes — as softly as the mark of your breath on the windowpane.

Like every Anglaise she's rather pinched and prim in public; but it's easy to see that when no one's looking *elle ne. demande qu'à se laisser aller!* Whenever she wants it I'm always there, and I've given her to understand she can count upon me. I've reason to believe she appreciates the assurance, though I'm bound in honesty to confess that with her the situation's a little less advanced than with the others. *Que voulez-vous?* The English are heavy and the Anglaises move slowly, that's all. The movement, however, is perceptible, and once this fact's established I can let the soup simmer, I can give her time to arrive, for I'm beautifully occupied with her competitors. *They* don't keep me waiting, please believe.

These young ladies are Americans, and it belongs to that national character to move fast. "All right — go ahead!" (I'm learning a great deal of English, or rather a great deal of American.) They go ahead at a rate that sometimes makes it difficult for me to keep up. One of them's prettier than the other; but this latter — the one that takes the extra-private lessons — is really *une fille étonnante. Ah par exemple, elle brûle ses vaisseaux, celle-là!* She threw herself into my arms the very first day, and I almost owed her a grudge for having deprived me of that pleasure of gradation, of carrying the defences one by one, which is almost as great as that of entering the place. For would you believe that at the end of exactly twelve minutes she gave me a rendezvous? In the Galerie d'Apollon at the Louvre I admit; but that was respectable for a beginning, and since then we've had them by the dozen; I've ceased to keep the account. *Non, c'est une fille qui me dépasse.*

The other, the slighter but "smarter" little person — she has a mother somewhere out of sight, shut up in a closet or a trunk — is a good deal prettier, and perhaps on that account *elle y met plus de façons.* She doesn't knock about Paris with me by the hour; she contents herself with long interviews in the *petit salon,* with the blinds half-drawn, beginning at about three o'clock, when every one is *à la promenade.* She's admirable, cette petite, a little too immaterial, with the bones rather over-accentuated, yet of a detail, on the whole, most satisfactory. And you can say anything to her. She takes the trouble to appear not to understand, but her conduct, half an hour afterwards, reassures you completely — oh completely!

However, it's the big bouncer of the extra-private lessons who's the most remarkable. These private lessons, my good Prosper, are the most brilliant invention of the age, and a real stroke of genius on the part of Miss Miranda! They also take place in the *petit salon,* but with the doors tightly closed and with explicit directions to everyone in the house that we are not to be disturbed. And we're not, *mon gros,* we're not! Not a sound, not a shadow, interrupts our felicity. My cousins are on the right track — such a house must make its fortune. Miss Miranda's too tall and too flat, with a certain want of coloration; she hasn't the transparent *rougeurs* of the little Anglaise. But she has wonderful far-gazing eyes, superb teeth, a nose modelled by a sculptor, and a way of holding up her head and looking every one in the face, which combines apparent innocence with complete assurance in a way I've never seen equalled. She's making the *tour du monde,* entirely alone, without even a soubrette to carry the ensign, for the purpose of seeing for herself, seeing *à quoi s'en tenir sur les hommes et les choses* — on *les hommes* particularly. *Dis donc, mon vieux,* it must be a *drôle de pays* over there, where such a view of the right thing for the aspiring young bourgeoises is taken. If we should turn the tables some day, thou and I, and go over and see it for ourselves? Why isn't it as well we should go and find them *chez elles,* as that they should come out here after us? *Dis donc, mon gros Prosper. . .!*

## VIII

### FROM DR. RUDOLPH STAUB IN PARIS
### TO DR. JULIUS HIRSCH AT GÖTTINGEN

My dear Brother in Science.

I resume my hasty notes, of which I sent you the first instalment some weeks ago. I mentioned that I intended to leave my hotel, not finding in it real matter. It was kept by a Pomeranian and the waiters without exception were from the Fatherland. I might as well have sat down with my note-book Unter den Linden, and I felt that, having come here for documentation, or to put my finger straight upon the social pulse, I should project myself as much as possible into the circumstances which are in part the consequence and in part the cause of its activities and intermittences. I saw there could be no well-grounded knowledge without this preliminary operation of my getting a near view, as slightly as possible modified by elements proceeding from a different combination of forces, of the spontaneous home-life of the nation.

I accordingly engaged a room in the house of a lady of pure French extraction and education, who supplements the shortcomings of an income insufficient to the ever-growing demands of the Parisian system of sense-gratification by providing food and lodging for a limited number of distinguished strangers. I should have preferred to have my room here only, and to take my meals in a brewery, of very good appearance, which I speedily discovered in the same street; but this arrangement, though very clearly set out by myself, was not acceptable to the mistress of the establishment — a woman with a mathematical head — and I have consoled myself for the extra expense by fixing my thoughts upon the great chance that conformity to the customs of the house gives me of studying the table-manners of my companions, and of observing the French nature at a peculiarly physiological moment, the moment when the satisfaction of the *taste,* which is the governing quality in its composition, produces a kind of exhalation, an intellectual transpiration, which, though light and perhaps invisible to a superficial spectator, is nevertheless appreciable by a properly adjusted instrument. I've adjusted my instrument very satisfactorily — I mean the one I carry in my good square German head — and I'm not afraid of losing a single drop of this valuable fluid as it condenses itself upon the plate of my observation. A prepared surface is what I need, and I've prepared my surface.

Unfortunately here also I find the individual native in the minority. There are only four French persons in the house — the individuals concerned in its management, three of whom are women, and one a man. Such a preponderance of the *Weibliche* is, however, in itself characteristic, as I needn't remind you what an abnormally-developed part this sex has played in French history. The remaining figure is ostensibly that of a biped, and apparently that of a man, but I hesitate to allow him the whole benefit of the higher classification. He strikes me as less than simian, and whenever I hear him talk I seem to myself to have paused in the street to listen to the shrill clatter of a hand-organ, to which the gambols of a hairy *homunculus* form an accompaniment.

I mentioned to you before that my expectation of rough usage in consequence of my unattenuated even if not frivolously aggressive, Teutonism was to prove completely unfounded. No one seems either unduly conscious or affectedly unperceiving of my so rich Berlin background; I'm treated on the contrary with the positive civility which is the portion of every traveller who pays the bill without scanning the items too narrowly. This, I confess, has been something of a surprise to me, and I've not yet made up my mind as to the fundamental cause of the anomaly. My determination to take up my abode in a French interior was largely dictated by the supposition that I should be substantially disagreeable to its inmates. I wished to catch in the fact the different forms taken by the irritation I should naturally produce; for it is under the influence of irritation that the French character most completely expresses itself. My presence, however, operates, as I say, less than could have been hoped as a stimulus, and in this respect I'm materially disappointed. They treat me as they treat every one else; whereas, in order to be treated differently, I was resigned in advance to being treated worse. A further proof, if any were needed, of that vast and, as it were, fluid *waste* (I have so often dwelt on to you) which attends the process of philosophic secretion. I've not, I repeat, fully explained to myself this logical contradiction; but this is the explanation to which I tend. The French are so exclusively occupied with the idea of themselves that in spite of the very definite image the German personality presented to them by the war of 1870 they have at present no distinct apprehension of its existence. They are not very sure that there *are,* concretely, any Germans; they have already forgotten the convincing proofs presented to them nine years ago. A German was something disagreeable and disconcerting, an irreducible mass, which they determined to keep out of their conception of things. I therefore hold we're wrong to govern ourselves upon the hypothesis of the *revanche;* the French nature is too shallow for that large and powerful plant to bloom in it.

The English-speaking specimens, too, I've not been willing to neglect the opportunity to examine; and among these I've paid special attention to the American varieties, of which I find here several singular examples. The two most remarkable are a young man who presents all the characteristics of a period of national decadence; reminding me strongly of some diminutive Hellenised Roman of the third century. He's an illustration of the period of culture in which the faculty of appreciation has obtained such a preponderance over that of production that the latter sinks into a kind of rank sterility, and the mental condition becomes analogous to that of a malarious bog. I hear from him of the existence of an immense number of Americans exactly resembling him, and that the city of Boston indeed is almost exclusively composed of them. (He communicated this fact very proudly, as if it were greatly to the credit of his native country; little perceiving the truly sinister impression it made on me.)

What strikes one in it is that it is a phenomenon to the best of my knowledge — and you know what my knowledge is — unprecedented and unique in the history of mankind; the arrival of a nation at an ultimate stage of evolution without having passed through the mediate one; the passage of the fruit, in other words, from crudity to rottenness, without the interposition of a period of useful (and ornamental) ripeness. With the Americans indeed the crudity and the rottenness are identical and simultaneous;

it is impossible to say, as in the conversation of this deplorable young man, which is the one and which the other: they're inextricably confused. Homunculus for homunculus I prefer that of the Frenchman; he's at least more amusing.

It's interesting in this manner to perceive, so largely developed, the germs of extinction in the so-called powerful Anglo-Saxon family. I find them in almost as recognisable a form in a young woman from the State of Maine, in the province of New England, with whom I have had a good deal of conversation. She differs somewhat from the young man I just mentioned in that the state of affirmation, faculty of production and capacity for action are things, in her, less inanimate; she has more of the freshness and vigour that we suppose to belong to a young civilisation. But unfortunately she produces nothing but evil, and her tastes and habits are similarly those of a Roman lady of the lower Empire. She makes no secret of them and has in fact worked out a complete scheme of experimental adventure, that is of personal license, which she is now engaged in carrying out. As the opportunities she finds in her own country fail to satisfy her she has come to Europe "to try," as she says, "for herself." It's the doctrine of universal "unprejudiced" experience professed with a cynicism that is really most extraordinary, and which, presenting itself in a young woman of considerable education, appears to me to be the judgement of a society.

Another observation which pushes me to the same deduction — that of the premature vitiation of the American population — is the attitude of the Americans whom I have before me with regard to each other. I have before me a second flower of the same huge so-called democratic garden, who is less abnormally developed than the one I have just described, but who yet bears the stamp of this peculiar combination of the barbarous and, to apply to them one of their own favourite terms, the *ausgespielt,* the "played-out." These three little persons look with the greatest mistrust and aversion upon each other; and each has repeatedly taken me apart and assured me secretly, that he or she only is the real, the genuine, the typical American. A type that has lost itself before it has been fixed — what can you look for from this?

Add to this that there are two young Englanders in the house who hate all the Americans in a lump, making between them none of the distinctions and favourable comparisons which they insist upon, and for which, as involving the recognition of shades and a certain play of the critical sense, the still quite primitive insular understanding is wholly inept, and you will, I think, hold me warranted in believing that, between precipitate decay and internecine enmities, the English-speaking family is destined to consume itself, and that with its decline the prospect of successfully-organised conquest and unarrested incalculable expansion, to which I alluded above, will brighten for the deep-lunged children of the Fatherland!

## IX

### MIRANDA HOPE TO HER MOTHER

*October 22.*

Dear Mother.

I'm off in a day or two to visit some new country; I haven't yet decided which. I've satisfied myself with regard to France, and obtained a good knowledge of the language. I've enjoyed my visit to Madame de Maisonrouge deeply, and feel as if I were leaving a circle of real friends. Everything has gone on beautifully up to the end, and every one has been as kind and attentive as if I were their own sister, especially Mr. Verdier, the French gentleman, from whom I have gained more than I ever expected (in six weeks) and with whom I have promised to *correspond.* So you can imagine me dashing off the liveliest and yet the most elegant French letters; and if you don't believe in them I'll keep the rough drafts to show you when I go back.

The German gentleman is also more interesting the more you know him; it seems sometimes as if I could fairly drink in his ideas. I've found out why the young lady from New York doesn't like me! It's because I said one day at dinner that I *admired* to go to the Louvre. Well, when I first came it seemed as if I *did* admire everything! Tell William Platt his letter has come. I knew he'd have to write, and I was bound I'd make him! I haven't decided what country I'll visit next; it seems as if there were so many to choose from. But I must take care to pick out a good one and to meet plenty of fresh experiences. Dearest mother, my money holds out, and it *is* most interesting!

*Born in New York City, Henry James (1843-1916) spent much of his youth in Europe, becoming a permanent resident there in 1876. A giant of nineteenth-century American literature, his two most famous works are THE TURN OF THE SCREW (1898) and THE AMBASSADORS (1903). This story first appeared in a magazine, PARISIAN, in 1879.*

# THE SEARCH

For a long time he had been looking for it. He had looked all over the village. The minute his mother had left him on the steps of Mr. Pomeroy's store, he had begun. He had looked around the church and the grange hall, around the post office where his father worked and around the consolidated school where he would go when he was bigger. He had looked around the service station where he wasn't supposed to loiter and peered down the blackened hole where Mr. Billing's garage had been.

Then, walking very slowly, he had looked up and down the streets and sidewalks, taking special pains on Elm Street, for once he had found a nickel there. After that he had searched the field behind Mr. Pomeroy's store, stumbling over the frozen hummocks. Then he had climbed the rail fence, almost as tall as he was, and covered every foot of the grove beyond. He had looked very carefully, lifting the low branches of the evergreens and stirring the dead leaves where they had drifted.

If only he could find it, he had kept thinking. If only he could burst open the door of Mr. Pomeroy's store and shout, "Guess what I've got, Mr. Pomeroy."

He liked Mr. Pomeroy. Mr. Pomeroy treated him with as much respect as though he went to school already. "Well, Boy," he would often say, "what do you make of that sky out there? Going to rain or ain't it?" Sometimes Mr. Pomeroy would ask his advice about decorating windows. "Take a look," he would say, "and give me your expert opinion." Mr. Pomeroy didn't tease, the way some grown-ups did, making you believe he was taking

you seriously, then giving a laugh or a wink to anyone listening.
When Mr. Pomeroy asked you a question, he wanted your answer, and when Mr. Pomeroy told you to stay and hang around
for a bit, he meant it.

Until today he had not realized about Mr. Pomeroy's loss. He
had been standing, watching the tarantula that Mr. Pomeroy kept
in a bottle while his mother matched up a sample to a spool of
thread. Leaving the bottle, his eyes had wandered to Mr. Pomeroy
himself and rested on a large safety pin set straight and firm
through the cuff of his sleeve. He had seen the pin before — in
fact, for as long as he could remember — and taken it quite for
granted as a part of Mr. Pomeroy. But suddenly it raised a question.

"Mama," he had asked, "why does Mr. Pomeroy wear that big
pin in—"

Before he could finish the question she had grabbed him by the
shoulder the way she did when he was bad. "Ssssh," she had
said, giving him a hard, firm shake. Then she had bent as though
to button his coat, and he could see her eyes. "Stop," they said.
"Not another word out of you."

"I didn't say anything," he protested, feeling injured. He had
looked again at Mr. Pomeroy, expecting him to take his part. But
Mr. Pomeroy didn't appear to be listening. The pin in his sleeve
looked bigger and brighter than ever before.

"Stop staring," his mother had whispered. "What's happened
to your manners?"

Manners meant saying "Please" and "Thank you," meant using
your napkin and excusing yourself when you walked in front of
anyone or stumbled over their feet. He couldn't see what manners had to do with Mr. Pomeroy's pin.

"But Mama," he said. "I just wanted to know."

She bent again and lowered her voice until it sounded angry.
"Mr. Pomeroy wears that pin because he has lost his hand. You
must never, never mention it in his hearing. Understand?"

He stared at her in astonishment. Then his eyes moved again
to the pin. He had heard of a great many things being lost, but
never a hand.

"Do you understand?" his mother had repeated.

But before he could answer Mr. Pomeroy had crossed the store and come over to where they were standing. "Sorry to keep you waiting, Boy," he had said as though *he* and not his mother was the important one. When Mr. Pomeroy said that, he liked him better than he had ever liked him before. It was right then that he had decided what he was going to do. He was going to find Mr. Pomeroy's hand.

He had very sharp eyes. People always said so. His grandmother said so when he picked up a needle or a button she had dropped. His mother said so when he brought her her glasses. Even his father admitted that. "If only your muscles was as good as your eyes," he often told him. He wondered if his father knew about Mr. Pomeroy's hand.

Stooping now to look under a bush, he wondered why Mr. Pomeroy himself hadn't found it. He must have missed it a great deal with so many boxes and crates to handle. Of course he didn't have much time to hunt, though. He was in his store from morning until bedtime, and on Sundays he opened up after church to accommodate the people who came in from the country. "If he had a wife," people sometimes said, "she would never put up with it." But Mr. Pomeroy had no wife. He lived alone in the three crowded rooms above his store.

The air was cold, but he did not feel it because of his warm, excited thoughts. He would find Mr. Pomeroy's hand and run back to the store with it.

"Guess what I found," he would say.

Mr. Pomeroy would stop whatever he was doing. "Now what would that be, Boy?" he would ask, looking puzzled.

"Just guess," he would tell him.

Mr. Pomeroy would smile a slow, thoughtful smile. "A beech nut," he might say. "Or a nice russet apple." He would smack his lips loudly. "Just the season for russets."

"No. Not those. Guess again."

And Mr. Pomeroy would keep on guessing. A gourd. An ear of pop corn. The tail feather of a pheasant.

And finally...

The thought of what would happen then made him quicken his steps.

Leaving the grove, he crossed into Mr. Peter's garden, working his way among the stiff brown stalks of corn. If only there was someone to tell him whether he was Hot or Cold. That was what happened when you hunted the thimble at parties. "You're Warm," people would say. "No, no, you're getting Cooler. Now you're Warm again. You're Hot now. Hotter." But there was no one to help him here. He was alone.

The wind was rising. He stood still and listened to it rattling among the corn stalks. He didn't like noises. He turned and looked back toward the village. Most of it was shut off by tall evergreens, but he could still see the church steeple, six or seven houses, and the roof of the consolidated school. He had never been so far away from home all by himself before.

He hesitated. Maybe he was too little to hunt for things lost outdoors. Maybe...

He saw two crows flying overhead and his spirits rose. "One crow sorrow, two crow joy," he said aloud and started on.

It had been a long time since Mr. Pomeroy had lost his hand. How could it be that no one had ever found it? He considered this soberly. Probably it was because grown-ups were the only ones who knew about it, and grown-ups were always busy, he decided. His father was much too busy to work puzzles with him. His mother didn't even have time to answer his questions. "Can't you see how busy I am?" she was always saying. His grandmother scolded about how she darned and mended from morning until night.

Mr. Pomeroy never seemed busy, even when the store was crowded. Mr. Pomeroy had time to stop and look at anything you had to show him. Especially animals. He liked animals and he was kind to all of them — even the tarantula. He never let the big boys shake the bottle or even snap their fingers against the glass.

He walked more slowly now, for his legs were beginning to feel tired. But his eyes never left the ground. If only he could find it.... He thought of Mr. Pomeroy's astonishment. "Why, Boy, where'd you come across that?" Mr. Pomeroy would say. "I thought sure that was gone for good."

A smile crinkled his cold, stiff face. He took a deep breath and made his legs go faster. Up a bank and down again. Through a cranberry patch. Over a smooth flat boulder...

Suddenly, straight ahead, in a bed of ferns, he saw something.

It looked like it. It might be. He hurried forward, one foot tripping the other until he all but fell, his heart pounding against his jacket.

But it was only a piece of bark stripped from a birch tree. He stood still, looking at it. Then in his disappointment, he pressed it with his heel among the crisp, brown bracken.

He turned and looked back at the village again. It seemed a long way off. He could see only the steeple now and a few roofs. Whose roofs they were, he couldn't tell.

Maybe he ought to go back. Maybe his mother would be mad at him. "Can't I count on you not to go traipsing off?" she'd say.

Slowly a thought came to him. Maybe the reason no one had helped Mr. Pomeroy was because you couldn't count on people any longer. His father said it all the time, especially about the clerks at the post office. His mother said it when Mr. Bowden left white eggs instead of brown. His grandmother said it more often than anyone. "Times have changed," she said, always sighing. "You can't count on anyone but your own folks these days."

Mr. Pomeroy didn't have any folks.

A lump rose in his throat. "You can count on me, Mr. Pomeroy," he cried so loudly that a partridge, startled, flew up out of the bush. He watched it for an instant and then hurried on.

In a little while he reached the brook, which was quiet now, hushed by the leaves that filled it. There were ragged shelves of ice among the rocks. He rubbed his eyes, for they were getting very tired, and looked carefully up and down both banks until they disappeared among the alders.

Feeling the cold now, he took off his mittens and buttoned the collar of his jacket. Then he put them on again and turned toward Bissett's lane. The ground was rougher here, for the cow tracks were frozen hard, but he was protected from the wind by the pine trees that grew on either side.

Going very slowly, he moved his eyes back and forth, back and forth. Every now and then he stopped and bent aside dried pods of milkweed and frozen clumps of grasses.

If only there was someone just to give him a hint. . . .

At the end of the lane was the pasture. He slipped through the bars and, in the open again, felt the full force of the wind on his ears and across his shoulders. He shivered.

Looking back, he could see no sign of the village. Looking ahead, he could see only rocks, juniper, a few clumps of pine trees, and the rough, hard path the cows had made.

Again he hesitated.

He had been in this pasture once before. That was last spring when his Sunday School teacher had brought his whole class to hunt for mayflowers. Mayflowers were hard to find, for they hid themselves among the leaves and mosses. He had been the first one to find a blossom, he remembered.

The remembrance gave him heart. He would keep on. He would keep right on looking.

He chose the widest path. Still, the going was rough, for the stones that bedded it had been loosened by the frost. His legs ached now from the jolts they got. His ankles kept turning. Blackberry vines caught at his stockings. Once, where the rocks gave suddenly away to pine needles, he slipped and almost fell. Every minute the wind seemed stronger.

If only he had stopped to have questioned Mr. Pomeroy. Yet he couldn't have done that, he realized, remembering what his mother had told him. Besides, if he had, there would have been no surprise. And the surprise was very important to him.

He thought again of Mr. Pomeroy's astonished face. Then, smiling, he thought of his gratitude. "I'm going to give you a reward, Boy," Mr. Pomeroy would say. "Just name it. Anything you fancy."

But he wouldn't take a thing. Not even a Hershey bar, much as he liked them. Not a bag of peanuts or even a popsicle. "Glad to do it for you, Mr. Pomeroy," he would say without a word about the wind and the cold.

In spite of his numbing feet he hurried faster. Around a dump of rusted cans and broken bottles. Across a swale.

And there it was, lying half hidden in a patch of bunchberries.

It hadn't been so bad, after all. It hadn't taken him long. Words sang in his head as he started forward.

*A present for you, Mr. Pomeroy . . .*

Then it moved — a tiny rabbit.

He watched it gravely as it leapt away. A single tear crept down his cheek and he caught it with his tongue. He had been so sure.

There was a log nearby, and he sat down on it. He had been disappointed many times before. Once he had missed the Sunday School picnic because of tonsilitis. Once the rain had come through the open window and soaked the lid of his butterfly box. Once he had exercised his muscles for days, lifting rocks in the orchard, and then had his father feel them. "Cat's muscles," was all his father said. But he had never known a disappointment like this. It burned in his eyes and throat. It ached in his legs. It stabbed at his stomach, making him sick all over.

He sniffed and wiped his nose on the back of his mitten. He would never find it. He would never see Mr. Pomeroy's pleasure or hear his praise. He couldn't even tell Mr. Pomeroy about it because of what his mother had said. Mr. Pomeroy would never know how hard he had tried.

Tears cut hot paths down his cheeks. He began to shiver. First his fingers, then his knees, then his whole body. He raised his right mitten to his teeth and yanked it off so that he could blow on his fingers. But his teeth were chattering so hard that it fell to the ground. While he was groping for it, he heard the sound of a whistle. Some one was coming.

He got up, brushed his left mitten quickly across his eyes and stood waiting. A man appeared, coming out of a grove of pine trees. He wore a red cap and blazer, and he carried a gun over his shoulder.

It was Mr. Varnum. Mr. Varnum was Mr. Pomeroy's friend. He owned a gravel pit somewhere, and anyone who wanted to reach him left a message at the store. Like Mr. Pomeroy, he had no wife, and on Sunday mornings on the way to church you could often see the two men sitting on the steps of the grain shed. Mr. Varnum was just the one to help him.

Mr. Varnum stopped suddenly, looking surprised. "Ain't you a long way from home, Son?" he asked.

He shook his head and squared his shoulders. "Mr. Varnum," he began, trying to control the shaking, "would you know about where Mr. Pomeroy was when he lost his hand?"

Mr. Varnum looked more surprised than before. "What's that again, Son?" he asked.

He felt impatient as he often felt with grown-ups, but he remembered his manners and repeated the question.

Mr. Varnum shifted his gun and took a long time answering. "Why, seems to me 'twas over to the old Leach place." He pointed eastward. "He was laying a wall there, as I recollect."

Now he knew.

All of a sudden the cold left him. In its place came a wave of heat and energy. The heaviness went out of his legs. They felt just the way they did the first thing in the morning.

Now he knew exactly.

Now he could really begin.

"Thank you," he cried. "Oh, thank you, Mr. Varnum." Then he started off over the rough road, running.

*The youngest of eight children, Virginia Chase (Perkins) (1902–1987) was born and raised in Blue Hill, Maine. A magna cum laude graduate of the University of Minnesota, with an M.A. from Wayne University, she won the Avery Hopwood Award for Fiction (1940), producing four novels and several volumes of nonfiction. This story first appeared in PUCKERBRUSH REVIEW in 1983.*

# STEP-OVER TOE-HOLD

E ven in mid-November when it was getting cold, I'd climb up the unpainted, broken-down shed stairs after supper with a flashlight to the shed chamber where I'd play for hours within my homemade television studio — so strong the pull of my fantasy world. There I'd plan variety, dramatic, and panel shows directed by me; design miniature sets for my cardboard actors attired in their aluminum-foil and crepe-paper costumes. Using mostly cardboard, scotch tape, toothpicks, foil, wax paper, multi-colored index cards, cookie package dividers, bits of cloth and glass, I devised an elaborate multi-floored dollhouse. I even wrote scripts for the shows and made dressing rooms for my stars.

One night, as I was making my way across the shed, amidst cries from my mother from the adjoining pantry that it was too cold to play up there, I hesitated briefly in front of my father who was busy skinning out a deer he had just killed early in the hunting season. He had most of the fur coat skinned off and was cutting the meat and putting pieces of it in a big enamel pan on the floor beside him. Newspapers covered the floor. My father, as usual, had on his old baseball cap and a cigarette hanging out of his mouth. The deer, which was a pretty fair-sized buck, was hanging from a bolt on one of the middle beams across the shed ceiling. I had once tried to help my father skin out a deer, but it had made me sick to my stomach, and so he didn't ask me anymore. "Where ya going?" he asked. "Up to the shed chamber to play with dolls?"

I didn't answer. I just went upstairs. Through the cracks in the floor I could see him hacking away at the deer; and because he was short of breath and always smoking, he'd cough and grunt. He had already suffered one mild heart attack and my mother was always worried about him. Finally, he'd hollar up at me, "O.K., I'm going in now and I'm turning the light off. You come down now."

He'd give my mother the fresh meat to wrap up in aluminum foil and label and put in the freezer compartment of our old Gibson refrigerator while he and I would go into the living room and watch television. A great outdoorsman who loved fishing and hunting, my father never liked team sports; and even when my older brother and I were on teams in school, he'd never go to see us play. But he did like boxing and wrestling matches on television. In the mid-fifties, there were boxing matches on Wednesday and Friday nights and wrestling bouts all the time. Two men beating each other around a ring made sense to my father. The Wednesday night matches were sponsored by Pabst Blue Ribbon and the Friday night fights were sponsored by Gillette. I'd go off to bed with their jingle of "Look sharp! Feel sharp! Be sharp!" ringing in my head. After one fighter was declared the winner, my father would always say, in his dry, dead-pan voice, "What a man!"

The wrestling matches I enjoyed more than the boxing exhibitions, because I enjoyed all the show biz and dress-up that went with them. Gorgeous George was like Liberace as a wrestler, and Ricki Starr wrestled in pink tights and ballet slippers. There were crazy midgets and tough women wrestlers in spangled bathing suits. The melodrama, week after week, was, of course, unending. There was always a grudge match that would continue for weeks; the villains were ever-so dastardly and the heroes so clean-cut and full of fair play. My favorite at the time was the handsome blond muscleman named Edouard Carpentier from Montreal who was billed as "The Flying Frenchman" because of the way he could execute back flips, drop kicks, and cartwheels mixed in with the more conventional takedowns, headlocks, and bearhugs. It was always very exciting when the "body beautiful" Frenchman tangled with the villainous Killer Kowalski, who would commit all manner of illegal atrocities against the handsome hero to the great boos and screams of the crowd. Kowalski's most punishing maneuver was the dreaded "claw hold," which, when applied to the other wrestler's stomach, was the end of the line for Kowalski's foe.

There were other wrestling terms, too, which were a part of the amusement: "flying double arm wringer," "double hiproll," "flying head scissors," and every wrestler's specialty hold. It might be Kowalski's "claw hold" or someone else's "cobra clutch" or "Congo butt" or "Italian pile driver." All of the wrestlers that we liked to watch in the fifties seemed to enjoy using airplane spins, flying dropkicks, and body scissors. And someone was always using the step-over toe-hold, a very ineffectual-looking hold, but one which was supposed to give some authority and power over an opponent. At least it held an opponent at bay until the wrestlers could think of what else to do before it was time for one or the other to win the pin.

My father also loved watching William Bendix of "The Life of Riley" and Jackie Gleason and Art Carney in the "Honeymooners" skits. He'd sit there in his rocking chair in his pajamas, sipping on his Narragansett, and laughing his head off as Gleason ranted and raved at his long-suffering wife played by Audrey Meadows. My mother hated Jackie Gleason.

When I was old enough, my father took me out in the back field and showed me how to shoot a rifle. When I was very little, he let me use a .22 and I would shoot at tin cans and bottles lined up on the neighbor's fence. One time I got to try his beloved .300 Savage, which literally knocked me on my rear end. The few times, however, that I went hunting with him — while I loved being in the November woods — I was scared to death, especially when the men would start drinking and then driving a deer, racing and yelling through the woods with their loaded rifles. My father would shoot at anything. One time walking down a woods road he spotted a chipmunk and shot it. I was horrified and ran over to the bloody body. With his dying breath, the chipmunk bit me. "For Christ's sake, that'll teach ya!" my father said. "Now you'll probably get rabies or something." That same walk he shot at a loon out on the lake. The other male relatives and neighbors really respected my father's prowess with a hunting rifle. He always got his deer, and usually more than one. So, once in the woods, with an audience, it was like he had to show off. He really lived all of his life for November.

One of the last times I went hunting with him and his boss and other men friends I really embarrassed him. I got scared and hid under a log when there was a drive on; and he found me there crouching. He was disgusted, even though he never said anything.

In the hunting camp where my father would hole up for a week or two, he always seemed to play the role of cook, or "cookee," as he called it. "Cookee" was a term used on the old Maine Central steamboats that my father used to work on as a young man.

And there was fishing. My father had once caught one of the biggest bass ever recorded from East Grand Lake Stream. We had pictures of the beast all over the house, and my father and uncles were always looking at the pictures and discussing the magnitude of the catch. Once, as a little fisher myself with a bamboo fishing rod, I wanted to impress the old man. So while he had gone off with his boss for an all-day fishing trip one summer day, I sat on the dock at the camp and caught about a dozen suckers, which I thought were a pretty impressive-looking fish. I put them in a pail which I hid out back of the woodshed to show him when he got back. But, alas, by the time he returned, a couple of cats had discovered my cache and removed all of the suckers. I had only an empty vessel to show him.

So I started taking piano lessons.

I was thirteen or so and I loved music. We had an old, untuned, upright piano with a couple of missing keys, and I wanted to know how to play it. So I talked my mother into letting me use some of my summer lawn-mowing money for the one dollar a week after-school lesson. My father hated the idea and he hated my practicing. The schoolbus from Taunton Corner would drop me off at Taunton Junction, where my father worked for the Rudolph Keen Fuel Oil Company, and I would walk the mile or so down the hill, across the Taunton Bridge, to West Hamlin and the big green house where Mrs. Scott, who reminded me of Loretta Young in both looks and mannerisms, would give me my lesson. Afterwards, I walked back across the bridge to the fuel oil company and hung around while my father "cashed up" with Virginia, the long-time, old-maid secretary and treasurer of the firm. Sometimes Virginia would give me little gifts if I had to wait for my father who was having an unexpected or late delivery. She once gave me a Planter's Peanut Coloring Book with Mr. Peanut cavorting about New York; and often she gave me money for a candy bar or a free Coke from the machine. When it was time for my father to go home, he let me sit up front with him with my red John Thompson music books while three of his greasy colleagues with their dinner pails (everyone was greasy around the garage and trucks, of course) would crowd into the back seat. There would always be a few humorous remarks about my music lessons, usually from my father. There I was embarrassing him again.

In the seventh grade, I announced one night at the supper table that I was going to become a writer. My father just looked across at me, his hair hanging in his face as usual, and said, "You'd better be a schoolteacher or minister." That was a major insult since he was always saying how stupid teachers were and how ministers were either crooks or queers. In the eighth grade I announced I was going to college. My father greeted this by saying, "Ya better get that notion out of ya head. Only rich kids go to college. Unless ya haven't noticed it, we ain't rich."

All of my younger life, and even up through high school, I had very few new clothes to call my own. I always wore hand-me-downs from my brother, family friends, or the summer people. But in the ninth grade I did buy with my own money my first pair of new Levis, and upon seeing me in them, my father said, "Those pants are too tight about the crotch! Take 'em off!" Also, up until high school, my father gave me all of my haircuts on Sundays in our "kitchen barbershop." And he made sure he gave me a haircut, all right. When he finished with me, I looked like a skinned monkey. When I'd complain, he'd say, "Well, ya wanted a haircut, didn't ya?"

When I made the JV basketball team in high school, my father tried to talk me into quitting by telling me repeatedly that I'd "break something and be maimed for life." I think he just didn't want to have to come pick me up after practices. As a member of the cross-country team, I'd often try to practice running, as I was supposed to, on the weekends; but my father made me stop. "Running down the road that way," he said, "the neighbors will think our house is on fire!"

One night I was holding the flashlight for him while he tried to fix the engine of our old 1951 Mercury. At one point, I moved the light a bit, and he yelled at me. "You think I'm stupid, don't ya?" I yelled back. "Yes, I think you're goddamn stupid if ya can't even hold a flashlight steady for five minutes," he said. I threw the flashlight down and ran into the house. Another time I swore at him at the kitchen table, and in an instant found myself on my back on the kitchen floor with my father on top of me, a cigarette dangling out of his mouth, and the ashes falling on my face. I was sixteen by then and around six feet, so I was shocked by my father's ability to take me down so fast and pin me so solidly. And I was surprised to realize how strong he was, how I couldn't move a muscle under him. "You're lucky I didn't give ya a goddamn super piledriver!" he said.

I'd watch him eat in the morning. He always made this oatmeal concoction with brown sugar, melted butter, the whole thing swimming in canned milk. At supper he loved to sop up the gravy with pieces of bread. He loved anything soggy, sweet, and fattening.

I helped him paint and shingle our house. I helped him with all the seasonal chores: banking the house with tarpaper and brush in the fall, taking the banking off in the spring, burning the backfield as soon as the snow was gone. I washed and waxed the car. As I got older, I gradually did all of the mowing, clipping and raking; and I helped both of my parents with their caretaking chores at two summer places on Taunton Point.

Once I accompanied him on one of his night fuel-oil deliveries in the middle of the winter down east to Cherryfield or Harrington or some place; and it seemed we drove forever. Dad sang a few of his tunes. He'd always sing the two lines or so that he knew over and over. One of them was, "I'm a poor little girl waiting for bread." He'd smoke his Camel cigarettes and keep asking me if I were too cold or too warm. He also drove that Texaco truck right in the middle of the road and at about twenty miles over the speed limit. He never drove all that fast when with Mom because she'd scream at him not to go over forty.

She'd also scream at him to cut his meat up into smaller pieces at supper and she'd scream at him when he'd come home every year drunk from his Texaco banquets.

I was thrilled to read after school one day a headline story on the front page of the Bangor *Daily News* about my father. Dad was a hero! COURAGEOUS TRUCK DRIVER STOPS BLAZE the headline read, and the story went on to relate how my father had stopped a potentially explosive gasoline fire which had started at the Texaco fuel-oil storage area in Bangor. When he came home that night, I congratulated him by saying, "Dad! You're a hero!" "Yeah," he said, "but you notice they forget to tell ya who started the fire." Then I noticed the ever-present cigarette dangling from his lips. "It's a wonder I didn't blow myself up," he said.

Spending a weekend home from college during my freshman year, I was sitting across the living room from my father watching him reading a Rommel book with his W. T. Grant three-dollar eyeglasses on when he looked at me and said, "Yes, I know. I'm a complete failure."

But he actually never failed to help me when I really needed help.

When the battery on my first car, a 1959 Ford Galaxie, which I bought the last semester of my senior year at the University of Maine, went flat the night before I was to start my student teaching in Bangor, he drove all the way to Orono after work to install a new battery in my car and make sure everything was going to go o.k. in the morning.

By the time I was in my mid-twenties, and Dad was nearing sixty, I realized that I didn't have much more time in which to try and become friends with him. I knew we would never be close pals, that he'd never hug me or say he loved me; but I did want him to look upon me at least once with some faint glimmer of approval.

From one of my first paychecks I sent him a ten-dollar check for his birthday, and it bounced. I sent him books: General Mac-Arthur's *Reminiscences,* Truman Capote's *In Cold Blood,* and other books I thought he'd enjoy and that we could talk about. Whenever I was home for occasional vacations, I'd try to get him to talk about his life working on the steamboats, working on the old lumber wharves over to Ellsworth, driving his trucks all over Maine.

One summer when I was home from my teaching job in New York, I got him to go with me for a beer and a boxing match in Ellsworth. The beer was good, and he seemed to be enjoying himself; but the boxing matches disgusted us both. The Job Corps

then had an outlet in Bar Harbor, and an Ellsworth boxing promoter, who also ran the movie theater, sold foundation garments,
and served as the Boy Scout leader, arranged to have the black and
Puerto Rican Job Corps boys fight some Maine Indian boys in the
old Grand Theatre before a predominantly white redneck audience. The promoter kept taking up a collection for the Jimmy
Fund, and the boys pounded each other around the ring while the
worst kind of racist comments were hurled back and forth. My
father and I left early.

When he turned sixty-one, and had been holding down a regular
job since he was thirteen, I asked my father about his plans. "I'm
going to retire next year," he said, "and then drop dead the year
after."

He sure knew how to call 'em.

We were sitting together two years later on the couch at my
brother's place outside of Cape Kennedy in Florida right after
Christmas, 1969, when Dad suddenly said, as he and Mom were
talking about visiting along the way back to Maine, "I'd like to
drive up to Syracuse and see An-day's apartment and have a few
beers with him."

Ah, the line I had been longing to hear all of my grown-up life.
My father actually wanting to do something with me in my world.
I was thrilled.

But he never made it. That Christmas vacation was the last time
I saw him alive. Shaking his hand just before I got into my brother's
car to drive to the Orlando Airport to return to Syracuse, I sensed
this was it. And so I stared back at him, standing there next to a
palm tree, his hair in his face, the cigarette dangling from his lips,
his hands in his pockets, his stomach hanging over his belt, un-
smiling forever, as my mother beside him waved and waved good-
bye.

He died of a heart attack a few days later, in a South Carolina
motel on the way back Downeast. My mother told me that he
had cried uncontrollably the night before and that it had frightened
her. The night that my brother called to tell me of our father's
death, I did the same.

*Raised in Maine, Sanford Phippen (1942-    ) was an English major at the University of Maine. He currently teaches at Orono High School. His works include A HISTORY OF THE TOWN OF HANCOCK, MAINE (1978) and THE POLICE KNOW EVERYTHING (1982), a collection from which this story is taken.*

# WINTER

*So they waited, marooned in their consciousness, surrounded by a monstrous tidal space which was slowly, slowly closing them out.*

The Ledge

# THE LEDGE

On Christmas morning before sunup the fisherman embraced his warm wife and left his close bed. She did not want him to go. It was Christmas morning. He was a big, raw man, with too much strength, whose delight in winter was to hunt the sea ducks that flew in to feed by the outer ledges, bare at low tide.

As his bare feet touched the cold floor and the frosty air struck his nude flesh, he might have changed his mind in the dark of this special day. It was a home day, which made it seem natural to think of the outer ledges merely as some place he had shot ducks in the past. But he had promised his son, thirteen, and his nephew, fifteen, who came from inland. That was why he had given them his present of an automatic shotgun each the night before, on Christmas Eve. Rough man though he was known to be, and no spoiler of boys, he kept his promises when he understood what they meant. And to the boys, as to him, home meant where you came for rest after you had had your Christmas fill of action and excitement.

His legs astride, his arms raised, the fisherman stretched as high as he could in the dim privacy of his bedroom. Above the snug murmur of his wife's protest he heard the wind in the pines and knew it was easterly as the boys had hoped and he had surmised the night before. Conditions would be ideal, and when they were, anybody ought to take advantage of them. The birds would be flying. The boys would get a man's sport their first time outside on the ledges.

His son at thirteen, small but steady and experienced, was fierce to grow up in hunting, to graduate from sheltered waters and the blinds along the shores of the inner bay. His nephew at fifteen, an overgrown farm boy, had a farm boy's love of the sea, though he could not swim a stroke and was often sick in choppy weather. That was the reason his father, the fisherman's brother, was a farmer and chose to sleep in on the holiday morning at his brother's house. Many of the ones the farmer had grown up with were regularly seasick and could not swim, but they were unafraid of the water. They could not have dreamed of being anything but fishermen. The fisherman himself could swim like a seal and was never sick, and he would sooner die than be anything else.

He dressed in the cold and dark, and woke the boys gruffly. They tumbled out of bed, their instincts instantly awake while their thoughts still fumbled slumbrously. The fisherman's wife in the adjacent bedroom heard them apparently trying to find their clothes, mumbling sleepily and happily to each other, while her husband went down to the hot kitchen to fry eggs — sunny-side up, she knew, because that was how they all liked them.

Always in winter she hated to have them go outside, the weather was so treacherous and there were so few others out in case of trouble. To the fisherman these were no more than woman's fears, to be taken for granted and laughed off. When they were first married, they fought miserably every fall because she was after him constantly to put his boat up until spring. The fishing was all outside in winter, and though prices were high the storms made the rate of attrition high on gear. Nevertheless he did well. So she could do nothing with him.

People thought him a hard man, and gave him the reputation of being all out for himself because he was inclined to brag and be disdainful. If it was true, and his own brother was one of those who strongly felt it was, they lived better than others, and his brother had small right to criticize. There had been times when in her loneliness she had yearned to leave him for another man. But it would have been dangerous. So over the years she had learned to shut her mind to his hard-driving, and take what comfort she might from his unsympathetic competence. Only once or twice, perhaps, had she gone so far as to dwell guiltily on what it would be like to be a widow.

The thought that her boy, possibly because he was small, would not be insensitive like his father, and the rattle of dishes and smell of frying bacon downstairs in the kitchen shut off from the rest of the chilly house, restored the cozy feeling she had had before she was alone in bed. She heard them after a while go out and shut the back door.

Under her window she heard the snow grind drily beneath their boots, and her husband's sharp, exasperated commands to the boys. She shivered slightly in the envelope of her own warmth. She listened to the noise of her son and nephew talking elatedly. Twice she caught the glimmer of their lights on the white ceiling above the window as they went down the path to the shore. There would be frost on the skiff and freezing suds at the water's edge. She herself used to go gunning when she was younger; now, it seemed to her, anyone going out like that on Christmas morning had to be incurably male. They would none of them think about her until they returned and piled the birds they had shot on top of the sink for her to dress.

Ripping into the quiet pre-dawn cold she heard the hot snarl of the outboard taking them out to the boat. It died as abruptly as it had burst into life. Two or three or four or five minutes later the big engine broke into a warm reassuring roar. He had the best of equipment, and he kept it in the best of condition. She closed her eyes. It would not be too long before the others would be up for Christmas. The summer drone of the exhaust deepened. Then gradually it faded in the wind until it was lost at sea, or she slept.

The engine had started immediately in spite of the temperature. This put the fisherman in a good mood. He was proud of his boat. Together he and the two boys heaved the skiff and outboard onto the stern and secured it athwartships. His son went forward along the deck, iridescent in the ray of the light the nephew shone through the windshield, and cast the mooring pennant loose into darkness. The fisherman swung to starboard, glanced at his compass, and headed seaward down the obscure bay.

There would be just enough visibility by the time they reached the headland to navigate the crooked channel between the islands. It was the only nasty stretch of water. The fisherman had done it often in fog or at night — he always swore he could go anywhere in the bay blindfolded — but there was no sense in taking chances if you didn't have to. From the mouth of the channel he could lay a straight course for Brown Cow Island, anchor the boat out of sight behind it, and from the skiff set their tollers off Devil's Hump three hundred yards to seaward. By then the tide would be clearing the ledge and they could land and be ready to shoot around half-tide.

It was early, it was Christmas, and it was farther out than most hunters cared to go in this season of the closing year, so that he felt sure no one would be taking possession ahead of them. He had shot thousands of ducks there in his day. The Hump was by far the best hunting. Only thing was you had to plan for the right conditions because you didn't have too much time. About four hours was all, and you had to get it before three in the afternoon when the birds left and went out to sea ahead of nightfall.

They had it figured exactly right for today. The ledge would not be going under until after the gunning was over, and they would be home for supper in good season. With a little luck the boys would have a skiff-load of birds to show for their first time outside. Well beyond the legal limit, which was no matter. You took what you could get in this life, or the next man made out and you didn't.

The fisherman had never failed to make out gunning from Devil's Hump. And this trip, he had a hunch, would be above the ordinary. The westerly wind would come up just stiff enough, the tide was right, and it was going to storm by tomorrow morning so the birds would be moving. Things were perfect.

The old fierceness was in his bones. Keeping a weather eye to the murk out front and a hand on the wheel, he reached over and cuffed both boys playfully as they stood together close to the heat of the exhaust pipe running up through the center of the house. They poked back at him and shouted above the drumming engine, making bets as they always did on who would shoot the most birds. This trip they had the thrill of new guns, the best money could buy, and a man's hunting ground. The black retriever wagged at them and barked. He was too old and arthritic to be allowed in December water, but he was jaunty anyway at being brought along.

Groping in his pocket for his pipe, the fisherman suddenly had his high spirits rocked by the discovery that he had left his tobacco at home. He swore. Anticipation of a day out with nothing to smoke made him incredulous. He searched his clothes, and then he searched them again, unable to believe the tobacco was not somewhere. When the boys inquired what was wrong he spoke angrily to them, blaming them for being in some devious way at fault. They were instantly crestfallen and willing to put back after the tobacco, though they could appreciate what it meant only through his irritation. But he bitterly refused. That would throw everything out of phase. He was a man who did things the way he set out to do.

He clamped his pipe between his teeth, and twice more during the next few minutes he ransacked his clothes in disbelief. He was no stoic. For one relaxed moment he considered putting about and gunning somewhere nearer home. Instead he held his course and sucked the empty pipe, consoling himself with the reflection that at least he had whiskey enough if it got too uncomfortable on the ledge. Peremptorily he made the boys check to make certain the bottle was really in the knapsack with the lunches where he thought he had taken care to put it. When they reassured him, he despised his fate a little less.

The fisherman's judgment was as usual accurate. By the time they were abreast of the headland there was sufficient light so that he could wind his way among the reefs without slackening speed. At last he turned his bow toward open ocean, and as the winter dawn filtered upward through long layers of smoky cloud on the eastern rim his spirits rose again with it.

He opened the throttle, steadied on his course, and settled down to the two-hour run. The wind was stronger but seemed less cold coming from the sea. The boys had withdrawn from the fisherman and were talking together while they watched the sky through the windows. The boat churned solidly through a light chop, flinging spray off her flaring bow. Astern the headland thinned rapidly till it lay like a blackened sill on the grey water. No other boats were abroad.

The boys fondled their new guns, sighted along the barrels, worked the mechanisms, compared notes, boasted, and gave each other contradictory advice. The fisherman got their attention once and pointed at the horizon. They peered through the windows and saw what looked like a black scum floating on top of gently agitated

water. It wheeled and tilted, rippled, curled, then rose, strung itself out and became a huge raft of ducks escaping over the sea. A
good sign.

The boys rushed out and leaned over the washboards in the
wind and spray to see the flock curl below the horizon. Then they
went and hovered around the hot engine, bewailing their lot. If
only they had been already out and waiting. Maybe these ducks
would be crazy enough to return later and be slaughtered. Ducks
were known to be foolish.

In due course and right on schedule they anchored at mid-morn-
ing in the lee of Brown Cow Island. They put the skiff overboard
and loaded it with guns, knapsacks, and tollers. The boys showed
their eagerness by being clumsy. The fisherman showed his in bad
temper and abuse which they silently accepted in the absorbed
tolerance of being boys. No doubt they laid it to lack of tobacco.

By outboard they rounded the island and pointed due east in the
direction of a ridge of foam which could be seen whitening the
surface three hundred yards away. They set the decoys in a broad,
straddling vee opening wide into the ocean. The fisherman warned
them not to get their hands wet, and when they did he made them
carry on with red and painful fingers, in order to teach them. Once
they got their numbed fingers inside their oilskins and hugged
their warm crotches. In the meantime the fisherman had turned
the skiff toward the patch of foam where as if by magic, like a
black glossy rib of earth, the ledge had broken through the belly of
the sea.

Carefully they inhabited their slippery nub of the North American continent, while the unresting Atlantic swelled and swirled as
it had for eons round the indomitable edges. They hauled the skiff
after them, established themselves as comfortably as they could in
a shallow sump on top, lay on their sides a foot or so above the
water, and waited, guns in hand.

In time the fisherman took a thermos bottle from the knapsack
and they drank steaming coffee, and waited for the nodding
decoys to lure in the first flight to the rock. Eventually the boys got
hungry and restless. The fisherman let them open the picnic lunch
and eat one sandwich apiece, which they both shared with the
dog. Having no tobacco the fisherman himself would not eat.

Actually the day was relatively mild, and they were warm

enough at present in their woolen clothes and socks underneath oilskins and hip boots. After a while, however, the boys began to feel cramped. Their nerves were agonized by inactivity. The nephew complained and was severely told by the fisherman — who pointed to the dog, crouched unmoving except for his white-rimmed eyes — that part of doing a man's hunting was learning how to wait. But he was beginning to have misgivings of his own. This could be one of those days where all the right conditions masked an incalculable flaw.

If the fisherman had been alone, as he often was, stopping off when the necessary coincidence of tide and time occurred on his way home from hauling trawls, and had plenty of tobacco, he would not have fidgeted. The boys' being nervous made him nervous. He growled at them again. When it came it was likely to come all at once, and then in a few moments to be over. He warned them not to slack off, never to slack off, to be always ready. Under his rebuke they kept their tortured peace, though they could not help shifting and twisting until he lost what patience he had left and bullied them into lying still. A duck could see an eyelid twitch. If the dog could go without moving, so could they.

"Here it comes!" the fisherman said tersely at last.

The boys quivered with quick relief. The flock came in downwind, quartering slightly, myriad, black, and swift.

"Beautiful —" breathed the fisherman's son.

"All right," said the fisherman, intense and precise. "Aim at singles in the thickest part of the flock. Wait for me to fire and then don't stop shooting till your gun's empty." He rolled up onto his elbow and spread his legs to brace himself. The flock bore down, arrowy and vibrant, then a hundred yards beyond the decoys it veered off.

"They're going away!" the boys cried, sighting in.

"Not yet!" snapped the fisherman. "They're coming round."

The flock changed shape, folded over itself, and drove into the wind in a tight arc. "Thousands —" the boys hissed through their teeth. All at once a whistling storm of black and white broke over the decoys.

"Now!" the fisherman shouted. "Perfect!" And he opened fire at the flock just as it hung suspended in momentary chaos above the tollers. The three pulled their triggers and the birds splashed into the water, until the last report went off unheard, the last smoking shell flew unheeded over their shoulders, and the last of the routed flock scattered diminishing, diminishing, diminishing in every direction.

Exultantly the boys dropped their guns, jumped up and scrambled for the skiff.

"I'll handle that skiff!" the fisherman shouted at them. They stopped. Gripping the painter and balancing himself he eased the skiff into the water stern first and held the bow hard against the side of the rock shelf the skiff had rested on. "You stay here," he said to his nephew. "No sense in all three of us going in the boat."

The boy on the reef gazed at the grey water rising and falling hypnotically along the glistening edge. It had dropped about a foot since their arrival. "I want to go with you," he said in a sullen tone, his eyes on the streaming eddies.

"You want to do what I tell you if you want to gun with me," answered the fisherman harshly. The boy couldn't swim, and he wasn't going to have him climbing in and out of the skiff any more than necessary. Besides, he was too big.

The fisherman took his son in the skiff and cruised round and round among the decoys picking up dead birds. Meanwhile the other boy stared unmoving after them from the highest part of the ledge. Before they had quite finished gathering the dead birds, the fisherman cut the outboard and dropped to his knees in the skiff. "Down!" he yelled. "Get down!" About a dozen birds came tolling in. "Shoot — shoot!" his son hollered from the bottom of the boat to the boy on the ledge.

The dog, who had been running back and forth whining, sank to his belly, his muzzle on his forepaws. But the boy on the ledge never stirred. The ducks took late alarm at the skiff, swerved aside and into the air, passing with a whirr no more than fifty feet over the head of the boy, who remained on the ledge like a statue, without his gun, watching the two crouching in the boat.

The fisherman's son climbed on the ledge and held the painter. The bottom of the skiff was covered with feathery black and white bodies with feet upturned and necks lolling. He was jubilant. "We got twenty-seven!" he told his cousin. "How's that? Nine apiece. Boy —" he added, "what a cool Christmas!"

The fisherman pulled the skiff onto its shelf and all three went and lay down again in anticipation of the next flight. The son, reloading, patted his gun affectionately. "I'm going to get me ten next time," he said. Then he asked his cousin, "Whatsamatter — didn't you see the strays?"

"Yeah," the boy said.

"How come you didn't shoot at 'em?"

"Didn't feel like it," replied the boy, still with a trace of sullenness.

"You stupid or something?" The fisherman's son was astounded. "What a highlander!" But the fisherman, though he said nothing, knew that the older boy had had an attack of ledge fever.

"Cripes!" his son kept at it. "I'd at least of tried."

"Shut up," the fisherman finally told him, "and leave him be."

At slack water three more flocks came in, one right after the other, and when it was over, the skiff was half full of clean, dead birds. During the subsequent lull they broke out the lunch and ate it all and finished the hot coffee. For a while the fisherman sucked away on his cold pipe. Then he had himself a swig of whiskey.

The boys passed the time contentedly jabbering about who shot the most — there were ninety-two all told — which of their friends they would show the biggest ones to, how many each could eat at a meal provided they didn't have to eat any vegetables. Now and then they heard sporadic distant gunfire on the mainland, at its nearest point about two miles to the north. Once far off they saw a fishing boat making in the direction of home.

At length the fisherman got a hand inside his oilskins and produced his watch.

"Do we have to go now?" asked his son.

"Not just yet," he replied. "Pretty soon." Everything had been perfect. As good as he had ever had it. Because he was getting tired of the boy's chatter he got up, heavily in his hip boots, and stretched. The tide had turned and was coming in, the sky was more ashen, and the wind had freshened enough so that whitecaps were beginning to blossom. It would be a good hour before they had to leave the ledge and pick up the tollers. However, he guessed they would leave a little early. On account of the rising wind he doubted there would be much more shooting. He stepped carefully along the back of the ledge, to work his kinks out. It was also getting a little colder.

The whiskey had begun to warm him, but he was unprepared for the sudden blaze that flashed upward inside him from belly to head. He was standing looking at the shelf where the skiff was. Only the foolish skiff was not there!

For the second time that day the fisherman felt the deep vacuity of disbelief. He gaped, seeing nothing, but the flat shelf of rock. He whirled, started toward the boys, slipped, recovered himself, fetched a complete circle, and stared at the unimaginably empty shelf. Its emptiness made him feel as if everything he had done that day so far, his life so far, he had dreamed. What could have happened? The tide was still nearly a foot below. There had been no sea to speak of. The skiff could hardly have slid off by itself. For the life of him, consciously careful as he inveterately was, he could not now remember hauling it up the last time. Perhaps in the heat of hunting, he had left it to the boy. Perhaps he could not remember which was the last time.

"Christ —" he exclaimed loudly, without realizing it because he was so entranced by the invisible event.

"What's wrong, Dad?" asked his son, getting to his feet.

The fisherman went blind with uncontainable rage. "Get back down there where you belong!" he screamed. He scarcely noticed the boy sink back in amazement. In a frenzy he ran along the ledge thinking the skiff might have been drawn up at another place, though he knew better. There was no other place.

He stumbled, half falling, back to the boys who were gawking at him in consternation, as though he had gone insane. "God damn it!" he yelled savagely, grabbing both of them and yanking them to their knees. "Get on your feet!"

"What's wrong?" his son repeated in a stifled voice.

"Never mind what's wrong," he snarled. "Look for the skiff — it's adrift!" When they peered around he gripped their shoulders, brutally facing them about. "Downwind —" He slammed his fist against his thigh. "Jesus!" he cried, struck to madness by their stupidity.

At last he sighted the skiff himself, magically bobbing along the grim sea like a toller, a quarter of a mile to leeward on a direct course for home. The impulse to strip himself naked was succeeded instantly by a queer calm. He simply sat down on the ledge and forgot everything except the marvelous mystery.

As his awareness partially returned he glanced toward the boys. They were still observing the skiff speechlessly. Then he was gazing into the clear young eyes of his son.

"Dad," asked the boy steadily, "what do we do now?"

That brought the fisherman upright. "The first thing we have to do," he heard himself saying with infinite tenderness as if he were making love, "is think."

"Could you swim it?" asked his son.

He shook his head and smiled at them. They smiled quickly back, too quickly. "A hundred yards maybe, in this water. I wish I could," he added. It was the most intimate and pitiful thing he had ever said. He walked in circles round them, trying to break the stall his mind was left in.

He gauged the level of the water. To the eye it was quite stationary, six inches from the shelf at this second. The fisherman did not have to mark it on the side of the rock against the passing of time to prove to his reason that it was rising, always rising. Already it was over the brink of reason, beyond the margins of thought — a senseless measurement. No sense to it.

All his life the fisherman had tried to lick the element of time, by getting up earlier and going to bed later, owning a faster boat, planning more than the day would hold, and tackling just one other job before the deadline fell. If, as on rare occasions he had the grand illusion, he ever really had beaten the game, he would need to call on all his reserves of practice and cunning now.

He sized up the scant but unforgivable three hundred yards to Brown Cow Island. Another hundred yards behind it his boat rode at anchor, where, had he been aboard, he could have cut in a fathometer to plumb the profound and occult seas, or a ship-to-shore radio on which in an interminably short time he would have heard his wife's voice talking to him over the air about homecoming.

"Couldn't we wave something so somebody would see us?" his nephew suggested.

The fisherman spun round. "Load your guns!" he ordered. They loaded as if the air had suddenly gone frantic with birds. "I'll fire once and count to five. Then you fire. Count to five. That way they won't just think it's only somebody gunning ducks. We'll keep doing that."

"We've only got just two-and-a-half boxes left," said his son.

The fisherman nodded, understanding that from beginning to end their situation was purely mathematical, like the ticking of the alarm clock in his silent bedroom. Then he fired. The dog, who had been keeping watch over the decoys, leaped forward and yelped in confusion. They all counted off, fired the first five rounds by threes, and reloaded. The fisherman scanned first the horizon, then the contracting borders of the ledge, which was the sole place the water appeared to be climbing. Soon it would be over the shelf.

They counted off and fired the second five rounds. "We'll hold off a while on the last one," the fisherman told the boys. He sat down and pondered what a trivial thing was a skiff. This one he and the boy had knocked together in a day. Was a gun, manufactured for killing.

His son tallied up the remaining shells, grouping them symmetrically in threes on the rock when the wet box fell apart. "Two short," he announced. They reloaded and laid the guns on their knees.

Behind thickening clouds they could not see the sun going down. The water, coming up, was growing blacker. The fisherman thought he might have told his wife they would be home before dark since it was Christmas day. He realized he had forgotten about its being any particular day. The tide would not be high until two hours after sunset. When they did not get in by nightfall, and could not be raised by radio, she might send somebody to hunt for them right away. He rejected this arithmetic immediately, with a sickening shock, recollecting it was a two-and-a-half hour run at best. Then it occurred to him that she might send somebody on the mainland who was nearer. She would think he had engine trouble.

He rose and searched the shoreline, barely visible. Then his glance dropped to the toy shoreline at the edges of the reef. The shrinking ledge, so sinister from a boat, grew dearer minute by minute as though the whole wide world he gazed on from horizon to horizon balanced on its contracting rim. He checked the water level and found the shelf awash.

Some of what went through his mind the fisherman told to the boys. They accepted it without comment. If he caught their eyes they looked away to spare him or because they were not yet old enough to face what they saw. Mostly they watched the rising water. The fisherman was unable to initiate a word of encouragement. He wanted one of them to ask him whether somebody would reach them ahead of the tide. He would have found it possible to say yes. But they did not inquire.

The fisherman was not sure how much, at their age, they were able to imagine. Both of them had seen from the docks drowned bodies put ashore out of boats. Sometimes they grasped things, and sometimes not. He supposed they might be longing for the comfort of their mothers, and was astonished, as much as he was capable of any astonishment except the supreme one, to discover himself wishing he had not left his wife's dark, close, naked bed that morning.

"Is it time to shoot now?" asked his nephew.

"Pretty soon," he said, as if he were putting off making good on a promise. "Not yet."

His own boy cried softly for a brief moment, like a man, his face averted in an effort neither to give nor show pain.

"Before school starts," the fisherman said, wonderfully detached, "we'll go to town and I'll buy you boys anything you want."

With great difficulty, in a dull tone as though he did not in the least desire it, his son said after a pause, "I'd like one of those new thirty-horse outboards."

"All right," said the fisherman. And to his nephew, "How about you?"

The nephew shook his head desolately. "I don't want anything," he said.

After another pause the fisherman's son said, "Yes he does, Dad. He wants one too."

"All right —" the fisherman said again, and said no more.

The dog whined in uncertainty and licked the boys' faces where they sat together. Each threw an arm over his back and hugged him. Three strays flew in and sat companionably down among the stiff-necked decoys. The dog crouched, obedient to his training. The boys observed them listlessly. Presently, sensing something untoward, the ducks took off, splashing the wave tops with feet and wingtips, into the dusky waste.

The sea began to make up in the mountain wind, and the wind bore a new and deathly chill. The fisherman, scouring the somber, dwindling shadow of the mainland for a sign, hoped it would not snow. But it did. First a few flakes, then a flurry, then storming past horizontally. The fisherman took one long, bewildered look at Brown Cow Island three hundred yards dead to leeward, and got to his feet.

Then it shut in, as if what was happening on the ledge was too private even for the last wan light of the expiring day.

"Last round," the fisherman said austerely.

The boys rose and shouldered their tacit guns. The fisherman fired into the flying snow. He counted methodically to five. His son fired and counted. His nephew. All three fired and counted. Four rounds.

"You've got one left, Dad," his son said.

The fisherman hesitated another second, then he fired the final shell. Its pathetic report, like the spat of a popgun, whipped away on the wind and was instantly blanketed in falling snow.

Night fell all in a moment to meet the ascending sea. They were not barely able to make one another out through driving snowflakes, dim as ghosts in their yellow oilskins. The fisherman heard a sea break and glanced down where his feet were. They seemed to be wound in a snowy sheet. Gently he took the boys by the shoulders and pushed them in front of him, feeling with his feet along the shallow sump to the place where it triangulated into a sharp crevice at the highest point of the ledge. "Face ahead," he told them. "Put the guns down."

"I'd like to hold mine, Dad," begged his son.

"Put it down," said the fisherman. "The tide won't hurt it. Now brace your feet against both sides and stay there."

They felt the dog, who was pitch black, running up and down in perplexity between their straddled legs. "Dad," said his son, "what about the pooch?"

If he had called the dog by name it would have been too personal. The fisherman would have wept. As it was he had all he could do to keep from laughing. He bent his knees, and when he touched the dog hoisted him under one arm. The dog's belly was soaking wet.

So they waited, marooned in their consciousness, surrounded

by a monstrous tidal space which was slowly, slowly closing them out. In this space the periwinkle beneath the fisherman's boots was king. While hovering airborne in his mind he had an inward glimpse of his house as curiously separate, like a June mirage.

Snow, rocks, seas, wind the fisherman had lived by all his life. Now he thought he had never comprehended what they were, and he hated them. Though they had not changed. He was deadly chilled. He set out to ask the boys if they were cold. There was no sense. He thought of the whiskey, and sidled backward, still holding the awkward dog, till he located the bottle under water with his toe. He picked it up squeamishly as though afraid of getting his sleeve wet, worked his way forward and bent over his son. "Drink it," he said, holding the bottle against the boy's ribs. The boy tipped his head back, drank, coughed hotly, then vomited.

"I can't," he told his father wretchedly.

"Try — try —" the fisherman pleaded, as if it meant the difference between life and death.

The boy obediently drank, and again he vomited hotly. He shook his head against his father's chest and passed the bottle forward to his cousin, who drank and vomited also. Passing the bottle back, the boys dropped it in the frigid water between them.

When the waves reached his knees the fisherman set the warm dog loose and said to his son, "Turn around and get up on my shoulders." The boy obeyed. The fisherman opened his oilskin jacket and twisted his hands behind him through his suspenders, clamping the boy's booted ankles with his elbows.

"What about the dog?" the boy asked.

"He'll make his own way all right," the fisherman said. "He can take the cold water." His knees were trembling. Every instinct shrieked for gymnastics. He ground his teeth and braced like a colossus against the sides of the submerged crevice.

The dog, having lived faithfully as though one of them for eleven years, swam a few minutes in and out around the fisherman's legs, not knowing what was happening, and left them without a whimper. He would swim and swim at random by himself, round and round in the blinding night, and when he had swum routinely through the paralyzing water all he could, he would simply, in one incomprehensible moment, drown. Almost the fisherman, waiting out infinity, envied him his pattern.

Freezing seas swept by, flooding inexorably up and up as the earth sank away imperceptibly beneath them. The boy called out once to his cousin. There was no answer. The fisherman, marvelling on a terror without voice, was dumbly glad when the boy did not call again. His own boots were long full of water. With no sensation left in his straddling legs he dared not move them. So long as the seas came sidewise against his hips, and then sidewise against his shoulders, he might balance — no telling how long. The upper half of him was what felt frozen. His legs, disengaged from his nerves and his will, he came to regard quite scientifically. They were the absurd, precarious axis around which reeled the surged universal tumult. The waves would come on; he could not visualize how many tossing reinforcements lurked in the night beyond — inexhaustible numbers, and he wept in supernatural fury at each because it was higher, till he transcended hate and took them, swaying like a convert, one by one as they lunged against him and away aimlessly into their own undisputed, wild realm.

From his hips upward the fisherman stretched to his utmost as a man does whose spirit reaches out of dead sleep. The boy's head, none too high, must be at least seven feet above the ledge. Though growing larger every minute, it was a small light life. The fisherman meant to hold it there, if need be, through a thousand tides.

By and by the boy, slumped on the head of his father, asked, "Is it over your boots, Dad?"

"Not yet," the fisherman said. Then through his teeth he added, "If I fall — kick your boots off — swim for it — downwind — to the island...."

"You...?" the boy finally asked.

The fisherman nodded against the boy's belly. "— Won't see each other," he said.

The boy did for the fisherman the greatest thing that can be done. He may have been too young for perfect terror, but he was old enough to know there were things beyond the power of any man. All he could do he did, trusting his father to do all he could, and asking nothing more.

The fisherman, rocked to his soul by a sea, held his eyes shut upon the interminable night.

"Is it time now?" the boy said.

The fisherman could hardly speak. "Not yet," he said. "Not just yet...."

As the land mass pivoted toward sunlight the day after Christmas, a tiny fleet of small craft converged off shore like iron filings to a magnet. At daybreak they found the skiff floating unscathed off the headland, half full of ducks and snow. The shooting *had* been good, as someone hearing on the mainland the previous afternoon had supposed. Two hours afterward they found the unharmed boat adrift five miles at sea. At high noon they found the fisherman at ebb tide, his right foot jammed cruelly into a glacial crevice of the ledge beside three shotguns, his hands tangled behind him in his suspenders, and under his right elbow a rubber boot with a sock and a live starfish in it. After dragging unlit depths all day for the boys, they towed the fisherman home in his own boat at sundown, and in the frost of evening, mute with discovering purgatory, laid him on his wharf for his wife to see.

She, somehow, standing on the dock as in her frequent dream, gazing at the fisherman pure as crystal on the icy boards, a small rubber boot still frozen under one clenched arm, saw him exaggerated beyond remorse or grief, absolved of his mortality.

*Born in Haverhill, Massachusetts, Lawrence Sargent Hall (1915-      ), earned an undergraduate degree from Bowdoin College and a Ph.D. from Yale University. An English professor who retired from Bowdoin in 1986, he received the Faulkner Award for his novel STOWAWAY (1962) and the O. Henry Memorial Award (Best Short Story 1960) for this story. It first appeared in THE HUDSON REVIEW, Winter 1958-1959, and was reprinted in O. HENRY PRIZE STORIES OF 1960 and THE BEST SHORT STORIES OF THE MODERN AGE (1962).*

# WHEN DUSTIN "CALLED ON"

O ld Swanton happened to be loafing in the men's room of the Osney Corners tavern — "How-be-ye Bill" Fogg's house — when Ben Belmore came home that time after his forty years of wandering.

Ben stumped in, so old Swanton relates, straddled his fat legs in front of the portly form of "How-be-ye Bill," who continued to rock calmly on the hind legs of his chair without getting up, and demanded:

"Know me?"

"Can't say so."

"Well, you've heard of Banjo Ben, the minstrel man!"

"Can't say so."

"Say, has the news got to this place yet that Jeff Davis is dead?" This with biting sarcasm.

"Die of anything ketchin'?"

"Now, look here, Bill, soften up a little for once in your life. You *know* me, and you *know* you do. I'm Ben Belmore who used to sit with you in school. For forty years since then as good a black-faced minstrel as ever stuck a thimble on his finger."

"How be ye?" inquired Fogg listlessly, using the phrase that had given him his nickname among travelers.

"Sixty-five, money enough to pay my board in some quiet place for the rest of my life, old bach, and can beat the best man that ever lapped a thumb, playing cribbage."

"You're a liar," he said briefly. "I mean about cribbage," he added.

"Oh, you only *think* you can play — I've met a lot like you," replied the rover with irritating condescension.

"But you wait a minute," he cried, holding up his hand to check a retort. "Are there still hornpouts in the mill pond? Are there pickerel in Branscomb crick? Do you set a good table and what will you charge a week for a boarder who will stay here the rest of his life?"

"Five dollars a week, and you can find out the rest of it for yourself," growled Fogg, "includin' the crib part."

"Consider it settled — I've got three trunks and a banjo down at the railroad station — here's five dollars for the first week," rattled the old minstrel.

"Do I look hard up enough to have to take board money in advance?" snorted the landlord. "Just because I've stuck by the old town and ain't gone flum-ti-flumin' around on a banjo with black paint on my face it ain't no sign I ain't done a little money-makin' myself."

He stood up and scowled at his old schoolmate.

"If you've made money it must be that your wife's a mighty good cook," snapped Belmore. "You ain't calculated to attract large crowds of loving guests if you meet 'em all the same as you have me."

"I ain't married and never have been — and if you ever saw a woman who can cook meats the way I can I'll give ye the tavern," said Fogg.

The two stood and looked at each other a long time. This mock crustiness that had deceived so many casual acquaintances in the past did not fool them. The deep lines on the smoothly-shaved face of the old minstrel began to curve into a quiet grin. Fogg reached down his upper lip and nipped at his short chin beard. Deep in their eyes something quivered — mystic flames springing up from the almost extinguishable embers of mirth of the old days. Hand slowly reached and grasped hand.

"You don't seem very glad to see me, Bill," said Ben softly.

"What do you want me to do — kiss ye?" demanded Fogg — and then they laughed and struck at each other as awkwardly as a couple of playful bears.

"You hard-shelled old Yankee turtle!" jeered Belmore. "Half the time a chap never knows whether a State of Maine man is glad to see him or not. But I tell you, Bill," he added, stroking the land-lord's plump shoulder, "being pretty much of granite and iron and other hard stuff, they usually stay put where you leave 'em and I've been round the world enough and been fooled enough times by the feathery sort to appreciate the difference. God bless me, it's good to be home again!"

He scruffed his fist across his eyes, went along and scrawled his name on the dog's-eared old register — and there and then by that writing became for the rest of his life the friend and guest and fidus Achates of "How-be-ye Bill." Every Tuesday after breakfast the five-dollar bill was laid across the register and as regularly the landlord unlocked the cigar case and handed his guest " a smoke on the house."

So on, through the weeks and the months! And everlastingly the cribbage game, with the supremacy swinging from side to side like a pendulum.

It was a Tuesday morning. The two old men came out from the dining room, slap-slupping in their slippers, the comfortable sense of a ham and egg breakast with them.

On the north windows of the men's room sounded the sharp clatter of snow pellets. The fire, tossing its banners of flame into the black throat of the Franklin stove, "whummled" like a softly neighing horse.

"She's going to be an old pelter," said "How-be-ye Bill," his chin beard brushing the glass as he peered without. "Startin' fine and drivin' straight and they've been grindin' the grist in that cloud bank for two days."

He finished stuffing the tobacco into his pipe and dusted his hand against his trousers.

"Banjo Ben" was lighting his Tuesday gift cigar from a wood spill that he had kindled at the stove.

"Even old baches like you have something to be thankful for," he said, rolling his eyes to take survey of the big room. The fire-light flashed on the windows of the little bar closet — relic of the old days when the stage coach folks called for "nips." The time-stained wood gave back a cosy glow. Even the snow that had begun to nest in the corner of the little window panes had a cheer-ful sparkle.

"As old Seth Blaisdell used to say when he'd come home some

summer night from a hard cider junket and clung to a tree in front of his house, 'Lord help the poor sailors on a night this!'" said the landlord, pushing their crib table before the Franklin.

With the smoke curling about their heads and flattening in strata on the warm air, they began their eleven hundredth game — according to the records — with "Banjo Ben" enjoying the quiet triumph of three games lead. When the snow clattered on the windows with a bit more emphasis they simply looked out into its swirling clouds and snuggled over their table with a new sense of the comfort of things within.

The muffled hoot of the belated up-train under the hill did not disturb them. It wasn't the sort of weather that encouraged folks to stop off at Osney Corners.

But there was a passenger who stopped. He was a tall, thin, old man who wavered in the wind on the station platform. The gusts that swept down the river valley spatted the snow into his eyes and tossed his long hair. His garments were thin for such weather and were shabby. But there was a certain dignity about his lean, shaven face, a something in his deep gray eyes that would cause even a careless observer to look twice at him. He carried an unprosperous-looking valise and hugged a battered violin case to this breast. His progress up the long hill from the railroad station was a stagger rather than a walk and the station agent, gazing after him, remarked to his helper that he cut the whistling wind like a jack-knife blade.

The feeble thunking of his feet on the tavern porch, as he beat off the snow, startled the men within-doors from their game.

"Who is there?" asked Ben, whose back was turned toward the window.

"It looks like a blue her'n," said Bill. "It's got legs like one but its head is like a man's."

And then the stranger came in.

He stood by the door and gazed at the two of them with a sort of piteous hesitancy that checked certain jests they were about to crack.

"It's about as it was when your father was landed here, Will," ventured the new arrival. "And you look as your father did before you. I suppose I cannot blame you for not remembering me — but I'm Francis Dustin — one of the old boys."

He took off his broad hat and smiled at them wistfully.

"'Fiddling Francis!'" blurted Belmore. He got up and walked along to the man and shook him by the hand. "Frank," he said heartily, "they still call me 'Banjo Ben,' just as they did in the old days here. Three years after you went away with your fiddle under your arm, to make your living, I started out with my banjo on my back to make mine. You had all the talent and I had all the brass and I had to make good with my cheek."

With the courtesy of the man of the world he affected to take no note of the other's seediness. He pulled a chair to the fire and pushed him down in it.

"Yes, you had all the talent," he repeated.

"Talent!" sneered Dustin. His blue hands trembled before the blaze. The melting snow dripped off his gray hair upon the threadbare shoulders of his coat. "Boys, don't say that to me! Why didn't my father make me what he was himself, a carpenter — anything rather than keep hammering that damnable word "talent" in my ears from the time I was able to understand? What's the use of trying to carry on this folly with you, the boys who went to school with me? I never had talent. I was only a lazy fool with long fingers and long hair and my folks spoiled me."

His lank jaws quivered with his passion and with the chill that was still in the marrow of his bones.

"Oh, my God," he complained, "when will fathers and mothers stop trying to make silk purses out of swine's ears? Think of it! They sacrificed all their lives to make me something that they dreamed I could be — something I was foolish enough to believe I was. Put me on a pedestal!" His lips curled. "And I fell — and broke!"

"Bus'ness ain't been so good with ye as ye hoped, then?" soothingly queried the matter-of-fact landlord, reaching for a match.

"Who is the first selectman in this town now?" asked Dustin with a sort of desperate bluntness.

"Columbus Jepson," said Fogg. "Honors in this town are sort of passed down through the Jepson family. Remember how long Columb's father was selectman?"

"I'm done with make-believe in this world for what little time is left to me," Dustin proceeded, his eyes straight before him. "I

started out wrong. I have always been wrong. Who is the first selectman in this town?''

"I said, Columbus Jepson," replied Fogg, a bit testily.

"Wrong — wrong — all the way to the end," moaned Dustin.
"After it all I've got to go to a Jepson."

He sat for a little time weaving his thin fingers together and
then, setting his teeth, he gritted.

"Where is he — does he live —?"

"Still keepin' store where his father did," replied Fogg laconically. "It's a great place to hang to the old things — is Osney Corners."

He cast a quick glance at Ben and there came a little wrinkle of
the old hectoring spirit under his beard.

"They do say that the reason why Lepha Jepson ain't ever got
married is because she is still hangin' onto that ole flame for you
that her father put his foot down on."

But there was contrition in his face when Dustin pinched his
narrow shoulders still farther forward and murmured, "Don't,
boys!" in that familiar old-time tone when he had been the butt of
the school on account of his long hair and his spoiled-child airs.

"Take off your coat, Frank, and visit," said the landlord. Some
notion of the man's plight came to him now. "We'll make — say, a
week of it — or till after Christmas — Ben and you and I, and talk
over old times. I don't want you to put your name on the book,
there. It's goin' to be just a nice little visit. We —"

"It's no use, Will," wailed the other, struggling out of his chair,
"I'm going to be honest at last with myself and the rest. I'm a
pauper. That's the truth of it. I've come out of the hospital with
these fingers twisted by rheumatism — and *that's* all my people
gave me to earn my living with in this world." He shook his fist at
the battered violin case lying beside his chair. "And now I've
become what an old orchestra hack must expect to become if he
isn't lucky enough to die at the right time. I don't have to tell you,
Ben," he cried, whirling on the old minstrel man. Ben wagged his
head in thoughtful assent.

Dustin stooped and cracked his bony knuckles on the fiddle
case, a queer, weak and childish anger at last bursting bounds
within him.

"It has ridden to and fro on my shoulders all these years," he gasped, "it hasn't let me stop long enough to know a home of my own. Always its whine in my ear — and the soul of it mocking me. It wouldn't come out at my touch! Talent! Boys, I haven't ever been a mere fiddler that could hold his place! And I've come back. There's no other place in the world that will have me. I've come back to go to the poor farm — and I've got to talk with Columbus Jepson and — and you know what that means for me!"

"You are goin' to stay right here and —"

"You'll drive me mad, Will, if you talk like that any longer," Dustin cried, his voice breaking shrilly. "I'm a pauper. There's only one place in all the world where I can rightfully call on for help, and it's where my father lived and paid his taxes. I'm not a beggar from my friends. I've earned my living, boys. There's what I did it with." He spread his long, crooked fingers before them. "They can earn no more dollars for me. But I'll cut them off before I'll take with them dollars or food from my friends. There's this much about a town pauper: he's so by the law and isn't sailing under false pretences. I'm going to see Columbus Jepson."

But when he started Ben pushed him back into his chair.

"Wait a minute, Francis," he entreated. "Jepson isn't at the selectman's office. He's at his store. And that store is always full of loafers. Columbus is the same sort of man you would expect from the boy he used to be. He would insult and abuse you in front of his loafers. I'll call him here. He must come, for it is town business. And we'll have it amongst ourselves. You stay here."

The next moment he had dragged his fur cap from its hook and was out into the smother of storm.

Jepson came promptly, for he had scented something interesting from the old minstrel's vague hints.

He stamped in boisterously, slatting the snow from his hat in a wide sweep.

"I reckon I'd have known your long hair, even if it is gray," he said without warmth or without taking the hand of the man crouching before the stove. "I can remember this feller, Fogg," he went on, "when he used to play for the dances. Used to have to sneak out of his house, for old Dustin thought he had too much talent and genius to play for kitchen break-downs. And he'd set there and saw catgut with his eyes rolled up like a sick cat and his long hair dancin' around and all the girls thinkin' he looked foreign. It didn't pay, did it, Dustin?" His tone was cruel.

"I'm not here to talk over old times, Columbus," said the musician. He had recovered from the grief that old memories had awakened in him and now fronted the town officer with quiet dignity. "I sent for you to tell you that I must call on the town of Osney for help. I cannot earn my living with these hands crippled this way and, as much as I hate to come back on my old town, there seems to be no other way."

"Where did you vote last?" demanded the selectman.

"Here."

"Do you mean to tell me that you haven't gained residence anywhere and haven't voted for more than forty years?"

"That is the truth."

"I can remember father sayin'" growled the selectman with fine scorn, "that the Dustin family never had any more practical ideas in 'em than you could find in a last year's bobolink's nest — and I reckon father knew what he was talkin' about."

"It strikes me," remarked the old minstrel, narrowing his eyes, "that end jokes and monologues aren't called for now. The question is, what are you going to do for our friend, here?"

The selectman simply eyed the rebuker insolently and turned again on the shrinking man at the stove.

"So the cricket has fiddled all summer, eh, and now comes home to the ants for food for the winter? You've had all the fun and now expect us to pay for it."

"We know that your idea of a howlin' good time in this world, Columb, would be settin' on a gravestun' and eatin' snowballs," interrupted the landlord brusquely. "You're just cold-blooded enough to like that kind. But what you are and what other folks are not is not the matter before the meetin'. Here's poor Frank Dustin back home amongst us and needy. We were all boys together. We've called you across here away from the loafers and peekers in your store so as to talk this over all friendly. He's been unfortunate and we three know why better than most folks. I'd like to make him an offer but I know he won't accept it. He's shown that much already. Columb, you don't need to send him to the poor farm. There's kind of a disgrace in that that a true Yankee hates to stand. The people there now are only bums and are proud of it. Here's my word to you, Columb. This town has boarded other people out. Put Frank here with me and you and I won't quarrel over the price per week."

He put his back toward Dustin and winked appealingly and meaningly at the selectman. But that functionary disregarded this opportunity to be lenient or to employ the subterfuge that the tavern-keeper plainly intended to quiet Dustin's scruples.

"Whenever they want you to run town business they'll probably elect you to office, Fogg," snapped Jepson, with covert and insulting allusions to a past and gone political difference and defeat. The brick-red that crawled up from under the landlord's collar told how the shot took effect. "Dustin, you have called on the town for help," the selectman went on. "I shall have to take you to the poor farm as soon as this storm clears away. I'll look for you here." He went out promptly as though to avoid further discussion and plowed across the street.

It was truly an inspiration with a touch of divinity in it that occurred to the old minstrel just then, as he stood there, his mind groping for some word, some diversion to smooth the dreadful embarrassment of that moment when that stricken man sat cowering there, looking from one to the other, waiting for them to speak.

"Say, Frank," volleyed Ben with a sudden boyish heartiness, "I reckon your hands aren't so bad but what you can play some of the old pennyroyals?"

Dustin bent over his violin case, welcoming this chance to hide his face from them.

"Bill and I have played together once in a while," the minstrel went on, "played just as we used to in school days, but I tell you, Frank, we missed your fiddle. Now once again, for old times sake, and we'll forget all the years that have passed."

He fetched his banjo out of a closet behind the stove and the tavern-keeper came up from under the little counter of the ancient bar, bringing a dusty old drum.

"Make her 'Hull's victory,' boys," he puffed, tucking the drum into the crook of his fat legs and propping himself on the edge of his arm chair. "There's plenty of drum part to it."

And the next moment this remarkable orchestra was off!

When men straggled over from the store, hearing the stirring strains above the howl of the storm, the players kept on, their eyes on each other's face, not heeding their audience, for the long, long thoughts that galloped in time to the old tunes had hurried them away from the present.

"Fiddlin' Francis" did not go to the poor farm that night. The town officers did not come after him. The roads were blocked and the storm still screamed.

In the night some one joggled the landlord's elbow that jutted invitingly under the patchwork quilt of his head. The old minstrel stood over him, his earnest face lighted by the candle that he carried.

"Bill, I can't sleep," said Ben. "Just you listen to that gad-awful wind!"

"She's a snorter," yawned Bill, listening a moment to the shuddering rush of the blast.

"I just looked in on Frank," said Ben. "He's sound asleep and forgetting his troubles. I reckon there was never a man who needed a good night's rest any more. Say Bill, it's tough to think of, ain't it?"

The landlord did not say anything, but his eyes, from which sleep had now gone, answered sufficiently.

Ben set his candle on the stand and muffled himself more closely in the quilt he had wrapped around his shoulders.

"You and I might do something for him, but he's just as big a fool about practical things as he ever was, as he showed out at your first hint. I reckon that kind of foolishness goes with his long fingers and womanly ways."

"He never was like the rest of the boys," assented Bill.

"But we are all more or less foolish," proceeded Ben. "I'm foolish to be roaming around this time of night like an old cat, haired up by the wind. Perhaps sitting down today and playing all those old tunes over and over has made all three of us a little foolish."

"Second childhood!" grunted Bill gruffly, but all the time winking at moisture in his eyes.

"Say, look-a-here, Bill," Ben blurted, leaning forward on his elbows, "I've got more foolish ideas in my head tonight than — well, you'll get up and bat me with a pillow pretty quick."

The landlord stared at him.

"You will, I say. Now down to cases, Bill — down quick and hard. There are some men that are peculiar and some women that are, too. Hey? Sure! You courted Lepha Jepson. You couldn't get her. In love with Frank Dustin! I courted Lepha Jepson. I didn't get her. Still in love with Frank Dustin, and that old tiger of a father of hers ready to eat her if she showed a sign of it. You went off and minded your business. I didn't mind mine."

His voice trembled.

"Beats all how foolish a man can get to be, thinking over the old times when they're thrown up to him all of a sudden. Just hear that wind, Bill! It's bad enough in here, but think of that old, yellow, poor-house breasting it out in that bare field!"

"What about this mindin' your bus'ness and not mindin' it," insisted the landlord, his eyes gleaming curiously.

"It's just this, Bill —" the old showman gulped — "you know I was naturally pretty much of a satan when I got mad in the old days. I broke it up between Lepha and poor Frank. Perhaps it wasn't much to break up — considering what would have been his chances of getting her away from the old man. But I broke it up. I told the truth to old Jepson and lied to Frank and Lepha and — no matter! That's what I did. And you and I know 'em well to know that they, being — what did I call it? — *peculiar* would be just fools enough to let it spoil their lives. There are some folks built that way. Of course, you and I ain't marrying men — never have been!" There was a queer break in his voice. "But I reckon Frank would have been different with a home."

"Ben, that was a mean trick — meaner'n I've got the disposition to work," said Bill.

The minstrel stood up and tossed the quilt off his shoulders.

"Bill," he cried, "you were speaking just now of second childhood. I'm in it. But if anyone is going to be a fool there's nothing like being one good and hard." He closed his fists and shook them into the steam arising from his breath. "I'm going to — I'm going to — listen! I'm going to have Frank Dustin and Lepha Jepson married inside of a week and that's just as true as it sounds crazy."

The landlord struggled up in bed. There was a strange glint in his eye. A quiver crept through his beard about his mouth.

"I won't stand for that," he said bluntly.

"You're going back on me?"

"I'll have to, Ben, because — well, you saw today how we stand toward each other, Columb and I, — I shall have to prevent that marriage because I love Columb and it will kill him if it ever comes off."

The quip was the true Yankee way of breaking a tense situation that was harrowing their feelings. Ben cuffed at Bill and Bill retaliated by shying a pillow. At the door the old minstrel turned and held his candle above his head. His eyes were shining.

"It's sort of good — this being foolish, ain't it, Bill?" he said softly, and went away down the corridor chuckling.

The next morning the neighbors of Miss Lepha Jepson were surprised to see a man whose features were nearly covered by a fur cap and scarf go plunging through the drifts of her yard. Aunt Ruth Howe, peering through the glitter of sun on snow, thought this person walked like Ben Belmore.

A little before noon there was a jangle of bells in front of the tavern and "How-be-ye Bill" answered a hail from the man in the sleigh. It was First Selectman Jepson.

"I've come for that pauper," he said to Fogg as he stuck his head past the edge of the shielding front door.

"Ain't able to go," returned Fogg.

"Well, he's got to go," stormed Jepson, sticking his red-tipped nose out over his fur collar.

"I say he ain't — I say he can't, and —" the landlord threw the door wide and stood on the threshold, his breath streaming far on the frosty air, "if you think you are man enough to take him out of this house you hitch your horse and come right in."

The selectman did not accept this truculant invitation. He lashed his horse and drove away.

There was always more or less mystery about the rest of this affair.

The first selectman came the next day and demanded the pauper. The pauper was not visible. But for long hours there was the mumble of voices in a room upstairs. And the neighbors had counted five trips to Lepha Jepson's little house by that man who wore the big fur cap.

On the evening of the third day, flushed and beaming, Ben and Bill went apart by themselves and clasped hands.

"Talk about bein' minister to Chiny and envoy to Pee-ru," said Bill, "why, me and you can give 'em diplomatic points that they never knew before!"

"As I said to you in the first place," said Ben, "they are peculiar — those two — but dig in, and they were loving each other all the time — the two old fools. Now you can trust that town clerk, can't you?"

"He hates Columb Jepson worse than I do," replied Bill. "He wouldn't tell Jepson his barn was on fire, much less show him them marriage intentions."

They were married Christmas eve in the little house on the hill, and the two wedding guests came away with the parson and left them there.

In front of Jepson's store on their way home, Guest Bill tugged at Guest Ben's arm.

"I reckon it's best for me and you to break the news to him," he chuckled. "We can do it in such a soothin' way, ye know. Then we can tell him we'll kill him if ever we hear that he's disturbed 'em and can come away wishin' him a Merry Christmas. There's a whole lot in knowin' how to do those things right, Ben."

Of all the loafers who were present in the store on that occasion Uncle Benson Huff tells most vividly of what happened. He relates — but, that is a story by itself.

When the two diplomats were back before the Frankin and were calming their nerves with a before-bed-time smoke, Bill said after awhile:

"That remark of yours to Columb that he couldn't very well make a pauper out of a man that had fifteen hundred dollars in the bank sort of struck me. You ain't been playin' any underhanded game on me have you, Ben?"

The minstrel flushed.

"That was the hardest part of the diplomacy," he stammered, half-guiltily. "I had to lie about owing his father money. Had to talk two days before I made him believe it. Couldn't have made him believe it even then if he'd known anything about business. But I finally tripped him and downed him and rammed it into his pocket — that is, it amounted to that."

"How much money have you got, anyway?" demanded Bill surily.

"None of your business."

"You've gone to playin' underhanded with me," persisted Bill. "All is, I don't want to have any more bus'ness transactions with you. I refuse to do bus'ness with you. If ever — now you under-stand me — if ever — " he leaned forward and shook his pipe stem under Ben's nose, "you offer to pay me another week's board I'll take that register of mine and peg you right down through the floor. Do you understand that?"

Ben did not reply to this indignant query. He leaned back in his big chair and smiled into the fire.

"Say Bill," he murmured, his round face glowing through the smoke clouds like an autumn sun, "I believe this is the Christmassiest Christmas I ever remember."

"It will do for a couple of hard-shelled old baches," assented Bill.

They stooped forward and rapped out their pipe dottles on the hearth of the Franklin, hiding their faces for a moment.

When Bill straightened and yawned obtrusively he gulped, "It is goin' to be a good night to sleep, Ben."

And it was. Not even the reindeer bells awakened them for their gift had come on ahead — the consciousness of a deed well done, to fill their brimming hearts.

*Holman Day (1865-1935), a native of Vassalboro, Maine, graduated from Colby College and for a number of years was employed as a correspondent by the LEWISTON SUN. Author of more than a dozen novels and many short stories, his work is noted for humor and use of dialect. This story first appeared in PINE TREE MAGAZINE in 1906.*

# "OLLIE, OH . . ."

E rroll, the deputy who was known to litter, did not toss any Fresca cans or Old King Cole bags out this night. Erroll brought his Jeep to a stop in the yard right behind Lenny Cobb's brand-new Dodge pickup. The brakes of Erroll, the deputy's, Jeep made a spiritless dusky squeak. Erroll was kind of humble this night. The greenish light of his police radio shone on his face and yes, the froggishly round eyes, mostly pupil because it was dark, were humble. His lips were shut down over his teeth that were usually laughing and clicking. Humbleness had gone so far as to make that mouth look almost *healed* over like the holes in women's ears when they stop putting earrings through. He took off his knit cap and lay it on the seat beside the empty Fresca can, potato chip bag, and cigar cellophanes. He put his gloved hand on the door opener to get out. But he paused. He was scared of Ollie Cobb. He wasn't sure how she would take the news. But she wasn't going to take it like other women did. Erroll tried to swallow but there was no saliva there to work around in his throat.

He looked at Lenny Cobb's brand-new Dodge in the lights of his Jeep. It was so cold out there that night that the root-beer-color paint was sealed over every inch in a delicate film like an apple still attached, still ripening, never been handled. Wasn't Lenny Cobb's truck the prince of trucks? Even the windshield and little vent windows looked heavy-duty . . . as though congealed inside their rubber strips thick and deep as the frozen Sebago. And the chrome was heavy as pots. And the plow! It was constricted into travel gear, not yet homely from running into stone walls and frost heaves. And on the cab roof an amber light, the swivel kind, big as a man's head. Of course it had four-wheel drive. It had shoulders! Thighs. Spine. It might be still growing.

The Jeep door opened. The minute he stood up out in the crunchy driveway he wished he had left his cap on. The air was like paper, could have been thirty below. His breath leaving his nose turned to paper. It was all so still and silent. With no lights on in Lenny Cobb's place, a feeling came over Erroll of being alone at the North Pole. Come to his ears a lettucelike crispness, a keenness. . . so that to the top arch of each ear his spinal cord plugged in. A cow murred in the barn. One murr. A single note. And yet the yard was so thirsty for sound. . . all planes gave off the echo: a stake to mark a rosebush under snow. . . an apple basket full of snow on the top step. He gave the door ten or twelve thonks with his gloved knuckles. It *hurt*.

Ollie Cobb did not turn on a light inside or out. She just spread open the door and stood looking down at him through the small round frames of her glasses. She wore a long rust-colored robe with pockets. The doorway was outside the apron of light the Jeep headlights made. Erroll had to squint to make her out, the thin hair. It was black, parted in the middle of her scalp, yanked back with such efficiency that the small fruit-shape of her head was clear: a lemon or a lime. And just as taut and businesslike, pencil-hard, pencil-sized, a braid was drawn nearly to her heels. . . the toes, long as thumbs, clasped the sill. "Deputy Anderson," she said. She had many teeth. Like shingles. They seemed to start out of her mouth when she opened it.

He said: "Ah. . ."

Erroll couldn't know when the Cobb house had rotted past saving, yet more certain than the applewood banked in the stove, the smell of dying timbers came to him warmly. . . almost rooty, like carrots. . .

"What *is* it?" she said.

He thought of the great sills of that old house being soft as carrots. "Lenny has passed away," he said.

She stepped back. He was hugged up close to the openness of the door, trying to get warm, so when the door whapped shut, his foot was in it. *"Arrrrr!"* So he got his foot out. She slammed the door again. When he got back in his Jeep, his coffee fell off the dash and burned his leg.

## II

The kitchen lights came on. All Ollie's white-haired children came into the living room when she started to growl and rub her shoulder on the refrigerator. This was how Ollie grieved. She rolled her shoulders over the refrigerator door so some of the magnetic fruits fell on the floor. A math paper with a 98 on top seesawed downward and landed on the linoleum. The kids were happy for a chance to be up. "Oh, boy!" they said. All but Aspen who was twelve and could understand. She remained at the bottom of the stairs afraid to ask Ollie what the trouble was. Aspen was in a lilac-color flannel gown and gray wool socks. She sucked the thumb of her right hand and hugged the post of the banister with her left. It was three-fifteen in the morning. Applewood coals never die. All 'round the woodstove was an aura of summer. The socks and undershirts and mittens pinned in scores to a rope across the room had a summer stillness. They heard Ollie growl and pant. They giggled. Sometimes they stopped and looked up when she got loud. They figured she was not getting her way about something. They had seen the deputy, Erroll, leave from the upstairs windows. They associated Erroll with crime. Crime was that vague business of speeding tickets and expired inspection stickers. This was not a new thing. Erroll had come up in his Jeep behind Ollie a time or two in the village. He said "Red light" and she bared her teeth at him like a dog. She was baring her teeth now.

There was an almost Christmas spirit among the children to be wakened in the night like that. There was wrestling. There was wriggling. Tim rode the dog, Dick Lab. He, Dick Lab, would try to get away, but hands on his hocks would keep him back. Judy turned on the TV. Nothing was on the screen but bright fuzz. The hair of them all flying through the night was the torches of after-dark skiers: crackling white from chair to couch to chair to stairway, rolling Dick Lab on his side, carouseling twelve-year-old Aspen who sucked her thumb, Eddie and Arnie, Tim and Judy.

The herdsman's name was Jarrell Bean. He was like all Beans, silent and touchy, and had across his broad coffee-color face a look that made you suspect he was related somehow, perhaps on his mother's side, to some cows. The eyes were slate color and were of themselves lukewarm-looking, almost steamy, very huge, browless, while like hands they reached out and patted things that interested him. He inherited from his father, Bingo Bean, a short haircut...a voluntary baldness: the father's real name was also Jarrell, killed chickens for work and had the kind of red finely lined fingers you'd expect from so much murder. But Bingo's eyes everybody knows were yellow and utility. It was from his mother's side that Jarrell the herdsman managed to know what tact was. He came to the Cobb's door from his apartment over the barn. He had seen the deputy Erroll's Jeep and figured Lenny's time had come. He was wearing a black- and red-checked coat and the spikes of a three-day beard, auburn. It was the kind of beard men adrift in lifeboats have. Unkind weather had spread each of the hairs its own way.

He had travelled several yards through that frigid night with *no hat.* This was nudity for a man so bald.

In his mouth was quite a charge of gum. He didn't knock. The kitchen started to smell of spearmint as soon as he closed the door behind him. Ollie was rolled into a ball on the floor, grunting, one bare foot, bare calf and knee extended. He stepped over the leg. He made Ollie's children go up the stairs. He dragged one by the arm. It howled. Its flare of pale hair spurted here and there at the herdsman's elbow. The entire length of the child was twisting. It was Randy who was eight and strong. Dick Lab sat down on the twelve-year-old Aspen's ankles and feet, against the good wool. Jarrell came down the stairs hard. His boots made a booming through the whole big house. He took Dane and Linda and Hannah all at once. Aspen kept sucking her thumb. She looked up at him as he came down toward her, seeing him over her fingers. She was big as a woman. Her thumb in her mouth was longer and lighter than the other fingers from twelve years of sucking. He fetched her by the blousey part of her lilac gown. She came away from the banister with a snap: like a Band-Aid from a hairy arm... "Cut it out!" she cried. His hands were used only to cattle. He thought of himself as *good* with cattle, not at all cruel. And yet with cattle what is to be done is always the will of the herdsman.

## III

When Jarrell came downstairs, Ollie was gone. She had been thinking of Lenny's face, how it had been evaporating for months into the air, how the lip had gotten short, how the cheeks fell into the bone. While Jarrell stood in the kitchen, he picked up the magnetic fruits and stuck them in a row on the top door of the refrigerator. He figured Ollie had slipped into her room to be alone.

He walked out into the yard past Lenny's new root-beer-color truck. He remembered how it roared when Leo at the Mobil had fiddled with the accelerator and everyone — Merritt and Poochie and Poochie's brother and Kenny, even Quinlan — stood around looking in at the big 440 and Lenny was resting on the running board. Lenny's neck was getting much too small for his collar even then.

Jarrell went up to his apartment over the barn, his head stinging from the deep-freeze night, then his lamp went out and the yard was noiseless.

Under the root beer truck Ollie was curled with her braid in the snow. She had big bare feet. Under the rust-color robe the goosebumps crowned up. Her eyes were squeezed shut like children do when they pretend to be sleeping. Her lip was drawn back from the elegantly twisted teeth, twisted like the stiff feathers of a goose are overlaid. And filling one eyeglass lens a dainty ice fern.

## IV

It was Ollie whose scheduled days and evenings were on a tablet taped to the bathroom door. Every day Ollie got up at 4:30 A.M. Every evening supper was at 5:45. If visitors showed up late by fifteen minutes, she would whine at them and punish them with remarks about their character. If she was on her way to the feed store in the pickup and there was a two-car accident blocking the road up ahead, Ollie would roll down the window and yell: *"Move!"*

Once Aspen's poor body nearly smoked, 102 temperature, and blew a yellow mass from her little nose holes...a morning when

Ollie had plans for the lake...Lenny was standing in the yard
with his railroad cap on and his ringless hands in the pockets of
his cardigan, leaning on the new root beer truck...Ollie came out
on the porch where many wasps were circling between her face
and his eyes looking up: "She's going to spoil our time," Ollie said.
"We've got to go down to the store and call for an appointment
now. She couldn't have screwed up the day any better." Then she
went back inside and made her hand like a clamp on the girl's
bicep, bore down on it with the might of a punch or a kick, only
more slow, more deep. Tears came to Aspen's eyes. Outside Lenny
heard nothing. Only the sirens of wasps. And stared into the very
middle of their churning.

Oh, that Ollie. Indeed, Lenny months before must have planned
his cancer to ruin her birthday. That was the day of the doctor's
report. All the day Lenny cried. Right in the lobby of the hospital...a scene...Lenny holding his eyes with the palms of his
hands: "Help me! Help me!" he wailed...she steered him to a
plastic chair. She hurried down the hall to be alone with the snack
machine...HEALTHY SNACKS: apples and pears, peanuts. She
despised *him* this way. *This* was her birthday.

V

In the thirty below *zero* morning jays' voices cracked from the
roof. Figures in orange nylon jackets hustled over the snow. They
covered Ollie with a white wool blanket. The children were steady
with their eyes and statuesque as they arranged themselves
around the herdsman. Aspen held the elbow of his black and red
coat. Everyone's breath flattened out like paper, like those clouds
cartoon personalities' words are printed on. It may have warmed
up some. Twenty below or fifteen below. The cattle had not been
milked, shuffling and ramming and murring, cramped near the
open door of the barn...in pain...their udders as vulgar and
hard as the herdsman's velvet head.

VI

At the hospital surgeons removed the ends of Ollie's fingers, most
of her toes and her ears. She drank Carnation Instant Breakfast,

grew sturdy again, and learned to keep her balance. She came home with her thin hair combed over her earholes. In the back her hair veiled her ruby coat.

She got up every morning at 4:30 and hurtled herself out to the barn to set up for milking. Jarrell feared every minute that her hair might fall away from her missing ears. He would squint at her. Together they sold some of the milk to the neigborhood, those who came in cars and pulling sleds, unloading plastic jugs and glass jars to be filled at the sink, and the children of these neighbors would stare at Ollie's short fingers. Jarrell: "Whatcha got today, only two...is ya company gone?" or "How's Ralph's team doin now?...that's good ta hear," or "Fishin any good now? I ain't heard." He talked a lot these days. When they came around he brightened up. He opened doors for them and listened to gossip and passed it on. They teased him a lot about his lengthening beard. Sometimes Tim would stand between Jarrell and Ollie and somehow managed to have his hands on the backs of Jarrell's knees most of the time. As Ollie hosed out the stainless-steel sink there in the wood and glass white white room, Tim's eyes came over the sink edge and watched the water whirl.

At night Jarrell would open Mason jars and slice carrots or cut the tops off beets. Ollie would lift things slowly with her purply stubs. She set the table. She would look at Jarrell to see if he saw how slick she did this. But he was not looking. The children, all those towheads, would be throwing things and running in the hall. There had come puppies of Dick Lab. Tim and a buff puppy pulled on a sock. Tim dragged the puppy by the sock across the rug. Ollie would stand by the sink and look straight ahead. She had a spidery control over her short fingers. She once hooked small Marsha up by the hair and pressed her to the woodbox with her knee. But Ollie was wordless. Things would usually go well. By 5:45 forks of beets and squash were lifted to mouths and glasses of milk were draining.

After supper Jarrell would go back to his apartment and watch *Real People* and *That's Incredible* or *60 Minutes* and fall asleep with his clothes on. He had a pile of root beer cans by the bed. Sometimes mice would knock them over and the cans would roll out of the room, but it never woke him.

Jarrell could not go to the barn in the morning without thinking of Lenny. He would go along and pull the rows of chains to all the glaring gray lights. He and Lenny used to stand by the open door together. The black and white polka-dot *sea* of cows would clatter between them. And over and between the blowing mouths and oily eyes, Lenny's dollar-ninety-eight-cent gloves waved them on, and he'd say: "Oh, girl...oh, girl..." Their thundering never ever flicked Lenny's watered-down auburn hair that was thin on top. And there were the hairless temples where the chemotherapy had seared from the inside out.

Jarrell could recall Lenny's posture, a peculiar tired slouch in his pea coat. Lenny wore a watch cap in midwinter and a railroad cap in sweaty weather and the oils of his forehead were on the brims of both.

Jarrell remembered summer when there was a big corn-on-the-cob feast and afterward Lenny lay on the couch with just his dungarees on and his veiny bare feet kicking. His hairless chest was stamped with three black tattoos; two sailing ships and a lizard. Tim was jumping on his stomach. A naked baby lay on its back, covering the two ships. Lenny put his arm around the baby and it seemed to melt into him. Lenny's long face had that sleepy look of someone whose world is interior, immediate to the skin, never reaching outside his hundred and twenty acres. That very night that Lenny played on the couch with his children, Jarrell left early and stayed awake late in his apartment watching Tim Conway dictating in a German accent to his nitwit secretary.

Jarrell heard Ollie yelling. He leaned out his window and heard more clearly Ollie rasping out her husband's name. Once she leaped across the gold square of light of their bedroom window. Jarrell knew that Lenny was sitting on the edge of the bed, perhaps with his pipe in his mouth, untying his gray peeling workboots. Lenny would not argue, nor cry, nor turn red, but say "...oh, girl...oh, Ollie, oh..." And he would look up at her with his narrow face, his eyes turning here and there on his favorite places of her face. She would be enraged the more. She picked up the workboot he had just pulled off his foot and turned it in her hand...then spun it through the air...the lamp went out and crashed.

Lenny began to lose weight in the fall. In his veins white blood cells soared. The cancer was starting to make Lenny irritable. He stopped eating supper. Ollie called it fussy. Soon Ollie and Jarrell were doing the milking alone. Sometimes Aspen would help. Lenny lay on the couch and slept. He slept all day.

## VII

One yellowy morning Ollie made some marks on the list on the bathroom door and put a barrette on the end of her braid. She took the truck to Leo's and had the tank filled. She drove all day with Lenny's face against her belly. Then with her hard spine and convexed shoulders she balanced Lenny against herself and steered him up the stairs of the Veterans' hospital. She came out alone and her eyes were wide behind the round glasses.

## VIII

Jarrell had driven Lenny's root beer Utiline Dodge for the first time when he drove to the funeral alone. Lenny had a closed casket. The casket was in an alcove with pink lights and stoop-shouldered mumbly Cobbs. They all smelled like old Christmas cologne. There must have been a hundred Cobbs. Most of the flowers around the coffin were white. Jarrell stood. The rest were sitting. The herdsman's head was pink in the funny light and he tilted his head as he considered how Lenny looked inside the coffin, under the lid. Cotton was in Lenny's eyes. He probably had skin like those of plaster-of-Paris ducks that hike over people's lawns single file. He was most likely in there in some kind of suit, no pea coat, no watch cap, no pipe, no babies, no grit of Flash in his nails. Someone had undoubtedly scrubbed all the cow smell off him and he probably smelled like a new doll now. Jarrell drove to the interment at about eighty to eighty-five miles per hour and was waiting when the headlighted caravan dribbled into the cemetery and the stooped Cobbs ambled out of about fifty cars.

## IX

Much later, after Lenny was dead awhile and Ollie's fingers were healed, Ollie came into the barn about 6:10. They were running late. The dairy truck from Portland was due to arrive in the yard.

Ollie was wearing Lenny's old pea coat and khaki shirt with her new knit pants. Tim was with her. Tim had a brief little mouth and freakish coarse hair, like white weeds. His coat was fastened with safety pins. Ollie started hooking up the machines with her quick half-fingers. They rolled like sausages over the stainless-steel surfaces. Jarrell, hurrying to catch up, was impatient with the cows when they wanted to shift around. Ollie was soundless but Jarrell could locate her even if he didn't see her, even as she progressed down the length of the barn. He had radar in his chest (the heart, the lungs, even the bladder) for her position when things were running late. God! It was like trying to walk through a wall of sand. Tim came over and stood behind him. Tim was digging in his nose. He was dragging out long strings of discolored matter and wiping it on his coat that was fastened with pins. One cow pulled far to the right in the stanchion, almost buckling to her knees as a hind foot slipped off the edge of the concrete platform. The milking machine thunked to the floor out of Jarrell's hands. Ollie heard. Her face came as if from out of the loft, sort of downward. *Her hair was pulled back* caught up by her glasses when she had hurriedly shoved them on. *She did not have ears. He saw for the first time they had taken her ears.* His whole shape under his winter clothes went hot as though common pins were inserted over every square inch. He squinted, turned away...ran out of the milking room into the snow. The dairy truck from the city was purring up the hill. The fellow inside flopped his arm out for his routine wave. Jarrell didn't wave back, but used both hands to pull himself up into the root beer truck, slid across the cold seat, made the engine roar. He remembered Lenny saying once while they broke up bales of hay: "I just ordered a Dodge last week, me and my wife...be a few weeks, they said. Prob'ly for the President they'd have it to him the next day. Don't it *hurt* to wait for somethin like that. Last night I dreamed I was in it, and was revvin it up out here in the yard when all of a sudden it took off... right up in the sky...and all the cows down in the yard looked like dominoes."

## X

That afternoon Jarrell Bean returned. He came up the old Nathan Lord Road slow. Had his arm out the window. When he got near the Cobb place he ascended the hill in a second-gear roar. As he turned in the drive he saw Ollie in Lenny's pea coat standing by the doorless Buick sedan in which the hens slept at night. She lined the sights of Lenny's rifle with the right lens of her glasses. One of her sausage fingers was on the trigger. She put out two shots. They turned the right front tire to rags. The Dodge screamed and plowed sideways into the culvert. Jarrell felt it about to tip over. But it only listed. He lay flat on the seat for a quarter of an hour after he was certain Ollie had gone into the house.

Aspen and Judy came out for him. He was crying, lying on his stomach. When they saw him crying, their faces went white. Aspen put her hard gray fingers on his back, between his shoulders. She turned to Judy . . . Judy, fat and clear-skinned with the whitest hair of all . . . and said: "I think he's sorry."

## XI

Ollie lay under the mint-green bedspread. The window was open. All the yard, the field, the irrigation ditches, the dead birds were thawing, and under the window she heard a cat digging in the jonquils and dried leaves. She raised her hand of partial fingers to her mouth to wipe the corners. She had slept late again and now her blood pressure pushed at the walls of her head. She flipped out of the bed and thunked across the floor to the window. She was in a yellow print gown. The sunrise striking off the vanity mirror gave Ollie's face and arms a yellowness, too. She seized her glasses under the lamp. She peered through them, downward . . . *startled.* Jarrell was a few yards from his apartment doorway, taking a pair of dungarees from the clothesline. There were sheets hanging there, too, so it was hard to be sure at first . . . then as he strode back toward his doorway, she realized he had nothing on. He was corded and pale and straight-backed and down front of his chest dripped wet his now-full auburn beard. The rounded walls of his genitals gave little flaccid jogglings at each stride and on all of him his flesh like unbroken yellow water paused satisfyingly and seldomly at a few auburn hairs. On top, the balded head, a seamless hood, trussed up with temples all the way in that same seamless fashion to his eyes that were merry in the most irritating way. Ollie mashed her mouth and shingled teeth to the screen and moaned full and cowlike. And when he stopped and looked up, she screeched: *"I hate you! Get out of here! Get out of here!"*

She scuttled to the bed and plunked to the edge. Underneath, the shoes that Lenny wore to bean suppers and town council meeting were still crisscrossed against the wall.

## XII

That summer Jarrell and the kids played catch in the middle of the Nathan Lord Road. Jarrell waded among them at the green bridge in knee-deep water, slapped Tim a time or two for persisting near the drop-off. They laughed at the herdsman in his secondhand tangerine trunks and rubber sandals. He took them to the drive-in movies in that root beer truck. They saw *Benji* and *Last Tango in Paris.* They got popcorn and Good and Plentys all over the seat and floor and empty paper cups were mashed in the truck bed, blew out one by one onto different people's lawns. He splurged on them at Old Orchard Beach, rides and games, and coordinated Aspen won stuff with darts: a psychedelic poster, a stretched-out Pepsi bottle and four paper leis. Then under the pier they were running with huge ribbons of seaweed and he cut his foot on a busted Miller High Life bottle . . . slumped in the sand to fuss over himself. It didn't bleed. You could see into his arch, the meat, but no blood. Aspen's white hair waved 'round her head as she stooped in her sunsuit of cotton dots, blue like babies' clothes are blue. She cradled his poor foot in her fingers and looked him in the eye.

Ollie *never* went with them. No one knew what she did alone at home.

One afternoon Ollie stared through the heat to find Jarrell on the front porch, there in a rocking chair with the sleeping baby's open mouth spread on his bare arm. Nearly grown puppies were at his feet. He was almost asleep himself and mosquitoes were industriously draining his throat and shirtless chest. On the couch after supper the little girls nestled in his auburn beard and rolled in their fingers wads of the coarse stuff. The coon cat with the abscesses all over his head swallowed whole the red tuna Jarrell bought for him and set out at night on an aluminum pie plate. Jarrell whenever he was close smelled like cows.

## XIII

Ollie drove to the drugstore for pills that were for blood pressure. Aspen went along. The root beer truck rattled because Jarrell had left a yarding sled and chains in the back. Ollie turned her slow rust-color eyes onto Aspen's face and Aspen felt suddenly panicked. It seemed as though there was something changing about her mother's eyes: one studied your skin, one bored dead-center in your soul. Aspen was wearing her EXTINCT IS FOREVER T-shirt. It was apricot colored and there was a leopard's face in the middle of her chest.

"Do you want one of those?" Ollie asked Aspen, who was poking at the flavored Chap Sticks by the cash register.

"Could I?"

"Sure," Ollie pointed somewhere. "And I was thinking you might like some colored pencils or a...you know...movie magazine."

Aspen squinted. "I would, yes, I would."

A trio of high-school-aged Crocker boys in stretched-out T-shirts trudged through the open door in a bowlegged way that made them seem to be carrying much more weight than just their smooth long bones and little gummy muscles. One wore a baseball hat and had sweat in his hair and carried his sneakers. He turned his flawless neck, and his pink hair cropped there in a straight line was fuzzy and friendly like ruffles on a puppy's shoulders where you pat. He looked right at Aspen's leopard...right in the middle and read: "Extinct is forever."

His teeth lifted in a perfect cream-color line over the words and his voice was low and rolled, one octave above adulthood. Both the other boys laughed. One made noises like he was dying. Then all of them pointed their fingers at her and said: "Bang! Bang! Bang!" There are the insightful ones who realize a teenager's way of flirting, and then there was Aspen who could not. To see all the boys' faces from her plastic desk in school was to Aspen like having a small easily destructible boat with sharks in all directions. Suddenly self-conscious, suddenly stoop-shouldered as it was for all Cobbs in moments of hell, Aspen stood one shoe on top of the other and stuck her thumb in her mouth. There is something about drugstore light with its smells of sample colognes passing up like moths through a brightness bigger and pinker than sun that made Aspen Cobb look large and old, and the long thumb there was nasty looking. The pink-haired Crockers had never seen a big girl do this. They looked at each other gravely.

She walked over to where her mother was holding a jar of vitamin C. Her mother was arched over it, the veils of her thin black hair covering her earholes, falling forward, and her stance was gathering, coordinated like a spider, the bathtub spider, the horriblest kind. She lifted her eyes. Aspen pulled her thumb out of her mouth and wiped it on her shirt. Ollie put her arm around Aspen. She never did this as a rule. Aspen looked at her mother's face disbelievingly. Ollie pointed with one stub to the vitamin C bottle. It said: "200% of the adult minimum daily requirement." Aspen pulled away. The Crocker boys at the counter looked from Ollie's fingers to Aspen's thumb. But not till they were outside did they shriek and hoot.

On the way home in the truck Aspen wished her mother would hug her again now that they were alone. But Ollie's fingers were sealed to the wheel and her eyes blurred by the glasses were looking out from a place where no hugging ever happened. There was a real slow Volkswagen up ahead driven by a white-haired man. Ollie gave him the horn.

## XIV

The list of activities on the bathroom door became more rigidly ordered. . . with even trips to the flush, snacks and rests, and conversations with the kids prescheduled. . . peanut butter and saltines: 3:15. . . clear table: 6:30. . . brush hair: 9:00. . . and Ollie moved faster and faster and her cement-color hands and face were always across the yard somewhere or in the other room. . . singular of other people. And Jarrell looked in at her open bedroom door as he scooted Dane toward the bathroom for a wash. . . Ollie was *cleaning out the bureau again; the third time that week*. . . and she was doing it very fast.

In September there was a purple night and the children all loaded into the back of the truck. Randy strapped the baby into her seat in the cab. The air had a dry grasshopper smell and the truck bed was still hot from the day. Jarrell turned the key to the root-beer-color truck. "I'm getting a Needham!" he heard Timmy blat from the truck bed. He pulled on the headlights knob. He shifted into reverse. The truck creaked into motion. The rear wheel went up, then down. Then the front went up and down. Sliding into the truck lights was the yellow gown, the mashed gray arm, the black hair unbraided, the face unshowing but with a purple liquid going everywhere from out of that hair, the half-fingers wriggling just a little. She had been under the truck again.

From the deepest part of Jarrell Bean the scream would not stop even as he hobbled out of the truck. Oh, he feared to touch her, just rocked and rocked and hugged himself and howled. The children's high whines began. They covered Ollie like flies. As with blueberry jam their fingers were dipped a sticky purple. The herdsman reached for the twelve-year-old Aspen. He pulled at her. Her lids slid over icy eyes. Her breath was like carrots into his breath. He reached. And her frame folded into his hip.

*Carolyn Chute (1947-      ) was born in Portland, Maine. She has worked as a correspondent for the Portland newspapers. THE BEANS OF EGYPT, MAINE (1985), her first novel, was a national best seller. This story first appeared in PLOUGHSHARES in 1982, and was reprinted in BEST AMERICAN SHORT STORIES OF 1983.*

# THEY GRIND
# EXCEEDING
# SMALL

I telephoned down the hill to Hazen Kinch. "Hazen," I asked, "are you going to town today?"

"Yes, yes," he said abruptly in his quick, harsh fashion. "Of course I'm going to town."

"I've a matter of business," I suggested.

"Come along," he invited brusquely. "Come along."

There was not another man within forty miles to whom he would have given that invitation.

"I'll be down in ten minutes," I promised him; and I went to pull on my Pontiacs and heavy half boots over them and started downhill through the sandy snow. It was bitterly cold; it had been a cold winter. The bay — I could see it from my window — was frozen over for a dozen miles east and west and thirty north and south; and that had not happened in close to a score of years. Men were freighting across to the islands with heavy teams. Automobiles had beaten a rough road along the course the steamers took in summer. A man who had ventured to stock one of the lower islands with foxes for the sake of their fur, counting on the water to hold them prisoners, had gone bankrupt when his stock in trade escaped across the ice. Bitterly cold and steadily cold, and deep snow lay upon the hills, blue-white in the distance. The evergreens were blue-black blotches on this whiteness. The birches, almost indistinguishable, were like trees in camouflage. To me the hills are never so grand as in this winter coat they wear. It is easy to believe that a brooding God dwells upon them. I wondered as I ploughed my way down to Hazen Kinch's farm whether God did indeed dwell among these hills; and I wondered what He thought of Hazen Kinch.

This was no new matter of thought with me. I had given some thought to Hazen in the past. I was interested in the man and in that which should come to him. He was, it seemed to me, a problem in fundamental ethics; he was, as matters stood, a demonstration of the essential uprightness of things as they are. The biologist would have called him a sport, a deviation from type, a violation of all the proper laws of life. That such a man should live and grow great and prosper was not fitting; in a well-regulated world it could not be. Yet Hazen Kinch did live; he had grown — in his small way — great; and by our lights he had prospered. Therefore I watched him. There was about the man the fascination which clothes a tight-rope walker above Niagara; an aeronaut in the midst of the nose dive. The spectator stares with half-caught breath, afraid to see and afraid to miss seeing the ultimate catastrophe. Sometimes I wondered whether Hazen Kinch suspected this attitude on my part. It was not impossible. There was a cynical courage in the man; it might have amused him. Certainly I was the only man who had in any degree his confidence.

I have said there was not another within forty miles whom he would have given a lift to town; I doubt if there was another man anywhere for whom he would have done this small favour.

He seemed to find a mocking sort of pleasure in my company.

When I came to his house he was in the barn harnessing his mare to the sleigh. The mare was a good animal, fast and strong. She feared and she hated Hazen. I could see her roll her eyes backward at him as he adjusted the traces. He called to me without turning:

"Shut the door! Shut the door! Damn the cold!"

I slid the door shut behind me. There was within the barn the curious chill warmth which housed animals generate to protect themselves against our winters.

"It will snow," I told Hazen. "I was not sure you would go."

He laughed crookedly, jerking at the trace.

"Snow!" he exclaimed. "A man would think you were personal manager of the weather. Why do you say it will snow?"

"The drift of the clouds — and it's warmer," I told him.

"I'll not have it snowing," he said, and looked at me and cackled.

He was a little, thin, old man with meager whiskers and a curious precision of speech; and I think he got some enjoyment out of watching my expression at such remarks as this. He elaborated his assumption that the universe was conducted for his benefit, in order to see my silent revolt at the suggestion. "I'll not have it snowing," he said. "Open the door."

He led the mare out and stopped by the kitchen door.

"Come in," he said. "A hot drink."

I went with him into the kitchen. His wife was there, and their child. The woman was lean and frail; and she was afraid of him. The countryside said he had taken her in payment of a bad debt. Her father had owed him money which he could not pay.

"I decided it was time I had a wife," Hazen used to say to me.

The child was on the floor. The woman had a drink of milk and egg and rum, hot and ready for us. We drank, and Hazen knelt beside the child. A boy baby, not yet two years old. It is an ugly thing to say, but I hated this child. There was evil malevolence in his baby eyes. I have sometimes thought the grey devils must have left just such hate-bred babes as this in France. Also, he was deformed — a twisted leg. The women of the neighbourhood sometimes said he would be better dead. But Hazen Kinch loved him. He lifted him in his arms now with a curious passion in his movement, and the child stared at him sullenly. When the mother came near the baby squalled at her, and Hazen said roughly:

"Stand away! Leave him alone!"

She moved back furtively; and Hazen asked me, displaying the child: "A fine boy, eh?"

I said nothing, and in his cracked old voice he mumbled endearments to the baby. I had often wondered whether his love for the child redeemed the man; or merely made him vulnerable. Certainly any harm that might come to the baby would be a crushing blow to Hazen.

He put the child down on the floor again and he said to the woman curtly: "Tend him well." She nodded. There was a dumb submission in her eyes; but through this blank veil I had seen now and then a blaze of pain.

Hazen went out of the door without further word to her, and I followed him. We got into the sleigh, bundling ourselves into the robes for the six-mile drive along the drifted road to town. There

was a feeling of storm in the air. I looked at the sky and so did
Hazen Kinch. He guessed what I would have said and he answered
me before I could speak.

"I'll not have it snowing," he said, and leered at me.

Nevertheless, I knew the storm would come. The mare turned
out of the barnyard and ploughed through a drift and struck hard-
packed road. Her hoofs beat a swift tattoo; our runners sang
beneath us. We dropped to the little bridge and across and began
the mile-long climb to the top of Rayborn Hill. The road from
Hazen's house to town is compounded of such ups and downs.

At the top of the hill we paused for a moment to breathe the
mare; paused just in front of the big old Rayborn house, that has
stood there for more years than most of us remember. It was
closed and shuttered and deserted; and Hazen dipped his whip
toward it and said meanly:

"An ugly, improvident lot, the Rayborns were."

I had known only one of them — the eldest son. A fine man,
I had thought him. Picking apples in his orchard, he fell one
October and broke his neck. His widow tried to make a go of the
place, but she borrowed of Hazen and he had evicted her this
three months back. It was one of the lesser evils he had done. I
looked at the house and at him, and he clucked to the mare and we
dipped down into the steep valley below the hill.

The wind had a sweep in that valley and there was a drift of
snow across it and across the road. This drift was well packed by
the wind, but when we drove over its top our left-hand runner
broke through the coaming and we tumbled into the snow, Hazen
and I. We were well entangled in the rugs. The mare gave a
frightened start, but Hazen had held the reins and the whip so that
she could not break away. We got up together, he and I, and we
righted the sleigh and set it upon the road again. I remember that
it was becoming bitter cold and the sun was no longer shining.
There was a steel-grey veil drawn across the bay.

When the sleigh was upright Hazen went forward and stood
beside the mare. Some men, blaming the beast without reason,
would have beaten her. They would have cursed, cried out upon
her. That was not the cut of Hazen Kinch. But I could see that
he was angry and I was not surprised when he reached up and
gripped the horse's ear. He pulled the mare's head down and

twisted the ear viciously. All in a silence that was deadly.

The mare snorted and tried to rear back and Hazen clapped the butt of his whip across her knees. She stood still, quivering, and he wrenched at her ear again.

"Now," he said softly, "keep the road."

And he returned and climbed to his place beside me in the sleigh. I said nothing. I might have interfered, but something had always impelled me to keep back my hand from Hazen Kinch.

We drove on and the mare was lame. Though Hazen pushed her, we were slow in coming to town and before we reached Hazen's office the snow was whirling down — a pressure of driving, swirling flakes like a heavy white hand.

I left Hazen at the stair that led to his office and I went about my business of the day. He said as I turned away:

"Be here at three."

I nodded. But I did not think we should drive home that afternoon. I had some knowledge of storms.

That which had brought me to town was not engrossing. I found time to go to the stable and see Hazen's mare. There was an ugly welt across her knees and some blood had flowed. The stablemen had tended the welt, and cursed Hazen in my hearing. It was still snowing, and the stable boss, looking out at the driving flakes, spat upon the ground and said to me:

"Them legs'll go stiff. That mare won't go home tonight."

"I think you are right," I agreed.

"The white-whiskered skunk!" he said, and I knew he spoke of Hazen.

At a quarter of three I took myself to Hazen Kinch's office. It was not much of an office; not that Hazen could not have afforded a better. But it was up two flights — an attic room ill lighted. A small air-tight stove kept the room stifling hot. The room was also air-tight. Hazen had a table and two chairs, and an iron safe in the corner. He put a pathetic trust in that safe. I believe I could have opened it with a screwdriver. I met him as I climbed the stairs. He said harshly:

"I'm going to telephone. They say the road's impassable."

He had no telephone in his office; he used one in the store below. A small economy fairly typical of Hazen.

"I'll wait in the office," I told him.

"Go ahead," he agreed, halfway down the stairs.

I went up to his office and closed the drafts of the stove — it was red-hot — and tried to open the one window, but it was nailed fast. Then Hazen came back up the stairs grumbling.

"Damn the snow!" he said. "The wire is down."

"Where to?" I asked.

"My house, man! To my house!"

"You wanted to telephone home that you—"

"I can't get home tonight. You'll have to go to the hotel." I nodded good-naturedly.

"All right. You, too, I suppose."

"I'll sleep here," he said.

I looked round. There was no bed, no cot, nothing but the two stiff chairs. He saw my glance and said angrily: "I've slept on the floor before."

I was always interested in the man's mental processes.

"You wanted to telephone Mrs. Kinch not to worry?" I suggested.

"Pshaw, let her fret!" said Hazen. "I wanted to ask after my boy." His eyes expanded, he rubbed his hands a little, cackling. "A fine boy, sir! A fine boy!"

It was then we heard Doan Marshey coming up the stairs. We heard his stumbling steps as he began the last flight and Hazen seemed to cock his ears as he listened. Then he sat still and watched the door. The steps climbed nearer; they stopped in the dim little hall outside the door and someone fumbled with the knob. When the door opened we saw who it was. I knew Marshey. He lived a little beyond Hazen on the same road. Lived in a two-room cabin — it was little more — with his wife and his five children; lived meanly and pitiably, grovelling in the soil for daily bread, sweating life out of the earth — life and no more. A thin man, racking thin; a forward-thrusting neck and a bony face and a sad and drooping moustache about his mouth. His eyes were meek and weary.

He stood in the doorway blinking at us; and with his gloved hands — they were stiff and awkward with the cold — he unwound the ragged muffler that was about his neck and he brushed weakly at the snow upon his head and his shoulders. Hazen said angrily:

"Come in! Do you want my stove to heat the town?"

Doan shuffled in and he shut the door behind him. He said: "Howdy, Mr. Kinch." And he smiled in a humble and placating way.

Hazen said: "What's your business? Your interest is due."

Doan nodded.

"Yeah. I know, Mr. Kinch. I cain't pay it all."

Kinch exclaimed impatiently: "An old story! How much can you pay?"

"Eleven dollars and fifty cents," said Doan.

"You owe twenty."

"I aim to pay it when the hens begin to lay."

Hazen laughed scornfully.

"You aim to pay! Damn you, Marshey, if your old farm was worth taking I'd have you out in the snow, you old scamp!"

Doan pleaded dully: "Don't you do that, Mr. Kinch! I aim to pay."

Hazen clapped his hands on the table.

"Rats! Come! Give me what you've got! And, Marshey, you'll have to get the rest. I'm sick of waiting on you."

Marshey came shuffling toward the table. Hazen was sitting with the table between him and the man and I was a little behind Hazen at one side. Marshey blinked as he came nearer, and his weak nearsighted eyes turned from Hazen to me. I could see that the man was stiff with the cold.

When he came to the table in front of Hazen he took off his thick gloves. His hands were blue. He laid the gloves on the table and reached into an inner pocket of his torn coat and drew out a little cloth pouch and he fumbled into this and I heard the clink of coins. He drew out two quarters and laid them on the table before Hazen, and Hazen picked them up. I saw that Marshey's fingers moved stiffly; I could almost hear them creak with the cold. Then he reached into the pouch again.

Something dropped out of the mouth of the little cloth bag and fell soundlessly on the table. It looked to me like a bill, a piece of paper currency. I was about to speak, but Hazen, without an instant's hesitation, had dropped his hand on the thing and drawn it unostentatiously toward him. When he lifted his hand the money — if it was money — was gone.

Marshey drew out a little roll of worn bills. Hazen took them out of his hand and counted them swiftly.

"All right," he said. "Eleven-fifty. I'll give you a receipt. But you mind me, Doan Marshey, you get the rest before the month's out. I've been too slack with you."

Marshey, his dull eyes watching Hazen write the receipt, was folding the little pouch and putting it away. Hazen tore off the bit of paper and gave it to him. Doan took it and he said humbly: "Thank'e, sir."

Hazen nodded.

"Mind now," he exclaimed, and Marshey said: "I'll do my best, Mr. Kinch."

Then he turned and shuffled across the room and out into the hall and we heard him descending the stairs.

When he was gone I asked Hazen casually: "What was it that he dropped upon the table?"

"A dollar," said Hazen promptly. "A dollar bill. The miserable fool!"

Hazen's mental processes were always of interest to me.

"You mean to give it back to him?" I asked.

He stared at me and he laughed. "No! If he can't take care of his own money — that's why he is what he is."

"Still it is his money."

"He owes me more than that."

"Going to give him credit for it?"

"Am I a fool?" Hazen asked me. "Do I look like so much of a fool?"

"He may charge you with finding it."

"He loses a dollar; I find one. Can he prove ownership? Pshaw!" Hazen laughed again.

"If there is any spine in him he will lay the thing to you as a theft," I suggested. I was not afraid of angering Hazen. He allowed me open speech; he seemed to find a grim pleasure in my distaste for him and for his way of life.

"If there were any backbone in the man he would not be paying me eighty dollars a year on a five-hundred-dollar loan — discounted."

Hazen grinned at me triumphantly.

"I wonder if he will come back," I said.

"Besides," Hazen continued, "he lied to me. He told me the eleven-fifty was all he had."

"Yes," I agreed. "There is no doubt he lied to you."

Hazen had a letter to write and he bent to it. I sat by the stove and watched him and considered. He had not yet finished the letter when we heard Marshey returning. His dragging feet on the stair were unmistakable. At the sound of his weary feet some tide of indignation surged up in me.

I was minded to do violence to Hazen Kinch. But — a deeper impulse held my hand from the man.

Marshey came in and his weary eyes wandered about the room. They inspected the floor; they inspected me; they inspected Hazen Kinch's table, and they rose at last humbly to Hazen Kinch.

"Well?" said Hazen.

"I lost a dollar," Marshey told him. "I 'lowed I might have dropped it here."

Hazen frowned.

"You told me eleven-fifty was all you had."

"This here dollar wa'n't mine."

The money-lender laughed.

"Likely! Who would give you a dollar? You lied to me, or you're lying now. I don't believe you lost a dollar."

Marshey reiterated weakly: "I lost a dollar."

"Well," said Hazen, "there's no dollar of yours here."

"It was to git medicine," Marshey said. "It wa'n't mine."

Hazen Kinch exclaimed: "By God, I believe you're accusing me!"

Marshey lifted both hands placatingly.

"No, Mr. Kinch. No, sir." His eyes once more wandered about the room. "Mebbe I dropped it in the snow," he said.

He turned to the door. Even in his slow shuffle there was a hint of trembling eagerness to escape. He went out and down the stairs. Hazen looked at me, his old face wrinkling mirthfully.

"You see?" he said.

I left him a little later and went out into the street. On the way to the hotel I stopped for a cigar at the drug store. Marshey was there, talking with the druggist.

I heard the druggist say: "No, Marshey, I'm sorry. I've been stung too often."

Marshey nodded humbly.

"I didn't 'low you'd figure to trust me," he agreed. "It's all right. I didn't 'low you would."

It was my impulse to give him the dollar he needed, but I did not do it. An overpowering compulsion bade me keep my hands off in this matter. I did not know what I expected, but I felt the imminence of the fates. When I went out into the snow it seemed to me the groan of the gale was like the slow grind of millstones, one upon the other.

I thought long upon the matter of Hazen Kinch before sleep came that night.

Toward morning the snow must have stopped; and the wind increased and carved the drifts till sunrise, then abruptly died. I met Hazen at the post office at ten and he said: "I'm starting home."

I asked: "Can you get through?"

He laughed.

"I will get through," he told me.

"You're in haste."

"I want to see that boy of mine," said Hazen Kinch. "A fine boy, man! A fine boy!"

"I'm ready," I said.

When we took the road the mare was limping. But she seemed to work out the stiffness in her knees and after a mile or so of the hard going she was moving smoothly enough. We made good time.

The day, as often happens after a storm, was full of blinding sunlight. The glare of the sun upon the snow was almost unbearable. I kept my eyes all but closed, but there was so much beauty abroad in the land that I could not bear to close them altogether. The snow clung to twigs and to fences and to wires, and a thousand flames glinted from every crystal when the sun struck down upon the drifts. The pine wood upon the eastern slope of Rayborn Hill was a checkerboard of rich colour. Green and blue and black and white, indescribably brilliant. When we crossed the bridge at the foot of the hill we could hear the brook playing beneath the ice that sheathed it. On the white pages of the snow wild things had writ here and there the fine-traced tale of their morning's adventuring. We saw once where a fox had pinned a big snowshoe rabbit in a drift.

Hazen talked much of that child of his on the homeward way.

I said little. From the top of the Rayborn Hill we sighted his house and he laid the whip along the mare and we went down that last long descent at a speed that left me breathless. I shut my eyes and huddled low in the robes for protection against the bitter wind, and I did not open them again till we turned into Hazen's barnyard, ploughing through the unpacked snow.

When we stopped Hazen laughed.

"Ha!" he said. "Now, come in, man, and warm yourself and see the baby! A fine boy!"

He was ahead of me at the door; I went in upon his heels. We came into the kitchen together.

Hazen's kitchen was also living-room and bedroom in the cold of winter. The arrangement saved firewood. There was a bed against the wall opposite the door. As we came in a woman got up stiffly from this bed and I saw that this woman was Hazen's wife. But there was a change in her. She was bleak as cold iron and she was somehow strong.

Hazen rasped at this woman impatiently: "Well, I'm home! Where is the boy?"

She looked at him and her lips moved soundlessly. She closed them, opened them again. This time she was able to speak.

"The boy?" she said to Hazen. "The boy is dead!"

The dim-lit kitchen was very quiet for a little time. I felt myself breathe deeply, almost with relief. The thing for which I had waited — it had come. And I looked at Hazen Kinch.

He had always been a little thin man. He was shrunken now and very white and very still. Only his face twitched. A muscle in one cheek jerked and jerked and jerked at his mouth. It was as though he controlled a desire to smile. That jerking, suppressed smile upon his white and tortured countenance was terrible. I could see the blood drain down from his forehead, down from his cheeks. He became white as death itself.

After a little he tried to speak. I do not know what he meant to say. But what he did was to repeat — as though he had not heard her words — the question which he had flung at her in the beginning. He said huskily: "Where is the boy?"

She looked toward the bed and Hazen looked that way; and then he went across to the bed with uncertain little steps. I followed him. I saw the little twisted body there. The woman had been keeping it warm with her own body. It must have been in her arms when we came in. The tumbled coverings, the crushed pillows spoke mutely of a ferocious intensity of grief.

Hazen looked down at the little body. He made no move to touch it, but I heard him whisper to himself: "Fine boy."

After a while he looked at the woman. She seemed to feel an accusation in his eyes. She said: "I did all I could."

He asked "What was it?"

I had it in me — though I had reason enough to despise the little man — to pity Hazen Kinch.

"He coughed," said the woman. "I knew it was croup. You know I asked you to get the medicine — ipecac. You said no matter — no need — and you had gone."

She looked out of the window.

"I went for help — to Annie Marshey. Her babies had had it. Her husband was going to town and she said he would get the medicine for me. She did not tell him it was for me. He would not have done it for you. He did not know. So I gave her a dollar to give him — to bring it out to me.

"He came home in the snow last night. Baby was bad by that time, so I was watching for Doan. I stopped him in the road and I asked for the medicine. When he understood he told me. He had not brought it."

The woman was speaking dully, without emotion.

"It would have been in time, even then," she said. "But after a while, after that, baby died."

I understood in that moment the working of the mills. And when I looked at Hazen Kinch I saw that he, too, was beginning to understand. There is a just mercilessness in an aroused God. Hazen Kinch was driven to questions.

"Why — didn't Marshey fetch it?" he asked.

She said slowly: "They would not trust him — at the store."

His mouth twitched, he raised his hands.

"The money!" he cried. "The money! What did he do with that?"

"He said," the woman answered, "that he lost it — in your office; lost the money there."

After a little the old money-lender leaned far back like a man wrenched with agony. His body was contorted, his face was terrible. His dry mouth opened wide.

He screamed!

Halfway up the hill to my house I stopped to look back and all round. The vast hills in their snowy garments looked down upon the land, upon the house of Hazen Kinch. Still and silent and inscrutable.

I knew now that a just and brooding God dwelt among these hills.

*Ben Ames Williams (1889-1953), a Mississippian, took a job as reporter for the Boston AMERICAN after graduating from Dartmouth College. Eventually moving to Maine, he produced more than thirty-five novels (several of which were filmed) and four hundred short stories, many of which formed a series about a mythical Maine community, Fraternity Village. This story first appeared in THE SATURDAY EVENING POST in 1919 and was reprinted in O. HENRY MEMORIAL AWARD STORIES, 1919.*

# SPRING

*The murmur of the pine's green branches is in her ears,
she remembers how the white heron came flying through
the golden air and how threy watched the sea
and the morning together, and Sylvia
cannot speak; she cannot tell
the heron's secret . . . .*

A White Heron

# SMALL POINT BRIDGE

It was March 31 and Isaac Bates had survived still another Maine winter. Now, his solitary lunch finished, he stood for a moment by the large living room window and looked down over the white stubble of glazed brush, farther down to the ledges along the shore and out to the churning sea, and enjoyed his one cigar for the day. He also savored their consternation: sons and daughters in Connecticut, Tennessee, California, and all over, neighbors back on the town road, all amazed that a man of his age who could easily afford to live anywhere would stick it out for the length of another winter. He had been snowed in for two months and three days. The old dirt road between his place and the highway was too steep for truck or tractor plowing; and even now, with the partial thaw, it was only fit for Jeep travel. There weren't many who would put up with all of that.

"No *sir*," he said aloud.

It hadn't been easy. It never was, of couse, but this year the snows had come early and the oil truck couldn't make a December delivery so by January he was using the kerosene space heater and by February he was back to coal in the cookstove and wood in the fireplaces. The children were forever writing him to get out of there; but what the hell, generations had lived in that house on the heat of good oak firewood. Better for you anyway. Oil heat cakes the lungs.

So now he was almost up to another April. During the dark months he'd told himself that if he stuck it to April he'd last another year and, as he told the children, a man past seventy bargains for short-term leases. The low point had come when the pipes froze and he had to shut off the water. That meant shoveling a path to the outhouse. In the old days he and the boys kept that path open morning by morning, which was easier in the long run than cutting through three months' accumulation. . . . Well, that was all behind him now.

But the winter wasn't through yet. There was still a kick to it. A March gale had begun the previous day and had built up strong during the night. Now, spitting sleet and rain, it churned the bay into an ugly froth. Only a month ago the ice had been thick enough for deer to wander out to the islands, and one young fool had driven his Ford pick-up out past Peniel Island just for the dare of it. But now the gale had broken that white valley up into slabs of forty and fifty tons and was grinding them against the shore. Tide and wind had jacked them up into weird angles like a nightmare of train wrecks. But unlike boxcars, they were forever moving — slow as a clock's hand and with a force you could hardly believe.

There was one year when the ice had caught hold of the marine railway he used to haul his fishing boats. Within an agonizing week it had pried those railroad tracks from the ties spike by spike and had slowly twisted them into hairpin shapes. The memory of it made him grimace even now.

From where he stood in his living room he could hear the inhuman whine and grunt as ice heaved blindly against ledge. The sound had been loud enough to pry its way into his dreams the night before.

"Snarl all you want," he muttered and blew cigar smoke against the window where it broke like surf. "You can't move granite." His shore line was solid ledge, and there was satisfaction in that. It was solid like his house, like the plate glass that stood between him and the driving sleet — he had seen full-grown pheasants break their necks against that glass.

The storm would do damage at the cannery. He knew that. He had seen the ice lock onto the base of a pile two feet thick and work it back and forth with the incoming tide, pulling it clear out of the muck and lifting the pier above it as well. He'd seen the oak hull of a lobster boat crushed like a beer can in a young man's grip. No sir, he wouldn't get by a winter like this without getting hurt somewhere. But there was money for repairs. In half a century he had built his cannery with solid blocks of effort: first, fresh crab-meat for the summer hotels; then canned crabmeat statewide; finally frozen seafood of all types coast to coast. As his billboards said, "You Can't Beat Bates for Frozen Fishcakes." And no one had. No matter what they threw at him, there was always the satisfaction that he had insured himself with bank accounts. "There's more than one way to build a sea wall," he said, and nodded, serving as his own audience.

But he was talking to himself again. That wasn't good. It meant he was getting weak-headed. "Keep your mouth shut," he said. What he needed was a little activity.

Then he remembered that this was the 31st. This was the day he had to see Seth. He probably should have taken care of it before this, but now they were at the deadline. And he had almost forgotten it.

It was a small business matter and Seth would be surprised that such details are important — Seth being a simple man. But a debt's a debt and all the world knew that. If you let the little things go — well, it's like not tending to a small leak.

"Rotten day to be out," he said, but he felt no deep resentment. He never expected the weather to give him an even break.

He went to the front hall and began burrowing in the cluttered closet. "Where's those boots?" he muttered. "Damn it, Ella, where's those boots?" Then he clamped his jaw on his cigar, cursing himself silently. Ella was dead — dead, buried, and gone two years now. It was weak-headed to call her name. Besides, it wouldn't do to let her know he was still living here. "Promise," she had said, looking up at him from that ugly hospital bed, and he had promised: he would move out of the old place when she was gone. And he would, too — when the time came to join her.

"Where the hell. . .?" And he spotted his boots just where he had left them on the chair — together with his coat, his lumber-man's cap, his tool box, his axe, his snow shovel, the broken car jack, his extra set of chains, and an empty anti-freeze can. Of course. "Got to clean up this goddamn mess," he said with the tone he used to use on the children.

The old barn was dark and colder than the outside air; but for all this his Jeep started easily enough. During the winter months

Isaac had run the motor for an hour each week with religious regularity; that, plus the recent trips to the store, had left the battery charged. All it took was a little foresight.

He backed out and drove past the barn through the apple orchards and down into the spruce grove. At the bottom of the ravine by the brook he stopped and shifted into four-wheel drive. The long, twisting ascent was a brutal challenge. It took two wild runs, wheels whining and spewing half-frozen cakes of mud; but he made it, finally, with a grunt of satisfaction.

"Crazy road," he muttered to himself, as he had said to every visitor who had ever come over it. It was the only route out from the farm to the highway and thus the only link with the store, with the town, and even with his cannery. He had cursed it and repaired it every spring; but it had its uses. It moved the assessors to pity, kept salesmen out, turned back summer tourists, and intimidated talkative neighbors. There was no gate or sign that could do all that.

Once on the tar road, he made good time. He had to dodge fallen branches and allow for sleet on the pavement, but it was not long before he came to the turn which led back onto his own acreage again, back down to the sea again where his cannery stood gray and silent on ice-caked piles, dormant and waiting like his orchard.

Small Point Road ran parallel to the sea from the cannery to Seth's place, less than a quarter-mile. It was a godforsaken bit of coastline with a few unpainted houses, a dump, and only scrub oak and choke cherry for coverage.

Isaac owned that entire section of the coast including Small Point itself, a useless nob of land cut off from the shore by muck at low tide and six feet of water at high. Seth had built his house out there with permission. It was made from driftwood and used lumber collected over the years he had spent working at the cannery. It didn't look like much — just a wood-shingled shack actually — but you could see it was put together with care. None of the windows matched, for example, but they were well fitted and puttied and not a cracked pane in the lot.

He had also built the ramshackle footbridge which led out to the house. As Isaac started to walk across it he could feel the ice heave against the untrimmed spruce piling. The cold wind seared his lungs and made his eyes tear and he wondered what drove a man to live like this. He hung on to the railing as if it were a lifeline and watched his footing carefully. Sections of the footbridge were already out of alignment, leaving gaps and twisting the planks.

"Goddamned thing ought to be condemned," Isaac muttered. But he forgot all that when his feet touched solid ground again. "Ah!" he said, and headed for the shack.

Seth opened the door even before the knock. His eyesight had grown poor and at first he only squinted, not recognizing Isaac. Then he nodded as if he had known all along. Isaac stepped in quickly and shut the door against the wind.

"Just having breakfast," Seth said. As night watchman, his day began in the afternoon. He was a short man and stooped, so he had to peer up at Isaac when he spoke. "Got some hot coffee going."

"It'll take more than coffee," Isaac said, struggling with his boots.

"I've got some of that too."

"Just a thimble, Seth. Can't stay long."

It was a one-room place, furnished only with necessities: wood stove, kitchen table, two straight chairs, and a bunk of two-by-fours built against the wall. Along the opposite wall were hooks on which his clothes and foul-weather gear were hung neatly. It was all snug enough until you looked out the front window and saw the ominous blocks of ice shoved in a jumble up the ledge to within twenty feet of the house.

Seth poured coffee from the percolator on the stove and then got a fifth of King's Whiskey from a cupboard and added a liberal jigger. They sat down at the table.

"Hasn't let up much," Isaac said.

She's got another night to run."

"Bad time for it," Isaac said. "One more week and we'd be free of that ice." They nodded. "That bridge of yours has heaved a bit."

"Always does."

"I don't suppose you'd consider staying ashore till this ice clears out?"

"I don't suppose," Seth said, closing the subject.

"How's the cannery pier?" Isaac asked.

"Well now, we've got some work to do there. One or two piles are loose. Don't know just how much yet."

"If it's bad enough, we might raise it up a foot or so. Wouldn't do any harm."

"We could get more rock underneath. It's weight we need."

And they were off on a familiar topic. Seth had spent most of his life working at the cannery as general maintenance man and had finally shifted to watchman with reluctance; but his real asset to the plant was still as planner and adviser in the endless task of rebuilding the pier. And for a hobby he worked on his own footbridge. It was the best game he knew — a sustained and personalized conflict. When they survived a bad winter gale he would say, "We got her licked that time"; and when the hurricane of 1954 smashed two sections of the pier and carried off the ice houses as well he said, "She sure as hell got us this time." That with a wry grin too.

So the two of them spent an hour, sipping spiked coffee and talking timbers and bracing, hardly hearing the gale outside.

But there was the business part of the meeting too, and Isaac had a mind for business.

"Say," he said at last, "there's a small matter I don't want to forget."

"What's that?"

"Well, you might call it rent."

There was a pause. The ice grinding against the ledge out front was now clear as if someone had opened the door. The house shuddered a bit as a gust slammed by.

"I don't believe you've asked for that before," Seth said at last, speaking slowly. "Seems like when I inquired about building out here, you just nodded. That was a long time ago, of course."

"Twenty years ago this April first. Tomorrow."

"That's quite a memory for dates you have. And how much were you figuring I might owe you?"

"A dollar would do it, Seth."

"Dollar a year?"

"No, for the whole twenty." He finished his mug. "It's just a fluke of the law, Seth. Law says a man takes possession after twenty years unless he's renting." Seth didn't answer. "What I mean is, if a man lives in a place for twenty years . . . ."

Seth raised his hand for silence. "You're not telling me anything." He went to the wall where there was a calendar advertising "Granite Farms Pure Milk and Cream." He lifted the March sheet and pointed to the date of April 1. It was circled in red crayon.

"You sure as hell caught me this time," he said. "You've got more of the bastard in you than most folks realize." This with a wry smile. But then the smile vanished and he sat down again.

He squinted at Isaac, though at that distance he could see perfectly well. Then a hesitant smile came over his face again and he said, "Ike, is this your idea of an April Fool's trick? We're gettin' a bit advanced for that...."

"No trick," Isaac said. He hadn't expected the resistance — just a dollar, after all. "This here's my land."

"Well for Lord's sake." It was as if Seth had only just then believed it. "You're serious."

"It's only a dollar I'm talking about."

"You can talk blue — you're getting no dollar from me."

"If it's the money, Seth, I could lend it to you."

"And hold possession for another twenty years? I don't fancy that."

"Then I'll deduct it from your pay."

"You'll deduct nothing. Not without my say-so."

"I've got the law, Seth, clear and straight. The land's mine."

"I've got the law too, when it comes to that. If I'm still sitting here at midnight, this here point is mine outright. I'm telling you, I'm not leaving. Not without being dragged. And you're not the man for dragging even the likes of me."

"For God's sake!" Isaac stood up, caught without words. Seth hadn't moved; he just looked up with a face flushed red. Then Isaac said in a rush, "You must be getting weak-headed. One dollar! You want me to go to court for one damn dollar?"

"You can go straight to hell for a dollar."

Isaac seized his coat and struggled into it, trembling with silent fury. He flung the door open. The wind slapped his face. "You're crazy out of your mind," he said and slammed the door behind him.

He stood there a moment, his rage sending tremors through his entire body. What could you do with a man like that? What the hell would it take to budge him?

Then he noticed that the wind had swung into the east a bit. Some of the ice slabs were being shifted, heaving murderously against the cannery pilings. From where he stood he could see that one corner of the loading platform had been weakened and now sagged. A wooden barrel of sawdust had already been dumped into the jumble of ice. No matter, he knew there'd be damage.

Then like the wind his mind shifted into a new quarter. There was hope after all.

Abruptly he turned and pounded on the door. "Seth," he called out. "Seth!" And as the door opened: "The pier. The cannery pier. We've got to get stuff out of there before the whole thing goes."

Seth peered by him, eyes squinting. "Something's smashed already," he said. "Wait up."

He disappeared but reappeared again in an incredibly short time, dressed in foul weather gear and boots. "Hurry up," he said, surging ahead along the footbridge, lumbering awkwardly in his boots. Isaac kept step right behind him as if driving him on.

They were halfway across the bridge when Seth stopped dead. Isaac piled into him with a grunt of surprise. "Go on," he said roughly.

"I remembered. I just remembered." Seth was almost whining. "You can't . . . ."

Isaac didn't want to hear him. He just pushed, grunting, "Go on," he kept saying, "Go on. Move. Go on." He pried at Seth's hand which was locked onto the railing.

They heaved against each other, almost evenly matched, senseless in their rage. Then Isaac raised his hand high and brought the edge of it down hard on Seth's wrist like a cleaver.

That did it. A squeal, a falling back, and a great rumbling like a line of boxcars being suddenly nudged, the sound resounding against his chest. Isaac felt a deep surge of power and then, catching sight of something larger out of the corner of his eye,, turned just in time to see the whole front wall of his cannery pier buckle and slide toward the saw-tooth jumble of gray ice.

The freight-car rumble continued as the wall was wrenched free, slowly as in films, so that he could now see right into those rooms where he had spent his life. The floor heaved forward and objects started sliding toward the sea: a mop, two cleaning buckets, chairs, now the stainless-steel vat — the new one — and the freezer itself was beginning to rip from its fastenings. Upstairs the parts room dumped whole shelves of nuts, bolts, small hardware, and cases of empty cans on the ice like pepper; and there, incredibly, was his office and his old oak desk and swivel chair with green cushion sliding faster now with filing cabinets and then splintering down the back of a littered plank of ice. A file drawer split open like a flowerpot and the records of a lifetime flew like snow.

He neither moved nor spoke. It was outrageous. The brutality of it shocked him. It wasn't like other storms. There had been no contest. How was a man to fight back?

Then the bridge on which they were standing gave a sudden shudder.

"Seth!" he said, half in warning and half in fear. But Seth was clinging onto the railing and staring at the remains of the cannery with his mouth open. He was paralyzed. Isaac would have to act for them both.

He looked first toward the shore and then toward the island. The distance was equal. The planks under them lurched to a severe angle. He swung his arm around Seth and firmly guided him back out to his house.

By the time they were at the front door, the bridge behind Seth was on its side and going through slow convulsions.

"It too," Isaac muttered in disbelief. He held tighter to Seth as if they were still in immediate danger. Then he stumbled into the protection of the house and shut the door against all that brutality.

Inside, neither of them spoke. They sat there, panting, one on the bed and the other in a chair, staring at their own thoughts.

And why, Isaac asked himself, did I do a damn fool thing like that? If we were ashore now, I'd have broken his hold on this place easy as. . . .

Some great slab of gray ice in the twilight outside bellowed like a live thing — like Isaac himself when crossed. He shuddered and then tensed again as if reliving the crisis they had just passed through. Then he shook his head. Crazy thoughts, he muttered to himself, for a man my age.

"You're a hard, cold sonofabitch," Seth said, speaking slowly, staring at the floor. Isaac looked over at him sitting there on the edge of the bed. He was still in his foul weather gear, a crumpled

pile of black rubber like something washed up after a storm. . .
like bits and pieces from the wrecked cannery.

Alarm struck Isaac as unexpectedly as a slap of spray. Had he
spent a lifetime on that miserable coast only to end up harsh as the
sea itself?

"That's not so," he said sharply. "I brought you back out here,
didn't I? The place will be yours."

"I don't want no gift."

"I don't take to giving."

"I've noticed."

"Fact is," Isaac said, thinking aloud now, "you wouldn't be
worth a pile of rags if you were forced back into town."

"Nor would you." His voice was still no more than a mutter.

"Well, we'll get your bridge built again," Isaac said, lighting a
kerosene lamp against the growing darkness. "Hell, I have to re-
build my own road every spring. No different. And the cannery —
I can get that rebuilt too. There's money."

"But is there time?" Seth said.

They looked at each other squarely, but they chose not to
answer the question. Seth stood up, finally, and shrugged off his
foul weather gear. Then he lit the other lamp.

Later that night, after supper together, they played cards and
drank hot whiskey. And when the sound of the ice occasionally
broke through, Isaac sang ballads which he had known as a boy
and which had lain dormant in him like seeds through the course
of a long, hard winter.

*Born in Boston, Stephen Minot (1927-     ) completed undergraduate work
at Harvard University and earned an M.A. from Johns Hopkins University.
Formerly a professor of English at Trinity College in Hartford, he summers in
Maine. CROSSINGS (1974) is a collection of his short stories, many of which
have won honors. This story first appeared in VIRGINIA QUARTERLY
REVIEW in 1969.*

# HEAD
# OF THE LINE

It was early in May but extra warm for the season. Dave dropped onto the door rock and sat doing nothing but let his breath go in and out. When he could make up his mind to move, he pulled a faded blue handkerchief from his hip pocket and waved it slowly back and forth to cool. Then he took off his hat and wiped his head, unbuttoned his shirt and rubbed the wet from his chest and shoulder blades. He sighed, spreading the handkerchief across his knee to dry. Hot, that was what it was; hot as Tophet.

He was still there an hour later when Harry, Shem Wilkins' boy, rode into sight over the hill, hind seat piled high with phosphate bags.

"Looks like you're ready for business," Dave shouted.

"Business enough," Harry answered. He jerked on his hand brake. Harry generally stopped to talk with Dave a few minutes, whenever he was headed home. "Awful hot this mornin'. Feels more like Fourth of July than plantin' time."

"Don't it! I s't out to get a little seed into the furrers, but time I'd emptied one pail of potaters I was done. S'I to myself, no more stuff than I need to see me through the winter, there ain't no great rush to be at it, weather like this is. So I drifted back here and sot down."

"Don't blame you," Harry said. He yawned and stretched. The steering wheel cut into his stomach. "Different with me, though. I got to keep humpin'. Seven mouths to my table every meal."

"Yes," Dave agreed comfortably. "There's spells a feller has to skurry round. I know. I been there, years back. Though anybody wouldn't hardly think it now."

He made a broad, mild gesture to indicate the sunny quiet of his place. He had two gaping cellar holes; one of the barn which had caved in six years ago come February, from snow too heavy on the roof, the other of the house in which Dave and Dave's father before him had been born, and which had burnt to the gound last spring when the chimney caught while Dave was down at the spring after his supper water and stopped by the way to rest a mite and must have fell asleep. He had a dozen gnarled apple trees, old past any bloom. He had a small woodpile, a grindstone part way off its trucks, horse sleds and rake long empty; in color all alike, gray, warm, and weatherbeaten. Wolf grass from the fields and juniper from the pasture crept into the yard together, feathers and prickles, soft and bright, side by side. This flat granite rock Dave had brought on a drag from the front door of the old house. It looked fine and big before the tar-papered door it led to now. His home itself, once a chopper's shanty, had been hauled out of the woods within two days after the fire and set close to the road where Dave could see Harry and Harry's young ones whenever they went by, even if it was night and he lay abed.

They were his only neighbors. Sometimes trucks passed, going into the woods or to the sandpit. Anyway, whatever did go along the road these days Dave saw. It was a good deal better than being back in there behind Sed's woodbine and lilac bushes. Women-folks would always clutter up window glass with flowers one side or the other, but a man kept his panes clear to know what was going on.

Dave had a real snug room in there, with a bed, a stove, a table, a lamp, and two chairs. All he needed. Plenty. But he could remember a time when it wouldn't have been enough. Not near.

He took off his hat and wiped his head again. The lids of his pale eyes crinkled.

"Yes," he said. "I had 'most that many, Harry. Twice . . . But they go. They come . . . and they go . . . ."

"Makes me think," Harry said. "Heard in the village this morning Chester Averill's dead. Funeral's tomorrow, they said."

*"Chet!"* Dave exclaimed. "Why, can't be. He's just a young feller still. Why, Chet —"

"'Tain't always age takes 'em out," Harry said.

"Well, he couldn't have been thirty —"

"Oh, yes, he was, Uncle Dave. He was older'n I am. I'm forty-four, forty-five next December, so Chet must have been forty-six anyway, I don't know but forty-seven. He was in school here at Number Four at the same time as Orrin and me, but he was 'way ahead —"

"Well, Chet was smart. I recollect hearin' the teachers always told his mother he was an awful quick one to learn. Picked everything right up soon as he heard it, you know. Some is like that. . . . Good boy, too. Awful good boy. And everybody always liked him. . . . Never heard anybody in my life say a word against Chet Averill. Never. . . . Chet gone — why, it don't seem possible!"

Dave wiped his eyes and blew his nose, and no sooner was his handkerchief back in his pocket than he had to fumble for it again.

"Old feller's kind of going to pieces, seems like," Harry thought. He said, "Yes, Chet was all right, near as I remember. Of course he's been gone from here a good while. They said his mother there, Grace, couldn't get him away fast enough after his father died. She said there wasn't no life for a boy on a farm these times, so she took him over to Wythe there, and put him into a city school. . . . I don't thinks likely he was over twelve or fourteen then, and I never seen him since."

"Nor I, neither," Dave said. "Heard well of him, though. Always heard he done fine. . . . My soul, Chet Averill gone already and an old staver like me left a-clutterin' up the earth. . . . I don't know, Harry. . . . Sometimes, I don't know what to think. . . ."

"Just as well not to think, I guess," Harry said. "Don't seem to get us anywheres. . . . Heard from Horace lately?"

" . . . What say?"

"I say, you hear anything from Horace?"

"No. . . . No, I guess it's been a year. Maybe more. Must be he's still out there to Cleveland, Ohio. I'd heard likely, if he'd made a change. But Horace ain't no hand to write. Never was. No more'n I am."

"Well. . . The girls'll get home this summer, I s'pose."

" . . . What's that?"

"The girls. Min. Lucy. I s'pose they'll get back around before long."

"Oh, I don't know. Lucy may. Min's been plannin' on it, so she says, ever since she was here to her mother's funeral, but her plans don't always come through. It costs somethin', of course, to get so fur, and they don't have no car. I guess that feller she married ain't much. Min, she has to work out all the time herself. . . . Lucy'll probably call around, with her young ones. I look for 'em two or three Sundays, course of the summer. She likes to bring flowers to fix up the graves. I tell her I don't know what it 'mounts to. Where we bury's all out of sight from the road. Can't nobody see in there, you know, without they let down the bars and go clear down around by where that point of pines runs out. Have to walk, too. Can't take any of those newfangled cars acrost my low ground. Not except right in hayin' time, anyway. And nobody ever tries to. Only her."

"No. Well, I got to be goin', Uncle Dave. Got to stick somethin' into furrers or first thing we know it *will* be the Fourth, and no peas."

"Yes, that's right, Harry. That's right. Well — see ye again!"

The car rocked away through the sand ruts. The town did not do much for a road on which only one family lived, and one old man alone in a tar-papered shanty.

Dave sat a while longer on the door rock. When the sun hung almost overhead he went around to the end of the house and lay on the grass in the shade. He may have slept part of the time, but most of the time he was thinking about Chet Averill.

Chet's mother was sister to Milly, Dave's first wife. When Dave first started going over there to Morton's, different ones thought it was Grace he was making up to. She was a little the oldest, and, a good many thought, the smartest and the handsomest of the two of them, and at first they would both sit into the buggy with Dave to ride out in the evenings. But when he got to where one was all he had room for in his buggy, it was Mil he wanted, and Grace begun to go around with Laurence Averill, a fellow from the village that everybody thought must be all right because she met him on a church picnic. He was a nice-looking fellow, too; the kind Grace took to; dressed up neat, waxed mustache, big talker. All four of them rid out together some for a month or so; then Lon and Grace got married, very sudden, and went off proud to live with his folks in the village. But soon after that his father died, and Lon never seemed to find any work. Had no trade of any kind. There was nothing coming in, and, for one reason and another, when Dave and Mil got around to marry, Grace come back up here to stay with them. Her folks kind of held out against her, at that time, because she'd gone off so quick and unexpected, and acted for a while as if she felt above them and everybody else. So she come to stay with Dave and Milly, and she was here when Chet was born.

Dave recalled that night very well. February. High wind. Snowing like all get out. He'd drove down after the doctor in the afternoon, plenty soon enough, but the doctor was out on another case of the same kind. His wife said he would be up as soon as he got home, but by then the Junction road must have been blocked full. Anyway, he never come. When Dave got home and unharnessed and into the house he found Milly and Grace both crying and taking on, Milly begging Grace to let her send for their mother, old Mis Morton, and Grace saying she would rather die, by far, than ask a single favor. When Dave had listened to this long enough, he went out and hitched into the sleds and went after Mis Morton anyway, brought her back all bundled up in hoods and shawls, holding a bag of bottles and soap and torn-up sheets in her lap. Which was a good thing because Grace turned out to be a hard one to do for, and at the end of it Milly had her hands full with Chet.

He was a pindling little tyke the first time Dave saw him. Milly washed and dressed him, front of the oven door, and Dave set there wishing he would make more noise. He sounded awful weak and sick, to Dave. But Milly never let up. She kept right on, tears running down her face, and her hands never trembled. Dave could see now, forty years and more afterwards, that pink in her cheeks, from the heat, and her hair getting loose and shining in the lamplight but not so shiny as the tears that ran down and had to drop off her chin because she was too busy to wipe them away.

When Milly had the young one clean and warm, she dropped a little sweetened water into his mouth and she and Dave both saw his lips pucker against the spoon. That heartened them.

"See if Ma thinks Grace ought to have him now," Mil said. "He's ready."

Dave went to the bedroom door and spoke, and old Mis Morton come out and took the baby, but right afterwards she brought him back.

"Grace don't seem to know what to do with him," she said. "Can't even shift herself a mite to let him try to get aholt. Never see a woman so onhandy with her own young one in my life. Anybody wouldn't think she'd ever come anear him before."

So Milly set and held Chet all night long. When it come breakfast time she carried him over to Dave, who had just come in from the chores. They kept handing him back and forth between them that way, waiting for the doctor to get through. When he did, and was finished with Grace so he could take a look at the baby, he shook his head and said, "Ain't at all likely you can raise him." But Milly and Dave kept right on taking turns like that, doing their work between times, for a week or more, so Chet was never put down, not for a minute, and all the time Milly and Dave felt as if it was their hearts under his that kept his a-going. Anybody gets braided in with a young one pretty close that way.

Well, he made out. By the time Grace was able to be up around, Dave had a stove set up in the parlor so she and her mother could sleep in there, and he and Milly took their own room back. They kept Chet with them because their bed was right off the kitchen, and they were so used to doing for him now that it wouldn't have seemed natural any other way. Dave bought a new cow, just come in, about all Jersey. Chet was getting along all right. Milly fixed up that Jersey milk with some water and a little sugar and a drop or two of paregoric and he begun to gain right off. Got so he could cry like a good one, and kick out some, and wave his fists.

"Take me in the jaw, want to?" Dave would say. "Take the old man right in the jaw?"

Joe Morton was so put out with his wife for coming over to Dave's that she didn't feel free to go home, except to get her clothes and patchwork, for six months, and even then she could never stay there more than a few days before they would have words and back she would come again. Dave didn't exactly enjoy keeping her around. She and Grace didn't get along any too peaceable, and she was kind of a fussy eater. But Milly said it eased her mind to have an older woman in the house in case anything went wrong with Chet, so Dave let it run along. Even when Lon would come walking in, as he did sometimes, pale as a ghost and his face all lined up like a man twice his age, and Grace would cry and old Mis Morton would rage, Dave and Milly put up with it some way as long as the fuss was kept to the other end of the house. Dave didn't believe but what a young one needed his own father around when he could have him, and Lon did have a good way of laying his hand up against the back of Chet's head. Kind of cupped it round. His hands were cleaner than Dave could ever get his to look, however much he scrubbed. Clay and axle grease and chimney soot make their own creases and dig into them, best a man can do.

One thing they, every one of them, agreed on. Anyway, out of all this, they had a fine young one.

Even old Joe hobbled in one day when he had seen the womenfolks go off huckleberrying and knew the house was clear. Old Joe stood there by the bed, so bent up with rheumatism any other man aggravated that bad would have sunk right down, and he looked at Chet a long time, and then he said, kind of broken, "That boy, Dave, he'll make his mark in the world."

"I guess he will," Dave answered. "He will, Joe. Sure."

Chet got up so he was about a year and a half old, trotting around underfoot, the summer Joe finally give in to lay down, and old Mis Morton had to go home to see to him. That time she stayed, and as winter begun to come on she felt afraid to be there alone with him, so she had Grace come back. Like enough by then Joe was glad to have her, too. Dave never heard he said anything indicating different.

Of course Grace took Chet.

That was natural enough. Dave and Milly understood it all right. She was his mother. They felt kind of bad, but what was there to say? Milly washed and ironed all his clothes, his blankets and such like, as if he were going a hundred miles, and combed his hair into a roll the length of his head, and carried him over the road herself, in her arms. Grace went ahead, wheeling their belongings in the baby carriage, and Dave come behind, leading the Jersey cow. He didn't intend to have the young one's milk changed, not yet a while, when he was thriving so.

Dave didn't go into Joe's. He just hitched the cow to the stanchion and give her a forkful of hay, and by the time he got out into the yard, Milly was running down the steps, crying as hard as she could cry. They went back over the road together, not saying anything, because they couldn't, until they got almost home.

Then Dave said, "You've got to stop it, Milly. You can't carry on like this now, you know."

And Milly answered him, trying to smile. "I know it. I've got our own to think of now, ain't I, Dave?" But then she burst out, "Only seems as though I know they can't any be more our own, maybe not so much, as he was!" And there she was crying again, harder than ever, so he had to set down on the door rock and hold her in his arms to tend her. He was glad it was getting dark, in case anyone went by.

Until now Dave hadn't thought over these things, much, for a good many years.

Because when Milly's time come she didn't get through like Grace, though she made less fuss, and the doctor was there, and her mother too, and old Mis Titus and Clara Goodwin from down the road a piece. Milly had three days of it, and then she died.

It was December, and they come to Dave and said the ground was froze too hard to dig a grave. They thought it might be best to put the coffin in the tomb at the village cemetery. But Dave said Milly wasn't acquainted any down there. He said he could dig her a grave on their own place. Give him a shovel; he could dig. Then they said they'd help him, but he wouldn't have none of their help. He worked down there most of two days, alone, and the pasture pines did not run out so far then. He could have seen the road and house all plain, as he worked, but he never looked up.

After that he went over to Joe's almost every day for a while. He would set and whittle out boats and whistles for Chet and listen to him talk. In time he got heart to fiddle again and Chet liked hearing that. He got so he wasn't satisfied if Dave ever come without the fiddle. Chet had sick spells, every once in a while, and Dave would go over and set there night after night by his bed. Once they didn't know as the boy would live until morning. He hadn't taken any notice, much, for almost a week. But as Dave set there, along about four o'clock, all of a sudden Chet come to, bright as a dollar, and first thing he said was, "Bring your fiddle, Da?" And Dave said, "You bet you," and got it and played him "Comin' Round the Mountain." About four o'clock, it was. Fall of the year, and not daybreak. Dave didn't have to light a lamp, either. He could have played then in his sleep, he guessed, with his hands tied behind his back.

But that was the winter after Joe died, and his womenfolks made talk about their planting and haying and how they were going to manage, and pestered Dave for this and that until at last he said, "Look here, you can't count on me to handle this place and my own too. I'm willing to do what I can to help out, but that's beyond all reason. I'm single-handed myself. You'll have to plan some other way."

Then Mis Morton looked down at the floor and said, kind of hesitant, "I didn't know, Dave, but you might think some of movin' over here with us. Bein' as we're *all* single-handed —"

This frightened Dave so that he got right up out of his chair and cast about for his hat.

"No," he said. "No. I'll tend to my place. You — you tell Grace she better send for Lon. He needs a roof over his head and I guess he'd make out to see you don't starve. I'll do what I can to help. I don't aim to shirk. But — you tell Grace best thing she can do is send for Lon."

"I don't think she will," old Mis Morton said sharply. "And if ever he comes, he shan't set food on my land. Not if I have to get out Joe's shotgun."

"Well, of course that's as you say," Dave answered, opening the door. "I'm just warnin' you not to count too much on me. I'll do what I can — but I'm — I'm goin' to have responsibilities of my own —"

"Going to get married again, I thinks likely," cried old Mis Morton, "and poor Milly not a year in her —"

Dave shut the door behind him. He tried all the way home to think who it could be that he was going to marry, and finally he lighted on Sed Turner. Sed was a likely woman. She had two young ones but that so much the better. They'd help fill up the house. He'd stop by there in a day or so and see if she wanted to pasture her stock in with his. That way she could let her fences go, and save herself trouble all around.

Dave and Sed were married the next spring, and about the same time Lon Averill come up to stay at Mortons'. At first Dave helped him what he could, but as soon as Lon was straightened around he seemed to get along all right, and there was always a kind of coolness. Old Mis Morton and Grace no more than passed the time of day with either one of them. Dave never went into the house.

Chet would come out and follow the men around, but Lon was always making great of him. Them two, Lon and Chet, had a nice way with each other. Lon would carry the boy out of the field on his back when he was so tired himself he could hardly walk, and Chet would look up when he put him down and say something about "my father," kind of big, like Lon himself, and brace back and kind of stride. It got so there wasn't much need of Dave over to Mortons', and he went less and less.

Sed kept him busy. She wanted the house painted and fixed up and the chimneys topped out neat. That took time, with all the rest there was to do. Dave had not been built to work fast. She had the two girls, Min and Lucy, and after a while she had another girl, by Dave. They called that one Flora. Then Horace come along. When he was about a year old, Flora died, and afterwards Sed had another girl that didn't live a day out. Dave put that one and Flora down by Milly. His mother and father and two brothers and one of their wives was already down there, but he had room enough. When Sed went, ten years ago, he put her on the other side of the little girls. There was a place for Dave over by the fence, next to Milly, and that only filled up the west end. The whole east side would still be empty, for Min and Lucy and Horace and their folks if they should ever want it. Though that wasn't likely. They would buy burying places off where they lived, up in New Hampshire, and down near Boston, and off out in Cleveland, Ohio.

The sun dropped and Dave went inside to light the fire and fry himself some fritters. Then he went out to milk his cow where she had stood all day in the shed. Hot as it was, there still was no feed in the pastures. He put the milk away and started to get his clothes off, to go to bed. But all that time he kept thinking about the years back there when Chet Averill was born just across the yard above the nigh cellar hole, and grew up over to Mortons' and used to run back and forth, and how he liked to hear a fiddle play. And the more Dave thought of it, the more it seemed as if he ought to go to the funeral.

"Of course nobody's sent me word of it, direct," he told himself, "but then, I s'pose I'm kind of hard to get ahold of, from 'way over there to Wythe. . . . Of course Grace might not happen to think of it, worked up as she'd be, time like this, and Chet's wife nor any of them, they may never have heard of me, being as I ain't no actual blood relation. . . . Still, exceptin' for Grace and any young ones he may have had, I guess I'm as near as there is. Because I know I always heard Lon was an only child, and Milly being all the other one to Mortons' besides Grace. . . . Lon may have had some cousins, but they wouldn't be very near to Chet. . . . I kind of think I ought to go."

So he laid out his suit of clothes and washed himself, and then he went to bed. In the morning he blacked his shoes and brushed his hat. When he was all ready but his necktie, he took that in his hand and went down to get Harry's wife to loop it up for him and button his 'ris'bands. He had Harry drive him into the village and paid him a dollar bill. All the way from the village to Wythe, he could ride on the bus. That only took him two hours and cost a half a dollar. People in settled places could get around awful quick and cheap these times.

Dave thought about the day he and Sed had taken their three young ones and Chet to the beach, thirty, thirty-five years ago. About the greatest outing any of them had ever had, up to that time. They were an hour and a half or more getting to the village, all piled into the democrat wagon. But they had started early. There wasn't any rush. They just rode along. The sky was clear as a bell, turning from pink to blue. They met old Charlie Tuttle, walking home from night watch down at the shop, carrying his lantern.

"Off airly," old Charlie sung out.

"Bound for the beach," Dave told him.

"That so. Well, you got a great day for it."

The birds sung like all possessed in the swamps that morning. As they rid into the village, a great truck drove by, stuck all over like a pincushion with bottles full of pink and brown and yellow and purple drinks. A clerk in a white coat was setting out boxes of strawberries in front of the grocery store; cultivated ones, big as a man's thumb.

"I hear the car," Chet said, low but excited. "Don't I hear it, Dave?"

"That's the old lady's whistle," Dave answered.

He stabled the horse as quick as he could. They all climbed on the electric car, and off it went.

The sun shone and the whistle blew and the wheels sung, and

Dave knew all the time that it would be dark when they come back. Down in the bottom of the biggest box, here beside him, he had his fiddle, and he would wait on the cliffs to play it after the moon come up. Chet would play some, too. He had picked up quite a few tunes lately. It didn't make any difference how late they come home. Chet was having him a day today all right, one he wasn't likely to forget.

Dave still remembered it, anyway, close on to forty years afterwards, riding over the same route the electric car had followed, but this time in a bus which turned off at the Y to take him to Wythe to Chet's funeral. Dave missed the whistle and the singing wheels, but quiet was of course more suitable today. He sighed, and ran his finger in around his collar. It was beginning already to chafe his neck.

"Wythe Railroad Station," the driver said.

That seemed to Dave as good a place as any to step out. He stood a while on the sidewalk, looking around, and tried to place himself, but it was fifteen or twenty years since he had been in Wythe. Cars were parked thick, and coming and going all directions. There was no telling which way would be toward Averills'. He had never even heard which side of town they had their house on. At last he went in and inquired of the station agent.

"You happen to know whereabouts Averills' is?"

"Certainly do," the man answered back, right off. "Is it the house you want? Or the church? Got something to deliver, have you?"

"No. No, I'm a — well, a relative, as you might say. There's going to be a funeral to that place today. Chet — Chet Averill — he —"

"A relative?. . . Well, the funeral isn't at the house. Mr. Averill's going to be buried from the church. Congregational Church. No, he had the biggest house in town, but it isn't big enough to hold the people that want to pay respects to him today. Very active, he was, you know — church and city affairs — big club man. . . . You're a relative, you say?"

Dave wasn't took back for more than a half a minute. It wasn't a bit more than he might have expected that the first one he spoke to should know Chet and speak well of him. Even in a town this size. Streets jammed with cars. Sidewalks thick with people. Thousands of them. But the very first man he asked knew Chet and all about him.

"That boy," old Joe had said, "he'll make his mark —"

"Maybe that ain't quite as I should rightly say," Dave answered. "We wa'n't blood relation. Chet's mother, Grace, was sister to Milly, my first wife. Chet, he was born over to our house, as it happened. Milly and I kind of tended out on him for quite a spell and got to think as much of him as if he'd been our own. Sometimes I guess we forgot he wa'n't. The kind of a little feller, he was, you know, that goes right into anybody's heart. Never was anybody, I don't care who, ever knew him but felt close to him, some way or 'nother. Smart boy, growing up. Good boy, too. I was thinking, comin' over here today, I never knew anybody meant so well, and was as able as he was willing. Why, the last few months before Lon died — his father you know — after he took sick — spring of the year it was, and plantin' time, just like 'tis now — well, Chet he knew there was work ought to be gettin' done and wa'n't, so he out into that field with a horse, and now I tell you he —"

"Sorry I'll have to ask you to move back from the window," the agent said. "Train's in and these people are waiting for their tickets. As soon as I've taken care of them, I can direct you. Or ask anywhere along the street. Almost anybody'll know."

Then Dave noticed the long line behind him.

"Well, thank you, thank you," he said. "Didn't know I was holding you folks up. . . . Didn't realize. . . . Got to talkin' there —"

He stepped outside the door and spoke to a man that stood beside his car. It was a bright, handsome car and the man was a neat, nice-looking fellow; had on a stiff visored cap. Dave thought how seldom he saw caps like that late years. Used to be men that never wore any other kind.

"I'm looking for Chester Averill's house. You know where that's at, do you? Kind of a big place, they say —"

"Oh, yes, sir. Number Four, Concord. I've had a quite a few going there today. Get right in."

He opened one of his hind doors.

"Well, much obliged," Dave said. "I'll be glad of a lift. Unless you're car'in' somebody else, I'll get in front. Like to see something of Wythe as we ride along. I'm quite a stranger here nowadays. Used to get over once in a while when I was younger."

"Sad thing," the man remarked, "Mr. Averill's going."

"Wa'n't it?" Dave said. "You're a friend of his, of course?"

"Well, I — yes, I —"

"I guess you was, all right. Same as everybody else that knew him. He was just that lovable kind. Everybody always liked him and nobody ever forgot him. Just the same way over home where I come from. Over in Derwich. He growed up there in the back part of the town. Left when he wa'n't over a dozen years old and none of us has seen much of him since, he's been so busy, but, well, as you might say, a lot of folks over there has got heavy hearts today, same as if we hadn't ever lost him out of the neighborhood. In a way, you know, we kind of went right along with him through the years. We knew how well he was gettin' along over here. We've kind of worried about him, afraid he'd overdo. But we've been awful proud he done so well. . . . Well, we've had reason to be. Good reason to be. . . . And I kind of think he's always knowed we was thinkin' of him, and appreciated it. He was one that never took things like that for granted. . . . Like what you're doin' today, meetin' trains and buses and takin' folks to his house, he'd appreciate that, high, if he knew it. Little things, you know, what you might call neighborly things, they meant an awful lot to Chet. More than to most. I didn't know as folks could do like that for each other in a place this big, but I guess it's just the same every-wheres. . . . Well, I'm glad 'tis. I'm glad Chet ain't ever had to be without it, because I know he'd missed it. He was that kind. . . . Handsome houses along this street, ain't there?"

"Oh, yes, sir. Best residential street in the city, Concord is. That's Mr. Averill's ahead there, on the corner."

Dave slid as far down in his seat as he could, and still the top of the car cut off the roof of Chet's house, but he could see the ground floor and the second story. Biggest, handsomest house he ever laid his eyes on. Built of cut stone, new-looking, with great big swinging windows full of little tiny panes of glass. Lawns and flowers all around it. Must have been full an acre of ground there, right in the heart of the city, almost.

The man stopped at an iron entrance gate. It was closed, but Dave could see through it the long flight of stone steps that led up to a heavy oak door set in under the wall of the house. Like some European castle.

"Here we are, sir," the man said.

"I don't know as I'll go in," he said apologetically. "I ain't exactly fit. Can't you ask Grace if she feels like stepping out to speak to me? Or p'r'aps she'd ruther I'd go right down to the church. Either way suits me. Just tell her I'm here and whatever she says —"

"Grace? That's —"

"That's Chet's mother, you know. It's through her I'm connected. She was sister to Milly, my first wife."

"Mrs. Laurence Averill? I don't know whether she'll be here, but I'll see."

While Dave waited, he studied Chet's house. This would be something to tell Harry Wilkins of, along with all the rest. Handsomest house he ever saw.

The man talked a minute with a woman in a white cap and apron. Might have been a nurse. They sometimes stayed through the funeral to settle things down. One had when Sed went.

The man came back to the car.

"She isn't here, sir. I didn't think she would be. I didn't know before it was her you wanted. You see, this was Mr. Chester Averill's. Mrs. Laurence Averill lives in a house of her own, over on Beekman Avenue —"

"So? Why, Chet's family must be some size, if there wa'n't room here for Grace. How many young ones has he got?"

The man hesitated.

"I don't exactly know, sir. I've heard of two. Two daughters, I believe. But they haven't been here for some time. Some years it must be. I believe they live abroad. . . . With their mother."

"With their mother?. . .Why, did Chet separate from his wife?"

"I don't know, sir. She hasn't been here for a long time."

"That so." Dave looked sober, and then began to smile, rather small and knowing. "Chet stayed here by himself then, and let Grace have her own place. . . . Well, I can't wonder at it. I done the same. I didn't have near so much of a house as this one is here, but there was room enough for Mortons, them times. Same as there was room enough over to Mortons' for me. But I kind of thought I'd sleep better if they stayed under a different roof. Likely Chet figured just the same. . . . Not to say any hard of Grace, you understand. 'Twa'n't her fault, I s'pose, she happened to be one of them kind that. . .Well. . ."

Dave let it go. Any man would know what he meant.

"Shall I take you round to the Avenue, then, sir? Of course, Mrs. Averill may not be there either. May be at the church. It's getting on to two o'clock now."

"What time is the funeral?"

"Two, I think."

"Well, then, drop me off at the church, I guess. If it's right on your way. You're goin' back to the station, be ye, to pick up any of the rest that may have gathered there?"

"Yes, I —"

"All right, then. All right. Just drop me right off any corner we go by that's nigh onto the church."

They rode back down Concord Street, past many handsome houses, but none as handsome, near, as Chet's. They rode up Main between two long rows of great stores with plate glass windows running across the whole front of them. Dave noticed the sign on one:

C. M. AVERILL CO.

"Why," he said, "that Chet's store?"

"Yes, sir."

"Well, I never heard he'd give his name to it. Never s'posed it was quite that size. Big one, ain't it?"

"Only department store we have in the city. Yes, very good size. Nice assortment in there, my wife says. Things may cost a few cents more than in the chain stores, but the quality's dependable."

"I bet 'tis. I bet she's right there. Chet would be behind anything he sold. I'd be as sure of that as I would of my own name. . . . Kind of like to get in there and look around a mite before I go back. Maybe while I'm waitin' for the bus —"

"Afraid you couldn't today, sir. It's closed, you see. On account of the funeral."

"You don't say so! That whole great big store! Why, don't seem — but there, of course, I s'pose they don't hardly know which way to turn, with Chet gone —"

"It isn't that, I wouldn't say. He's got good men. It's organized to run all right. He's been sick some months, and they've got along. . . . No, of course it's closed in tribute to him. Been closed all day. All the rest have closed, too, for the afternoon —"

"All the stores in town?"

"Yes, sir."

Now Dave was more took back than he would have wanted to admit. He had never heard of such a thing. Every single store in a place this size to close up its doors! What would Harry think when he heard that?

"Why," Dave muttered, "don't seem — don't hardly seem as if —" But then he pulled himself up. "Still, I ain't a mite surprised. Not a mite. One like Chet — smart as he was, and good, too — why, his grandfather said to me when Chet wa'n't a year old, old Joe said, 'Dave, you mind what I'm tellin' you, that boy'll make his mark in the world!'"

"This is the church, sir."

"Well, you brought me right to the spot, didn't ye?" Dave exclaimed, getting out. "That wa'n't needful, as you might say, but it comes in handy. I ain't quite so spry as I used to be."

The other man had got out, too, very polite, and Dave shook hands with him.

"I certainly appreciate the trouble you've took," he said. "Chet would, too, if he knew about it. Hope I can do you a turn some way some time. . . . Well, I s'pose you'll be back here by and by, soon as you can. So — see ye again!"

The Congregational Church was a mighty one. Built of stone a good deal like Chet's house. They seemed to run to stone over here in Wythe. Must be a good granite quarry right close by somewhere.

Dave started briskly up the walk and then, remembering himself, slowed down. A man in a long black coat stood in the doorway. Dave knew he must be the undertaker.

"How do you do," Dave said to him in a low voice.

The undertaker inclined his head.

"Relative, sir?" he asked.

"Well," Dave answered, "I don't know as I could rightly. . . I'll tell you how it is. Chet's — Mr. Averill's mother was sister to my first wife. . . . I don't s'pose that makes me — Well, you figure it out however it seems to you. I'll set wherever you say. . . . Only thing, he was born to my house, kind of growed up along with me, and bein' as his own father's gone, I don' know but I come about as — Well, you just figure it out as you think best."

The undertaker turned to another man, dressed just the same, who stood near. It must be that for funerals this size they needed two.

"We'd better speak to Mrs. Averill," the second one said, "If you don't mind waiting, sir. Just over here."

Dave stepped back out of the way. He waited there perhaps ten minutes, and all the time people were coming in. Not a soul had been in sight on the street when Dave rode up, but now they were coming steady, like a parade. He watched their faces. All nice-looking people, all sober, but none of the women wore black clothes, and nobody was crying.

"Will you come this way, sir? Mrs. Averill would like to see you."

The undertaker went ahead down one flight of stairs and up another, some back way. Dave followed after. And in a little room, sitting there all by herself, was Grace.

"Well — hullo — dear," Dave said.

"Oh, Dave. Dave. . . .Oh, I'm so glad you've come. . . .I was afraid you wouldn't. . . .I had them write to you, but we didn't get any answer. . . .I didn't know. . . .It had been so long since I saw you. . . .I didn't know. . . ."

"Letter must be down there to the mailbox," Dave said, as soothing as he could. "I don't get over the road very often. Never thought, of course, of anything like this. But it don't make no difference. Word got to me all right. I'm here. Harry — Harry Wilkins, Shem's boy — brought me as fur as the village this mornin', and I come over on the bus —"

Grace got right up from where she had sat listening to him, and watching him, and she put her arms right around his neck and leaned her head against his cheek.

"Oh, Dave," she sobbed, "I'd forgotten. . . .It has been so long . . . .Your voice sounds so. . .Your face looks. . .Oh, God bless you for coming. . . .If you hadn't, I don't know how I'd — I don't know, Dave. . . .There's nobody else that — nobody in the world —"

"There now," Dave said. "Now, you mustn't go on so, Grace!"

He was patting her back. She felt like Milly against him. That was what she felt like. When they were growing up, she had been different. Always thin as a rail. But now she was rounded out, as

Milly had been. Not young like that, of course. But Milly wouldn't have been young, either, if she had lived to be here today.

"We've got to pull ourselves together, dear," he said. "You can't carry on like this, you know."

She kept on crying and he kept on patting her. He felt awkward at it, and glad the door was shut in case anyone went by, but he could tell he was a comfort to her. She cried softer and softer, and when the undertaker come to call them, she had stopped altogether. He helped her pull down her veil.

"Will the gentleman —"

"It's Mr. Caswell," Grace said. "My — brother. He found at the last minute he could come. He'll sit with me."

And after that Grace didn't shed another tear. Dave never see the beat of it in his life. She lifted up her head as she went in front of him into the church, and then she turned and laid her hand on his arm, and the way she walked in and sat down in front of all that crowd of people, she might have been a queen. She was no more the way she had seemed for a minute there alone with him, no more as he had expected, no more as Milly would have been, no more as Sed was when she lost that little Flora — no more than nothing at all.

And the funeral was nothing like any Dave had ever been to, though he had been to a good many. If he hadn't kept reminding himself, he wouldn't have known what it was or who it was for.

The church was a mighty one, packed full. Up in front, all there was to see was flowers. The greatest lot of flowers Dave had ever laid his eyes on. He couldn't have given the name of half of them. Organ music played a long time, kind of cold and far off. That was the way it all seemed to Dave, cold and far off. It didn't seem to have anything to do with Chet. A man — he must have been the minister — read off poetry and Scripture, but he never mentioned Chet's name once, nor said a thing about him. When the minister was through, the organ played again. Nobody sung. Well as Chet had always liked singing, not a voice was raised. After a while people begun marching down the aisle in a long line. Nobody had called them out, so Dave did not know who they were. Probably the men and women who had worked for Chet. The men who belonged to his club. Other folks who lived up on Concord Street. Like enough the mayor. Maybe the governor. They all climbed the steps among the flowers, stopped a minute, and went down the other side. Dave studied them. They were all nice-looking folks. Sober and respectful. But not a one of them cried.

When everybody else had gone, Grace stood up. The minister come and offered her his arm but she shook her head and leaned on Dave. He straightened himself and walked as steady as he could, to help her. But she didn't tremble a mite. They went up the steps nice and smooth, and stopped where the other ones had stopped.

It was the handsomest coffin Dave had ever seen. Looked like silver, all embossed, and fixed up inside with white satin heavy enough for royalty's marriage clothes. The face of the man who lay there had some of the look of Lon Averill when he died, Dave thought, but rather more of old Joe about the time Dave first begun going over to Mortons'. Seemed strange to see the Morton look after so many years. Both Joe's girls had favored their mother's side.

Grace moved away, drawing Dave with her. They were almost out of the door when all of a sudden he thought of Chet. Where was the boy? What had they done with him? *Why, Chet! Nobody never even said good-bye!*

Dave must have been slowing up. He felt the pull of Grace's hand, and went on again, with her, out into the bright sun.

Cars lined the street, and every one had a white flag blowing against the left headlight. A man in a black coat opened a door for Grace and Dave and spoke low to the driver.

"Head of the line," he said.

They rode off a little way and then the car stood still again. Dave did not know why, and did not ask. He saw there was a long row of old brick houses on both sides of the street, each one built so close to the next that anybody could hardly walk between. Women and children sat thick on the steps, staring into the cars and making remarks back and forth as if nobody but them had ears to hear.

"His store's been closed all day, ain't it?" one woman called across to a neighbor.

"Yes. They're all closed this afternoon. Even the bakeshops. I forgot to get any bread for supper and I don't know what I'm going to do."

Dave thought, "Can't you bake some biscuits like I'm going to?"

He saw three boys sprawled on the grass, three bicycles beside them. He thought how bad Chet had wanted a bicycle when he was their age. He and Lon had helped Chet plant a piece of his own one spring and told him what come of it he could have to spend as he pleased; but only a day or two after that, Lon's sickness come on, and the family needed to eat whatever come off their place that summer as well as all Dave could spare off his. So nothing more was said or done about a bicycle. And not a word out of Chet about it either. No complaint.

Dave took out his handkerchief and wiped his eyes.

"Look at that old man in there," one of the boys said. "He's crying."

Dave turned his face away. He wished he was to home. There was things there he ought to be tending to. Then he saw Grace with her head drooped down. She must feel, as he did, that a good deal might have been said and done which hadn't. He cleared his throat.

"He was an awful good boy, Grace," he said. "Chet was. An awful good boy."

"Yes, Dave. . . . Yes, he was."

A big black car drove by with flowers at every window. Their driver pulled in behind it, and they rode out onto the Avenue.

"That was his store, Dave," Grace said. "Over there."

"Big one, ain't it? . . . Well, he done fine. Got further in half a lifetime than most folks would in two. . . ."

"Yes. . . . Yes, I've been proud of him. Of course I have. . . . I — never understood him very well, though. Not since he grew up. Not since he got married, anyway. . . . I never knew why he and Else couldn't get along. She was a lovely girl. Came of one of the big mill families here. Of course it was her money that . . . Well, I don't know, Dave. I thought the day they were married was the happiest day of my life and his. But it didn't last long. I don't know why. I never could find out. He wouldn't say anything about it . . . . Yes, he did well. But he had a hard life. Short as it was, it was hard. He wasn't ever strong, you know, and he took everything so seriously. . . ."

They rode into a cemetery, through a mighty iron gate. There were great statues and marble stones as far as Dave could see. The black car ahead stopped. Masses of flowers were taken out and laid on grass unnaturally soft and green, almost like velvet. A coffin was lifted out and placed among them. The cars moved on again and as each one passed by a man in a black coat, he took off its white flag.

This was the end of it then. This was all there was to it. This was all Wythe could do for Chet.

"The last ten years," Grace was saying, "he spent day and night, almost, down in that old office. I used to beg him to leave it and get a rest, but he'd say, 'Where is there for me to go? This is all I've got that belongs to me. I might as well stick by it.' I always wanted him to take me to Europe. There wasn't any reason why he couldn't." Her voice took on a familiar note, hopeless and kind of long drawn out. "But I never got there and now I don't suppose I ever shall. I'm too old to start off alone. . . . I know it would have done him good to get away. I told him so, over and over. But he'd just say, 'Where is there for me to go?'"

"Let me off whatever corner's nigh the railroad station." Dave spoke up louder than he had meant. "I'll get the bus there."

Grace turned to him, surprised. He hadn't noticed her face much before. It was pink and soft. Not right for an old woman. She didn't resemble either the Mortons or the Poultneys. Didn't look like anybody he ever knew.

"Why, I thought you'd come up to the house with me, Dave," she said. She put her hand on his knee. "What have you got to hurry you back? You've never seen my little house. It's not like Chester's, but I guess he thought it was good enough. I want you to stay to supper anyway."

"No. No," Dave answered, "Harry's going to be down to the Square to meet me. I got to get right back. I've got my chores to see to. My cow's waitin' to be milked."

What did a man do who had no cows to call him?

"We can send word to Harry. This man can leave us and go right on over to Derwich and find Harry and tell him. Harry can milk your cow."

"Oh, no. No. Can't nobody handle that there Blossom very well but me. She's kind of techy. I wouldn't want to trust — No, there's the station now. You just let me off, Grace. Let me off right —"

"Wait! Don't open the door yet!"

"No, I just got my hand on it.... There, here we are.... Well ...good-bye, Grace. You — keep your spirits up. You — might drive over and see me some Sunday this summer. I'm doing business at the same old stand. Glad to see you, any time. Course I can't ask ye to stop overnight. No room where I am now. But call in sometime. I'll fry ye a good fish and stir ye up some biscuits.... There's the bus coming! See ye again!"

All the way over Dave sat very straight, and all the way up from the village he talked a steady stream to Harry Wilkins, telling him about what the Wythe station agent said, about the man who met every bus and train all day to take Chet's friends to his house, and about the funeral.

"Master great house, Harry. Biggest one-family house I ever see, but there wasn't room for all them that wanted to be there today, not near.... Most an acre of grounds.... Heart of the city.... Averill's store fills a whole block. Closed all day. Every store in town shut up this afternoon.... Mighty church.... Crowds of people.... Tears raining down their faces.... Bet them flowers would 'a' filled both my cellar holes.... Minister said it was a terrible loss to Wythe.... Best man he ever knowed.... Honest, upright, good citizen, good neighbor.... If anybody was in heaven today, it was Chester Averill.... Yes, Grace was able to be there. All broke up, of course.... Yes, nice wife. Comes of a big mill family over there. Yes, two daughters. Handsome young ones as ever you saw.... Percession a mile long. A good mile long...."

Harry didn't notice that anything seemed wrong with Dave. He always talked a good deal when he was excited and of course this trip had been quite a thing.

It was a little unusual, perhaps, that when they got home to Dave's place he should ask Harry if he could stop long enough to milk the cow. That was something he had never given in before to having anybody do, even last winter when he was sick enough to be in bed, with the grippe. But Dave explained it, reasonable enough, and Harry never thought until afterwards how strange it was he paid so little attention to it at the time.

"I've got my best clothes on," Dave said. "I hadn't ought to get in around the barn, I don't s'pose. If you want to do something to ease up on me a little mite today, you could see to my milkin', Harry. I can take care of the rest of it all right myself."

"Sure," Harry answered. "Well as not. Where's your pail?"

"Hangs right there on the shed door. When you git through, leave it here on the door rock, and get along to your own work. I'll set it in."

So Harry milked, fed, and bedded down for Dave that night. When he set the pail up by the door, he noticed that Dave was sitting on a chair inside and only nodded at him; did not speak. There was no smell of supper cooking.

"Tired out, I guess," Harry thought. "Well, he's gettin' 'long."

He drove on home. Dave watched him go. He sat quiet for a few minutes more. Then he stood up and offered his arm to Milly.

"Don't mind me, Dave," she said in her sweet, husky voice. "I'm all right. I'll keep up with you."

He went over to the bed and took up a long, white, shining box into his arms. With Milly beside him he stepped out into the yard.

Four men came toward him, but he shook his head.

"I'll carry it myself," he said. "'Tain't heavy. Not for me."

He and Milly walked across the yard and through the dust of the road a little way. She let down the bars for him. They went slow over the hill, across the meadow and up again, around the point of pasture pines running out. There was a long line of people following. Mis Morton and old Joe. Lon and Grace. The Wilkinses and Tituses and Goodwins. Cousins and neighbors and schoolmates. The teacher and the minister. With every step Dave's burden grew heavier but he only held it gentler. His heart beat harder. Milly was so near his shoulder he could feel hers beating too. Beating for Chet, to hold him, and keep him, as long as they could.

Now they were there, among the others.

"This is the place," Dave said, stopping by a mat of pinks which had spread out from the mounds marked MILDRED J. CASWELL and LITTLE FLORA. "I've got the place fixed, Elder. Been here all day a-gettin' ready."

"I brought the flowers down last night," said Milly. "Roses. From the bush he set out under my window there. He knew how I loved a rosebush, and mine all winter-killed two years ago, so he set out this, and last night it was full of bloom for him."

"He was the thoughtfulest boy," Mis Morton said. "Always the thoughtfulest —"

"Best pupil in the school," the teacher said. "Honest. Dependable. Willing —"

"Good son," sobbed Grace, "he always did as near as he could just what we wanted —"

"Like a man," Lon said. "More of a man than I ever was."

"Made his mark," said Joe. "Made his mark, all right. I said he would."

"Near as our own," wept Milly. "Nearer."

"He was our own," said Dave. "It's us he has come back to, ain't it? He said, where had he to go? Why, he had home. And he's come home."

"The Lord giveth," said the Elder, "and the Lord taketh away. Blessed be the Lord. He maketh me to lie down in green pastures. He leadeth me beside the still waters. . . . "

One minute they were all standing there together, Mortons, Caswells, Tituses, Goodwins, and the rest, crying and singing. The next minute the only voice raised up was Milly's. She kept singing stronger and lighter all the time. So light at last that Dave put his fiddle against his chest and begun to play with her. Lighter and lighter, faster and faster, until Chet stirred and opened his eyes.

"Dave! Dave!" cried Milly. "Look!"

But Dave kept right on playing, swung into "Comin' Round the Mountain," and Chet smiled all of a sudden at him, bright as a dollar.

"Brought your fiddle, Da?" he asked. "Thought you would."

The next day when Harry stopped at the camp and found nobody there, and the cream rising on the pail, he knew something had happened. Then he saw the bars open across the road and followed the track through the grass down to where Dave was.

He was some taken aback, of course, but it was nothing he hadn't been expecting.

Going home he thought of what Dave had said. *". . . If you want to do something to ease up on me a little mite today. . . I can take care of the rest of it all right myself."*

"Now jest what was he thinking of?" Harry wondered.

He handed the long box to his wife. Such a box as flowers are sent in. Charred at one corner. Must have come near getting caught in the fire that time Dave's house went. Must have been the only thing he saved.

"I never thought it meant that much to him," Harry said. "His fiddle. He ain't played it for twenty years that I know of. But he had it down there. I kind of think we'd better see it's buried with him.''

"Poor old Dave,'' Maudie sobbed. "We all used to go in there when we was young ones, and beg him to tune up. Sometimes he would and sometimes he wouldn't. He was always kind of odd about it. But oh, my, when he did!''

She took out the fiddle tenderly. It felt very smooth against her fingers. She stood there stroking it. Then she saw there were other things in the bottom of the box.

A pair of homemade baby shoes. A long white dress and an embroidered flannel petticoat. Things Sed must have kept to remember one of the babies by, Maudie guessed. Nothing a man would bother to lay up.

And a whole year of district school report cards. Gray from mildew. As if, having lain a long time in the litter that always strews the floors of empty houses, they had at last been picked up and saved.

English, 95; History, 98; Arithmetic, 92; Spelling, 98; Geography, 95; Deportment, 100; Effort, 100 —

The name across the top of every card was Chester Averill.

*A graduate of Bates College, Lewiston, Gladys Hasty Carroll (1904-    )
was born in Rochester, New Hampshire, and has spent most of her life in New
England. AS THE EARTH TURNS (1933) is the most famous of her more
than twenty books of fiction. It has been translated into sixty languages. This
story first appeared in her collection HEAD OF THE LINE (1942).*

# THE SOLDIER SHOWS HIS MEDAL

I saw him coming up the driveway between the lines of the horse chestnut trees in bloom, a pint-sized soldier, thin and gawky as a young crane. He walked a little stiffly and his blond hair looked bleached white against his tan and against the rich green of the leaves behind him. His uniform was a private's, but the splendid cap in his hand had a visor — the kind officers wear.

A Maine kid doesn't use a hat much, this time of year. He's enjoying being bareheaded again, I thought. But he put the cap on as he came closer, very likely so he could tip it to a lady, as a proper soldier should.

"Well, hello!" he said. A note or so higher, and his voice would have broken like a thirteen-year-old's. He grinned a wide, toothy grin, and he almost wrung my hand off my wrist. Somewhere, probably in the Army, he had got himself a set of false teeth.

"Hello, yourself. How are you?" I said. I was poking hastily around in my memories of the lanky kids of the town. I had been away myself, for three years, and they grow up so. The teeth weren't any clue, because most of our Depression crop of children had had bad teeth. For ten years following '29, the village hadn't had two cents to rub together, and the only dentist within twenty miles charged summer people's prices the year around.

Besides, this boy had me puzzled. Most of the Maine men, particularly the young ones, no matter when you saw them last, say, "Hi," laconically, in greeting, and nod one or two little bobs of the head. If it's to a woman, they don't shake hands unless she puts out her hand first.

Maybe this isn't a local boy, I thought. Must be someone I've met somewhere else.

He saw me thinking it and the pleasure went out of his face, leaving his eyes bewildered and hurt. "I guess you don't remember me so good," he said.

"I guess I *do*," I said quickly. "I was just surprised to see you so grown up." That was safe, because three years ago this kid couldn't have been much over fifteen — seventeen, at the most.

"Well," he said. He was through with me. He'd been glad to see me and I hadn't remembered him. Now he was trying to think of something final to say, so he could go. "I guess we wasn't on good terms when we saw each other last."

"No, I guess not." (Which of the youngsters had run afoul of me, three years ago?) I grinned at him. "But I never saw the grudge I could hold for three years, did you?"

He just stood there.

That, I said to myself, was about the damndest-fool thing you've ever said in your life. Whoever this boy is, wherever he's been, he's just come home from a war. Maybe one day you'll get it into your head for good that there's a war on.

"Well," he said, "what I come in for, I wanted to see the teacher."

One of my sister's boys. Before she'd been married, she'd taught for a long time in the high school.

"Sure," I said. "She's inside. Come on in."

"Why, Joe!" my sister said. "Joey Hinckley." She had just taken the baby up and had him on her arm.

Joe Hinckley said, "Hi," and nodded at her, two little short bobs of his head. He didn't shake hands until she put out her hand.

"It's nice to see you," my sister said. "You've been gone two . . . three . . . Where've you been all this long time?"

He sat down, holding his cap carefully rightside up on his lap. He kept looking at my sister as if he were puzzled — first at her and then at the baby.

"Oh, I've been all over," he said. "Pearl Harbor. The Solomons. Mostly Guadal."

She nodded. "I knew you were at Pearl Harbor. Your mother was worried for a long time after, because she didn't hear from you."

"Took a long time to get word through." He ducked his head shyly. "That your baby?"

"Why, yes. I got married the summer after you graduated in the spring, Joe, to Harland Peters. I've got another baby, nearly two — a little girl."

The distant bewildered look was back on his face. "I never graduated, remember? I quit school and enlisted the spring of my senior year. I ain't been home since then."

"Of course!" my sister said. "I remember I tried to get you to wait till June, and you wouldn't."

"That's right." But you could see he was hurt because she hadn't remembered exactly.

Oh, I knew him now, all right. The skinny, tow-headed little devil he was, with wisecracks to shrivel you right at the tip of his tongue. I remembered the early November night when we'd got "not on good terms" — a night crisp with frost; a full moon; and the best of the Northern Spy apples that I'd left on the tree because they taste better with a touch of frost on them. I was planning to hand-pick them the next day, and that night I happened to glance out an upstairs window, and here was some scalawag up the tree.

I went out the front door, sneaked around the barn, and arrived at the foot of the tree. When he slid down with his blouse and pockets full, I grabbed him by the collar and shook apples in all directions.

Joey Hinckley was slight, and his bones under my hands felt like bird bones, but he was pretty indomitable even in those days. He landed a full kick on my shin and I howled and sat flat down.

"Ole apple-hog," he said succinctly. "Ole apple hog with a big nose."

He was gone before I could pull in my breath, a supple shadow in the moonlight, his sound a light rustling over the frost-crisped grass.

I remembered sitting there, madder — as Joey had known I'd be — over the reference to my practical-sized nose than I was over the apples or the whack on the shin.

Now here he was, home from his wanderings and the foreign wars, sitting in our kitchen, on his knees the visor cap he'd probably bought with his own money to dress him up for his coming home. He was saying to my sister in that voice of puzzlement, "I didn't even know you'd been married."

He'd been gone a long time and he wanted to pick up where he'd left off, with nothing changed. Some things had changed — not the Maine village, for that's been the same in June for a hundred and fifty years: the same high sky with big clouds ballooning over; the arm of the sea slicking up past it, blue and lazy in the afternoon; the white houses folded in against the hill. Even the horse chestnuts couldn't have changed much — at least, not within Joey's memory, or mine — proud in their white blooms, each bloom itself a proud, perfect little tree.

Except for the tide going in and out, the seasons and the weather, the village doesn't change; but different people are born and grow up and die, and Private Joe Hinckley couldn't seem to catch up with them.

"You saw some fighting, I guess, Joe," my sister said.

"Why, yes. I did."

"Was it bad?"

"Got tough sometimes. Them Japs, they don't give up easy."

"You get along all right?"

"Well, I got my arm scraped some in a ruckus. Had some malaria. Not bad."

I could see she wanted to ask him more about what it had really been like out there. You do, you know, when they come back, but somehow it's hard to phrase the questions. She didn't and I was glad she didn't. She said instead, "Does it seem good to be home?"

"I'll say." He fiddled with his cap. "Don't seem's if I know people's good's I use to. Most of the boys my age, they're gone in the Army or Navy."

"The girls, too," my sister said. "A lot of them have got jobs, away."

"Ayeh. Well, I better be on my way." He got up and moved toward the door. "Sure seems funny to think of you married and with two kids. And me not even know it."

My sister laughed. "Well — time goes by. And, you know, I kind of like it, Joe."

"Oh, sure. It's swell." But he didn't think it was swell. He wanted things the same as when he'd left. As his teacher, she'd meant something to him, the Lord knows what. It's hard to figure what a teacher ever does mean to a harum-scarum youngster. My sister'd been good at her job — she'd brought her university degree and her Phi Beta Kappa back to the one-horse country high school, and she'd worked her head off trying to drum some values and some maturity into the helter-skelter bunch of kids she was faced with. Maybe something she'd taught him *had* been of use to him out where he'd been. Whatever it was, now she was just another married woman.

"Well. . .so long," he said.

"So long, Joe. Drop by again if you have time."

"Sure will."

He went away down the aisle of horse chestnut trees, and I knew it was better to leave things alone, but I took out after him. It isn't done in Maine villages, for a bespectacled, middle-aged lady to take out running down a driveway after a boy of twenty. I could see he thought that, but he waited politely until I caught up with him.

"Joe —" Oh, damn that reticence that ties up the tongues of us all, when the heart wants to out with what's next to it. Even cities can't teach us different. "How long you home for?"

"Ten days."

"Have a good time on your leave, Joe. Find the prettiest girl in town — she'll be proud to go out with a soldier."

Old fool, with your glib glab! Not to have known better than to mention girls — and pretty ones, at that — to a Maine man! I watched the face of Private Hinckley grow red from the tip of his chin to the edge of his bleached hair. It made me realize how pale he'd been, under that tan.

"Thanks," he said carefully.

"Joe. . .once in the city, in the hard times, I was looking for a job and I ran out of money. I didn't eat for most three days. It was tough. . .not like a war, I know that. But all I could think of, one night, was Spy apples, how they crackle when you bite into them."

He had been turning away, but he stopped in his tracks.

"Gee, I done that one night in the jungle. I got to thinking about that and I like to died. Did you —?"

"I sure did," I said. "I got so homesick I bawled like a calf."

"I guess anyone does." If he had, he wasn't going to say so. Not, anyway, to a woman.

"The tree's in blossom now. I kind of wish it was November, Joe. You could have all the apples you could lug away."

He grinned, suddenly, and light was like a flare in his blue eyes. "I'd sure have the juice running down my chin," he said. He looked around slowly at the village, at the harbor, at the houses lying peacefully against the hill. "It don't change much, does it?"

"It doesn't change at all, Joe."

"Well," he said. "I — Look, I got this." He fumbled at something pinned carefully to the inside of his shirt pocket and held it out to me on the palm of his hand. The ribbon glinted in the bright sun. I don't know soldiers' medals, but it was the Distinguished Service Cross, I think. Anyway the words on it were: FOR VALOR.

The underside of his arm wasn't tanned, and along it ran a livid scar where the flesh had been ripped and shredded.

I just looked, I couldn't say anything. Then I said, "How... how'd you do it, Joe?"

"That scar, that's shrapnel." He explained patiently, putting it into simple terms, as Maine men do explain to womenfolk the men's affairs in which the women have no part. "When a bomb or a shell busts, pieces of iron, like, fly around."

"Oh," I said, as if I hadn't known. "This — couldn't you wear it on the outside, Joe, so folks would know?"

"Well, my own folks do know. But you know how the neighbors are... what they'd say: Joe's home. Guess he thinks he's something, going round trimmed up like a Christmas tree."

I nodded. He was right. That was just what they would say. Not meaning anything ugly, but only what they — and we — had had drilled into us from the time we could understand words. "Don't put yourself forward. It's kind of cheap." Born in the flesh and bred in the bone.

The year I myself was twenty, I published a poem in a little magazine, dead now these many years, both poem and magazine forgotten. It wasn't much — not like the things of war — but I remember how I wanted people to know. They never did, for whenever it was on my lips to tell, I kept hearing the neighbors: "Guess she thinks she's something, bragging about her writing being printed, somewhere to the west'ard." Oh, I knew what Joe meant, all right.

"Joe," I said, "I'll tell my sister, if you'd like it. I'll tell everyone." I silenced his quick protest. "I'll say I saw that pin in your pocket and made you tell me what it was you had there."

"Gee." He hesitated. "I guess so, if you put it like that. I would kind of like to have folks know."

He went away down the line of the horse chestnuts, walking a little stiffly, his cap carried carefully in his hand. A Maine kid, this time of year, hasn't much use for a hat.

*Born on Gott's Island, Maine, Ruth Moore (1903–1989) was a graduate of what is now called New York State University at Albany. Her literary output included fifteen novels, two volumes of poetry, and a book of ballads. Perhaps her most famous book is SPOONHANDLE (1946). This story first appeared in THE NEW YORKER in 1945.*

# A WHITE HERON

## I.

The woods were already filled with shadows one June evening, just before eight o'clock, though a bright sunset still glimmered faintly among the trunks of the trees. A little girl was driving home her cow, a plodding, dilatory, provoking creature in her behavior, but a valued companion for all that. They were going away from the western light, and striking deep into the dark woods, but their feet were familiar with the path, and it was no matter whether their eyes could see it or not.

There was hardly a night the summer through when the old cow could be found waiting at the pasture bars; on the contrary, it was her greatest pleasure to hide herself away among the high huckleberry bushes, and though she wore a loud bell she had made the discovery that if one stood perfectly still it would not ring. So Sylvia had to hunt for her until she found her, and call Co'! Co'! with never an answering Moo, until her childish patience was quite spent. If the creature had not given good milk and plenty of it, the case would have seemed very different to her owners. Besides, Sylvia had all the time there was, and very little use to make of it. Sometimes in pleasant weather it was a consolation to look upon the cow's pranks as an intelligent attempt to play hide and seek, and as the child had no playmates she lent herself to this amusement with a good deal of zest. Though this chase had been so long that the wary animal herself had given an unusual signal of her whereabouts, Sylvia had only laughed when she came upon Mistress Moolly at the swamp-side, and urged her affectionately homeward with a twig of birch leaves. The old cow was not inclined to wander farther, she even turned in the right direction for once as they left the pasture, and stepped along the road at a good pace. She was quite ready to be milked now, and seldom stopped to browse. Sylvia wondered what her grandmother would say because they were so late. It was a great while since she had left home at half past five o'clock, but everybody knew the difficulty of making this errand a short one. Mrs. Tilley had chased the horned torment too many summer evenings herself to blame any one else for lingering, and was only thankful as she waited that she had Sylvia, nowadays, to give such valuable assistance. The good woman suspected that Sylvia loitered occasionally on her own account; there never was such a child for straying about out-of-doors since the world was made! Everybody said that it was a good change for a little maid who had tried to grow for eight years in a crowded manufacturing town, but, as for Sylvia herself, it seemed as if she never had been alive at all before she came to live at the farm. She thought often with wistful compassion of a wretched dry geranium that belonged to a town neighbor.

"'Afraid of folks,'" old Mrs. Tilley said to herself, with a smile, after she had made the unlikely choice of Sylvia from her daughter's houseful of children, and was returning to the farm. "'Afraid of folks,' they said! I guess she won't be troubled no great with 'em up to the old place!" When they reached the door of the lonely house and stopped to unlock it, and the cat came to purr loudly, and rub against them, a deserted pussy, indeed, but fat with young robins, Sylvia whispered that this was a beautiful place to live in, and she never should wish to go home.

*       *       *

The companions followed the shady woodroad, the cow taking slow steps, and the child very fast ones. The cow stopped long at the brook to drink, as if the pasture were not half a swamp, and Sylvia stood still and waited, letting her bare feet cool themselves in the shoal water, while the great twilight moths struck softly against her. She waded on through the brook as the cow moved away, and listened to the thrushes with a heart that beat fast with pleasure. There was a stirring in the great boughs overhead. They were full of little birds and beasts that seemed to be wide-awake, and going about their world, or else saying good-night to each other in sleepy twitters. Sylvia herself felt sleepy as she walked along. However, it was not much farther to the house, and the air was soft and sweet. She was not often in the woods so late as this, and it made her feel as if she were a part of the gray shadows and the moving leaves. She was just thinking how long it seemed since she first came to the farm a year ago, and wondering if everything went on in the noisy town just the same as when she was there; the thought of the great redfaced boy who used to chase and frighten her made her hurry along the path to escape from the sha-dow of the trees.

Suddenly this little woods-girl is horror-stricken to hear a clear whistle not very far away. Not a bird's whistle, which would have a sort of friendliness, but a boy's whistle, determined and some-what aggressive. Sylvia left the cow to whatever sad fate might await her, and stepped discreetly aside into the bushes, but she was just too late. The enemy had discovered her, and called out in a very cheerful and persuasive tone, "Halloa, little girl, how far is it to the road?" and trembling Sylvia answered almost inaudibly, "A good ways."

She did not dare to look boldly at the tall young man, who carried a gun over his shoulder, but she came out of her bush and again followed the cow, while he walked alongside.

"I have been hunting for some birds," the stranger said kindly, "and I have lost my way, and need a friend very much. Don't be afraid," he added gallantly. "Speak up and tell me what your name is, and whether you think I can spend the night at your house, and go out gunning early in the morning."

Sylvia was more alarmed than before. Would not her grand-mother consider her much to blame? But who could have foreseen such an accident as this? It did not appear to be her fault, and she hung her head as if the stem of it were broken, but managed to answer "Sylvy," with much effort when her companion again asked her name.

Mrs. Tilley was standing in the doorway when the trio came into view. The cow gave a loud moo by way of explanation.

"Yes, you'd better speak up for yourself, you old trial! Where'd she tuck herself away this time, Sylvy?" Sylvia kept an awed silence; she knew by instinct that her grandmother did not comprehend the gravity of the situation. She must be mistaking the stranger for one of the farmer-lads of the region.

The young man stood his gun beside the door, and dropped a heavy game-bag beside it; then he bade Mrs. Tilley good-evening, and repeated his wayfarer's story, and asked if he could have a night's lodging.

"Put me anywhere you like," he said. "I must be off early in the morning, before day; but I am very hungry, indeed. You can give some milk at any rate, that's plain."

"Dear sakes, yes," responded the hostess, whose long slumbering hospitality seemed to be easily awakened. "You might fare better if you went out on the main road a mile or so, but you're welcome to what we've got. I'll milk right off, and you make yourself at home. You can sleep on husks or feathers," she proffered graciously. "I raised them all myself. There's good pasturing for geese just below here towards the ma'sh. Now step round and set a plate for the gentleman, Sylvy!" And Sylvia promptly stepped. She was glad to have something to do, and she was hungry herself.

It was a surprise to find so clean and comfortable a little dwelling in this New England wilderness. The young man had known the horrors of its most primitive housekeeping, and the dreary squalor of that level of society which does not rebel at the companionship of hens. This was the best thrift of an old-fashioned farmstead, though on such a small scale that it seemed like a hermitage. He listened eagerly to the old woman's quaint talk, he watched Sylvia's pale face and shining gray eyes with ever growing enthusiasm, and insisted that this was the best supper he had eaten for a month; then, afterward, the new-made friends sat down in the doorway together while the moon came up.

Soon it would be berry-time, and Sylvia was a great help at picking. The cow was a good milker, though a plaguy thing to keep track of, the hostess gossiped frankly, adding presently that she had buried four children, so that Sylvia's mother, and a son (who might be dead) in California were all the children she had left. "Dan, my boy, was a great hand to go gunning," she explained sadly. "I never wanted for pa'tridges or gray squer'ls while he was to home. He's been a great wand'rer, I expect, and he's no hand to write letters. There, I don't blame him, I'd ha' seen the world myself if it had been so I could.

"Sylvia takes after him," the grandmother continued affectionately, after a minute's pause. "There ain't a foot o' ground she
don't know her way over, and the wild creatur's counts her one o'
themselves. Squer'ls she'll tame to come an' feed right out o' her
hands, and all sorts o' birds. Last winter she got the jay-birds to
bangeing here, and I believe she'd 'a' scanted herself of her own
meals to have plenty to throw out amongst 'em, if I hadn't kep'
watch. Anything but crows, I tell her, I'm willin' to help support,
— though Dan he went an' tamed one o' them that did seem to
have reason same as folks. It was round here a good spell after he
went away. Dan an' his father they didn't hitch, — but he never
held up his head ag'in after Dan had dared him an' gone off."

The guest did not notice this hint of family sorrows in his eager
interest in something else.

"So Sylvy knows all about birds, does she?" he exclaimed, as he
looked around at the little girl who sat, very demure but increasingly sleepy, in the moonlight. "I am making a collection of
birds myself. I have been at it ever since I was a boy." (Mrs. Tilley
smiled.) "There are two or three very rare ones I have been hunting for these five years. I mean to get them on my own ground if
they can be found."

"Do you cage 'em up?" asked Mrs. Tilley, doubtfully, in re-
sponse to this enthusiastic announcement.

"Oh, no, they're stuffed and preserved, dozens and dozens of
them," said the ornithologist, "and I have shot or snared every
one myself. I caught a glimpse of a white heron three miles from
here on Saturday, and I have followed it in this direction. They
have never been found in this district at all. The little white heron,
it is," and he turned again to look at Sylvia with the hope of discovering that the rare bird was one of her acquaintances.

But Sylvia was watching a hop-toad in the narrow footpath.

"You would know the heron if you saw it," the stranger continued eagerly. "A queer tall white bird with soft feathers and long
thin legs. And it would have a nest perhaps in the top of a high
tree, made of sticks, something like a hawk's nest."

Sylvia's heart gave a wild beat; she knew that strange white
bird, and had once stolen softly near where it stood in some bright
green swamp grass, away over at the other side of the woods.
There was an open place where the sunshine always seemed

strangely yellow and hot, where tall, nodding rushes grew, and her grandmother had warned her that she might sink in the soft black mud underneath and never be heard of more. Not far beyond were the salt marshes and beyond those was the sea, the sea which Sylvia wondered and dreamed about, but never had looked upon, though its great voice could often be heard above the noise of the woods on stormy nights.

"I can't think of anything I should like so much as to find that heron's nest," the handsome stranger was saying. "I would give ten dollars to anybody who could show it to me," he added desperately, "and I mean to spend my whole vacation hunting for it if need be. Perhaps it was only migrating, or had been chased out of its own region by some bird of prey."

Mrs. Tilley gave amazed attention to all this, but Sylvia still watched the toad, not divining, as she might have done at some calmer time, that the creature wished to get to its hole under the doorstep, and was much hindered by the unusual spectators at that hour of the evening. No amount of thought, that night, could decide how many wished-for treasures the ten dollars, so lightly spoken of, would buy.

*       *       *

The next day the young sportsman hovered about the woods, and Sylvia kept him company, having lost her first fear of the friendly lad, who proved to be most kind and sympathetic. He told her many things about the birds and what they knew and where they lived and what they did with themselves. And he gave her a jackknife, which she thought as great a treasure as if she were a desert-islander. All day long he did not once make her troubled or afraid except when he brought down some unsuspecting singing creature from its bough. Sylvia would have liked him vastly better without his gun; she could not understand why he killed the very birds he seemed to like so much. But as the day waned, Sylvia still watched the young man with loving admiration. She had never seen anybody so charming and delightful; the woman's heart, asleep in the child, was vaguely thrilled by a dream of love. Some premonition of that great power stirred and swayed these young foresters who traversed the solemn woodlands with soft-footed silent care. They stopped to listen to a bird's song; they pressed forward again eagerly, parting the branches, — speaking to each other rarely and in whispers; the young man going first and Sylvia following, fascinated, a few steps behind, with her gray eyes dark with excitement.

She grieved because the longed-for white heron was elusive, but she did not lead the guest, she only followed, and there was no such thing as speaking first. The sound of her own unquestioned voice would have terrified her, — it was hard enough to answer yes or no when there was need of that. At last evening began to fall, and they drove the cow home together, and Sylvia smiled with pleasure when they came to the place where she heard the whistle and was afraid only the night before.

## II.

Half a mile from home, at the farther edge of the woods, where the land was highest, a great pine-tree stood, the last of its generation. Whether it was left for a boundary mark, or for what reason, no one could say; the woodchoppers who had felled its mates were dead and gone long ago, and a whole forest of sturdy trees, pines and oaks and maples, had grown again. But the stately head of this old pine towered above them all and made a landmark for sea and shore miles and miles away. Sylvia knew it well. She had always believed that whoever climbed to the top of it could see the ocean; and the little girl had often laid her hand on the great rough trunk and looked up wistfully at those dark boughs that the wind always stirred, no matter how hot and still the air might be below. Now she thought of the tree with a new excitement, for why, if one climbed it at break of day, could not one see all the world, and easily discover whence the white heron flew, and mark the place, and find the hidden nest?

What a spirit of adventure, what wild ambition! What fancied triumph and delight and glory for the later morning when she could make known the secret! It was almost too real and too great for the childish heart to bear.

All night the door of the little house stood open, and the whip-poorwills came and sang upon the very step. The young sportsman and his old hostess were sound asleep, but Sylvia's great design kept her broad awake and watching. She forgot to think of sleep. The short summer night seemed as long as the winter darkness, and at last when the whippoorwills ceased, and she was afraid the morning would after all come too soon, she stole out of the house and followed the pasture path through the woods, hastening toward the open ground beyond, listening with a sense of comfort and companionship to the drowsy twitter of a half-awakened bird, whose perch she had jarred in passing. Alas, if the great wave of human interest which flooded for the first time this dull little life should sweep away the satisfactions of an existence heart to heart with nature and the dumb life of the forest!

There was the huge tree asleep yet in the paling moonlight, and small and hopeful Sylvia began with utmost bravery to mount to the top of it, with tingling, eager blood coursing the channels of her whole frame, with her bare feet and fingers, that pinched and held like bird's claws to the monstrous ladder reaching up, up, almost to the sky itself. First she must mount the white oak tree that grew alongside, where she was almost lost among the dark branches and the green leaves heavy and wet with dew; a bird fluttered off its nest, and a red squirrel ran to and fro and scolded pettishly at the harmless housebreaker. Sylvia felt her way easily. She had often climbed there, and knew that higher still one of the oak's upper branches chafed against the pine trunk, just where its lower boughs were set close together. There, when she made the dangerous pass from one tree to the other, the great enterprise would really begin.

She crept out along the swaying oak limb at last, and took the daring step across into the old pine-tree. The way was harder than she thought; she must reach far and hold fast, the sharp dry twigs caught and held her and scratched her like angry talons, the pitch made her thin little fingers clumsy and stiff as she went round and round the tree's great stem, higher and higher upward. The sparrows and robins in the woods below were beginning to wake and twitter to the dawn, yet it seemed much lighter there aloft in the pine-tree, and the child knew that she must hurry if her project were to be of any use.

The tree seemed to lengthen itself out as she went up, and to reach farther and farther upward. It was like a great main-mast to the voyaging earth; it must truly have been amazed that morning through all its ponderous frame as it felt this determined spark of human spirit creeping and climbing from higher branch to branch. Who knows how steadily the least twigs held themselves to advantage this light, weak creature on her way! The old pine must have loved his new dependent. More than all the hawks, and bats, and moths, and even the sweet-voiced thrushes, was the brave, beating heart of the solitary gray-eyed child. And the tree stood still and held away the winds that June morning while the dawn grew bright in the east.

Sylvia's face was like a pale star, if one had seen it from the ground, when the last thorny bough was past, and she stood trembling and tired but wholly triumphant, high in the tree-top. Yes, there was the sea with the dawning sun making a golden dazzle over it, and toward that glorious east flew two hawks with slow-moving pinions. How low they looked in the air from that height when before one had only seen them far up, and dark against the blue sky. Their gray feathers were soft as moths; they seemed only a little away from the tree, and Sylvia felt as if she too could go flying away among the clouds. Westward, the woodlands and farms reached miles and miles into the distance; here and there were church steeples, and white villages; truly it was a vast and awesome world.

The birds sang louder and louder. At last the sun came up bewilderingly bright. Sylvia could see the white sails of ships out at sea, and the clouds that were purple and rose-colored and yellow at first began to fade away. Where was the white heron's nest in the sea of green branches, and was this wonderful sight and pageant of the world the only reward for having climbed to such a giddy height? Now look down again, Sylvia, where the green marsh is set among the shining birches and dark hemlocks; there where you saw the white heron once you will see him again; look, look! a white spot of him like a single floating feather comes up from the dead hemlock and grows larger, and rises, and comes close at last, and goes by the landmark pine with steady sweep of wing and outstretched slender neck and crested head. And wait! wait! do not move a foot or a finger, little girl, do not send an arrow of light and consciousness from your two eager eyes, for the heron has perched on a pine bough not far beyond yours, and cries back to his mate on the nest, and plumes his feathers for the new day!

The child gives a long sigh a minute later when a company of shouting cat-birds comes also to the tree, and vexed by their flut-tering and lawlessness the solemn heron goes away. She knows his secret now, the wild, light, slender bird that floats and wavers, and goes back like an arrow presently to his home in the green world beneath. Then Sylvia, well satisfied, makes her perilous way down again, not daring to look far below the branch she stands on, ready to cry sometimes because her fingers ache and her lamed feet slip. Wondering over and over again what the stranger would say to her, and what he would think when she told him how to find his way straight to the heron's nest.

*          *          *

"Sylvy, Sylvy!" called the busy old grandmother again and again, but nobody answered, and the small husk bed was empty, and Sylvia had disappeared.

The guest waked from a dream, and remembering his day's pleasure hurried to dress himself that it might sooner begin. He was sure from the way the shy little girl looked once or twice yes-terday that she had at least seen the white heron, and now she must really be persuaded to tell. Here she comes now, paler than ever, and her worn old frock is torn and tattered, and smeared with pine pitch. The grandmother and the sportsman stand in the door together and question her, and the splendid moment has come to speak of the dead hemlock-tree by the green marsh.

But Sylvia does not speak after all, though the old grandmother fretfully rebukes her, and the young man's kind appealing eyes are looking straight in her own. He can make them rich with money; he has promised it, and they are poor now. He is so well worth making happy, and he waits to hear the story she can tell.

No, she must keep silence! What is it that suddenly forbids her and makes her dumb? Has she been nine years growing, and now, when the great world for the first time puts out a hand to her, must she thrust it aside for a bird's sake? The murmur of the pine's green branches is in her ears, she remembers how the white heron came flying through the golden air and how they watched the sea and the morning together, and Sylvia cannot speak; she cannot tell the heron's secret and give its life away.

Dear loyalty, that suffered a sharp pang as the guest went away disappointed later in the day, that could have served and followed him and loved him as a dog loves! Many a night Sylvia heard the echo of his whistle haunting the pasture path as she came home with the loitering cow. She forgot even her sorrow at the sharp report of his gun and the piteous sight of thrushes and sparrows dropping silent to the ground, their songs hushed and their pretty feathers stained and wet with blood. Were the birds better friends than their hunter might have been, — who can tell? Whatever treasures were lost to her, woodlands and summer-time, remember! Bring your gifts and graces and tell your secrets to this lonely country child!

*Born in South Berwick, Maine, Sarah Orne Jewett (1849-1909) wrote novels, short stories, poems, and essays. Her best work is considered to be THE COUNTRY OF THE POINTED FIRS (1896), a collection of related tales, and this short story, which first appeared in A WHITE HERON AND OTHER STORIES (1886).*

# THE PEOPLE OF WINTER

## *Sanford Phippen*

O n the surface, Maine has been described to death. The wonderful light in the summer on the coast that painters talk about, the smell of an old woods trail in the fall, the feel of a gritty clam hoe on a cold spring morning on the flats of a Downeast shore, the deep woods after a heavy winter storm — these have all been described in book after article after story.

Capturing the essence of Maine on paper, however, is as elusive a task as there is for language. Edward M. Holmes, a Maine writer, has said: "No one is going to know Maine by reading about it . . . nor even by visiting here for a few months. He will have to live here ten years and develop the right rapprochement with his neighbors." Even then, among people knowledgeable about Maine there will be vast differences in perspective — determined, for example, by ethnicity and income.

Although popular literature has not shown Maine as diverse, its cultural heritage is rich. We are not all WASPs. Missing in this book — and to some extent in the literature — are stories about and by Maine's French, a group that has played and still plays a very important role in the life of the state. But Willis Johnson's "Prayer for the Dying" is set among the Russians in Richmond and Rebecca Cummings' "Berrying" features Finnish people near South Paris. These stories present unusual perspectives on Maine.

Because the state has great disparity between rich and poor and a relatively small middle class, some say it is like an undeveloped country, perhaps a colony of Boston and New York. It is hard to zone Maine; mansions and shacks exist side by side. On the one hand there is Louis Auchincloss's portrayal of Anchor (read Bar) Harbor:

> . . . clouded in the haze of unreality that hung so charmingly over the entire peninsula. It was indeed a world unto itself . . . it was an Eden in which it was hard to visualize a serpent. People were never born there, nor did they die there. The elemental was left to the winter and other climes . . . it was a land of big ugly houses, pleasant to live in, of very old and very active ladies, of hills that were called mountains, of small, quaint shops and of large, shining town cars.

On the other hand, in Gladys Hasty Carroll's "Head of the Line" there is an impoverished old man living in a cobbled-together shack on the side of an out-of-the-way road. Both accurately represent Maine — specifically, the Maine coast.

We can understand perspective much more easily than essence, and understanding perspective leads to an understanding of essence. There are numerous Maines in literature. For the range of perspectives in these stories, compare "The Search" by Virginia Chase, "A Bundle of Letters" by Henry James, and "A White Heron" by Sarah Orne Jewett. But the different literary views of Maine can be sorted in general categories. First, there is the long romantic tradition. Then there is what I call the realistic view of Maine, a newer outlook. The other way to categorize Maine literature is to look at the seasonal influence, which is so pervasive this book is organized around it.

The romantic version of Maine is very strong and no doubt will continue as long as the state remains rural and beautiful. Several Maine "transplants," who were once summer boys but have now lived here year-round for a long time, have told me that the reason they wanted to live Downeast was it always seemed a much "realer place" than, say, Manhattan, where people shuffled papers but didn't "produce" anything with their hands. As New York and Maine author José Yglesias puts it, "from a distance Maine is not a place but a metaphor." Yglesias recalls Thoreau, inspired by climbing Katahdin, Maine's highest mountain: "Here not even the surface has been scarred by man, but it was a specimen of what God saw fit to make this world." Although paper companies have now scarred this view, it is still magnificent.

During World War Two and for at least fifteen years afterward, there was a flurry of sentimental, popular books published about Maine, many of them by people who had found great happiness in moving from urban areas to rural Downeast. These include John Gould's *Farmer Takes a Wife* (1942); Louise Dickinson Rich's *We Took to the Woods* (1942), its sequel *My Neck of the Woods* (1950), and *The Peninsula,* (1958); Chenoweth Hall's *The Crow on the Spruce* (1946); Margaret Henrichsen's *Seven Steeples* (1953); and Gertrude McKenzie's *My Love Affair with the State of Maine* (1955). Similar books by natives include Mary Ellen Chase's *Windswept* (1941) and Robert P. Tristram Coffin's *Maine Doings* (1950). Such works promoted an unrealistic perspective.

Those who dream of Maine — as opposed to, say, California — tend to see it not as presenting a life of ease but as a simplification. Some of the well-fixed summer or retired folk with well-insulated homes with picture windows framing Currier and Ives views do manage to have their Maine just as simple as they anticipated. But younger and poorer people are confronted with loneliness in a cold climate, low pay and limited job opportunities. This Maine is my own, and this outlook likely to be far closer to reality.

This Maine is cold, dark and often deformed, recognizable not in the sunny seascapes of so many Sunday painters but in the dramatic forms of Marsden Hartley or the muted earth tones of Andrew Wyeth. This Maine is frustrating; it is hard on people. It is a life of poverty, solitude, struggle, lowered aspirations, living on the edge. One realizes that at any moment, despite all one's efforts, one can lose everything. Most of the Maine writers of my generation, people now in their late thirties and early forties — Carolyn Chute, Stephen King, Margaret Dickson, and others — know poverty firsthand, and have written movingly about it.

My case is no doubt typical. My family was poor, but because we had enough to eat, and just about the entire population of the town was in the same boat, we didn't know it. Even the owners of the lobster pounds and lumber yards lived pretty much the same as their employees. Being poor in a coastal town meant eating a lot of clams we dug ourselves, and in winter a lot of deer meat. Being poor was getting a box of a summer boy's used clothes to wear to school. It was taking up a collection around town to help pay for someone's hospital bills or for a neighbor's funeral. It was watching a neighbor's house burn down in the dead of winter, then collecting clothes, furniture, and money to give to the deprived and uninsured family. Being poor meant sharing: it was keeping a cot in the kitchen for someone, even a stranger on the road, who needed a place to stay; or several people sharing a bed. It was a full car of people going shopping on Saturday or sightseeing on a Sunday afternoon.

Indoor plumbing and electrical outlets were uncommon. My family had to labor to get water, to keep things cool, to heat the house, to prepare meals, to wash and clean. For many years we had no car, just the use of my father's boss's pick-up truck or the uncertainty of rides with relatives or neighbors. Repairs to house or car were made by the owner or with a neighbor's help. There were no regular doctor's or dentist's appointments. The family kept a tab at the local grocery, and if you couldn't pay a bill in cash you obtained a money order from the post office. Our house was filled with cast-off furniture. My mother, who did domestic work for the summer rich, took in laundries, sewed, and did any other odd job she could find.

While some may see Carolyn Chute's story "Ollie, Oh . . ." as grotesque and utterly bleak, I am impressed by Ollie's stubbornness and toughness of spirit in the playing out of a life that was but a poor hand to begin with. Chute's characters seem perfectly realistic to me.

There is a positive side to this life: sharing, strong family and community ties, generations of traditions, a spirit of self-sufficiency, a life rich in the ways of the outdoors, and there is the earthy humor of the underdog. Maine people are hard-working, self-sacrificing, no-nonsense, and usually skeptical. They do not expect hand-outs or happy endings. They are usually appreciative of the great natural beauty of the ocean and woods.

But I don't for a minute believe the romantic notion that living a hard life in a hostile climate makes people better. A mean life breeds meanness, poverty breeds bitterness, suffering does not ennoble. Maine people are not essentially different from other people. In small towns people tend to be honest and dependable because everyone knows everyone. It is the family-oriented familiarity and interdependence that keep people honest. One gets a reputation fast. Unlike much of America, there is still community here. This is the essence of the positive side of Maine life.

Most Maine people are well aware that from November to April they are ruled by the elements, that they could die if lost in the woods or on the ocean. If this situation breeds fatalism and a feeling that good fortune may be followed by a downfall, it also provides an exciting battlefield, a proving ground for strength and will. A friend says: "People who live like this have to have the sharp vision. Sunsets are intense, food tastes good." Of course, even the tough and experienced can fall victim to *hubris,* as happens in Lawrence Sargent Hall's "The Ledge." Still, fatalism is not passivity, and unlike protagonists so prominent in much current literature who throw up their hands in despair, Maine people tend to fight on. "The Ledge," one of the most powerful stories in all literature, shows just how far they are capable of carrying that fight.

Maine's climate means less mobility, more waiting, and a reduction in physical and psychological space as family members are pressed in upon each other. The result is that people pull in, become reticent. Feelings are held back, lest they shatter delicate balances. In "The Soldier Shows His Medal," the narrator exclaims: ". . . damn that reticence that ties up the tongues of us all, when the heart wants to out with what's next to it."

But beyond the winter there really is spring. Not surprisingly, some stories of spring and summer are happier or have a lighter tone. Summertime Downeast is a brilliant and joyful season when everything seems vividly green, alive, and sharp. It also is a time when millions of visitors from around the world pour into the state. Ever since people from "westward" started summering in Maine, conflicts between the locals and visitors have arisen. As both "The Lesson" by Sam Brown, Jr., and "The Viking's Daughter" by Arthur Train illustrate, such conflicts have been the source of some of the best stories.

The party ends by Labor Day, however, and afterward the resort streets are largely deserted. Fall is coming and it is time to begin digging in for the cold season. Crops are stored away, houses are winterized. In Maine the winter hovers over all the seasons. In a few lines of Auchincloss's "Greg's Peg" there is rendered the distinct Maine coloration of the impending cold and darkness.

"Getting through the Maine winter" has as much to do with molding Maine character as the long Russian winter has to do with

Russia. If one knows only the rhythms of summer, one cannot write realistically about Maine. Here is the bridge between, on the one hand, realism and romanticism in Maine literature and, on the other hand, the influence of the elements in this literature. Although in this book there are dark tones in the stories set in the warmer months, the grimly realistic and tragic stories are likely to take place in the cold seasons. I am thinking of "The Ledge" and "Ollie, Oh. . . ." As Auchincloss wrote, "the elemental was left to the winter."

I personally feel that after so many years of romantic treatment it is time to redress the balance. It is not that the Real Maine has never been glimpsed. One of the stories just cited was written many years ago. But it is time that Maine's winter and the people of winter be fully recognized.

"About Maine we are all romantics," José Yglesias wrote, appropriately, in *The New York Times,* and Maine *is* a romantic place of great natural beauty. It is understandable that anyone falling in love with such a place would want to try to capture romantically in word and image the object of this affection. But while rhapsodizing about its land, Maine's romanticists tend to do the same about its people. While it is true that Maine people on the surface appear as straight as their pines and as independent as their seagulls, they are complex creatures of flesh and blood, full of sin as well as of good deeds. Their lives deserve complex treatment. Only then, with a balancing of perspective, can we approach the mysterious essence of Maine.

Orono, Maine
1986

# The Anthologists

SANFORD PHIPPEN, who wrote the Afterword, "The People of Winter," is also the author of THE POLICE KNOW EVERYTHING (1982), PEOPLE TRY- ING TO BE GOOD (1988), and CHEAP GOSSIP (1989), as well as editor of HIGH CLOUDS SOARING, STORMS DRIVING LOW: THE LETTERS OF RUTH MOORE (1993). Phippen's story in this anthology, "Step-Over Toe-Hold," was selected by the other anthologists. He writes the regular column "Voices from the East" for the MAINE TIMES, and he lives and works in Hancock and Orono, Maine.

CHARLES WAUGH, who has published over 170 anthologies, teaches speech and psychology at the University of Maine at Augusta.

MARTIN GREENBERG teaches political science at the University of Wisconsin at Green Bay. He has worked on over 700 anthologies, co- editing many of them with Charles Waugh.